Embracing Euphoria

by

C. Becker

Euphoria Series

Cover Art by *The Wild Rose Press, Inc.*

The Wild Rose Press, Inc.
PO Box 708
Adams Basin, NY 14410-0708
Visit us at www.thewildrosepress.com

Publishing History
First Edition, 2025
Trade Paperback ISBN 978-1-5092-5980-9
Digital ISBN 978-1-5092-5981-6

Euphoria Series
Published in the United States of America

Dedication

To Paul,
Thank you for supporting my dreams, no matter how crazy they seem.

Acknowledgments

Thank you to my talented editor, ELF, for her guidance and expert feedback. I'm grateful to Rhonda Penders and the hardworking team at The Wild Rose Press for the opportunity and your support. A special thank you to RJ Morris, the brilliant artist who designed the cover.

A huge debt to my insightful writers' group: Sandra Woods, Nancy Hall, Gene Turchin, Pepper Hedden, Lindsey Minardi, and Joanie Raisovich. Words cannot express how appreciative I am for your suggestions with this novel, and the entire trilogy. Now we can move on and let Hailey and Mark live their lives.

To my long-time friend and Spanish teacher Brenda Gibson and to my beta readers who read the early drafts, Dan Becker and Brooke Driscoll, I give many thanks.

Thank you to my readers, for allowing Hailey and Mark to find a home in your hearts and minds.

Special thanks to my wonderful children, Kevin, Ashley, Brian, and Brooke, for your never-ending encouragement. I'm proud to be your mom. Brooke, your expertise as an occupational therapist helped shape Mark's story. The residents you support each day are fortunate to have such an empathetic OT.

Thanks to Paul, my loving husband for your patience and support. You plowed through many overcooked dinners, and sometimes no dinner, as I worked on the manuscript, and you never complained. I can still smell the potatoes burning in the pan when the water boiled out. Thank goodness for takeout. I love you!

And most importantly, thanks to God who created me with a vivid imagination, making all my stories possible.

Dedication

To Paul,
Thank you for supporting my dreams, no matter how crazy they seem.

Acknowledgments

Thank you to my talented editor, ELF, for her guidance and expert feedback. I'm grateful to Rhonda Penders and the hardworking team at The Wild Rose Press for the opportunity and your support. A special thank you to RJ Morris, the brilliant artist who designed the cover.

A huge debt to my insightful writers' group: Sandra Woods, Nancy Hall, Gene Turchin, Pepper Hedden, Lindsey Minardi, and Joanie Raisovich. Words cannot express how appreciative I am for your suggestions with this novel, and the entire trilogy. Now we can move on and let Hailey and Mark live their lives.

To my long-time friend and Spanish teacher Brenda Gibson and to my beta readers who read the early drafts, Dan Becker and Brooke Driscoll, I give many thanks.

Thank you to my readers, for allowing Hailey and Mark to find a home in your hearts and minds.

Special thanks to my wonderful children, Kevin, Ashley, Brian, and Brooke, for your never-ending encouragement. I'm proud to be your mom. Brooke, your expertise as an occupational therapist helped shape Mark's story. The residents you support each day are fortunate to have such an empathetic OT.

Thanks to Paul, my loving husband for your patience and support. You plowed through many overcooked dinners, and sometimes no dinner, as I worked on the manuscript, and you never complained. I can still smell the potatoes burning in the pan when the water boiled out. Thank goodness for takeout. I love you!

And most importantly, thanks to God who created me with a vivid imagination, making all my stories possible.

Chapter One

Shielding her eyes from the morning sun, Hailey Langley crouched behind a dense thicket of thorny shrubs and peered down at Manuel Mendoza's mansion. Hard to determine how tightly the owner secured the Colombian property.

The plantation was too vast for a manufactured fortification. One guard stood in the stone observation tower next to the main house. Was another sentry posted nearby? The U-shaped house with its distinctive clay roof tiles looked exactly like the pictures her former colleague at the Special Crimes Agency had emailed.

She reviewed the outline of the security system from the blueprints. One mistake and Rose might die.

Colleen Toole, Rose's mother, squatted beside a bush and wheezed. "I need a few minutes to catch my breath." She grabbed a low-lying branch and shrieked when a dozen hummingbirds zoomed away, disappearing into the foliage.

Hailey wiped her brow and shrugged the knapsack off her shoulders. She pulled out a canteen, gulped the tepid water, and passed Colleen the container. "Show restraint."

Colleen should've dressed more practically for the rescue. Designer slacks and a cable-knit sweater weren't ideal clothing for trekking in the tropics. At least she'd bought sensible hiking boots at the hotel shop.

Hailey crammed the canteen into the knapsack filled with water-treatment pills, compass, lighter, rope, flashlight, energy bars, and a hunting knife. She might need her training in knife-combat tactics. They were also bound to come across snakes in the woods.

"I promise. I'll keep you safe," she'd rashly assured Rose eight weeks ago, just before the girl's criminal father kidnapped the child.

Hailey replayed the still-fresh memory. Yes, she had promised. "Break's over." She adjusted the ball cap on her head. With a pat, she checked the burner phone in her pants pocket. Then she tugged her khaki pants over her boots and hoisted the sack on her back. "Ready?"

The sooner she rescued Rose, the sooner Hailey could return to Virginia and focus on her own family. For a second, she closed her eyes, fantasizing a group hug with her husband, Mark, and their two kids. When Mark vanished from the picture, her eyes opened, and her muscles tensed. Ethan and Anna were safe visiting cousins, but Mark's whereabouts while he recovered from his injuries were still a mystery. He'd said staying away would be easier on her, but his absence only made her reckless. Was she down here trying to save Colleen's five-year-old to prove something to Mark or to herself?

Colleen looped her hair into a ponytail holder. She had grown gray during her six years in prison, but it was now styled and colored back to blonde with little swirls framing her face. She smeared the last splotches of sunscreen onto her cheeks, returned the lotion tube to her waist pack, and slapped a gnat that had landed on her arm. "I'd better not get malaria out here. Or yellow fever. Or—"

Blood pressure rising, Hailey glared until Colleen

closed her mouth. "Watch out for land mines along the way." *God, give me strength.* She should've demanded Colleen stay with their guide near the garage. Getting into the mansion would be hard enough without this spoiled woman's constant whining.

Hailey led the way down the steep path. The heady fragrance from the surrounding hibiscuses triggered the memory of six years ago when Colleen held her hostage and tried to kill her.

What had Mark's best friend, CIA agent David Smith, warned her about Colleen? *"A chameleon might change colors, but it's still a chameleon. When things get rough—and they will—Colleen will double-cross you, first chance she gets."*

Hailey shook away the distrust. David had to be wrong. Colleen was only a mother trying to rescue her daughter from the drug-lord father who kidnapped her.

In the backyard, Hailey scurried behind a tuft of prickly flowering bushes and pulled her wool socks higher, covering her gun assembled from 3D printed parts.

Five years had passed since her last mission. For this trip, she compressed three weeks of groundwork into three days. A myriad of factors could bungle her plan: traveling through the region, navigating the security system, evading guards, accessing the mansion, and determining Rose's location. *Too many variables.* The odds weren't in their favor, but if she could trust their guide's intelligence, at least Manuel Mendoza's mother was at work in the orphanage today. Rose would be alone with the nanny.

Colleen tugged Hailey's sleeve. "There's Rose! There's my baby!" She stood and pointed to the long-haired girl on a lawn chaise, not far from a young woman dancing to Spanish-style music by the pool.

Hailey gripped Colleen's arm, pulling her back beneath a bush. She motioned at a surveillance camera on the patio staircase. "Get down! They'll see us."

"No one's here but my daughter and her disco-bopping nanny."

"We don't know that for sure." *If this were my child, would I wait?*

A loud boom shook the air.

Colleen jumped. "What was that?"

Hailey's stomach clenched. *Gunshot.* "Stay down." She checked her phone. Their hired guide hadn't texted about any trouble. "Follow me."

They used the tall grasses as a shield and skirted the mansion's perimeter. As they crept toward the high shrubs around the infinity pool, another blast thundered in the air.

Darn. Two shots now. Better get my gun.

"Our guide said Manuel's out of town. We need to act now," Colleen whispered. "Use your knife and threaten the nanny."

"Wait until Rose is alone." Hailey rolled down her sock and palmed the handgun.

"We're losing valuable time. I say we go."

Hailey pulled at the heel of her boot for the bullets the guide had supplied. "I said, stay until—"

Click.

Dammit! At the sound of a round being chambered, Hailey left the heel intact and pushed the firearm back into her sock.

"Ah! We have visitors." A deep gravelly voice thundered from behind.

Hailey quickly retied the leather bootlace and turned.

A man punched her in the abdomen with his gun, knocking the wind out of her. He had a familiar face, harsh and weather-beaten. *José Mendoza.* Manuel's father. His gray moustache needed a trim, but his piercing eyes were as jet-black as his son's. Damn. The security sensors must've alerted them.

José hooked his gnarly hand around Hailey's arm and gnashed his teeth as she yanked. "Two more trespassers, Luis."

The gunshots. Please, by some miracle, let our guide be okay.

A muscular man with tanned skin, Luis looked to be in his midthirties. He grabbed Colleen's waist as she struggled to run.

José's grip dug deeper into Hailey. "Look who's here. Hailey Langley, the troublemaker who cracked into my computer files." He coughed and ogled Colleen. "And you must be the *puta* who bewitched my son. I'd like to see how you romp in my bed."

Colleen spat in his eye. She had spunk after all.

José slapped Colleen's face hard. "Is that anyway to treat your daughter's *abuelo*?"

Hailey wrenched her wrist from José's grasp. "We're not here to cause any trouble. Give us Rose, and we'll go."

For a moment, the old man seemed to consider the request. "I have a better idea." He coughed again. "My contacts pay *mucho dinero* for North American bitches."

José spoke rapidly to Luis in a broad Spanish accent.

Hailey fingered her shirt over the scar where Manuel Mendoza had stabbed her two months ago. The blood in her veins chilled as she translated pieces of the men's conversation. Branding. Smuggling. Transfer. From the fear in Colleen's wide eyes, she understood, too.

Colleen squirmed against Luis's grip. "Please. Give me my daughter. Then we'll go."

José scoffed. "The only place you're going is to the Caribbean—with all the other worthless *prostitutas.*" He jerked the knapsack from Hailey's shoulders and pulled out the knife inside. He held up the blade, rotating it to stare at the sharp edges.

Smirking, he turned to Hailey. "You shouldn't carry such a weapon unless you are skilled at using it." He jammed the blade into his belt and pointed his gun at them. "Phones."

Not many options. If she refused, José would frisk her and confiscate the firearm hidden in her sock. Hailey pulled the burner phone from her pocket and tossed it onto the ground.

Colleen copied her movements.

Luis collected the phones and put them into his pants.

José howled in a high-pitched voice. "Doesn't this pool music make you want to dance?" He fired his gun three times at their feet.

Colleen screeched as she jumped.

Near the pool, the nanny grabbed Rose's arm and raced into the house.

José jerked Colleen's forearm, his eyes sinister and cold. "If you try anything funny, next time I won't miss. Now, start walking."

Luis wrenched Hailey's arm behind her back and pointed the way.

José spoke in Spanish again. "We'll keep them in

the old *basuco* shed until I make arrangements."

Hailey scratched at her arm. This couldn't be happening. *Stay calm. Say nothing.* She surveyed the area. If the guide managed to sneak away, he'd be the one surprise attack she had left.

They walked past the entranceway and slowed where a flock of birds feasted beyond the driveway.

Hailey peered where the scavengers gathered, and she gagged. It couldn't be. Bile rose in her throat at their hired guide sprawled on the grass with a bullet hole in his head.

Colleen spat at José. "You're a monster!"

José pushed her. "Keep walking."

Twenty yards away, another man lay on the ground, his shirt covered in blood.

Hailey spun to the empty observation tower overlooking the two-hundred-acre estate. The second gunshot. Had the guide's bullet killed him, or had José killed his own sentry?

José wouldn't hesitate to carry out his threats. Given his extensive connections in the Caribbean, if the man shipped her and Colleen there, no one would ever find them.

Remain calm. Outwit them and escape. Just like you got away from Manuel before. Patience and poise.

As they walked on the dirt path lined with trees, Colleen stumbled on a root and fell.

José kicked Colleen's legs. "Stand up."

Moaning, she curled into a fetal position and cried.

Poor Colleen. She couldn't buy her safety here like she did in prison.

Hailey bent to help, but Luis yanked her away.

They hiked down a winding hill, past a farm tractor

stranded beside an old truck with baled hay in the bed. The terrain became rockier, steeper. A split-rail fence bordered pastures where horses and cattle grazed.

José jerked Colleen's arm. "*Apúrate!* Faster!"

The path ended at a tin shed next to a brick firepit.

Sweat dripped down Hailey's cheeks and back. The temperature had to be over ninety degrees. This was like a bad scene in a movie. She should've told David about her plans. *Recklessness gets you killed.*

Think. If she could jerk her arm from Luis' grip and flip him, she could run into the woods. Make her way back to the guide's jeep down the road.

She glanced back at Colleen, lagging five feet behind. Even if Hailey rescued Rose, she couldn't abandon Colleen to be exploited by drug dealers or rebel forces. Like it or not, Colleen was her partner, her responsibility.

Luis opened the door of an 8'x10' metal shed and shoved Hailey inside.

A wave of heat slapped her face, and she blinked, letting her eyes adjust to the small rays of sunlight worming under the gaps of the corrugated roof. She crinkled her nose at the stench of a dead animal and tensed as a dark-colored furry creature with a long tail squeaked and scurried behind a wooden barrel.

Ignoring her protests, José thrust Colleen into the shed. He pulled rope from Hailey's backpack and tossed it to Luis. "Bind their hands and tie them together on the floor."

José held the gun while Luis looped rope around Hailey's arms.

What was this place? Old bricks were stacked along the wall, some broken or crushed into rusted coffee cans on the ground. A bucket of ash was tipped over. An antique metal container was labelled "Kerosene." She squinted at the lettering of a bag on a shelf—benzoin gum powder. This had to be where the Mendoza family processed some of their drugs.

Hailey gazed at her boots. If only she could draw her gun. "Let us go."

José sniggered and opened an energy bar from her bag. "Why should I?"

She met his glower with a hard glare. "Because I can be your worst enemy."

He stepped forward and slowly traced a hand along her breast. "You're in no position to make demands."

She refused to flinch at the touch. Damn pervert. "My contacts know I'm here."

José chomped on the snack. "Like the milksop with you today?"

How dare he talk about her guide that way. "You're a jackass." Hailey leapt toward him, but he kicked her in the chest. She dropped to the ground, hitting her face. Fear rankled her as she tasted salt on her lips. "There are others. When I don't check in, they'll come and search this place—in force. You'll regret this."

José hawked sputum on her legs. "I'll have to make sure you're shipped out before they arrive." He opened the canteen in the knapsack and took a swig.

After Luis finished securing Hailey's hands, he bound Colleen's wrists.

Colleen let out a sob. "You won't get away with this. Manuel's going to be pissed you hurt me."

José cackled. "If I have the chance, I'll send Manuel's little mixed-breed brat to the Caribbean, too. Young girls fetch a high price."

Hailey fought for control. *Asshole.*

Luis positioned her and Colleen with their backs together. While he secured a rope around the two women, his hand bumped against her leg. His eyes narrowed.

Hailey held her breath. *Don't discover my gun.*

"Hurry." José stepped closer and picked up an empty burlap bag from the ground. "Gag them."

Hailey exhaled. Her secret was safe for now.

Taking the bag, Luis ripped off strips of woven fabric and pressed them into her mouth.

Ugh! The material tasted like sand, but she dared not give José the satisfaction of coughing. The ropes binding her arms had a little slack. With time, she might be able to slip her wrists through the knots. The rake hanging on a metal wall might come in handy. She could bash one of her captors with a brick if she caught them off guard.

José tramped to the door. "Come, Luis. I need you to dispose of the bodies on the lawn while I make phone calls. Manuel won't be back until tomorrow. If we hurry, I can put these two *putas* on a boat before he returns. Maybe the girl, too." Jeering, he pulled another energy bar from the bag and tossed the canteen and backpack onto the floor with a thud.

The door slammed, and a lock clicked.

Memories of her abduction twenty years earlier flashed through Hailey's mind. She'd never been so afraid. So helpless. So alone.

Did Rose feel alone? Did Manuel try to act as a father?

Hailey's chest tightened. He'd stabbed her two months ago. She couldn't let Rose live with him. The little girl would never be safe. Especially with José close by. The violent sociopath was even more dangerous than his son.

A heightened sense of purpose coursed through her. Hailey used her teeth to nudge the moldy gag from her mouth. "Hurry. Slip your hands through the ropes."

"I'm trying." Colleen mumbled through the gag.

"Use your teeth. Pull down the gag. Luis didn't tie them very tight." *Be thankful for small favors.* Hailey twisted her hands beneath the bristly twine.

At last, Colleen freed the gag from her mouth. She yanked her arms back and forth. "Ouch! Dammit!" Her soft voice trembled. "What's going to happen to us?"

Sweat dripped down Hailey's back. "Nothing."

"I'm not stupid." Colleen shuddered. "I know what they plan to do with us in the Caribbean. If José doesn't give us to his rebels first."

Hailey knew, too. More sweat dripped down her face. Under the metal roof, the temperature had to be well over one hundred degrees. "Stay calm. Concentrate on getting out of the rope."

"I can't." Colleen's voice was now a high-pitched whine.

"Listen to me. I've been abducted before—twice. We can escape if we focus." Hailey wrenched her hands against the rope while keeping tabs on the shadows scampering near the barrel.

"You were kidnapped twice?"

"The first time I was seventeen." Hailey's voice faded to a whisper. "The kidnappers destroyed my life. The second time, you and Manuel tried to kill me. Did you forget?"

"I'm sorry. I wish I could take it all back." Colleen sniffled.

"We can only move forward. Now, keep it together. You didn't serve six years with good behavior to lose your daughter. We have to find a way out before they return."

Colleen's back rubbed against Hailey's with new determination. "I'm not leaving without my daughter."

"We won't. But we need a plan." Hailey gritted her teeth and tried pulling her hands through the rope. Something warm dripped down her hand. Blood.

"This is all your fault." Colleen shrieked. "Why didn't you have safeguards in place for the police to come if we got caught?"

"Are you for real? You knew the US government wasn't involved."

"You could've contacted the Colombian govern—"

"Stop! You asked me to help you because Rose's case is caught up in red tape. This mission isn't sanctioned. The Colombian government won't help two American women kidnap a child of a Colombian father to take back into the US."

"Did you tell David? He has his CIA resources."

Hailey shook her head. "When you visited my house and asked for help, he told you to let the Department of State handle Rose's rescue."

Colleen groaned. "He always loathed me."

Because you double-crossed his best friend when you cheated on Mark. Hailey tightened her lips. *Mark belongs to me now.*

"I can't believe you don't have a backup plan." Colleen whimpered.

"Why didn't *you* do something? I don't see you coming up with a better idea."

"I have plenty of ideas to get us out of here."

"Like what?"

"Give me a minute to think…" Colleen whimpered. "It's getting hotter. I don't feel so good."

"What's wrong?"

"My head's spinning."

"Could be from the heat. It will be a couple of hours before the sun shifts and the temperature lowers."

Colleen puffed air and shifted her arm, fingering the rope. "It's no use." She leaned forward and cried. "I'm never going to see my baby again."

Hailey's temples throbbed like a jackhammer pounded her brain. She could die of heat stroke before José and Luis returned. "I wish I had more time with my kids, too, but if we give up, we'll die here."

"I'm sorry about Mark. I shouldn't have dragged him into my problems. I made him promise to help me and Rose." Her sobs changed into weeping. "He died because of me…I'm such a selfish snob."

"Stop it! You can't break down now." Colleen didn't deserve to know Mark was alive.

"I had everything. Tons of money. Good looks. Status. Now look at me. I'm an ex-con with a record." Colleen sniffled. "I slept with a drug lord, for crying out loud. Now I'm either going to be turned into a sex slave or die in this hellhole while that drug lord raises my daughter." Colleen hiccupped. "Because of me, your kids not only lost Mark, but they'll also lose you."

Hailey sighed. The woman had a heart after all. But it was a little too late. Their desperate situation had zero chance of rescue. No one would be coming to save them. Even if the director at the SCA discovered she'd left the country and tried to track her, the GPS in her ear implant would be useless inside the tin shed. Hailey would fight to the end, but Colleen needed hope. No sense in pushing her further into desolation.

I better not live to regret this. Hailey exhaled. "We don't have time for this self-pity. Mark's alive."

After a long moment, Colleen stopped crying. "What did you say?"

"Mark pretended to die in the fire so he could trap Manuel."

"He's alive? You're not just saying that?"

"It's true."

"Thank God!" Colleen's voice brightened. "He'll save us."

Maybe telling her about Mark wasn't such a smart idea. "He can't."

"Why not?"

"First of all, he doesn't know we're here."

Colleen gasped. "You didn't tell him?"

Hailey bit her lip. Hard to communicate when Mark didn't return texts or calls. "Second, Mark's not well."

"What are you talking about?"

"Mendoza's goons tortured him. Beat him up. Broke both legs and set him on fire."

Colleen shook her head. "Stop!"

"Why are you so surprised? Violence is Mendoza's world. Mark has scars all over his body and needs rehab. He's seeing a counselor to deal with the PTSD he developed after his beating. I didn't tell Mark about the trip because I didn't want to worry him. He has enough going on."

Colleen wailed. "Oh God! We're doomed!"

"Stop blubbering!" Hailey twisted her wrists with more force. "Channel your energy into loosening the ropes."

After a few minutes, Colleen quieted. Her breathing slowed, and her shoulders slumped forward.

"Colleen? Colleen!" Hailey rocked against her back and forth. "Don't you pass out on me!"

Shit!

In a burst of anger, Hailey picked at the rope until sharp pain shot down her arm.

"Aargh!" Sweat dripped down her forehead, stinging her eyes. Her throat scratched like sandpaper. The headache throbbed worse, and her vision blurred. Nausea washed through her. The temperature seemed to rise with each passing minute, but goose bumps prickled on her clammy skin. If by some miracle she lost consciousness and didn't die of heat exhaustion, she'd wake up somewhere in the Caribbean. José wouldn't waste time, especially since he loathed her for accessing his private files.

Hailey's head began spinning. She'd never see her family again.

Mark, Anna, and Ethan, I love you.

She slumped forward as the darkness swallowed her.

Chapter Two

Atlanta, Georgia

Mark limped through the restricted hallway of Posterity Medical Innovations and unlocked the door to his small apartment. The blue light of the microwave glowed 11:48 AM. If he napped now, he'd have a hard time falling asleep later. Yawning, he flipped the kitchen light switch and scrolled through the screens. Three more voicemails from Hailey. That made fourteen over the past week.

Call her.

His therapies were demanding, but they didn't compare to the challenge of pretending life would someday return to normal. Two weeks had passed since he'd called his wife. One week since he last texted. *How can Hailey still love me?* He'd ruined everything with his lies, letting Hailey believe he'd died, and then by leaving her again to recuperate in solitude. If her former partner Parker hadn't died, she'd be with the guy.

Though Hailey claimed she didn't blame Mark for Parker's death, the pain in her voice was too hard to endure. Text messages were easier to ignore the disappointment in her voice—and easier to avoid discussions about his return.

He stared at the compression glove on his left hand. Every movement was harder since his injury. Even texting was cumbersome.

In the tiny kitchen, he opened the fridge and snagged a bottled water. This apartment had been his haven, his escape for the past two months. Would he ever feel safe to leave?

Mark drained half the water bottle and wandered into the living room. He picked up the old guitar he'd bought from a local pawnshop and sat on the sofa, slowly plucking the strings using the PIM arpeggio pattern he'd learned in high school.

Someone knocked on the door.

Panic poured through his veins. Mark dropped the stringed instrument onto the floor with a hard thud. *Focus on breathing. Don't hide in the closet. I'm safe here.*

He propped the guitar against the wall and walked to the entrance. When he peered through the peephole, an unexplained comfort flowed through him. He unlocked the dead bolt and opened the door. "Dr. Hanover. What a surprise."

"Please. Call me Bruce. We're past the formalities, especially since you're my guest here for the interim."

The man hadn't changed a bit. Bruce may have moved away to Georgia six years ago, but he still spoke with a pleasant Texas lilt.

Mark gestured him inside. "When did you get back?"

"Late last night." Bruce lightly shook Mark's gloved hand. His tanned, wrinkled face was a marked contrast to the snowy hair on the sides of his head. "I had a mountain of paperwork to attend to in my office. How have you been?"

"I'm doing okay." Mark led him to the living room.

Bruce settled onto the plaid sofa and looked around

the room. "How's this arrangement working out?"

Mark eased into his chair. "It's perfect."

"When you contacted me, I was boarding a plane. I didn't have much time to get your accommodations started. Do you need anything?"

"No. The receptionist and custodian get me everything I need—and more."

Bruce grinned. "That's great to hear. Sorry, the company's corporate apartments only provide the basics."

The dated sofa and well-worn chairs reminded Mark of his college apartment. His family photo on the end table was enough. "Don't apologize. The place is fine."

"Have you continued your therapies?"

"The agency I used in Virginia set me up with rehab services at the outpatient burn center downtown. I take a shuttle to my morning and afternoon treatments." Mark extended his fingers. Stretching felt like a constant part of his routine. He tugged his oversized T-shirt. "These baggy clothes don't look the neatest, but they're easy to get in and out of for the staff to change my pressure garments."

"Comfort is more important than fashion. My entire life has been without color." Bruce pointed to his white lab coat and laughed. "Tell me about your therapy."

"The physical therapist works on range-of-motion exercises for both hands even though my right side wasn't burned as badly as my left."

"PTs do amazing work. Regaining hand functionality is important for your quality of life. We take a lot of what our hands can do for granted."

"Like shaving and combing our hair. That's why I have a beard and moustache." Mark brushed his fingers against the whiskers growing below the clear silicone mask that covered his facial burns. "My OT helps me with cooking and food prep. Buttering a piece of bread is cringeworthy. Thank goodness for takeout." He raised his gloved hand. "It's hard to grasp things. Even picking up a water bottle is difficult. I don't know how I'll ever handle a gun again."

"Don't get discouraged. Physical and occupational therapy is very effective."

"I guess I'm living proof. Therapy got me out of the wheelchair. At least now I can walk without much limping."

"Do you use a cane?"

"Only when I'm fatigued. I'm seeing a psychologist, too—Dr. Kendrick."

"Have you found any relief from the PTSD?"

"A small improvement." No sense in telling him the episodes were still frequent. "The therapists are showing me interventions."

Bruce removed his wire-rimmed glasses and polished them against his dress shirt. "Have you told Hailey you're staying here?"

"No." Mark tensed. "I need to do this on my own."

Bruce's eyes carried a mixture of shock and sympathy. "Are you sure that's what's best for you?"

"I don't want to be a bother." Mark glanced at his left arm where pressure garments covered the skin.

"Did Hailey say you're a bother?"

"No, but I don't want her to feel trapped."

Bruce grinned as though he had a secret to tell. "Believe me. Hailey won't think that."

"What if she decides to leave me?"

"That's your insecurities talking. Don't push her

away. Hailey knows you can't do this alone. When she was a teenager, she relied a lot on Parker's support after her trauma."

Mark shuffled his feet on the carpet. "Sooner or later Hailey will blame me for Parker's death. I'm afraid she might change her mind about us."

"Parker was a friend. That's all. Hailey loves you. Let her help. I learned a long time ago that you can't live in 'what-ifs.' " Bruce pointed to the phone on the end table. "Call her."

"I'll give it some thought." He stared, unwavering, daring Bruce to question further. "How was your trip?"

"Tiring, but productive." Bruce slid on his eyeglasses.

"The receptionist said you went to the Amazon?"

"Peru. I went to see a shaman near Puerto Inco."

"Shaman…as in a medicine man?" Mark shook his head. "I'm not following."

"My *Bixa aparra* shrub was dying. I thought the shaman might know how to save it."

The Euphoria plant. A shiver ran down Mark's spine. "Did he have any suggestions?"

"Yes, but I'm too late. While I was away, my plant wilted away like a corn plant in a Texas drought. I hated to see it die."

Mark scoffed. "I'm not. I say good riddance. The shrub caused a lot of destruction."

Bruce's face twisted. "You may feel differently after you hear what I have to say."

"What do you mean?"

"I believe the plant can regenerate skin beneath your scars. That's the research I was working on before I left town."

"You think the Euphoria drug can cure me?"

"Not the drug made from the leaves, but the flowers from the plant might. *Bixa aparra* once flourished in Peru around Shanay-Timpishka—a river in the Amazon known as the 'boiling river.' "

A boiling river? Mark skimmed the room. Where was the hidden camera? "Is this some kind of con?"

"I'm serious."

"The river actually boils?"

Bruce shook his head. "It comes close. Temperatures reach 200 degrees Fahrenheit. *Bixa aparra* was indigenous to the banks along the river. The aborigines used the plant for hundreds of years to cure villagers scalded by the river."

"Did you find any shrubs growing there?"

"No, the shaman believes *Bixa aparra* is extinct, like many other plant species deforested in the Amazon. The shaman's grandfather used to gather the flowers from the shrubs. He'd boil the blooms, collect the oil, and make a thick paste."

Mark tilted his head. "Did the shaman actually see the paste cure people with burns?"

"He remembered his grandfather using a salve on a warrior who slipped on the rocks and fell into the river. He swears it regenerated the warrior's skin. Took away the pain, too."

Where was this miracle salve ten months ago? Mark pointed to his burn mask and pressure garments. "My scars have already formed. Even if the plant can regenerate skin, it's too late for me."

"Maybe not. Scars can take eighteen to twenty-four months to resolve and mature." Bruce rolled up his sleeves and extended his arms. "I used the salve. Look."

Mark gaped. The doctor's left arm was wrinkled and dotted with age spots, but the right arm showed no signs of aging.

Was it possible Mark's own scars could vanish? He could have his life back.

Realization struck him like a gut punch. "Your plant's dead."

Bruce reached in his trouser pocket and pulled out a vial and a folded paper. "The shaman gave me his last oil to make salve."

Mark eyed the small vial in Bruce's hands. There couldn't be more than two ounces of oil. "Is that enough to treat me?"

"No. Therein lies the problem." Bruce frowned. "If I analyze the oil to determine the structure, I run the risk of running out *and* not having any left to use on you. If I treat your scars, I won't have enough oil to determine the composition."

Mark swallowed the lump in his throat. He hadn't come this far to go home empty-handed. "Kind of gives being stuck between a rock and a hard place new meaning."

"That's not the entire issue. Even if I decide to use part of the oil and make a salve for you, I don't have the necessary approval to perform this research in the open. There are regulations, and the ethics committee needs to approve it."

"So do it under the table. Hailey has told me you're a genius at medical advancements."

"I hoped you would say that." Bruce unfolded the paper and passed Mark a pen from his jacket. "With your permission, I'd like to contact your former doctors to review your records."

Mark scanned the permission form and scrawled his signature. "Do whatever's necessary. Talk to my doctors at the Peachtree Wound Care and Burn Center, too."

"I'll make some phone calls. We can discuss this in more detail tonight." Bruce collected the form and slid it into the inside pocket of the lab coat. "I'll drop by your apartment later and give you an update. If you'd like, we can go out and eat."

"I haven't ventured into restaurants yet."

If Bruce noticed Mark's awkwardness, he didn't show it. "No problem. I'll order us some takeout. Are you fine with Chinese?"

"That'd be great. Thanks." He walked Bruce to the door. The skin under his arm garment itched like crazy. With any luck, the treatment would ease his pain and itchiness, too.

When Bruce left, Mark held the family picture against his chest, and he collapsed against the seat cushion. Was it possible a plant existed that could heal him? He might be able to reunite with Hailey, Ethan, and Anna sooner than he ever imagined.

His cell phone rang.

David. Mark swiped his finger across the screen. "Hey, buddy."

"Sorry to bother you."

"You're fine. I have some time before my next therapy. What's going on?"

"Hailey's gone."

"What do you mean 'gone'? Where'd she go?"

"I'm not sure. When I texted her yesterday morning, she planned to work on the yard all day."

"Okay…"

"It rained—the entire day." David's deep breathing

rasped through the phone line. "She didn't return my calls last night. Her car wasn't in the driveway this morning, either."

"Maybe she went shopping."

"At seven AM? She didn't go shopping."

Mark tensed. "Where do you think she went?"

"Colombia."

"Colombia?" Mark dropped the photograph onto his lap. "Why?"

"I think she went with Colleen."

Mark balled his hands into fists as dizziness passed over him. "Dammit! They went to find Rose."

"I thought the same. Last week, Colleen stopped by your house and asked Hailey for help."

Mark fought to keep his thoughts straight. "Why didn't you tell me sooner? You know what kind of assholes we're dealing with!"

"I thought I had talked her out of going. Hailey has a mind of her own."

Isn't that the truth. If his sweat glands could function, his body would be beading with moisture. "Dammit! Mendoza almost killed Hailey this spring. How could she risk going anywhere near him again? Contact the director at the SCA. Stefan must have connections with the Colombian government. Ask if he can track Hailey using the GPS from her ear implants. Call my supervisor at the DTA. Owen will provide support. Can any of your agents look for her?"

"I already coordinated plans with the agencies. Stefan Bruno's son Erik who works at the San Francisco field office is teaming with me. Hailey tried to get intel on Manuel's property last week, but Stefan had given Erik strict orders to keep her away from the investigation. I'll keep you posted." David hung up.

Mark couldn't keep his hand from shaking as he stared at the blank screen. *Call Hailey.*

He pressed in her number. He hadn't heard his wife's voice in over a week. A week!

The call went to her voicemail.

"Honey, please call me. It's important. I love you." He ended the call and buried his head in his palms.

He was powerless. Again.

Panic gripped him as he started trembling.

A goon punched his gut and flicked the lighter.

Mark was on fire again. He curled up on the sofa and rocked.

****

"Do we have an agreement?" Drawing in a heavy lungful on his cigar, José passed the bistro owner a bag of bills and leaned back in the rickety chair.

Two *gringas* would bring a high price. A young one like Manuel's bastard daughter even more. This sweet deal offset the hellacious treatment his son had handed him the past month.

The man locked the money in his bottom desk drawer. "Consider it done. You bring the women tonight. The boat carrying your…passengers…will dock in Jamaica."

José lowered his cigar onto the ashtray, shook the man's leathery hand, and exited through the rear door. He'd hold off celebrating until the deal was over. Too much could go wrong.

For months, the authorities had been confiscating his drug shipments. Even after he switched port locations, the officials continued to seize most of the cargo when the narcosubs departed. Someone on the inside could be betraying him. Someone he trusted.

José needed to be extra careful with this evening's venture. Dealing with the whore and the nosy troublemaker was personal. Trafficking them would be even better than killing them. They'd soon beg for mercy from the hell he'd forced them into.

He coughed and spat on the ground. The damn herbicide the government had been spraying was finally licking him.

The doctor had cautioned the scarring and cysts in the lungs would worsen. He even warned of digestion difficulties and skin lesions.

The treatment, however, would be more toxic on José's body than the disease. At seventy-three, he had too much work to do with the Resistance, too much to accomplish before he could slow down and spend his days confined to a hospital bed.

He could order the researchers in the mountain lab to find a cure. Shouldn't be too difficult since Manuel had insisted his precious *Bixa aparra* plant had curative powers.

José chuckled. *Curative powers. Hogwash!*

At a traffic light, he checked his phone.

His wife hadn't returned any messages. Why hadn't he noticed Camila's aloofness? While he worked with the insurgents in the jungle camps, she busied herself in the city.

Did she enjoy their estranged relationship? Their lack of intimacy? When they married, mutual sexual attraction warmed the bed. Camila wanted the power and prestige of a strong man who wielded brutal control. After Manuel was born, she complained how the government oppressed its people. She made the orphanage her refuge, working as though helping poor scullions was restitution for José's criminal life.

A life their granddaughter would never witness since Manuel didn't permit her to leave the ranch. Manuel even forbade her to meet José. A decision Camila supported. The denial stung more than the snap of the leather belt José used to whip Manuel with.

José grumbled. The only thread binding him to Camila was her father's legal perpetual trust stipulating José maintained control as long as he remained married and avoided any scandal. At the time, the idea seemed reasonable. Any public transgression on José's part, he'd lose everything—and his wife would take control of the estate. If Manuel had kids, the power would pass to him and then to his children, continuing down Camila's family line.

José spat. Camila's father had been slicker than spoiled caviar.

The property and holdings are mine. How dare Camila's father pass along his entire wealth to a whore's offspring.

When José transported Manuel's first love, Selena, to the Caribbean, he'd assumed his lovestruck son would never marry. The reckless boy couldn't keep his cock in his damn pants.

When the pedestrian light switched, José hiked down the block toward a marketplace that sold ammunition under-the-table. He crossed the road to his truck parked along a side street.

Luis lifted the last box of ammo and supplies onto the truck bed and wiped his brow. "Did you finalize the plans, *jefe*?"

José nodded. "There'll be a boat docked here in

Santa Marta at midnight. Got a price on the five-year-old, too, if we can sneak her out of the house."

Luis's expression remained stoic. No doubt he still remembered when José sent away Luis's sister.

If the man had a problem with sex trafficking, he wouldn't be working there. Luis was a loyal man. He understood the Resistance came first. Taking power from the Colombian government was the prime objective, no matter the cost. In many ways, Luis would've made a better son than Manuel.

"Do you need help ordering the other supplies? I can navigate the dark web and secure a courier until you find a tech replacement." Luis opened the driver's side door.

José frowned. Luis was resourceful, but he was merely a rebel drill leader. If his technical expert had been more competent, José wouldn't have lost his temper and shot him. "No. I'll bring in another tech specialist soon."

"As you wish." Luis reached into the truck and pulled out two bottles of liquor. "I found a street vendor down the road selling *aguardiente*." He twisted off the cap and handed José a bottle. Then he twisted the cap off the other container and raised his hand. *"¡Salud!"*

To our health. José raised his arm, clinking his bottle against Luis's. He pulled a long sip on the bottle, letting the liquor roll to the back of his throat. The tropical fruit spirit had an aroma of anise. Damned if he could recall the medicinal benefits of that herb.

He rotated the bottle in his hand, trying to ignore the area on his skin flaking away like spalling concrete. Was there a plant in the jungle that could heal him? *¡Jueputa!* Such crazy thoughts. His mind must already be intoxicated.

"Where are you shipping them?" Luis took a swig of his drink.

José paused a moment. Was Luis making small talk, or did he have an objective? "My connection in Jamaica is interested." He leaned his back against the truck and swallowed more *aguardiente*. "I want them out of here before Manuel returns."

Before Manuel decides to turn his whore into a wife.

José smirked. How fitting to sell Colleen Toole in the same manner as Manuel's first love.

Luis guzzled down the rest of his drink. "We should head back. We have a long night." He tossed the bottle into a trash can and secured the load with shock cords.

José threw his bottle onto the ground and climbed into the truck. He'd need to hurry. Already the sun dipped below the trees. A lot depended on shipping out the two women at midnight. The money he'd make could provision his rebels for the next two months. Shipping the overindulged girl would give him an additional three months.

Chapter Three

Slow deep breaths. Inhale. Exhale.

Hard knocks beat against the door. "Mark, it's me. Bruce. Can you please open the door?"

Mark jumped, his muscles tensing like tightropes. He wiped his tears, groped his way to the entrance, and unlocked the door.

Bruce rushed in carrying a white plastic bag. "Are you okay? I knocked for five minutes."

He raked a hand through his hair. "Uh...I was in the bathroom. I didn't expect you until this evening."

"It's seven o'clock." Bruce raised the bag in his hand and set it on the kitchen table. "I brought you dinner."

Damn. He'd been on the sofa all day. For the third time in a week, he'd become helpless, shaking on the sofa. "I must've lost track of time."

Bruce's bushy eyebrows knitted into one long brow. He flipped the overturned wastebasket upright and picked up two pillows from the floor. "You said your PTSD was getting better."

"I thought it was." Mark shrank from the pity on Bruce's face. Or was it disappointment?

The doctor lifted the guitar from the carpet and leaned it against a wall. "Want me to call Dr. Kendrick?"

Mark shook his head. "I'll call her in the morning. I'm all right. Really."

Bruce removed his jacket and laid it over the recliner. "You seemed fine earlier. What happened?"

Mark gestured at the living room sofa. "Let's sit. I have news about Hailey."

When Mark finished explaining where Hailey had gone, he paced. "Colombia's a dangerous country. Why did she take off without telling anyone?"

"She must've felt no one would help, especially since Colombian courts favor a Colombian parent. Stefan knows the Department of State handles the return of kidnapped children in foreign countries. He's always kept the SCA out of their affairs." Bruce massaged his temple. "Your kids must be worried sick."

Mark shook his head. "I doubt they know. They're visiting family in New Jersey for a few weeks. My sister's kids are just a little older than Anna and Ethan."

"Hopefully, they won't have to find out Hailey's missing. Do you have options?"

"Stefan's tracking Hailey's location—thanks to the GPS you put into her hearing implant."

Bruce glanced at his watch. "They should've located her by now."

"I'm expecting David to call any time." Mark walked into the kitchen and opened the fridge. "Would you like a drink while we wait? Sorry, I don't have any beer."

"Water's fine. Thanks." Bruce stepped into the kitchen.

Mark pulled out two plastic bottles and passed one to Bruce.

"Did you get to any therapies this afternoon?"

"No."

Bruce drained half his bottle in one gulp. "I know

you're worried about Hailey, but you can't miss your therapies. Your exercises are critical in your recovery."

Mark bowed his head. His life seemed to revolve around the therapies. "I know. But when these episodes rear up, I can't stop them."

"I'll call the center to see if someone can come over to change the garments and do some therapy before you go to sleep." Bruce opened the takeout bag and set white boxes onto the table. "In the meantime, you need to eat. Starving yourself won't help you or Hailey. We also need to discuss the consultations I had with your doctors."

When Mark finished eating, he moved into the living room and began his stretching exercises. Having discussed his options with Bruce, he'd decided to move forward with the salve treatment. Though Hailey's plight was still unresolved, hope of any kind was something to hang on to. If the worst happened, the kids would need him sooner. Better to start the experimental treatment while he had time.

Bruce phoned the doctor on-call at the burn center and joined Mark in the living room. "Someone should be here within the hour."

Mark's cell vibrated in his pocket, and he pulled out the phone. "It's David. Shit! They lost the signal. How'd they lose the fucking signal?"

Bruce slumped onto the sofa. "Hailey must be somewhere that's preventing the GPS from responding. Tell them to keep trying."

Mark texted David and paced the room.

"Sit." Bruce gestured to the vacant spot on the sofa beside him.

Mark squeezed his water bottle. "I don't want to sit."

"You're making me dizzy when you walk back and forth, crackling your plastic bottle like you're gripping hand weights."

"I'm pissed." Mark hurled the half-filled water bottle at the recycle basket, bouncing it off the side onto the floor.

Bruce folded his arms, gestured at the sofa, and waited.

Dammit! The old man was more stubborn than a mule. Mark exaggerated a loud huff and perched on the recliner instead.

Bruce leaned back in his seat. "Something else is bothering you. What is it?"

Mark's nerves were like springs priming to snap. "I can't believe Hailey left. How can she justify putting our family at risk for someone else's child?"

"She obviously wanted to help the little girl."

"I don't like it."

Bruce's eyebrow lifted. "*You* ran away."

Mark opened his mouth but quickly closed it. "That's different."

"How?"

"My leaving wasn't entirely voluntary. Hailey's was. I was doing my job. Trying to protect Hailey and the kids. My job has always entailed risks and secret operations." He ached to squeeze his fist tighter. "I should be the one in Colombia, not Hailey."

"But you're not there. She was also an agent. A damn good one."

Pride filled his chest. Mark picked up the family picture from the end table. "I know she's competent, but she's not working for SCA anymore. I feel useless that I can't protect her. Or Colleen. God help them. What were those two thinking? They're going to get killed—if they don't kill each other first."

"Give Hailey some credit. She's trying to find Colleen's daughter. She understands how it feels to be ripped apart from people you love."

Why hadn't he considered that? "I know about her kidnapping when she was seventeen."

"I'm glad she told you."

"She's the strongest person I've ever met. Can you tell me more about what she went through?"

Bruce's lips tightened, and he looked off into the distance.

"Come on. I know about her counseling. I even know how you and Parker helped her after she mentally shut down."

Bruce scrubbed a hand over his stubble. "She was frozen after her trauma. Much like you are. That's why I think she'd be able to help with your PTSD."

I love her too much to put her through my pain. "Our situations are different."

"Don't be too sure. Hailey dealt with her own self-esteem issues after the trauma. She still has scars."

"She's the bravest woman I know. How did she learn acceptance?"

"The therapists tried different treatments until they found something that worked. Exercise made a difference. Hailey tried yoga—and running. She and Parker ran together."

"She still runs. Every morning."

Bruce nodded. "The endorphins elevate her mood."

"Dr. Kendrick suggested I try yoga."

"It's not a bad idea."

Mark snorted. "Yoga's more of a women's activity."

"Not necessarily. It relieves stress. The breathing promotes healing." Bruce stood and dropped his water bottle into the recycling bin. "My advice is let Hailey help you. Your wife knows how it feels to be alone and scared."

Mark rested his head against the recliner cushion. Bruce had given him a lot to think about. "It's not fair to drag her down with my problems after everything she's been through."

"Hailey's your wife. She wants to help you, and you need her." The lines in Bruce's face softened. "Marriage is about being there for each other—for better, for worse, in sickness and in health."

"For now, I'd feel better if I knew Hailey was safe."

"Are you sure I can't call Dr. Kendrick for you?"

"No. I'm okay." He lied.

Bruce's eyebrow arched, and he zipped his jacket. "The nurse should be here soon to change the garments. Do you want me to stay and open the door?"

"Thanks, but I can handle it." Mark ushered him to the entrance.

"Text me if you hear anything. Drop by my office in the morning, and we'll begin the salve treatments. Eight o'clock okay?"

"That works. My shuttle comes at nine. Thanks for everything."

"Anytime. Try not to worry. Hailey's a professional. She's gotten out of tough scrapes before." Bruce patted Mark's back and closed the door behind himself.

Mark walked into the living room and picked up the family photo. Hailey didn't need any more adversity in her life. She'd been through too much already. *I can't lose her.*

He envisioned wrapping his arms around his wife, smoothing her wavy chestnut hair, easing away the tiny wrinkles under her enchanting hazel eyes, and taking in her soft feminine scent.

Honey, wherever you are, please be careful.

****

Hailey's eyelids fluttered open. The rope binding across her breasts dug into her skin. When she stretched her fingers, they tingled. Shoulders were stiff and achy. How long had she slept? Night had set in, but moonlight outlined shadows inside the shed. The temperature had cooled considerably, easing her piercing headache. The dizziness was gone.

A low clawing sound came from the corner, and a large possum-like animal with a long tail scurried across the floor and over her hiking boots.

"Aaah!" Hailey kicked her legs as the critter dashed back to the corner. "Colleen. You awake?"

"I am now."

"We have to get out of here. I don't know how much time we have. Lift your arms a few inches, and I'll try to untie you." Hailey tugged at the knots again, grimacing as the scabs on her wrists opened.

"I'm out." Colleen unraveled the ropes around their torsos. Next, she freed her ankles and untied Hailey's wrists.

Hailey loosened the ropes around her feet. "Check the canteen."

Colleen fetched the container. "Hallelujah! Yes!" She gulped like a desert cactus sucking up water after a rainstorm. Then she passed it. "Your turn."

Hailey drained the canteen and rubbed her thigh muscles in a quick massage. "Let's go."

Colleen reached the door first and rotated the doorknob. "It's locked."

"Grab me the backpack." Hailey slid her fingers along the hinges.

Colleen clutched the bag from the ground and handed it to her. "What are you doing?"

"I need a tool to open the door." Hailey reached into the bag and pulled out her flashlight and the six-inch screwdriver. She handed Colleen the flashlight. "Bring me a brick from the pile by the wall."

Colleen gathered one and hurried back. "Is this okay?"

"Yes." Hailey inserted the screwdriver tip under the bottom hinge and took the brick. "Shine some light over here." With a hard smack, she pounded the brick against the screwdriver's handle and popped the pin from the hinge. The pain in Hailey's wrists hurt like a blade sawed her bone. She removed the remaining two pins and tossed the screwdriver onto the bag. "Hold the door steady while I slide it away from the hinges."

When she detached the door, animal calls and insect buzzes flooded the room.

"Way to go!" Colleen stepped back as Hailey dropped the door to the ground.

Hailey tilted her head and peered outside. "It's clear." She zippered her backpack and adjusted it onto her shoulders. "The road is up the hill to the right. The trail's rugged."

Colleen brushed off dirt from her sweater. "I remember."

"Let's go." Hailey bolted, but at the firepit, she paused a moment to massage her legs once more before she ran.

Following close behind, Colleen aimed the flashlight onto their path while treading between the prickly bushes that stretched across the rocky ground.

As Hailey and Colleen neared the crest, they took a moment and caught their breath; the cacophony of loud chirps, croaks, and animal calls drowned out their heavy panting.

Colleen aimed the light at a farm tractor and old truck. "Do you think—"

"The truck looked to be in decent shape when we passed it earlier." Hailey took off running. "Let's go for it."

Hailey tested the door latch and fist-pumped a silent victory when the door opened. Settling onto the front seat, she laid the backpack next to her and leaned under the dash, fingering the wires. Mark would be proud she'd paid attention when he showed her how to hot-wire a car in the Langley garage.

Colleen slid into the passenger seat. "What if it doesn't start?"

Hailey peered out the window at the full moon. "There's enough light to walk to the main road. We'll have to find our way back to the nearest town on foot."

"In the dark? Are you crazy? There are snakes out there!" Colleen shuddered.

"It's either that or we wait here for José to find us. Cross your fingers. It's been years since I started a vehicle this way." Hailey connected the correct battery wires, sparked the starter wire, and the engine vroomed. With her foot pressing on the gas, Hailey revved the engine and detached the starter wire. Yes! It worked. She cranked the wheel hard to the left and broke the steering lock. "Buckle up."

Hailey tugged her seat belt, shifted into low gear, and drove the truck up the narrow hill. At the top, she steered onto the path and shifted gears. She pressed her foot harder on the gas pedal. Every minute they went unnoticed increased their chances of escaping.

Boom!

Hailey turned, and her pulse quickened.

José and Luis raced toward them with weapons raised. José fired his gun three more times.

One bullet ricocheted off the truck's tailgate.

Colleen ducked. "Oh my God. They're shooting at us."

"No shit." Hailey found the headlights on the dash. She fought to maintain control of the vehicle as José fired again and again.

The last shot thwacked the rear window and cracked the glass.

Colleen peeked over the seat. "Damn. That was close."

Hailey drove down the gravel lane and veered onto the main road, increasing the distance from their pursuers. Soon she neared the tall grasses and underbrush where the guide had parked his vehicle earlier that morning. She glanced at Colleen, still crouched in her seat. "I think it's okay now." As she navigated a sharp curve, she squinched her eyes from the bright lights shining in the other direction.

Colleen crossed her arms in front of her face and screamed.

Hailey hit the brake but sideswiped the car and veered off the road, landing in a copse of evergreen trees. She lurched forward, whacking her head on the steering wheel.

Son of a bitch! Her headache returned with a vengeance. Dazed, Hailey rubbed her brow and winced; a bump was already swelling. No bones felt broken, though her wrists and head throbbed something awful. "Colleen, are you okay?"

"I think so." Colleen slid back onto the seat. "Are we stuck out here?"

Hailey looked over the dash. The moonlight illuminated the smashed front end of the car against a tree. *What else could go wrong tonight?*

"Is anyone hurt?" A tall man with a deep voice shouted from his car and ran toward them.

Hair prickled on her neck as Hailey squinted in the darkness. *I recognize that voice.* She gathered her backpack, opened her door, and helped Colleen climb out.

The man stepped closer, peering at them through the cloudy headlights. "Bella?" His gaze remained fixed on Colleen like a starstruck lover, and his voice softened. "You came."

Bella? Hailey gasped. Dear God. Her day just got a million times worse. Manuel Mendoza was home. Called *Mendoza* within the US Intelligence community, he would forever be known to her as the man who shattered her world.

A truck sped toward them, gunshots firing from the windows.

When the vehicle slowed, José whipped open the passenger door and sprinted toward them, leaving Luis to park alongside the road. "Manuel. I wasn't expecting you."

"I flew back early. The nanny heard gunshots."

"That was me. Luis and I found these two *putas*

outside." José gestured toward Hailey and Colleen. "They were trying to kidnap Rose."

Colleen's shoulders squared as she spun to her former lover. "She is *my* daughter. You had no right to take her."

"She's *my* daughter." Mendoza's gruff voice was daunting. "You had no right to hide her existence from me. I lost five years getting to know her."

"I lost six years because of you!" Colleen beat her fists against his chest. "How dare you! You never even contacted me. No letters. No phone calls." She slapped his cheek. "I gave up my life for you. You owe me. I want my daughter back."

Mendoza's jaw tensed. "Rose stays with me. This is her home."

"Home?" Colleen gestured at José. "You trust your daughter with him? She's in prison here."

"*Papá* isn't allowed near Rose. He can't hurt her *or* you."

Hailey pursed her lips. *Wanna bet?*

"Don't be so naïve." Colleen stamped her foot. "He's already made plans to ship all three of us to the Caribbean tonight—and it's not for a vacation."

"Is that true, *papá*?"

José shrugged and spat at the ground. "They're trouble, *hijo*. We need to teach them a lesson."

"*We* are not doing anything. Luis, escort Bella and *señora* Langley back to my car. I want a word alone with my father."

With her eyes, Hailey shot daggers at the Mendoza men. Both were scum of the earth and deserved to rot in jail. Hard to tell which was worse. They each had a laundry list of crimes ten miles long.

Luis pulled a gun from his camouflage pants and steered the women through the grassy culvert across to the paved road. He opened the rear car door and stationed himself beside the vehicle as Colleen and Hailey slid into their seats.

Hailey turned her head closer to the half-open driver's side window as Mendoza shouted at José. Though he spoke fast, she could understand most of his Spanish.

"What the hell were you doing?"

"They have no reason to be here, *hijo*."

"Bella is Rose's mother. I'd like to hear why she came."

"She didn't come for a fucking social visit. She and that snitch were trying to break into the house."

"You should've called."

José coughed. "I can handle things while you're away."

"You arrogant old fool! I run this ranch now. You no longer have power over me—or anyone. The DNA tests proved Rose is my child. I'm the executor of *abuelo's* dynasty trust until Rose can take over. You're lucky the trust allots you money every month." The anger in his voice escalated. "You're not allowed to see Rose. I told you to stay away from the mansion. My generosity has ended. Vacate the ranch house by nightfall tomorrow. Now get out of my sight."

José grasped his son's arm. "You can't throw me out. What about your mother? This is her father's land."

"*Mamá* is welcome to stay, but you must go."

"And if I don't?"

Mendoza grabbed his father's shirt. "Then I give all the criminal evidence I have on you to the government.

Every drug trade. Every assassination. Your involvement with the revolu—"

José cackled. "I'll take you down with me."

"Don't count on it, old man." Mendoza hissed and pushed his father. "Now leave, before I change my mind and silence you forever."

Chapter Four

Hailey sat in the parlor, sneaking glances at Luis.

Every few minutes, he'd look up from his phone and then return his attention to the screen. He was shorter than Mendoza. His tanned broad forehead and crooked nose gave him a rugged look. Probably broke his nose once or twice. Muscular arms, but not too beefy. A gentle sadness dimmed his eyes. The man might be likeable if he didn't work for a family of criminals.

The tambour clock on the marble mantel inched to the next minute. What were Mendoza and Colleen discussing? An hour was a long time to hash over their parental roles about Rose, unless they were discussing other matters.

Hailey slid her thumb over the fabric of the wingback chair. Soft and velvety. The antique chair, with its carved claw feet, must've cost more than all the furniture in her home in Virginia. Her stomach rumbled, and she squirmed in her seat. Surely Luis heard the noise. Her knapsack was on the floor next to him, but José had scarfed down the protein bars. The canteen had been drained. If she didn't drink something soon, her headache would kill her.

She faked a cough. "Could I please have a glass of water?" When he ignored her, she raked a hand through her grubby hair and repeated her request in Spanish.

Luis stared at her for a moment. Then he strode to

the wet bar in the corner and pulled a bottle from the fridge.

She licked her lips as he handed her the cold water. It seemed like years since she'd eaten the pastries and tropical fruits at the hotel's buffet breakfast. No surprise she was lightheaded.

"*Gracias*." She untwisted the cap, guzzling the entire bottle of water. In an hour, she'd need to ask for a bathroom—if she wasn't poisoned first. "How long have you worked here?" As soon as the words came out of her mouth, the question sounded foolish. Did she really think her keeper would entertain conversation? Did he even speak English?

After an awkward silence, his green eyes warmed, but his expression remained stern as he returned to his seat.

Why wouldn't he speak?

The door swung open, and Mendoza stepped inside.

Colleen sashayed beside him, holding Rose's hand.

Dressed in a pink nightgown and fuzzy slippers, Rose rubbed her eye as if someone woke her from her sleep.

The child pulled away from Colleen's hand, and she dashed to Hailey. "You came!"

"I told you I would." Hailey scooped Rose into her arms and leaned back. The girl looked well. Thinner, but no bruises on exposed skin. "How are you? We're all worried about you. Anna misses you."

Rose wrapped her little arms around Hailey's neck and began to cry. "I miss her—and Samantha. And my other mommy. Are you taking me home?"

Blinking rapidly, Colleen stepped closer and smoothed Rose's hair. "D...darling, I told you we can

45

video chat with your friends after we settle in here."

"Settle in?" A band tightened across Hailey's chest, and she held Rose even tighter. *Oh my God!* Colleen was reuniting with Mendoza. David had been right. *Dammit! I should've listened to him.*

Stepping back, Hailey turned, shielding Rose from the bedlam. "Don't tell me—"

Colleen held Mendoza's hand and crinkled her nose at him. "We used to make a great team. We...we want to try again."

Mendoza's posture became more rigid. "Bella's agreed to live with Rose and me. She's going to head my research lab."

Hailey's head spun. "Your research lab?"

Colleen nodded. "Manuel has a lab in the mountains."

The implants had to be playing tricks on her. "You served six years in jail because of this man. How could you forget he's betrayed you?"

Colleen lowered her chin and fidgeted with her hands.

Mendoza massaged Colleen's back. "Because she'll get to see our daughter every day." His brusque reply sounded like a warning.

Hailey rubbed her temple. Her brain felt like it was exploding. "Do you really want this?"

Colleen draped her arm around Rose. "I want us to be a family. Yes, we had problems, but I never stopped...thinking of Manuel and our daughter."

The room slanted. Whether this decision was forced or voluntary, there was no sense arguing. Colleen had made her choice.

Where does this leave me? Even without José

46

around threatening to ship her to the Caribbean, Mendoza might not let her leave. How would she get out of Colombia?

Think of something convincing.

Hailey held Rose's hand. "I have an idea. Let's call Joyce and the girls and tell them you're okay. They'll want to talk to you. We can use my phone to call."

Rose started hopping. "Yay!"

Hailey turned to Luis and extended her hand. "Now that everything's fine, can you give us our phones back? Rose would like to talk to my daughter." At the very least, Anna could notify David that Hailey had found Rose.

Mendoza's smile vanished. "Nice try."

He leaned down and patted Rose's head. "Princess, go to the kitchen and ask your nanny to get you a snack."

"But I want to talk to my friends—"

Mendoza shook his head. "Rose, it's bedtime. We'll talk about it tomorrow."

When she left, Mendoza paced the marble floor, hands clasped behind his back. "You present quite a dilemma. Now I must decide what to do with you."

Easy solution. Hailey lifted an eyebrow. "You can let me go back to the US."

He grunted. "Why would I do that?"

"You have Colleen. Rose. Everyone important to you."

"If I recall correctly, I ordered you killed."

"Yes, you tried again after you stabbed me in my office. It's like double jeopardy. Can't say there's no hard feelings, but you and I have no reason to see each other anymore. You can let me go home, and I won't come back."

"Unfortunately, you were the agent who hacked into my family's files, nearly bankrupting us." Mendoza scrubbed his bristled jaw. "For personal reasons, I don't support my father's views on human trafficking—but that doesn't mean I'm ready to let bygones be bygones."

"But I don't know anything. I haven't seen you do anything corrupt…I have nothing to tell when I go back to the US." Hailey scratched her arm. "If I don't go back, my family and friends will come here and look for me."

Mendoza folded his arms across his chest. "Luis. Tie her up."

Hailey gaped. "What? Why?"

"Then blindfold her and put her in a car. Drive her to the airport and charter a plane to fly her to the States."

Yes! Hailey held back from jumping. She'd be home in a day or two.

Colleen gaped. "You can't be serious."

"She's right. I have everything I want. If she tries to cause any trouble, I'll charge her for trespassing."

"But you can't just tie her up and put her on a plane."

His finger caressed Colleen's cheek. "I want her out of our hair."

"Okay, but don't send her away tonight."

"Why not?"

Colleen gestured to Hailey. "L…l…look at her. She's filthy. Cuts all over her wrists. Her hair is grungy, and she smells like an overheated pig."

Hailey huffed. "Pig? You're one to talk. You smell as bad as me."

Colleen's lips tightened. "Give her a few days to recover before you send her back."

Hailey's mouth went dry. "No. Send me back now. I don't need a few days."

Mendoza exhaled. "I'll sleep on it, *querida*. Luis, show *señora* Langley to the servants' quarters. The staff left for the day. See that she's secured inside." He twisted a finger through Colleen's hair. "Tonight, I want to spend time with Bella."

"*Sí, señor*." Luis grabbed Hailey's arm.

"B…B…But wait." Hailey shook her arm free. "When are you going to release me?"

Mendoza slipped his hand across Colleen's backside. "We'll discuss it in the morning." He kissed Colleen on the cheek and listened politely as she whispered in his ear. "Oh, and Luis, please see that our visitor gets something to eat."

****

Luis led Hailey to a room across from the laundry area and locked the door before he left.

She jiggled the handle anyway and slammed her fist against the door. There had to be another way out.

A narrow door in the corner opened to a tiny powder room. Not the exit she was looking for, but at least she had a toilet to relieve her bladder. The ventilation ducts mounted on the ten-foot-high ceilings wouldn't be large enough to squeeze through even if she managed to reach them. Perhaps a key hidden in the desk? She opened the ebony drawers. Nothing. Not even a hidden compartment.

When footfalls approached in the hallway, she jumped onto the Victorian chaise and waited as the keys clinked in the lock.

Luis stepped into the room, carrying a food tray. For a moment, he looked as though he might speak. Instead, he placed the tray onto the desk and locked the door on his way out.

49

Eyeing the assorted fruit and bread, she picked up a juice container. The seal was intact. With a hard twist, she broke the cap's seal and drank. Tangy and tart. At this point, she'd drink anything. Next, she tore open a small loaf of cheese bread and peeled the skin from a dragon fruit. When the tray was empty, she could barely keep her eyes open.

She wiped dirt from her arms and headed into the bathroom. *Got to clean these gashes before I get an infection.*

After cleaning her wounds, Hailey left the bathroom light on as a nightlight. Then she flipped off the overhead light and settled onto the chaise, adjusting a pillow under her neck.

She was a prisoner, but at least tonight she had a bed. What had she been thinking, coming to Colombia with no backup? It was a foolhardy move.

Hailey rolled to her side, glancing down at her boots. Too risky to remove them. Mendoza and Luis might be spying with a hidden camera and see the 3D gun and bullets.

What would Mark do in her situation? He'd been in tough scrapes. If she tried hard enough, maybe she could connect with his thought process.

David's intuition never failed. He'd warned Colleen would double-cross her! If the bitch hadn't opened her big mouth, Hailey would be on a plane tonight. Granted, she'd be tied up on the flight home, but Mendoza had been willing to send her back. The traitor may have ruined any chance of Hailey returning home. *Wouldn't put it past her to convince Mendoza to ship me to the Caribbean.*

At least José wasn't living in the mansion. Him

being at odds with his son was an unexpected bonus. Something seemed off with the old man. He had walked slowly, panting often. His weathered arms had patches of dried crusted skin, and his hacking sounded worse than a typical cough.

Hailey plumped up the pillow again and stared at the shadows in the room. The place was eerie, but more comfortable than the shed.

She yawned as an unpleasant isolation cloaked her. She hadn't felt this lonely since her parents' death. Just as well Mark hadn't called before she left; he would've realized she was up to something.

Her eyelids became heavier. She'd think more clearly in the morning—assuming she survived the night.

Chapter Five

A knock rattled the door.

Hailey opened her eyes.

What? Where?

The events from the previous night flooded her mind. *Oh yeah. Mendoza. At least I wasn't poisoned.* She glanced at her watch. 7:07AM.

Luis unlocked the door and trod into the room. "*Señor* Manuel will see you now."

So he did speak a little English.

He escorted her into an open-style contemporary kitchen where the aroma of rice and roasted coffee filled the air. A woman bustled about, loading stainless-steel pots and pans onto a rack above the island. The young nanny stood near the glass table where Colleen and Mendoza chatted with Rose.

Rose lowered the last piece of a corn cake and egg sandwich onto her plate and licked her fingers. "There you are. Want to eat with us? The mango juice tastes really good." Her dark-blue eyes glistened as she pointed to the trays of fresh homemade pastries and assorted sliced fruits on the counter. "The pink fruit is my favorite."

Mendoza studied Hailey. His clean-shaven jaw tensed, emphasizing his chiseled features. He drank some coffee and instructed the nanny in Spanish to help Rose dress for the day.

With a slight nod, the nanny held Rose's hand and led her out of the room.

Hailey glowered. Beside him, Colleen was freshly showered with her damp hair untangled. No doubt, she slept soundly in Mendoza's bed, most likely after a long night of steamy sex. Her clothes were different, too. Mendoza must maintain an entire wardrobe to dress his overnight guests.

Mendoza tapped his fingers on the saucer. "I trust you slept all right?"

Hailey chose her words carefully. "I doubt you care about my sleeping habits."

"You're right. I don't."

Hailey glared. "I'd like to leave now so I can fly back to the US."

Colleen lowered her coconut pastry. "Babe, I want Hailey to come with us today when we fly to your lab."

No! Send me home.

Mendoza scowled. "The less she knows about our operation, the better."

Our operation. Hailey pursed her lips. *Definitely. Keep me out of this.*

Colleen caressed Mendoza's nape. "She can help watch Rose."

"Rose is staying here, Bella." Tension thickened the air at his stern tone.

Colleen shook her head. "You said your mother's working at the orphanage today. I don't want Rose here, in case your father comes back and tries to ship her to the Caribbean while we're away. The nanny's too young to stand up to him."

Mendoza eyed the two women.

Colleen leaned over and whispered, "Please? Rose

is comfortable with Hailey. She'll adjust easier. I bet she's never had a helicopter ride."

He frowned. "She probably hasn't."

"See? She'll enjoy it. Please, do it for our daughter. Besides, Hailey's resourceful. If we leave her, she'll find a way to escape, and she might try to take Rose with her. At the very least, she'll contact her boss, and we'll have agents swarming this ranch. We don't need that worry."

Mendoza sighed. "Fine, Bella. Luis will come along and guard her. I'll call ahead to have an escort meet us." He motioned to Luis, standing near the wall. "Take the day off from helping my father and ride with us to the mountains."

Luis cast a watchful look at Hailey.

She stared back. Hard to tell what was going on inside Luis's head. No doubt, he'd report their activities back to Mendoza's father.

****

José paced the floor in his family room, his foul mood hanging over him like he'd been sprayed by a polecat. Why hadn't Luis sent any texts regarding Manuel's decision to ship the *putas?* The contacts in Jamaica didn't tolerate delays. The snub would cost him money and reputation.

Storming into the kitchen, he poured whiskey into a glass and marched outside to the patio. His drink dribbled onto the stone pavers as he coughed. He hacked a gob of phlegm into a handkerchief and grimaced at the dark streaks. *¡Hijueputa! More blood.*

Slowly, he began to relax. Putting behind the previous evening's confrontation had been difficult. When Manuel defended Colleen, he'd treated José like a worthless minion. *Pack my bags*—mi culo!

José's loins heated at the thought of the striking, blonde-haired woman with sapphire eyes. Even covered with sweat, Manuel's whore was sexy. Full bosom. Thin waist. Curvy ass. No wonder Manuel bedded her. She lived up to the name his son called her—Bella. A stunning beauty. The SCA bitch didn't look bad either, just smaller assets.

José lowered his gaze to his erection. He'd find relief at a brothel later.

Camila had stopped sharing a bed with him years ago. She had trusted him when they married. Leaned on him, doting on his every word. Lately, she had become more headstrong and quarrelsome. Perhaps his wife had become a liability.

Wind gusted across José's face. Bitterness latched onto him like a fungus clinging onto moist skin. He swallowed the rest of his drink and stared at the magnificent residence on the knoll where he used to live. His life had fallen apart since Manuel returned with his bastard daughter. This ranch house built by his father-in-law on the two-hundred-acre property was too cramped.

He fisted his hands until the knuckles turned white. He was condemned to this...this...prison cell while Manuel lived in luxury like the new head honcho. *I lived there forty years! How dare he ban me from my mansion.*

Returning to the kitchen, he clinked the tumbler onto the granite counter. The place wasn't so awful—but he deserved better.

José scratched his arm. *¡Hijueputa! Another crusty outbreak. When will this itching end?* He needed a miracle drug. How ironic it would be if the so-called "medicinal powers" in Manuel's Euphoria plant could heal his ailments.

Stranger things could happen. *Bixa aparra* had different draws. The initial success Manuel found using the leaves to make a mind-altering Euphoria drug proved lethal, but the bixine from the plant's roots did create a brain fog t enabled José to traffic the homeless teenagers from the orphanage easier.

José rubbed his hands together. His sex-trafficking plan produced enough funds to provide the Resistance with weapons and supplies.

Anger boiled the blood in his veins. The military group was all he had left where he could exercise his authority. He couldn't even keep his wife from doting on Manuel's daughter.

How could Camila accept the *chica*?

José hawked another gob. His declining health wasn't his only battle. The war on cocaine had serious repercussions. When the Colombian government convinced FARC leaders to relinquish their weapons during the last peace agreement, gutless guerillas gave up control of many drug-trafficking routes.

Fucking shitheads.

He got vengeance. One by one, he ordered his betrayers' executions. They shouldn't have abandoned the Resistance. They should've held out and retained power, controlling the jungles and the rural citizens the government had betrayed.

Coca plants provided wealth and power. In selling out to the government, the others lost everything.

José scoffed. The US, with their "anything goes" mentality, was one of the world's worst abusers of illicit drugs. *Norteamericanos* would deal with the consequences of their foolishness when they fell down from their high horse.

He checked his phone. Still nothing from Luis.

As he jammed the phone into his pocket, a helicopter thundered above the house.

"What the—" José stepped to the kitchen window and followed the path of the noise.

As the copter descended to the mansion's helipad, his phone beeped an incoming text.

—Manuel wants me with him today. Flying to the lab with his guests.—

Guests? Pressure mounted inside José's body. Manuel didn't even like Luis. Never trusted him after José shipped Luis's sister to the Caribbean.

Luis texted again.

—I'll keep you posted. No decision yet on shipping the "goods."—

He snickered. Luis was his devoted right-hand man. Manuel should be careful whom he trusted.

José waited until the blades spun again and the helicopter headed east into the mountains. The flight to the lab took over two hours. They'd be gone all day.

When the chopper disappeared, José unrolled maps over his desk. The leaders in the other blocs were eager to unite rebels for another demonstration. He'd mobilize the men for the attack in Bogotá. Set off car bombs near the National Capitol. He had a few weeks before the new president took over.

After reviewing the tactics for the different encampments, he plucked the truck keys from the counter. Plenty of work to do. The camps needed supplies and instructions. Weapons and food. His top officers could distribute the provisions to the other campsites while the insurgents finished setting up land mines in the area. Drug gangs were becoming bolder, taking over rebel camps and broadening their territories.

In the evening, he'd contact the captains in the other four blocs, advising them to fortify their camps—and he'd text Luis with a plan to transport the two *putas* and Manuel's bastard to the docks.

Chapter Six

With his left foot dragging a bit behind his right foot, Mark paced Bruce's lab. A mixture of nerves and hope spiked his adrenaline. Hard not to be optimistic after seeing the change in Bruce's arm. *Bixa aparra*, the Euphoria plant that had caused so much devastation and sadness, might heal his skin.

The custodian entered the room, transporting a large cardboard box on a flatbed pushcart. "Morning, Mark. Catch the game last night?"

"Hi, Ronnie." Mark waved at the fifty-year-old man. "I caught the highlights. Exciting homerun during the last inning. We can watch the next game at my place if you'd like."

"Sounds good. I'll bring the brewski."

Mark chuckled. "Any idea where Bruce is?"

"No, but he should be here soon. Doc usually starts early. I brought up the shipment he's been expecting." Ronnie grunted as he lifted the box.

"Here, let me help you with that." Mark picked up an end and lowered the carton onto the counter.

"Thanks. That was a doozy." Ronnie shook dust from his hand. "Hey, man. Are you okay?"

What did okay feel like anymore? "Everything's moving so fast. Bruce thinks he may have developed a new scar-management plan for me."

"You're in capable hands. Doc knows his stuff."

Ronnie extended his arm. "The new cream he gave me for my psoriasis is helping."

Mark sighed. The only dark spot to his recovery was Hailey's absence.

A high-pitched noise sounded from the hallway.

A moment later, Bruce rolled a metal cart into the room, one wheel squeaking. "Sorry I'm late, Mark. I had a few phone calls to return. Hi, Ronnie." He eyed the counter. "Oh, good. My new equipment arrived."

"Safe and sound." The custodian tapped the box. "I told the warehouse guys I'd bring it up." He high-fived Mark. "I'll catch you later. You got this."

When Ronnie left, Bruce pulled out vinyl gloves from a box on the counter. "Any news about Hailey?"

"Not yet."

"She'll be okay. Hailey's too skilled an agent to be caught off guard."

"I wish I could help find her." Mark lifted the tin container from the cart. He'd be lucky if the salve lasted more than a few days. "Is this all you have?"

Bruce shook his head. "I kept a small sample to test. I know we discussed this last night, but I need to caution you again. This is experimental. Even if the salve regenerates your skin, there's no guarantee your scars will completely disappear."

A lump lodged in Mark's throat. Life was full of risks. "I understand."

"You're certain you want to treat your face and neck first? We can apply salve on your upper body where you had laser resurfacing last month, or we can work on your left leg where the dermis had the most damage."

"With the limited supply, I need to prioritize." In bed with Hailey, he could conceal his body with darkness and sheets. Pretend life was normal again for a moment.

Memories swam in Mark's head of the nights he caressed Hailey's silky skin. Her fingers roamed across his body, tracing his muscle lines as she touched him. How would his alligator skin feel to her now? Repulsive?

"Give me a minute to prepare everything." The circles under Bruce's eyes were dark. Just returned from Peru, he was already working long hours in the lab. No wonder Hailey joked he was married to his work.

At least that kind of marriage was easier. Mark fingered his pressure garments. He could never atone for the misery he caused Hailey.

He gazed out the window to the courtyard below, where the landscaper pruned rose bushes with a hand trimmer. The flowers looked like the ones Mark had given Hailey when he apologized after an argument.

Mark bowed his head. He tried so hard to protect her, but he only hurt her more.

Sliding onto the chair, he removed his face mask and fingered its smooth laminated silicone. The inside surface wasn't at all like the pockmarked texture of his face. Uneasiness crept over him like a slithering snake. If his skin grew back, what would the new "normal" be like? Would the pain that haunted him daily go away, too? He cleared his throat. "Do you know what's in the salve to make it regenerate skin?"

Bruce sat on a round stool and pulled the cart closer. "Not yet, but I'm almost certain the oil contains some type of growth factors and MMPs."

"MMPs?"

"Matrix metalloproteinases. They're involved in the ECM…extracellular matrix…when the collagen fibers are laid down."

Mark blinked. He ought to be used to Bruce's polysyllabic scientific jargon by now.

Bruce peered over his wire-rimmed glasses. "You didn't read the article I dropped off late last night?" Not waiting for a reply, he stirred the salve with a glass rod. "When you have a skin wound, your body releases different components to close the wound. White blood cells migrate to the area. Fibroblasts. Angiogenic endothelial cells—"

"I read that part. But the other twenty-six pages were a confusing mix of unpronounceable words and diagrams."

"Did you understand how these components move to the wound to create a new barrier from the outside environment?"

Mark shifted in his seat. "Are you serious? I struggled to get a 'D' in high school biology."

Wrinkles spread between Bruce's eyebrows. "I assumed you liked science, especially since your wife teaches it."

"I like watching Hailey's face light up when she talks about science."

"Touché." Bruce's blue eyes flickered. "Did you read the section on epithelialization?"

The man was a walking encyclopedia. "I tried. Can you explain it in layman's terms?"

"Epithelialization is the process where new skin forms over the wound. If the wound is deep enough, which it is in your case, granulation occurs and forms new blood vessels and connective tissues." Bruce stood and picked up a clipboard hanging from a cabinet door. "It might be easier if I draw a picture."

Mark nodded. Drawings would be much easier to

follow than trying to make sense of the scientific terms.

Bruce reviewed the process, and he pointed to the extracellular matrix. "In normal skin, the collagen fibers are oriented in a random basket-weave formation. The fibers cross-link, giving skin its strength and elasticity. In deep dermal wounds, inflammation and other factors cause the collagen to repair itself quickly. The collagen fibers are thicker and align in a single direction."

"Forming scars." That part he understood. Mark had plenty of scars where the flames had licked his skin.

Bruce nodded. "Your current scars have less flexibility and strength than regular skin. I think the oil from *Bixa aparra*'s flowers sends more fibroblasts to the wound and then scaffolds the collagen matrix in the correct formation."

Mark pointed to the honey-colored salve in the container. "It's hard to believe something in that ointment can regenerate my skin."

"I think enzymes in the oil degrade the scar tissue and direct the restructuring of the collagen fibers." Bruce held up the tin. "Do you have any other questions? Anything more you want to discuss about the risks?"

Bruce had reviewed the risks at least five times. "If I do nothing, my scars will remain."

"Correct. But your pressure garments and face mask will minimize the scarring."

And he'd have to wear the mask for another year. "Let's do it. Start with the face."

"I'll put on a small amount today, in case you have a reaction. Tell me if you notice anything unusual. Tomorrow, I'll apply more." Bruce cleaned Mark's face. Using a small, rounded spatula, he scooped out a tiny bead of salve from the tin. "This might nip a bit."

As the cold salve covered his skin, Mark stiffened, but then he relaxed at the sweet scent. "Will the salve reduce the itchiness and pain?"

Bruce smoothed the salve over Mark's cheek with great care. "I'm not sure. No one knows exactly how this oil works. We're lucky your skin hasn't finished forming. The extracellular matrix should break down easier."

Bruce covered the area with gauze. "If you notice any blisters or darker redness than usual, we'll stop the treatment."

Mark attached the burn mask over his face. "How soon until we know if this works?"

"I'll check the direction and pattern of the new collagen fibers in a few days."

"Perfect. I can't wait to stop wearing this mask."

"Whoa! Hold on to your britches. I'll determine that once the collagen fibers configure in a random fashion and new skin has formed."

The red cobweb of scars on Mark's arm wouldn't discourage his optimism. "You put in a lot of research. I can't thank you enough."

"I'm doing this for you *and* Hailey. She's like a daughter to me." Bruce screwed the lid onto the tin. "Besides, I'd like to see *Bixa aparra* yield something useful. The world knows only that this plant produced the drug Euphoria—and how deadly it was."

"What's the name of this salve?"

"The shaman called it *achachilla sisa*. 'Miracle flower' in Quechua, the language of the villagers."

Mark shook his head. "I'll never remember that—or pronounce the name correctly. Can we call the salve Euphoria? After all, that was the initial essence of this plant, right? We could redeem it—for something good. You know, give it a second chance?" Like his marriage.

"Works for me. It's time Euphoria transmitted a positive connotation anyway." Bruce looked at his wristwatch. "Dang! It's almost eight thirty. I have a meeting. I'll apply more salve when I drop by for dinner around seven. Italian subs okay? It's on the list of foods the dietician gave you."

"Sounds good."

"Let me know when you hear anything about Hailey. No news is good news."

Not necessarily. Mark nodded politely. For the sake of his mental health, he'd stay optimistic.

A calm assurance flowed through him as he rode the elevator downstairs to catch the shuttle. Not only did the Euphoria salve seem promising, but Bruce had a confident way about him. No wonder Hailey admired him.

Chapter Seven

Can't they keep their hands off each other? Hailey sat in the back seat of the helicopter and gagged at the overt groping of the lustful couple in the front row. If Mendoza grabbed Colleen's breasts again, Hailey's breakfast omelet would climb up her throat.

The pilot had issued headsets to reduce the cabin noise, but only Mendoza and Colleen had working sets to communicate. They sure looked cozy. If Mendoza uttered the name Bella one more time, Hailey would scream. The two frauds deserved each other.

I don't buy it.

Who was playing with whom? Was Colleen so desperate to be with Rose that she'd take Mendoza back? She served six years in prison for him! Mendoza wasn't naïve either. A ruthless drug lord couldn't be so stupid to think his former girlfriend would forgive and forget. Love couldn't be that blind. Was Mendoza toying with Colleen, or did he want to be a family? He did act nicer around her. Hard to believe this was the same man who stabbed Hailey two months ago.

Sitting in the middle seat between Hailey and Luis, Rose tapped Hailey's hand and pointed below. "The house is so tiny!" She squealed at the steep mountains, rocky cliffs, and tall trees. "Look. A waterfall!"

Hailey smiled and nodded. She'd have thought Rose would've been traumatized by being kidnapped and whisked off to another country, but the young girl acted so normally. Maybe Rose enjoyed living with her father, or maybe she was internalizing her emotions.

Hailey tilted her head, relying on her ear implant as she divided her time nodding at Rose and eavesdropping on Colleen and Mendoza's conversation.

Thirty minutes into the ride, Colleen began raising her voice. "I don't understand how I can take care of our daughter when you expect me to work in your lab."

"I'll remodel your office to make more room for her to play. Build some bookshelves. Toy bins. Nice girly furniture for you two."

Colleen crossed her arms. "What kind of life is that? She'll have no friends. Last night, you said I could be with Rose if I stayed. It will be impossible to get the project running and spend time with our daughter."

"You won't work every day." Mendoza kissed her hand. "Bella, I don't understand what the big deal is. Once you figure out the most efficient way to produce Euphoria, you can take time off. If you work faster, you'll be able to spend more time with her."

"How have you made Euphoria these past six years?"

"By harvesting the leaves, similar to cocaine. The process is very time-consuming. I gave the scientists your formula, but they haven't been able to synthetically manufacture the drug."

Colleen sighed. "That's because the formula was faulty. I'll do what I can, but I want Rose with me. I don't want strangers to babysit her. That was the deal."

"No. The arrangement was you could stay, but you're not taking Rose out of the country."

"I lost out on her early years when I was in prison. I

want to be with my daughter as much as possible. *Every day*."

"I'm aware of that. When my mother's not at the orphanage, she'll also help watch her."

"In the mountains? Be real, Manuel."

"Then Rose can stay with the nanny at the house." He massaged Colleen's neck.

Colleen pushed away his hand. "I'm not working in the mountains while my daughter is hundreds of miles away. And I don't want her anywhere near your father."

"Then she can stay with you in the mountains until you teach the other researchers to run the production more efficiently." Mendoza was quiet for a minute. "My scientists have extracted other compounds from *Bixa aparra*. They need your expertise, Bella. I'll build a smaller lab on the ranch later, but for now I need you in the mountains where the lab is hidden from the authorities."

"How many researchers do you have?"

"Three as of now. I can hire more." He curled her hair around his finger. "Whatever you want, I will make happen. I want us to be a family. You, me, and Rose."

Rose gripped Hailey's hand and pointed at the snowcapped peaks in the distance, jutting out from the forested mountainsides.

Hailey noted the steep, sloped ridges. Identifying the lab location in the Sierra Nevada de Santa Marta Mountains would be critical to the SCA.

As the pilot descended toward the trees and targeted a leveled section in the mountain ridge, Mendoza tapped Colleen's shoulder. "Look to your right."

Hailey stretched her neck and peered out the window, too.

Camouflaged in the middle of the forest stood a massive compound with a system of roadways snaking between concrete buildings with hunter-green roof tiles. The smallest building at the far end had a greenhouse attached.

When the copter landed, Hailey unbuckled Rose and waited as the others disembarked. Bracing against the fierce winds, Hailey grabbed Rose's knapsack, took the girl's hand, and stepped down onto the ground.

Mendoza led Colleen toward a dark-haired escort waiting by the landing pad. "This is one of our top researchers. I'll introduce you as *señora* Bella. I don't want tongues to wag about you and Rose. It's better to let people think you are married—or widowed."

After introductions, the man pointed to a jeep parked beside two trucks. "*Señor* Manuel, would your guests like to see the complex on the way to the lab?"

As they rode past workers harvesting crops in the fields, Hailey remained alert and noted the different-shaped buildings the driver pointed out. The tour was a welcome distraction. Anything was better than staring at Mendoza and Colleen's bedroom-flavored glances.

When they approached the researcher's offices, Colleen gestured at one of the older structures. "Manuel, what's in there?"

"Cocaine."

Colleen did a double take. "How much of your work is with the coca plant?"

"Ninety percent." Mendoza held her hand. "That will change. Now that you're here, I expect to start producing more Euphoria."

As they passed the lush coca fields terraced on the mountain slopes, Hailey ground her teeth. So many countries smuggled drugs around the world. The US was fighting a losing battle.

Colleen grabbed Mendoza's arm as the jeep swerved to avoid hitting a large rodent crossing the path. "Why do some plants look dead?"

"The government sprayed different herbicides over the years. They killed the crops and injured many workers, too." Mendoza pointed to a barren section of land. "My father has ailments because of the herbicide."

Hailey glared at the back of Mendoza's head. *José got what he deserved. Hopefully, you will, too.*

The escort drove to a steep field of broad-leaved shrubs with large pink-and-yellow blooms. He pulled off the road and parked behind a truck carrying a load of steel drums. "I'll see what's going on."

While they waited, Mendoza picked up a small box of cigar matches and a pocketknife from inside the center console. He plucked a cigar from his pocket, cut one end with the knife, and lit a match. Slowly, he rolled the end of the cigar near the flame. Leaning back in his seat, he drew in and let the smoke float out of his mouth.

Rose pinched her nose and gagged.

Mendoza smirked. "One day you'll get used to my cigars, princess." He pulled out another stick from his pocket and passed it to her. "Want to try one?"

"No, way!" Rose flung it to the floor. "It smells yucky!"

Mendoza laughed and inhaled again.

Minutes later, the escort returned.

Mendoza puffed, and more rank smoke came out of his mouth. "Problem?"

The driver slid into his seat and turned the key. "The engine died on the way to transport the gasoline shipment to the warehouse. The worker is waiting for another truck to pick him up so he can get some tools." He pulled onto the path and drove past four small buildings before parking the jeep beside an SUV. "Let me show you the project in the greenhouse. You'll be pleased with the progress."

Standing, Hailey grabbed Rose's hand and waited for Luis to jump out from the back row first.

Mendoza extended his arm. "Luis, keep them here. We won't be long." He lifted Colleen out of the jeep and walked with her into the glass structure.

When twenty minutes had passed, Rose rubbed her belly. "How much longer?"

Hailey glanced at the time. 11:42 AM. She folded a map she'd found under the seat and tucked it in her pocket. What snacks had the nanny packed? She unzipped Rose's backpack and pulled out a fruit bar and water bottle. "Snack time."

"Yippee!" Rose jumped from her seat and clapped.

After eating, Rose dug out a drawing pad and pencil from the bag. She tapped her cheek. "Hmm. What can I draw?" The corners of her mouth lifted, and she began sketching a picture of three girls.

Hailey opened the map again and memorized locations of nearby villages. "Do you like living here?"

The child shrugged as she drew a mouth on one of the faces. "It's okay, but I miss Sam and my other mommy and daddy."

"I'm sure they miss you too." Hailey peered at the picture. "Who are you drawing?"

Rose pointed at the figures. "Me and Sam and Anna." She rolled the pencil in her hand, and her chin trembled. "I want to go home."

A heavy ache swelled in her throat, and Hailey wrapped her arms around Rose, pulling the girl closer. Rose needed playtime with friends, not isolation with workers toiling in coca fields. What a horrible life this child would have being thrown into Mendoza's criminal dealings.

From the backpack, Hailey pulled out two water bottles. "*¿Agua?*" She passed a bottle to Luis standing guard near the jeep.

He chugged down the water and shifted his attention to his phone.

Must be texting José about shipping her out to the Caribbean. Dammit. Time was ticking. She drank the water and concentrated harder on learning the map.

When the driver returned with Mendoza and Colleen, he continued the tour, describing how laborers collected leaves in coca fields.

At the helipad where the pilot had landed earlier, the escort gestured to the flowering field beside the disabled truck. "The Euphoria crops are thriving."

Mendoza gave an arrogant nod. "The shrubs are resistant to the newest eradication tactics."

A dark shadow of dread settled inside Hailey. With Colleen's expertise on *Bixa aparra* plants, Mendoza would expand Euphoria's reach as wide as cocaine's.

The tour of the grounds ended when the jeep parked in a gravel lot. "The cook has prepared a lunch of *empanadas* and *fritanga* platters. Follow me."

Mendoza extended his arm to Colleen as she stepped onto the ground. He lifted Rose from the seat and kissed her forehead. "Here you go, princess." His stern expression seemed to soften as he held the child.

Don't be fooled. Has to be an act for Colleen's sake.

Hailey lagged, identifying the different dirt pathways winding the complex. The map showed a little village ten miles down the road. The getaway would go faster in a jeep, but the escort pocketed the key. Given the time, she could hot-wire it. Otherwise, she'd have to hike through the forest.

Uneasiness gnawed at her stomach. *How can I abandon Rose?* Hailey had no authority to bring the child back to the United States. Even if she could, Rose's passport was at the hotel.

Hailey caught Luis's stare. He trailed a foot behind her, monitoring every movement. If she didn't lose him, she'd never escape.

****

After lunch, the escort led them inside the complex's largest building.

Hailey stifled a gasp. *Dang.* Mendoza wasn't an amateur.

None of the labs she worked in after college came close to this place. Deep troughs extended into the floor. A score of men in hip boots and jeans mulched coca leaves with a weed-eater contraption. Balance scales, tools, and handwoven bags stuffed with leaves covered wooden tables. The place reeked of gasoline and ammonia.

Got to give Mendoza credit. This place functions like a well-oiled machine—even though it wouldn't pass inspection by an accrediting agency.

Instead of erecting makeshift labs near the fields, Mendoza concealed a dynamic operation in one building. As long as people demanded cocaine, he could supply it.

Colleen pointed to huge stainless-steel containers on the floor. "What's in those vats?"

Mendoza turned. "Gas. We soak the coca leaves in it."

Hailey wrinkled her nose at the noxious fumes. If addicts only realized they were ingesting this poison when they used cocaine. Maybe they were so desperate to get high they didn't care.

One small spark would ignite the flammable vapors, turning the building into a towering inferno. She shuddered as she pictured Mark burning in the warehouse.

The workers seemed to enjoy the commotion, scuttling around the vats as they shouted directives to the younger boys tramping in the troughs with bare feet. On the opposite side of the building, teenage boys stacked cement bags and bottles containing bleach and acid. The workers were thin, but not undernourished, and many wore casual shirts, jeans, and work boots. Hard to tell the supervisor from the others.

The escort walked beside Colleen, answering her stream of questions. He pointed to laborers spreading powdered cement over a trough of minced coca leaves, and he explained the process of making cocaine.

Hailey glanced at Rose who took in the operation with wide eyes. Shame on Mendoza and Colleen for exposing their daughter to this scene! Her throat tightened. *You fool. Rose might run this operation one day.*

Colleen tugged on Mendoza's sleeve. "When will I see my office?"

"Soon." Mendoza turned and lowered his voice to the escort. "Bella will be staying in your office. Go on ahead and clean out your desk. Do it quickly. Move into the vacant office down the hall. After I show Bella her room, I'll introduce her to the other scientists."

With a cursory nod, the man withdrew from the group and headed into the stairwell.

Mendoza took the lead. "Let's go upstairs where the primary focus is on Euphoria research."

Hailey's pulse raced. This had to be where Mendoza's father made the bixine from *Bixa aparra* that poisoned her.

Upstairs in the main workspace, archaic balance scales and stacked weight cups mingled amidst high-tech instrumentation. All the equipment needed to mass produce Euphoria.

Hair prickled on Hailey's neck. Cocaine might be problematic around the world, but Euphoria had the potential to create even more destruction. If other countries learned how to cultivate the plant and extract the drug from the leaves, global drug routes would explode. Once Colleen figured out how to manufacture Euphoria synthetically, there'd be no stopping its spread.

"*Señora* Langley, are you okay?"

"What?" Hailey's cheeks heated as everyone stared at her.

Colleen's eyebrow arched. "Manuel asked you a question."

"I'm sorry. I must have zoned out."

Mendoza scoffed. "I'm surprised this place bores you."

Colleen looped her arm around Mendoza's. "Darling, don't concern yourself with her. Show me my office. I'd like to see the space you have in mind for Rose and me."

Down the hall, Mendoza led them to a spacious room equipped with an ebony desk, floor-to-ceiling bookcases, leather office chairs, and contemporary framed oil paintings. Very masculine.

"This is your office, Bella."

Colleen's nose crinkled as she walked around the room. "We'll need to add a playroom in the corner for Rose. With smaller bookcases, toy shelves, and a daybed."

"Whatever you wish." Mendoza leaned against the desk. "I'll have a new computer installed this week. A secure internal network will link your computer to the others." He opened the window blinds. "The researchers share the central lab to run experiments. Their latest research was on *Bixa aparra's* roots…"

Hailey shrank back against the wall. Could she sneak away while Mendoza spoke? She inched toward the door…

In a quick moment, Luis strode beside her.

Damn. He stuck to her like fruit flies on overripe bananas. She'd never be able to make a run for it.

A woman with dusky skin and sleek, black hair knocked on the door. "Excuse me."

Mendoza waved her inside. "I'd like to introduce you to *señora* Colleen Toole, a researcher from the States. She will research *Bixa aparra* with you."

"Nice to meet you." The woman extended her hand and turned to Mendoza. "I'm sorry to interrupt, but we have an issue downstairs with one of the new machines."

Mendoza frowned. "I'm sorry, Bella. Duty calls."

"Hurry back." Colleen kissed his cheek and pulled a binder from the bookcase. "Rose and I will find something to do."

"I won't be long. Luis, keep them here until I return."

When Mendoza left the room, Hailey marched over to Colleen. "Thanks for nothing, *Bella*. I should've known you'd double-cross me."

Colleen pursed her lips. "I did what I had to do."

"What kind of life do you think you're going to have here, *Bella*?" Hailey glared. "Mendoza's father will kill you the first chance he gets."

Turning, Colleen brushed hard against Hailey's backside. "Watch it, bitch."

Hailey dug her fingers into Colleen's shoulder. "Who's calling who a bitch?"

Luis stepped forward. "Ladies, please."

Colleen stumbled backward and fell against the desk. "My foot!" She hobbled, wincing. "I think I broke a bone. Look, it's starting to swell." She scowled at Hailey. "I hope you're satisfied. You tried to kill me."

Heat flowed through Hailey's body. *The lying witch.*

Luis dragged a cushioned chair from the desk. "Here, *señora*, sit down."

Colleen tested her foot on the floor. "Ow! It hurts. I need some ice."

Luis's gaze volleyed between Hailey and Colleen.

"Please hurry." Colleen's voice trembled as she pulled up a pant leg. "Look, the swelling's getting worse." Moaning, she collapsed onto the chair and shot a glance at Luis. "Manuel will be furious if you don't help me." She lowered her leg onto the floor again. "Oh God. I really think it's broken! This hurts worse than childbirth. I need ice. Now, dammit!"

Luis rubbed his neck. "*Sí, señora.*" He marched out the door and down the hallway.

Colleen jumped from her seat and grabbed Rose's hand. "Hurry. To the jeep. We don't have much time."

Hailey jerked her head. "Wait… You're faking this?"

A sly grin spread across Colleen's face. "Of course. Now hurry. Take a left and go down the back stairwell."

Chapter Eight

Hailey didn't need to be told twice. She followed
Colleen and Rose as they stole down the uneven concrete
steps. At the bottom, Hailey tilted her head toward the
door. "Someone's coming. Quick. Duck behind these
crates." She crouched beside Colleen and Rose in the
corner behind a stack of wooden boxes. Turning to Rose,
she put a finger to her lips. They needed a plan.

"When the coast is clear, head for the jeep we rode
in this morning." Colleen held up a silver key. "I swiped
this from our tour guide's pocket."

Hailey blinked. Underneath that spoiled exterior,
Colleen had more layers than an onion. Maybe she
learned thievery skills in prison.

When the footfalls faded, they raced outside.

Rose whimpered. "Wait for me! You're going too
fast!"

Hailey hoisted the girl over her shoulders piggyback
style. "I got her. Go!"

Colleen ran to the jeep and started the engine.

Hailey placed Rose in the back seat. Any minute
now, Luis or someone would realize they'd fled and
sound the alarm. She buckled Rose's seat belt and slid
into the passenger seat. "Can I drive?"

"No." Colleen clicked her belt. "You almost killed
us the last time." She pressed her foot on the gas pedal.
"Hang on!"

Colleen careened down the road, veering left and right, and braking as she dodged laborers hauling coca leaves.

When they reached the field of *Bixa aparra* plants near the broken-down truck hauling gasoline drums, Hailey pocketed the box of cigar matches on the console. "Rose, can you reach the cigar you tossed on the floor earlier?"

Pinching her nose with one hand, Rose leaned over and handed it to her.

Hailey took the cigar and turned. Good. No one was chasing them yet. She had a little time. "Stop the jeep."

Colleen gaped. "What? Why?"

"There's no time for questions. Stop here."

"Are you out of your mind?"

"Trust me."

Scowling, Colleen pressed in the clutch and braked.

Hailey leapt out of her seat and backtracked fifteen feet to the truck.

"What are you doing?" Colleen shouted. "The truck's broken."

Hailey set the cigar on the bed rail, unlatched the tailgate, and jumped onto the bed. She loosened one of the two fittings on the drum head and unscrewed it. Then she unscrewed the other fitting.

Let's hope these tubs aren't too heavy.

She grunted and heaved the container off the truck. Gasoline poured down the hill. She pumped her fist in the air. *Yes!*

She had no time to celebrate. Pivoting, she unscrewed the fitting on another drum.

When the last barrel rolled off the truck, she jumped onto the ground and lit the cigar she'd placed on the rail.

After a few quick puffs, she hurled the tobacco stick at the *Bixa aparra* shrubs.

The fire spread across the field in a fiery sheet.

Relief flooded Hailey as she sprinted back to the jeep.

As she dropped onto her seat, an explosion rocked the vehicle. Dirt and rocks rained down on them.

Rose screamed.

"Holy shit!" Colleen crouched behind the steering wheel. "What was that?"

"Probably a land mine." Hailey buckled her belt. "Step on it."

As the jeep gained distance, Hailey pulled the gun from her sock. She lifted her boot and removed the ammo hidden in the heel. Even if she could take out some of Mendoza's men, getting down the mountain would be damn near impossible. This far into Mendoza territory, they were hopelessly outnumbered and outgunned. She won a battle, but the war had only just begun.

Colleen rotated the wheel at a tight curve and glanced at Hailey. "Why didn't you tell me you had a gun?"

"You're not the only one with a plan."

"Is that a 3D gun? Does it actually work?"

Hailey loaded five bullets into the cylinder. "I know the designer, so I'm betting it does." Turning, she checked on Rose, who was crouched and shaking. "Rose, listen to me. Don't be scared. I need you to stay down. Can you do that for me? Pretend we're playing Hide and Seek."

Lips quivering, the girl flattened her small frame against the bench seat and covered her eyes.

"Good girl."

Engines churned near the helipad, and Hailey raised her firearm.

Gunshots blasted in the air.

When a shot ricocheted off the jeep, Colleen pushed down on the gas. "Assholes! They don't care a child is riding with us."

Hailey turned. "One…two…three vehicles are heading right toward us. Come on! Push the pedal to the metal!"

Sandwiched between two pickups, Mendoza's jeep struggled to gain distance. Mendoza drove, shouting orders at Luis.

Luis aimed his gun and fired.

Missed. If he had a half-decent aim, she'd have worse trouble. Why did José keep him around if he was such a lousy shot?

"Stay down." Hailey stretched her hand over Rose's back and fired at the pickup in front, hitting the windshield.

The truck spun across the road and flipped.

Mendoza swerved out of the way.

Luis fired again.

As gunshots volleyed between the two vehicles, Colleen dodged the potholes. "How close are they?"

"Very. Only one vehicle left." Hailey fished out more shells from her heel and loaded the chamber, shoving the remaining ammo into her pants pocket. "Rose, stay down!" She fired again.

Mendoza swerved and lost control. His jeep skidded into a ditch.

"Bingo!" Hailey spun forward and exhaled. She bought some time. "Keep driving straight. There's a village not too far from here." She patted Rose's back.

"Your mom and I are going to keep you safe, honey. Stay down a little longer."

The trees and vegetation became denser as Colleen gained more distance. At a fork in the road, she braked. "Which way?"

Hailey dug out the map from the console. "Go left." She leaned back in the seat as her heartbeat slowed. "So, you put on an act the entire time?"

Colleen shrugged. "You told me if I had a better plan, I should use it."

"Not many things surprise me, but you had me fooled." Hailey grinned. "You're a good actor."

"Maybe you were so determined to see the worst in me, you didn't give me the benefit of the doubt." Colleen gave her the side-eye. "I'm sorry. I can't blame you."

At the next split in the road, Hailey studied the map. "I think we missed a turn. We're going up. Go back."

"There's no way in hell I'm turning back. Manuel will be waiting for us. There has to be another way out of here."

Hailey wiped the sweat from her forehead. "The only way to escape going up is to fly." She looked at the map again and pointed to a clearing in the trees. "Try this way. It should wind us back down the other side to a main road."

Colleen took the path and peered in the rearview mirror. "Rose, are you doing okay?"

The child lay trembling, hands covering her face. "Y…y…yes."

Hailey smoothed Rose's hair. Her own Anna wouldn't have handled the situation any differently at this age. "You've doing great, Rose. Just hide a little longer."

When they had driven a mile, the jeep sputtered. Colleen slammed her hand against the steering wheel. "Dammit. You've got to be kidding me!"

Hailey glanced up from the map. "What's wrong?"

"We're out of gas."

What else could go wrong! "We'll have to walk." Hailey shoved her gun in her waistband and tucked the map in her pocket. "There's a village a half mile from here."

Colleen lifted Rose from the jeep and hugged her. "Be brave a little longer, pumpkin. I'll protect you."

A sharp pang of jealousy twinged inside Hailey. She'd do anything to hug her children at this moment.

Thick vines snagged Hailey's clothes as she ducked under low branches and trekked along the wooded path. Soon daylight diffused through the canopy. She glanced at her watch. Five PM. The sun would be setting in a few hours. She sped up her steps. The village had to be close.

At the end of the trail, she stopped.

Damn. Double damn.

She stood at the edge of a steep cliff. No village. Only a rickety swinging footbridge made of braided twine spanned a deep ravine and connected to a bluff eighty feet away. Jagged boulders flanked a river five hundred feet below.

Colleen and Rose caught up with her. "Where's the village?"

Hailey pointed her index finger. "On the other side of this bridge, I hope."

Crying, Rose tugged Colleen's sleeve. "Hurry. Before the bad guys come."

Colleen groaned. "This isn't safe. Half the boards are missing."

"The rest look rotten." Hailey sighed. The bridge smelled of decaying wood. The flimsy vines connecting the railings and hangars probably weren't safe, either. The structure should've been condemned years ago. Hailey picked up a small stone, and with as much force as she could muster, threw it across the ravine. "Dammit!"

She gazed at the flaming orange sun dipping lower in the sky. They might have two more hours before sunset. "We have to go back."

As they walked back to the forest, an engine roared from not far away.

Hailey turned. "Someone's coming."

"Manuel?"

"I don't know." Hailey readied her gun. "We need to hide."

They ran toward the trees, but Rose tripped over a rock, scraping her knee. Colleen leaned over and carried her behind a thicket of shrubs. Hailey took cover beside them as Mendoza and Luis drove out of the wooded path.

Damn, too late!

Hailey readied her gun while Mendoza and Luis fired their weapons at them.

The pungent stench of ammunition hovered in the air as the gunfire rattled back and forth between the two groups.

Hailey reached into her pocket. "I'm out of bullets." She shook her head at Colleen as dread passed through her. "I'm sorry."

Colleen's face crumpled. "It's not your fault." She kissed Rose's forehead and covered the girl in her arms. She peered through the bushes. "Manuel, we surrender. Don't shoot."

Gun in hand, Mendoza jumped out of the passenger seat. "Stand with your hands in the air."

Slowly, Hailey, Colleen, and Rose raised their hands and stood.

Luis leapt out of his seat and aimed his firearm at Hailey. "I got this one covered."

Mendoza walked toward them, his face crimson. "I should've known you'd betray me, Bella. My father was right. You're nothing but a washed-up slut."

Colleen spat at him. "You make me sick."

Mendoza sneered and pointed his gun at Hailey. "Drop your weapon, or I'll shoot."

Rose wailed. "Don't shoot my friend!"

Colleen wrapped her arms around Rose. "How dare you scare her, Manuel! She's your daughter."

Hailey placed her gun on the ground. She couldn't lose her composure, even if this was the end.

Mendoza kicked the gun into the underbrush and slapped her face hard. "That's for burning my field. You cost me millions." His icy glare nipped her soul. "Luis, tie her to a tree—and shoot her. I'll deal with Bella."

Luis twisted Hailey's arms behind her back. "Move."

Pain radiated through her limbs as Luis dragged her across the dirt path. She'd have to escape on her own. Mendoza would give Colleen another chance, for Rose's sake. A flicker of tenderness still lit his angry eyes.

With his free hand, Luis lifted the bench seat and pulled a rope from a burlap bag. Blood oozed from Hailey's day-old sores as he secured her wrists. When he reached in the sack again, she delivered a lightning-fast kick to his groin with her heavy boot. *Take that, you scumbag.*

Luis buckled over and grunted.

As Hailey ran for cover under the trees, she glimpsed movement on the dilapidated bridge. Someone was holding on to the ropes, crossing the rickety bridge. "Rose, no!" She turned and bolted to the cliff.

Mendoza and Colleen stopped screaming at each other and raced to the bridge.

When Hailey met them, Luis was panting a few feet behind.

Colleen cupped her hands around her mouth. "Rose, stop!"

Mendoza placed his foot on the first plank, but the bridge swayed, and he removed it. *"¡Hijueputa!"*

Rose moved faster. Her foot slipped between the treads. Screaming, she grabbed the rope railing.

The muscles in Mendoza's neck tensed. "The bridge can't take much more weight."

Colleen gripped his sleeve. "Please. Save our daughter."

Mendoza removed his boots and inched forward with his bare feet. As the bridge teetered, he steadied himself with the railing. "Princess, hold on to the ropes. I'll get you."

Rose's face puckered. "I want Hailey and Mommy. Not you."

He kept his gaze on his daughter. "Daddy's coming. Don't move."

"Go away. You want to shoot me."

His face paled. "I didn't mean that. I'm sorry. I'd never hurt you."

"Manuel's going to bring you back, Rose. Listen to him." Colleen threaded a hand through her hair, and she looked up to the sky. "God, don't take her from me."

As Mendoza crawled across each tread, the bridge creaked with the weight of his body.

"Luis, we need rope." Hailey extended her arms. "Untie me so I can help."

He shook his head. "Not a chance." Turning, he sprinted to the jeep.

Colleen muffled a moan. "Oh God, not my baby!"

Hailey stifled her own groan. "You're doing good. Look at us, Rose. Don't look down."

"You're a brave girl, Rose." Colleen followed Hailey's cue. "Everything's going to be okay."

Can the bridge support the added weight? Hailey held her breath as Mendoza moved within a few feet of Rose.

Mendoza slid his foot over the next tread, and the plank snapped. He fell onto the adjacent plank, one leg dangling below the deck. "*¡Maldita sea!* The boards are rotted." Slowly pulling himself upright, he crept closer, extending his arm. "Take my hand, princess. Daddy won't let anything happen to you."

Rose whimpered.

Colleen shrieked. "Take his hand!"

Rose wiped her eyes, and she lowered her hand into Mendoza's open palm.

Crack!

In a quick swoop, Mendoza pulled Rose against him and kissed her as the board she was standing on broke. "I got you, princess. You're safe."

Hailey exhaled. *Thank God!*

Colleen clenched her hands against her breast. "Hurry. Please be careful."

Luis returned, holding a hank of thick rope.

As Mendoza led Rose back, the bridge began to arc

wider and two more boards snapped under his footing.

Hailey chewed her lip. They were only ten feet away, but the breach between planks was too wide.

Mendoza gripped the railing. "Luis, the force from the swinging motion is breaking the ropes. Get ready to grab Rose while I try to stabilize the bridge." He squatted down, eye-level with his daughter. "When I lay down on the planks, I want you to walk over my back. Luis will guide you."

He cast an uneasy glance at Colleen. Then he slowly positioned himself face down over the open space. "Okay, Rose. Walk over me."

She hesitated. "Come with me."

"After you get to safety, I'll come."

It seemed like an eternity as Rose's little feet padded across Mendoza's back. She tested each footstep and shuffled forward.

When Rose neared solid ground, Luis leaned over the deck and grabbed her.

Tears ran down Colleen's cheeks as she took Rose from Luis and smothered her in kisses. "Thank God you're safe."

Another loud crack whipped through the air. Halfway across the bridge, three ropes securing the treads popped and flapped haphazardly in the air.

Mendoza dragged his body across the boards until he spanned the breach. He rose to his feet and steadied himself.

The bridge swayed wider.

As he landed on the next plank, Mendoza's foot slipped below the deck. By some miracle, he grasped a dangling end of the rope and pulled his body over the next tread.

"Manuel! Oh my God! Be careful." Colleen lowered Rose onto the ground and stepped closer. "Luis, don't just stand there. Help him."

Luis unwound the loop of heavy rope he'd taken from the jeep, and he raised one end. "We'll pull you back."

Hailey grimaced. Any shift or added weight would jeopardize the bridge's frame.

"Manuel, be careful." Colleen's voice echoed.

His face tensed. "I love you, princess. I love you, Bella."

"*Señor*, catch." Luis heaved the rope.

Hailey caught her breath as the cord landed short. Geez. Where the hell did Luis learn to throw? "Untie me. I'll try."

A chill ran down her spine. If she rescued Mendoza, he'd turn around and kill her. What choice did she have? She couldn't let the man drop to his death in front of the daughter he'd just saved.

Luis reeled in the line and tossed it once more. This time the rope landed closer. "Can you reach it, *señor*?"

Sweat beading on his face, Mendoza swung his arm, gaining momentum as he gritted his teeth and reached again.

Boom!

The blast across the ravine sounded like a bomb detonating.

A railing snapped in two, and the base twine attached to the treads gave way. One after another, the boards dropped like dominoes.

Mendoza jerked backward, his arms flailing in the air. "Bella—"

Colleen reached for him. "Manuel—no!"

For a moment, the thrust suspended him in midair. Then gravity took over, and he plummeted.

Chapter Nine

"Manuel!" Colleen's high-pitched wails echoed throughout the gorge, and she collapsed onto her knees, clinging to her daughter.

Hailey closed her eyes a moment, and then she peered down at the jagged rocks protruding from the ravine's turbulent waters. Memories of Mendoza would be conflicted forever. Each passing moment shook her with a different emotion. He had tried to kill her. Multiple times. He was a ruthless drug lord. A cold-blooded killer.

So why did his death unsettle her?

Despite Mendoza's evil ways, his unselfish act reflected the greatest virtue: love.

Hailey tried to move her hands, but the rope dug into her wrists. Now that Mendoza was dead, she'd be free.

Turning, she eyed Luis a few yards away, talking into his cell.

"This is going to be easier than we anticipated. Meet me at the helipad in an hour. Plan to transport three." He ended the call, slipped the phone into his front pocket, and hustled toward them.

Sweat dripped down her face. Luis was free to help José with his plan.

Think fast. If she and Colleen ran in separate directions, Luis couldn't catch all of them. One would be able to find help—unless they died in the wild.

She could escape easier with the ropes off. "Psst. Colleen. Quick, untie me."

Luis wielded the gun from his pocket. "Get in the jeep. Everyone. You have a flight to catch."

Colleen's face paled as she grabbed Rose's hand. "P…Please. Let us go. I just got my little girl back. Manuel didn't want to send me away."

Hailey lowered her voice. "Luis is loyal to José."

A rumble sounded in the far distance.

Luis waved the gun toward his jeep. "*¡Apúrense!* Hurry."

With the extra rope, Luis secured Hailey and Colleen in the back seat.

When Luis gripped Rose's hands, Colleen cried. "Please, no. She won't run."

To Hailey's surprise, he buckled Rose in a seat belt between them.

The tires spewed dust as Luis steered onto a narrow path and spiraled up the mountain.

During the ride, Colleen sang nursery rhymes to Rose, like Hailey had done to comfort Anna as a young child.

When Rose drifted off, Colleen whispered, "What's going to happen to us?"

Hailey shrugged and swallowed the hard lump forming in her throat. No sense in upsetting Colleen. The SCA knew the atrocities of human trafficking. Victims were forced into sex or hard labor. News reports on TV mentioned occasional arrests, but the crime was more widespread than the media led the public to believe. Most victims died without escaping their horrible circumstances.

Would Luis split up her and Colleen? What would

become of Rose? Would they be drugged and beaten? So many questions but no answers.

Hailey trembled. She'd never see Anna or Ethan again.

Or Mark. He'd spend every minute searching for her instead of focusing on his recovery. He didn't even know she was in Colombia.

Why had she taken off without telling anyone her plan? David knew Colleen had asked her to help rescue Rose, but Hailey never told him they had left.

She'd been so busy trying to save Rose that she'd neglected her chief responsibilities—a family who needed her.

As twilight settled in, Luis slowed the jeep and entered a large clearing in the woods.

In the center of the field, a helicopter waited with its rotor blades spinning. A dull beating noise whipped the dark sky.

Hailey's pulse pounded. "Don't do this. Mendoza's dead." She jerked her hands against the ropes. "Where are you taking us?"

Beside her, Colleen pulled Rose closer and whimpered.

Luis cut the engine. "Santo Domingo." He opened his door and untied the cords binding Hailey's wrists.

Three men climbed out of the chopper and strode toward them.

Hailey peered through the darkness.

David?

What the hell was happening? Why was Stefan's son Erik with him?

A third man wore a flight suit and helmet. Maybe the pilot.

Hailey jumped out of the jeep and ran toward them.

David gave her a brief hug, but his expression was all business. "I can't wait to see how you're going to explain yourself this time." He scrubbed his fingers against his stubble. "Are you okay?"

She nodded, too choked up to speak. She felt like a five-year-old who'd been caught with a hand in the cookie jar.

The mystery man removed his helmet and crossed to the other side of the jeep. He introduced himself as the pilot and spoke with Colleen as he untied her wrists.

Hailey turned to Luis. "I thought you were going to send us away."

He shrugged. "I am."

David lifted Rose from the seat. "I told Luis to keep you in the dark. After your underhanded trick, you deserved to squirm a little."

Hailey blinked back tears as Rose hugged Colleen in a sweet embrace. The trip, all the risk, was worth it. "I can explain—"

David held up his hand. "Save it. We have a long trip after Santo Domingo, and I don't need my blood pressure to rise any higher."

"How did you find us?"

"After I notified Stefan, we used the GPS on your ear implant to track your location. He assigned Erik to work with me."

"But how did you know I had left? I've only been gone two days."

"The day you left, you texted you'd be mowing the yard."

She stared. Where was he going with this?

"It rained all day." His eyes glistened, with

admiration maybe? "Since you spoke with Colleen a few days before, I figured you two might head to Colombia."

She slapped her forehead. How could she forget the heavy downpour when she left that morning? "Ouch. That was dumb."

"Stupidity saved your life. We would've come sooner, but we lost the signal."

"We were held inside a metal shed."

"Fortunately, Luis has been working with the US to bring down the Mendoza family. He notified the Colombian Government to contact us."

Luis shook Erik's hand. "It's good to see you again, *señor*."

Hailey's jaw dropped. "You were on our side the entire time?"

Luis's face reddened. "I tried not to treat you too roughly, but I couldn't let on that I was undercover. Manuel and José would've killed me and my family."

So that's why he didn't bind her arms too tightly or tell José about her 3D gun.

Gesturing a five-minute departure, the pilot lifted a black bag from the jeep's trunk and accompanied Colleen and Rose to the copter.

Hailey followed with the others. "Did Luis tell you about Mendoza?"

Erik nodded. "He phoned an hour ago. He was going to slip the three of you out of the lab and drive you here. Make Mendoza believe you escaped. But you foiled his plan."

Luis pointed to the bag in the pilot's hand. "*Señora* Colleen mentioned the hotel where you stayed. Last night, I broke into your room. Your phones and passports are in there. I packed Rose's bogus passport from

Manuel's bedroom. I didn't have much time. José wanted to ship you out tonight. Your escape stunt—and fire near the lab—bungled my plan. I had to revise the strategy."

Hailey shook her head. *Fooled me the whole time.* "At the bridge, you tried to toss Mendoza the rope…"

Luis gave a crisp nod. "My aim is exact. It was easier to let nature take its course, especially since Manuel had decided to kill you after you set fire to his Euphoria field."

"How can I thank you?"

"Twelve years ago, José kidnapped my sister, Selena, the night before she was to marry Manuel. He sold her to one of his contacts in the Caribbean." Luis's eyes misted. "I know you opened José's records. Can you find out what happened to her?"

Hailey read the expression on the other men's faces. Twelve years was a long time for human trafficking survivors, but she owed Luis her life. "I'll do my best."

The lines on his forehead eased. "*Muchas gracias.*"

David stepped forward. "Hailey, we have to go. There's a plane waiting in Santo Domingo."

She shook Luis's hand. "How can I contact you?"

"David has my information. Please, *señora.* I need to know if Selena's alive. My mother still cries for her." Luis backed away from the chopper as David and Erik climbed inside.

Hailey waved goodbye and boarded.

As the helicopter lifted into the air, a heavy sadness cloaked her. Luis looked so desperate. She had to do something to pay him back.

****

—En route to U.S. with 3. Everyone's ok. Mission

complete. ETA tomorrow 1:00 PM CST in Austin—

Mark read David's text and whistled. Amazing how one message could lift his spirits. "Hailey's on her way home." He powered off his phone and returned his attention to Bruce and the subs on the table.

Bruce's eyebrows arched as he sipped his coffee. "Is she okay?"

"Yes, Thank God. She gets in tomorrow afternoon. I'll check on her then." Mark bit into his sandwich. The fresh-baked bread and the recent news must've had a synergistic effect on his appetite. Homesickness nipped him as an image of a family dinner flashed through his mind.

"What about Colleen?"

"She's safe, too. And Rose. All three are flying home."

"I knew Hailey would find her." Grinning, Bruce dived into his entree. "I hope Colleen finds some peace now. Losing her father to Parkinson's was tough."

"She'll probably stay with Joyce Rogers in Boston for a while. Joyce is the sorority friend who cared for Rose while Colleen was in prison."

"You need support, too." Bruce's bushy eyebrows arched. "Don't you think it's time to tell Hailey you're here?"

Mark's emotions had ping-ponged over the past forty-eight hours. He longed for his wife, but not if she felt obligated to come. He'd be a burden until he could pull his own weight. He couldn't expect to secure his career back at the Drug Trafficking Agency if he couldn't fire a weapon.

"Having Hailey here would complicate things. I'd rather wait until we see if the salve heals my skin."

Bruce peered over his eyeglasses. "My question isn't only for your well-being. Hailey's had a horrible year. She's lost you. For months, she thought you'd died. Then, Parker did die. She's had to maintain some sort of normalcy around the kids while coping with her own emotions. God only knows what hell she went through in Colombia. She's going to need someone."

"Are you saying Hailey could have another breakdown?"

Bruce wiped his mouth with a napkin. "I haven't spoken with her lately. I'm only saying she could use support."

"Thank you for telling me." Mark should've realized Hailey might need him. He finished eating his sub. "Have you made progress testing the Euphoria oil?"

"Afraid not. One of my analyzers is broken."

"Can you fix it?"

"No. But this morning, I submitted a purchase-order request. Unfortunately, the supply chain is backed up. I have no date when the part will ship. A lot of oil was wasted when I tried to get the machine to aspirate the sample, and now there are only a few drops of oil left."

"That's all?"

Bruce nodded. "Sorry. I doubt it will be practical for testing anyway. The heat used to destroy the toxins in the oil likely destroyed the chemical bonds in the original structure."

"Can you restore them?"

"No. It's like trying to unfry an egg. The bonds can't go back. I need to analyze raw oil." Bruce scratched his head. "Meanwhile, I'll try to figure out how the oil degrades collagen from scars and forms normal collagen."

"What does collagen do again?"

"It provides the framework for your skin. Gives the skin a smoother texture."

Mark looked at his arms where dark red scars hid beneath his fitted garments. "Sign me up for a whole-body special."

"Not possible." Bruce drank the rest of his coffee. "I'm sorry to be blunt, but I need more *Bixa aparra* blooms if we're going to collect more oil. I kick myself for not harvesting them when the plant was alive."

After Bruce left, Mark worked on his finger exercises, plucking patterns on his guitar. Funny how certain hand motions stayed in his memory. At one time he'd aspired to form a band with his friends. He'd even composed a ballad for Colleen Toole, the girl he dated.

Her mocking laughter killed his dream and his confidence.

Mark hummed along to a long-forgotten melody. One day he might build the courage to play for Hailey. Would she laugh at him, too? He gazed at the family photo on the end table. She'd be back in the United States before long. Tomorrow couldn't come soon enough.

****

José dodged a deep rut on the gravel road and rubbed his eyes. Twenty-two hundred hours and he was already falling asleep. He flipped on the radio to reggae music and leaned back into his seat.

The headlights of his truck illuminated another pothole, and he steered tight around it. The days he trained his insurgents were usually long, but today, he only partially focused on the military maneuvers. Manuel's trip to the mountains pulled at José's mind like an impatient child tugging at a parent's arm. What had his son decided to do with the two *gringas*? The group must've returned by now. When he had cell service, he'd call Luis.

As José stopped at a crossing a mile from the Mendoza estate, a news broadcast interrupted the music:

Investigations have been mounting after an explosion this afternoon east of the town of Pampillo set off a forest fire in the Santa Marta Mountains.

The cocaine lab? Typical! Manuel's left another mess for me to clean up.

He clenched his jaw and increased the volume.

According to one eyewitness, business entrepreneur Manuel de Mendoza is believed to be dead from an accident after leaving the area. Rescue units are searching for him.

The broadcast switched back to the music program.

José's gut buckled like he'd been horse kicked. Manny? Dead? Impossible. He pulled the phone from his pocket and powered it on. *There must be some mistake.*

His phone beeped repeatedly with text messages and unanswered calls.

He clicked on Luis's messages:

—*Bridge collapsed. Manuel caught in accident.*—

—*Talking with authorities. Many questions.*—

—*Where are you?*—

Luis had texted again five minutes later.

—*Where are you?*—

José's mouth went dry. *Oh God. It can't be true.*

One of the field foremen texted.

—*Colombian Government is searching for you.*—

The housekeeper messaged.

—*Police are everywhere. Señor Manuel and Rose haven't returned yet.*—

His lieutenant left a voicemail.

Cops raided the mansion. Stormed your ranch house. Beep.

He scrolled through the other posts. Nothing from Camila. She still hadn't returned texts from last week. If Manuel were really gone, she'd be devastated.

And blame me.

His muscles tensed. Would she contact the police like she'd threatened?

¡Maldita sea! He had just talked to Manuel the night before. It wasn't possible.

Or was it? José closed his eyes. He should've been tougher on the boy. Forced him to be stronger. Smarter.

This isn't my fault.

He'd done his best, but his son was weak.

Manuel trusted women.

José snorted. *Fool.*

What were the exact words from the radio broadcast... No mention about the *putas*—or Manuel's love child. They couldn't have escaped. Not in the mountains.

José rubbed his forehead. He'd made a deal with his connections in Jamaica.

What the hell happened? He slammed his fist against the steering wheel. Could his son really be...dead? He lowered his head and moaned as a vast hollowness emptied him.

A police car with its sirens blaring sped toward the Mendoza estate.

Got to hide! Pressing his foot on the gas pedal, he veered onto the main road and sped toward town.

Chapter Ten

Austin, Texas

What a day! Hailey fell backward onto the hotel bed. It was great to be back in the US, safe and sound. The room wasn't elaborate, but at least she wouldn't have to keep one eye open tonight while she slept.

An engine delay in Aruba and a layover in Santo Domingo made the last twenty-four hours seem like a week. David and Erik's cold-shoulder behavior made the flight even more unsettling. Neither man uttered a word about Rose's rescue.

Tomorrow's debriefing with Stefan would be like standing up against a firing squad. He'd verbally pummel her for not relying on the State Department. Good thing she wasn't still employed at the Special Crimes Agency—she'd receive a clearance level reduction and censure. She was in no position to request the SCA search for Luis's sister.

Hailey sighed. A stomach ulcer would probably develop during the night.

Maybe her plan hadn't been the smartest way to rescue Rose, but it had worked. Eight weeks, and the State Department hadn't had any success. She'd rescued Rose in less than one. Despite what Stefan thought, reuniting the girl with her mother had been worth the trouble.

During the flight back, Colleen gave her daughter

the toys she'd packed. Rose squealed when she saw her stuffed teddy bear and favorite book *Mommy, I Need a Hug*. Rose and Colleen were building a family, one that Hailey had helped birth. And gosh, what an incredibly hard labor this birth was.

Something stirred a sensation she hadn't experienced in a long time. The rush of adrenaline? Endorphins? Whatever it was—it felt invigorating.

The digital clock on the nightstand flipped to 8:08 PM.

Enough time to get ready for bed before she'd return Mark's call.

After a hot shower, Hailey opened her suitcase and wrinkled her nose at the pajama top's musty odor, but she slipped into it anyway. She applied antibiotic ointment onto her wrists and bandaged the wounds.

Her phone rang as she pulled down the covers.

She swiped her finger across the screen. "Mark? Are you okay?"

"I should ask *you* that question. Thank God you're back. I was so worried." The concern in his deep-velvet voice melted her fears.

She perched on the bed. "I'm fine. I guess David told you what happened?"

"He only said that you're okay. My God, Hailey. You could've been killed. Why did you go alone to save Rose?"

Hailey gripped the phone tighter. Would the image of the frantic child dangling on the escape ladder ever disappear?

"I wasn't alone. Colleen came with me."

Mark scoffed. "You know what I mean. You *both* could've been killed."

"I'm fine. We're all fine."

"Only because Stefan and David had your back. You're still recovering from the stabbing."

"Mark, please. Don't start. That was months ago. My doctor cleared me to go back to work. Yes, it was risky, but I couldn't leave Rose with Mendoza. Besides, if I hadn't found her, you would've tried to bring her back. I couldn't stand by and lose you again."

After a long pause, he exhaled. "I'm sorry, honey. I've been out of my mind with worry. How are you doing—for real?"

"I'm okay."

"Promise me you won't leave like that again."

Her pulse raced. He was still trying to protect her. "I promise." An easy pledge to make.

"Where are you now?"

"At a hotel in Austin."

"Tell me what happened. All of it."

"Okay, but it's a long story."

When she had finished talking, her nerves settled. "I meet with Stefan tomorrow before I fly back to Virginia. I'm trying not to think about him going off at me." She scratched her arm. "How are you doing?"

"Fine."

"Why did you stop calling?"

"I'm trying new therapies. I didn't want to get our hopes up."

"With the PTSD? Is it helping?"

"I don't know yet."

There had to be a therapy to help her husband. "Where are you?"

"Hailey, I can't—"

Heat ran up her neck. "Come on, Mark. That's not

fair. Why am I not supposed to go anywhere, but you can hide for months?"

"Because you leaving the country was reckless. I'm not in any danger."

Hailey frowned. "I wish you'd let me help you."

"You can—by staying safe at home."

"Home isn't the same without you. I miss you. We all do."

"I miss you, too."

The sweetness in his voice sated her for the moment. "Are you still in pain?"

"Yes, but the pain meds help."

"Is there anything I can do?"

"Take care of yourself. Are the kids okay?"

Hailey chuckled. "Of course. They're at Laura's. She's spoiling them too much."

"How are my parents?"

"The same." The cognitive decline in Mark's father would only upset Mark. "They can't wait to see you again."

"The feeling's mutual. Is Laura doing better?"

"She's slowly working her way through the divorce. Her kids and the job keep her from thinking about Jack and his new girlfriend. By the way, on the plane ride back David asked a lot of questions about her. I didn't realize he knew your sister that well."

"He had a huge crush on Laura when we were in high school."

Hailey grinned. *So that's why David blushed when he spoke about her.*

Mark cleared his throat. "Are Colleen and Rose at the hotel?"

"Yes. Down the hall. They fly to Boston tomorrow."

"Will they stay with Joyce?"

"Yes. Until Rose feels more secure. Joyce is the closest Colleen has to any family." Hailey scratched her arm. "Family's important."

"Did Colleen say anything about the witness protection program?"

"She doesn't think she needs it now."

"I wish she'd go into the program. The Mendoza clan is dangerous."

Hailey browsed photos on her phone and brought up a beach photo of Mark. He looked happy. Confident. "You promised you'd come home. I'm going to hold you to it."

He chuckled. "I hope you do. Meanwhile, I'll text and call more. I just don't want to bring you down."

"You won't. Besides, it's my job to pick you up." She slid under the covers. "What made you call?"

"I wanted to hear your voice—and tell you I love you."

"I love you, too." And like that, he was the passionate man she'd first met. Nothing else mattered but Mark. When she returned to Virginia, she'd find a way to bring him home.

Chapter Eleven

José pushed back the tarp on his tent and swatted at a red tanager chirruping overhead on a tree branch. He blinked at the sun beating down on his face. Seven o'clock. Already the day was stifling.

Adjusting the brim of his hat, he headed into the makeshift grub tent and claimed a mug from the table. A small breakfast might ease the nausea that had flared up again.

A seasoned soldier poured coffee into the mug and spooned cornmeal onto a plate.

José raised the cup and inhaled. Gak! The brew smelled nasty. He'd try it anyway. "Aargh!" He spat out the bitter coffee and flung the mug.

José marched outside past a group of rebels washing clothes in the river. So many unfamiliar faces.

More children and women had joined the Resistance since the peace treaty. Pop-up tents lined up across the base of a mountain. Kids as young as eight years old had come from neighboring villages, seeking to take part in the fight.

Who wouldn't want to hold a gun in their hands and feel power? Poverty-stricken people with no control over their lives would do anything to feel stronger.

At a nearby tree, young teens mimicked the howling sounds of a red howler monkey.

Normally, José would order the rebels to plant land

mines, but his chest ached from the damp nights and coughing fits. He paced the camp. How long could he hole up here? He marched past a group of older men assembling weapons and halted beside a run-down shed where his top sergeant gave orders to young insurgents.

The sergeant met José's gaze and dismissed the soldiers with a wave of his hand.

José stepped forward, mentally bracing for the information. "I'm surprised you're back. Any news?"

"Let's talk in my tent." The man led him inside a cramped, stuffy shelter. "A search team found Manuel's body in a ravine. *Lo siento, señor.*"

José's knees hitched. His only son—gone. He didn't want sympathies or pats on the back. No one would miss Manuel like he would. Except maybe Camila. "*Gracias.*"

The sergeant pulled a phone from his pocket and handed it to José. "Here's your cell. More messages downloaded when I got reception in town."

José scrolled through his texts. Nothing from his wife. Not even a "Go to hell!" He slid the phone into his pocket. "Any word on Luis? He should be able to tell us what happened."

"The authorities have him. We can't risk any communication. His phone could be compromised."

¡Maldita! Luis was one of his best men. "Did you contact the commander in Venezuela?"

"I did. He's agreed to fly you out of Colombia today."

"He'll make the necessary arrangements to smuggle me into the US?"

"Yes. Just like you asked. The *pollero* will take one leg of the journey. Move you across the Mexican and US border. Another contact in the US will set up your travels during the second half of your trip."

"Did you get the bank notes?"

The sergeant reached down to the backpack on the ground and handed him a paper bag. "The open exchange rate equals the amount you requested."

José reached inside the cloth bundles and flipped through the bills. Enough to smuggle him out of the country and pay all necessary traveling expenses and overheads—if the commander's contacts proved competent.

José clutched the bag. He had to fight his own war before he continued the battle in Colombia. Exacting vengeance on the *gringas* was the only way to quell the swelling rage in his blood. If the blonde hussy hadn't slept with his son and had his bastard, Manuel would be alive...and the coca plants would still be growing. Someone had to pay for this loss. "When do I leave?"

The sergeant adjusted the strap holding a machine gun on his back. "A helicopter will arrive at noon. You'll receive instructions on how to communicate with your contacts. With the authorities looking for you, it's better to transfer you to Mexico using cheap private planes. INTERPOL will contact other countries' agencies if word gets out you left Colombia."

A hard lump lodged in José's throat. He was weak to rely on others.

José stuffed the bag into his jacket. "I have a few hours. We can run the morning training maneuvers and uncrate the supplies. Spend the week setting up more land mines and continue the drills." He held his chin high. No one would catch his camp unprepared as long as he was in charge.

****

Car horns beeped amid the low thrum of engines. *Why is there traffic in the woods?* Strange. She must be dreaming. The images of Mark and her snuggling in a cozy cabin dissipated.

No! Come back.

Hailey groggily opened one eye and peeped at the digital clock sitting on the nightstand. 8:19 AM. "I forgot to set the alarm. Drat!"

Hurrying into the bathroom, she swept a brush through her hair. *Time to face Stefan.*

As she slipped into her loose-fitting safari pants, a tap rattled the door.

"Coming." She shrugged into a T-shirt that had been scrunched into her suitcase, and she smoothed the wrinkles. With a quick check in the peephole, she unlatched the lock and flung open the door. "This can't be the same Rose I saw yesterday! You look so much older in pigtails."

Dressed in a new plaid jumper and yellow shirt, Rose released her mother's hand and hugged Hailey. "I'm going to miss you."

Hailey breathed in Rose's strawberry-scented hair. "What a way to greet the day." She smiled at Colleen with more than politeness. "Are you leaving already?"

"The hotel shuttle is waiting downstairs. Joyce and her daughter will meet us when we land." Colleen reached into her purse and fished out a pair of sunglasses. "I'm truly sorry for the trouble I've caused. I should've warned Joyce about Manuel so she could protect Rose while I was in prison." Fine lines etched on the corners of her eyes. "But the bond between sorority sisters has limitations, and I was afraid Joyce wouldn't be Rose's guardian if she knew the truth. I used poor judgement."

Though no apology could ease the grief from losing Parker, the agony Mark suffered, or the time Hailey and her kids had lost with him, Colleen sounded sincere. "At least you're reunited with Rose now. Any career plans when you get to Boston?"

"I'm not sure yet. Possibly research if I can find a lab that will hire me. Daddy's inheritance will tide me over for a while. I've been thinking of him a lot lately. Did you know he named me after a neurotransmitter? Acetylcholine. Daddy said we'd always be connected, even after he passed on." Colleen's voice softened. "I wish I'd done something creative like that for Rose's name."

A.C. Toole's play on words would be tough to beat. "Rose is a lovely name. Though perhaps you can think of a nickname as creative and meaningful."

"I hope so." Colleen donned her sunglasses.

Despite the tumult of the last few days, Rose and Colleen had finally reunited. Motherhood and time in prison had made Colleen a better person.

Hailey dipped her chin. "Concentrate on Rose, and enjoy your time together."

Colleen ran her hand over Rose's braids. "We will. I wouldn't have my baby if it weren't for you. Thank you for everything."

Was there some kind of friendship forming? Stranger things had happened. "You're welcome. Text me and let me know how you're doing."

Colleen adjusted the purse strap over her shoulder. "I will. Rose and I are eager to explore Boston."

Rose's broad smile showed a mouthful of teeth. "I want to see the art museum."

Colleen patted her daughter's hand. "That's first on our list."

"And we're getting a puppy!" Rose's eyes sparkled like sapphire.

"I said once we settle in, we'll look into adopting one." Colleen nodded. "It's time to make some memories. When you talk to Mark again, please thank him. I hope he finds his way back to you soon."

Hailey waved goodbye and locked the door. Tears blurred her vision as she wrapped her arms around her chest and took a moment for a self-hug. *I hope he doesn't take too long.*

Chapter Twelve

"Of all the lamebrain ideas! What the hell were you thinking, Hailey?" Since her arrival, Stefan's surly language had downgraded from explosive to outraged to exasperated. "Dammit! Didn't you learn anything at the agency?"

Hailey's muscles tensed for the umpteenth time during Stefan's tirade. She dug her fingernails into her palms and glanced across the conference table where Erik and David behaved like tight-lipped minions. "I told you a hundred times already that I'm sorry. I promised Rose I'd keep her safe. I tried to go through the proper channels. I asked you to let me work the case."

Stefan banged his fist on the table. "And I told you I didn't want you involved. I had men working with the Colombian government, tracking both Mendoza and his father's movements. Besides, you could've been killed." He choked on the last few words.

"I said I'm sorry—"

"Please…don't say anything more." He leaned back in his chair and massaged his temples. "I lost Tom Parker two months ago. I can't lose you, too."

He was softening. Hailey wiped her clammy hands against her pants. *Here goes nothing.* "Permission to speak, sir."

Stefan huffed. "What now?"

"The man working undercover with the Colombian

Government, the one who helped me get away, made a personal request."

Erik cleared his throat. "Dad, I told you about him earlier. Luis Garvez."

Stefan's brow furrowed. "What does he want?"

Hailey scratched her neck. "José Mendoza sold Luis's sister to one of his human trafficking contacts in the Caribbean twelve years ago. Luis has worked for the Mendoza family, gaining their trust so he could find—"

Stefan bolted from his seat and stood within an inch of her. "No! Absolutely no—"

She leaned back. "B…But you haven't even heard what I'm asking."

"I don't have to. You want to fly to the Caribbean and search for her. Are you out of your mind? You don't even know if she's still alive."

"If we can help her, we should—"

"*You* are not doing anything *ever* again." Stefan spun to his son. "Is this legit?"

Erik nodded. "I searched the files last night and found José's business contacts. Most of his connections back then were with Haiti. I can have my division look into it."

The meeting ended, and Hailey hurried out of the room. When had she endured a reproach where she felt so mentally beaten? Stefan's loss of respect hurt worse than her own discontent. After she lost her parents, Stefan took her into his home, treated her like family. Now she'd disappointed him.

Erik and David stepped into the elevator cab with her. Both men looked as relieved as she felt that the meeting was over.

Erik patted her arm. "Don't worry. Dad will cool

down. He was worried about you. He thinks keeping you away from the SCA will keep you safe." He grinned. "Dad should know better by now."

When the elevator doors opened, she trudged into the lobby. "Nothing can make me feel any worse than I do right now."

Erik opened the front door. "Word got around the agency about what you did. If it makes you feel any better, most of us think you're a pretty gutsy woman."

Hailey sighed. "Right now, I feel like a pathetic loser."

****

Mark regarded the half-empty container beside the treatment bed. The salve would be gone within the week. "Sorry I overslept. Thanks for fitting me in after my morning therapies." He removed his face mask.

Bruce wheeled closer on his exam stool. "Not a problem." He inserted the metal spatula into the salve. "Have you noticed any redness where we applied the salve? Any pain? Burning? Itching?"

"Nothing more than usual." Mark touched his cheeks. With his bed of scars, how could he tell?

Bruce peered over his eyeglasses. "I'll wait a few days for the salve to degrade the scar's collagen, and then I'll biopsy it."

"You're going to cut into my face?" Grimacing, Mark leaned back and lifted his T-shirt where a patch of red keloid scars spotted his pecs. "Put the salve here for a few days and biopsy this."

"Don't worry." Bruce shook his head. "I'll use a non-invasive technique."

Mark exhaled. "Thank God. The last thing I need is a chunk of my cheek removed."

"No need for that extreme yet."

"Are you sure you can't get more oil? There must be more shrubs in Peru."

Bruce shook his head. "The shaman searched his entire village. *Bixa aparra* is extinct."

Mark peered at the container again. "Any luck in determining what's in the oil?"

"Not yet."

Disappointment hit Mark like a wrecking ball. "I guess we'll finish what we have, and I'll live with the results."

Bruce spread the salve over Mark's cheeks. "How was Hailey's meeting with Stefan?"

"I haven't heard, but she was dreading it when I called her last night."

"Stefan can seem rough, but he's a kind man. He and his wife encouraged Hailey to finish school and got her the support she needed to tame her scratching habit."

"Hailey still scratches when she's nervous."

"It's more than that. Distress triggers her scratching. Thinking about her parents. Reminders of loss. Emotional pain." Bruce smoothed the salve over Mark's jaw and set the container on the tray. "Okay, all finished."

Mark reattached his mask. "Why are you so invested in Hailey's happiness?"

Bruce stared a long moment, like he was caught in a memory. "I made a promise to Hailey's uncle a long time ago."

"If you want to talk to Hailey about her Uncle Henry, I think she could handle the truth now."

"She might be able to, but I'm not sure *I* could." Bruce was silent as he screwed the lid on the salve container. "What are your plans for the rest of the day?"

Mark glanced at the wall clock and stood. "My psychologist's appointment was rescheduled for three o'clock. I better head downstairs for the shuttle. See you later."

When he stepped off the elevator onto the main floor, Mark stopped at the front desk. "Hi, Desiree. Is the shuttle running on time?"

The thirty-year-old receptionist lowered her cell phone onto the counter. "No delays today."

He settled into the curved sofa and checked his text messages. Life was brighter now that Hailey was safe.

Ronnie pushed his cart of cleaning supplies through the lobby and emptied the trash bin. "Hey, Mark. Catch the game last night?"

"Sure did. The Braves are on a streak." When Ronnie left, Mark speed-dialed David. "Got your message. What's going on?"

"I wanted to let you know what went down at the debriefing. Stefan hit hard on Hailey. I felt bad for her."

Hailey's director has some nerve. Mark tightened his fists so tight that pain shot through his hands. "How is she now?"

David cleared his throat. "She's not looking forward to returning to an empty house. Anna and Ethan aren't home to lift her spirits. Hailey misses you. Your absence has taken a toll on her."

She deserves better. "I'll call her tonight. Thanks for letting me know."

"No problem, buddy. We all want you back. I'll catch up when you come home."

"I wonder what kind of life I'll have if I return home." Mark choked.

"What are you talking about? Hailey and the kids want you with them."

"I can't work." He stared at his hand, covered in nylon spandex fabric. "My reflexes are too slow. I can't even shoot my firearm."

"Focus on getting better. Everything else will fall into place."

Mark hung his head. "Feels like it's falling apart."

"Have faith. Tell me where you're staying, and I'll bring you a pizza and beer. That'll cheer you up."

It must be killing him not to have my address. "Not a chance."

David sighed. "Okay, but be warned, Hailey's determined to find you. She brought up the subject again on the ride to the airport. I reminded her that you don't want to be found."

Mark scowled. "You both should focus on your own lives."

"Funny you say that. I have a gut feeling my life's going to change soon."

"You never know." *Sheesh!* David's gut feelings were never wrong. Whatever it was, Mark couldn't handle any more surprises. He peered at the window. "Hey, my shuttle pulled up. Talk to you later."

As Mark ended the call and hurried to the bus, he couldn't shake the uncanny feeling both their lives were going to change.

Let's hope it's for the better.

Chapter Thirteen

Home again.
Juggling a handful of mail and a carry-on bag in her hands, Hailey unlocked the front door of her two-story home and dropped her luggage onto the foyer floor. She laid the bills and other envelopes on the console table and flipped the light switch. Silence gripped her as a grim sense of déjà vu hung over the room. Alone again. She'd taken Anna and Ethan to New Jersey only a week ago. The kids should be back from the zoo at seven. She'd call then.

The room was the same as she'd left it. She glanced up at Ethan and Anna's school portraits on the living room wall. Above the fireplace mantel, she touched a family photo of Mark, her, and the kids. If only Mark would tell her where he was staying, she'd join him during his recovery. Together they could get through anything.

Heaviness settled into her heart as she picked up one of her son's dirty sweat socks jammed under the recliner. *I'm not ready for Ethan to leave when he graduates in two years.* She leaned over next to the television stand and collected the stress-relieving coloring books she and Anna colored as part of their recent therapy. Anna would graduate two years after Ethan.

In one harrowing situation, she'd almost lost them both. The Mendoza family had come too close to ruining her family's happiness. Hailey scratched her hand and stopped. Destructive habits didn't go away—they only lay dormant.

Stillness thickened as she navigated the empty house.

Hailey carried the mail into the study where a stack of bills made a lopsided mountain on the desk. She played her latest voicemail as she opened the top envelope.

*Hi, It's Joyce. We just got back from the airport. Thank you again for finding Rose. Having her and Colleen here will cushion the loneliness of Oliver's deployment in Syria. We're slowly settling in. The house looks the same as when I was a kid. I took your suggestion and scheduled home health care for my dad. Samantha and I have been busy painting and doing small repairs around the house...*Beep.

Hailey sat in her padded office chair, opened her address book, and penciled in Rose and Colleen's name under Joyce Rogers. Her kids called her old-fashioned for not entering addresses into her phone, but a hard copy wouldn't crash and delete information like her last computer had.

When she flipped through the pages, she paused at Bruce Hanover's name on the worn, crinkled page. Would Bruce be back from Peru yet?

She perused more mail. A few more days and the mailbox would've been stuffed. *Next time, stop the mail.*

Hailey frowned. *I promised Mark there wouldn't be a next time.* Stefan also had made it clear.

She powered on the computer and sorted the mail into three stacks: junk, immediate attention, and look at later when she wasn't so tired. After she dumped the junk into the trash, she opened a formal-looking letter from a law firm in Chicago. Halfway through the letter she jumped from her seat.

…you are designated as the beneficiary on the life insurance policy…

"Oh, Parker." She lowered her head a moment. Tom Parker was one special man. She didn't deserve his generosity. Turning her address book to Parker's name, she kissed two fingers and touched his name. Life was too short. *Rest in peace, dear friend.*

She walked into the living room and traced a finger over a photo of her and Mark walking down the Appalachian Trail. It didn't matter if he couldn't hike any longer. *Mark, please come home. Wherever you are.*

She fished her cell phone from her purse and powered it on. The screen lit up with a series of incoming messages.

—*We made it to Boston. No delays. Thank you for everything. ~Colleen*—

—*Mom, Ethan and I had the best time at the zoo today. Want to talk at 8?*—

—*Hailey, it's Mom. Adam and I wanted to know if you're available for dinner Sunday. We thought since the grandkids are at Laura's, you could use the company.*—

—*Hi, honey. It's me. Did you make it home okay? I love you.*—

Talking with Mark the previous night felt as though he'd never left. At home without him, she felt cheated. How could he expect her to stay home and wait for his return?

Because you don't know where he's staying.

She was brushing breadcrumbs off her blouse when the phone rang. She clicked on a video call. "Anna!"

"Hi, Mom!"

Hailey peered at the giddy girl waving to her from the screen. "Hi, sweetie. How are you? Gosh, you look older."

"I'm good. We had fun at the zoo, but it was crowded today."

"As long as you had fun. I love your French braid."

Anna fingered the back of her head. "Thanks. Kayla did it."

"Hi, Aunt Hailey." The fourteen-year-old cousin leaned closer toward the screen.

"Hello, Kayla." Hailey waved. "Is Ethan there, too?"

"Right here, Mom." Ethan's head moved into the screen; the other cousins stood beside him.

So many happy faces. "Are you boys staying out of trouble?"

Three sweaty faces answered in unison. "Of course!"

After Ethan chatted a few minutes, Anna filled in their latest activities. "I'm glad we decided to visit."

"If you're ready to come home early, I can pick you up this week."

Anna chewed her fingernail. "Can we stay until school starts?"

Hailey gasped. Another month without her kids? "The plan was only for three weeks."

"I know, but we're having so much fun. I wish we lived closer. Please?" Anna's fingers intertwined as if she were begging. "Ethan wants to stay, too."

Anna's face glowed. How could Hailey disappoint her?

Hailey mentally weighed her loneliness against the

kids' happiness. Not fair to keep them at home for selfish reasons. "Let me talk to Aunt Laura first."

Anna jumped. "She's right here. Thank you, Mom. Thank you. Thank you. Thank you. Bye. Love you!" She threw kisses at Hailey and skedaddled.

Laura shifted into the screen, laughing. "Never a dull moment around here."

"Are you okay with the kids staying?"

"Oh my, yes! It's like a party every day. We haven't had this much laughter in the house since Jack…" Laura paused. "The question is, are *you* okay if they stay?"

Life would be empty without Ethan and Anna, but Laura had to be lonely, too. The divorce was less than two years ago. Laura and the kids deserved some fun memories.

"Don't worry about me." Hailey forced a smile. "I can always visit. School starts the end of August, so it's not too far away."

When Hailey ended the call, she opened an old photo album and ran a finger over her parents' faces. She flipped the page to black-and-white pictures of her father playing football with his older brother, Henry, and Henry's med school friend Bruce Hanover.

Henry's death was a mystery, rumored to do with drugs. Though she'd never met her uncle, Bruce had become one of her dearest friends. What was Bruce up to? He always asked for her help whenever he called. He even mentioned she could stay in one of the facility's corporate apartments.

She tapped her finger on a photo. Should she go? Her biochemistry background would prove useful. At least she'd feel needed. Visiting Bruce would be the perfect distraction.

Hailey slammed the album. Question settled. Once she researched the cheapest airfare, she'd head for Georgia.

Should she call Bruce first?

Nah. A surprise visit would be the best.

****

After Hailey returned home from dinner at her in-laws' house, her cell rang. She read the caller's name and tapped the screen. "Erik. Tell me you have some news about Luis's sister."

"I'm afraid it's not good."

She slumped back into her seat. "Is she dead?"

"I found one of Selena's sister wives at the brothel where she stayed in Haiti."

"Sister wives?"

"Yeah. The woman knew her when they worked for the same gorilla pimp. The wives were friends, but they weren't permitted to socialize much. One night the pimp brought some of his drunken friends into his apartment. They played a game to see if the prostitutes would choose up."

Hailey shook her head. "What does that mean?"

"It's a way the prostitute can choose a new pimp." Erik cleared his throat. "Selena looked up, meaning she chose a new daddy. The shithead beat and raped her in front of everyone before the new owner took her."

Her stomach clenched. "Did he kill her?"

"No, but she took months to recover. Unfortunately, her new pimp was worse. Police caught up with him three years ago in a drug sting and killed him. I tracked down some of his connections. He routinely raped his victims and sold them when the price was right. The sleazeball's cousin remembered Selena. Liked the name.

Told us his cousin beat Selena after she got pregnant and sold her to a merchant who traveled in the Caribbean circuit."

"How long ago was that?" She scratched her arm and stopped.

"Six years."

A long time in human-trafficking terms. Hailey chewed the lining inside her bottom lip. "Do you know where she went?"

"Not yet, but don't get your hopes up. These cases rarely turn up anything."

Hailey blinked back tears. Human trafficking involved women, children, and men. No one deserved that treatment. "What's your plan?"

"I have a description of the merchant. My men are running his data through the computer, trying to find a match. We'll go from there."

"Keep me posted. I'll tell Luis. Thank you."

Hailey took a moment for her nausea to pass and dialed Luis's number.

When he heard the news, he cried. "*Gracias, señora.* I know it's not likely Selena's alive, but I'm indebted to you and your friends for trying to find her."

She wiped a tear from her cheek. "There's always hope. Hold on to that."

"I will." A rumble sounded through the connection, like Luis blowing his nose. "Please call me if you learn anything."

Chapter Fourteen

In the lobby of Posterity Medical Interventions, a receptionist with red, curly hair offered Hailey a wide smile. "Good afternoon, can I help you?"

"Is Bruce Hanover available? We worked together in Austin. He's asked me a dozen times to come and visit." Hailey showed the woman her identification.

The receptionist's perfectly manicured eyebrows arched. "What a nice surprise! And you're in luck. Dr. Hanover recently returned from a trip." She lifted the handset on the phone. "Have a seat. I'll let him know he has a visitor."

Hailey chose one of the cushioned benches and tapped her fingers on her suitcase. She was finally accepting his invitation, for a few weeks anyway.

A familiar tenor voice interrupted her musing. "Hailey?"

Bruce's wide, inquisitive eyes made the impromptu visit worthwhile. She stood, extending her arms wide. "Surprise!"

The past years had been kind to the seventy-six-year-old man. Still the same guy. White tufts of hair on the sides of his head. A few deeper wrinkles on his forehead between his eyebrows. Same wire-rimmed spectacles. Thinner, though. Probably lost weight during his trip to Peru.

He stammered. "Hailey. What are you doing here?"

Hailey laughed as she hugged him. "Very funny. For five years, you've asked me to come and assist with your projects. Ethan and Anna are visiting their cousins, so I flew down to take you up on your offer." When he said nothing, she stepped back. "I hope that's okay... You said the company has corporate apartments where I can stay."

He placed a hand under her elbow and ushered her away from the reception area. "Usually it does. But...uh...all the rooms are filled for the next month at least."

Darn. "No worries. My bad. I can book a hotel room."

"How long do you plan to stay?"

Money wouldn't be too much of a worry since Parker's beneficiary payout would arrive soon. "I'm flexible. My kids won't be home for at least two more weeks."

Bruce's nose twitched. "I handed out most of my projects to colleagues when I went to Peru. Why don't we go somewhere and talk?" He gestured to the front desk. "First, I need to request a visitor pass. The cafeteria is down this corridor. We can talk there."

His discomfort was palpable. Had she misread Bruce? Was his offer to "come visit sometime" simply a social gesture?

"Wouldn't your office be quieter?" When he hesitated, she teased. "Unless you have something to hide."

He massaged his chest the way he used to avert a panic attack. "No. Not at all."

After she completed the visitor paperwork, she walked beside Bruce to the elevator behind the lobby.

She followed him into the cab and swiveled her suitcase beside her. "How have you been?"

"Fine." Bruce pushed his eyeglasses over the bridge of his nose.

"I know work consumes your attention. I hope you've been taking time to eat and sleep."

He pressed the button for the second floor. "I may be getting older, but I can take care of myself."

She shrugged. He seemed grumpier than Ethan and Anna when they woke up on the wrong side of the bed. Maybe she interrupted his research project. Maybe he was just shocked to see her. "How was your trip to Peru?"

His eyes softened under his reflective mood. "Useful. But I'm glad to be home."

"Were you able to save the *Bixa aparra* plant?"

As doors opened, Bruce motioned her to step out first. "When I came back to town, the plant was nothing but a withered piece of straw."

Hallelujah! She resisted breaking out into a little dance, and she faked a frown. "Oh, Bruce. I'm sorry."

"Nothing I can do about it." Bruce looked around nervously as he led her across the hall to his office. "Wait out in the hall a minute. Sometimes I forget to clean my desk."

Hailey sucked in her cheeks, trying not to grin. Since when did he worry about clutter?

He peeked inside and flipped on the light switch. "I guess it's not too messy."

The place was a typical office, with medical books and folders scattered over a desk.

Hailey parked her luggage next to a bookcase filled with thick binders.

Bruce brushed off a chair and waited until she sat. He settled into his chair across the desk and steepled his fingers. "I'm afraid you wasted a trip. With *Bixa aparra* dead, my skin regeneration project is on hold indefinitely."

She picked up a metal tin sitting next to a partially filled coffee mug. "Don't be silly. I can help with something else. What other projects are you working on?"

He grabbed the tin from her hand and placed it back on the desk. "Just reports I need to write for my director. Nothing important." Bruce started massaging his chest but, eyeing Hailey's gaze, quickly thrust his hand into his lab coat pocket.

Yep, he was hiding something. Maybe he was sick. More of a reason to stick around. "I'm sorry I disturbed your day. I should've called before coming. But since I flew all the way from Virginia, I'd love to see the place. Could you give me a tour when you're free?" She lifted her eyebrows. "I'll take you out to dinner afterward."

Bruce glanced at his watch. "I guess I can squeeze in an afternoon break. Let's start in the basement. The biomechanics and bioengineering labs are located there. We've designed some innovative medical devices that will interest you."

During the tour, Bruce became his old self, introducing Hailey to the other senior researchers in the building, engaging in conversation about the company's mission, and discussing the latest medical advancements.

"Next up is the bioinstrumentation research workroom." For the next hour, Bruce showed her the research areas on the first floor. "Dr. Pettorini was impressed with your work at the NIH. Don't be surprised if he contacts you in the future."

Hailey's cheeks heated. The afternoon had evoked fond recollections of her work with enzyme assays and protein purification. "His interest is flattering, but I can't uproot Ethan and Anna from their schools and friends."

Besides, Mark would need a familiar place when he returned—assuming he could maneuver his way around the house.

Bruce pointed to a long hallway. "This is where the clinical engineering and orthopedic labs are located."

Late afternoon, Hailey followed Bruce back to his office. "So much state-of-the-art equipment. How do you keep up with it all?"

"I don't." Flecks of jade twinkled in his eyes. "Sometimes I forget I'm getting older. My mind isn't what it used to be. I do most of my testing in the lab down the hall from my office. It has some older analyzers that my brain can still operate." He gestured to the hallway. "I'll show you my research area next."

Bruce's lab was more spacious than the lower-level areas, housing more computers, analyzers, and biosafety cabinets. Hailey stepped past the cell culture incubators and pointed at a door with a sign: GREENHOUSE. "Is this where *Bixa aparra* grew?"

"Yes." Bruce led her outside to a balcony constructed with glass walls and white acrylic roof panels. In the center of the room, he rested his hand on a dried-up branch in an oversized clay pot. "This is the shrub."

"How long have you had it?"

"Since 1972. But I only started researching the plant ten years ago."

"Why so late?"

Bruce pulled out a handkerchief from his coat pocket and wiped his brow. "I didn't have any interest when I was younger."

Hailey eyed the withered leaves on the soil and fingered a broken branch. "I'm sorry your project on skin regeneration is ruined."

He scratched his forehead. "I feel bad you wasted your time to come here."

She shook her head. "Don't apologize. I wish I'd come sooner."

Bruce glanced at his watch. "Suppertime. Let me drop off my lab coat in the office, and we can leave."

"Sounds good." Hailey exaggerated an enthusiastic voice. She should visit Bruce more often. He was getting old if five o'clock was now his dinnertime instead of nine.

As they walked to the elevator, Hailey crooked her neck and pointed to a RESTRICTED sign hanging from the ceiling. "What's down there? You said there were no more labs on this floor."

Bruce pressed the down arrow. "That's where the guest researchers stay."

"The corporate apartments you mentioned?"

"Yes. PMI has a few out-of-town researchers currently collaborating on projects."

Hailey tightened her lips. How odd. The other scientists hadn't mentioned any outside researchers.

Bruce's gaze lingered to the restricted corridor until the elevator dinged.

Something peculiar was going on with Bruce. Perhaps she could pry it out of him during dinner. "Where do you recommend we eat? I'm starved."

****

Mark shuffled down the hallway to the lab. Bruce should've stopped over at the apartment by now. *It's not like him to be late.*

He stared at his left hand where the burn glove concealed raised, red scars. Fat chance his left arm would ever look normal again, even with the miracle salve.

Using a rhythmic pattern from the ballad he'd been practicing, he knocked on the office door. "Bruce? You in there?" When no one answered, he flipped the light switch. *Where did he go?* They'd eaten together every evening since the doctor had returned from Peru.

I'll try again later.

Back in his apartment, Mark kept the lights off and stared out the window at twilight setting in. The cityscape, with its tall skyscrapers and buildings aglow in the distance, was magical. Hailey would enjoy the pink-and-orange evening sky—if she were here. She was a romantic softie for sunsets and sunrises.

Just as well Hailey wasn't with him. Being a recluse made handling his disfigurement easier. Other than going to the burn clinic for treatments and walking in the park, he hadn't often risked going out into the public. Owen, his supervisor at the DTA, checked in sporadically, but the man was fooling himself if he believed Mark would ever return to work. Rehab was a full-time job.

Besides, Mark would never be able to load and fire a weapon quickly. The mobility on his right side had gradually returned, but the action on his left side was still stiff.

He slumped his shoulders. Workers' compensation wasn't near to his full salary. Even with Hailey's income from teaching, they'd have trouble making ends meet.

His phone chirped an incoming text.

Mark switched on the lamp and read his messages from Anna and Ethan about their day at Ocean City. For the next ten minutes, he fumbled on the keypad.

—Miss u. Wish I could've built the sandcastle, too!—

Hailey still hadn't returned his morning text.

An image of her running through Colombian jungles raced through his mind. He paced the room, trying to keep his blood pressure from spiking. He could call his parents. Ask them if they knew where she was. Or maybe he'd only worry them. Mom and Dad weren't getting any younger. Hailey had hinted for months that Dad was showing signs of dementia.

My absence is only creating more stress.

He picked up a brochure on EMDR that Dr. Kendrick had handed him at the last meeting.

"Please read this over. I think you should consider the therapy for your PTSD," she had said.

He browsed through the medical literature. Eye Movement Desensitization and Reprocessing. The therapy had only been around for thirty-five years. Relatively new in the world of psychotherapy, though many patients found results. It used a different approach—changing the way one's memory processed disturbing images in the brain.

The cognitive behavior therapies he'd tried worked to some degree, but loud sirens, abrupt noises, and helplessness still brought panic. Firetrucks racing down the streets at night caused the worst reactions.

Mark shuddered and flipped to the last page.

The EMDR sessions occurred a couple of times a

week. He could start seeing results after the first few sessions—if it worked.

He crumpled the brochure. "What a scam." His kind of panic couldn't go away with simple eye movements and shoulder taps.

The microwave clock beamed 7:27 PM.

Plenty of time to call his parents and catch Bruce back in the lab.

Chapter Fifteen

Hailey laid the cloth napkin on her plate. Any remnant of the herbed roasted chicken, carbonara, and wild mushrooms couldn't be detected under a microscope. The charming Italian restaurant, with its elaborate paintings of the Mediterranean and sculptures throughout the room, was as alluring as the evening's conversation. She picked up her coffee cup and sipped the smoky-tasting brew. "Your trip to Peru sounds fascinating. So many deep-rooted customs in that village. I can't imagine what the shaman would say about our lifestyle in the US—and our technology."

Bruce's fork clanked on the dinner plate. "You'd be surprised how progressive some of his medicines are compared to our 'advanced' technology." He emptied his water glass. "I should head back to the lab and shut everything down for the night. I have a couch, but my place is cramped. Can I recommend a hotel close to the airport?"

Hailey choked on the coffee. Nothing like being pushed out the door. Why was Bruce defaulting on his invitation to have her help with his research? Surely he had something she could do for a week.

She pulled out her credit card. "When you went to the bathroom earlier, I booked a hotel room down the street from your workplace… Shoot. I left my suitcase in your office. I'll grab it when you close up the lab."

He glanced at his watch. "Okay…if you insist."

Insist? Was this the same man who invited her to come to Atlanta? She stifled a laugh and walked with him out of the restaurant. He'd been acting strange all day, massaging his rib cage in that odd motion.

Twenty minutes later, Hailey followed him into his office.

Bruce powered off the instruments and picked up the tin container from his desk. "I'll be back shortly, and then we can leave."

She pulled out a chair and scrolled through her text messages. Anna. Ethan. Mark. Mark had texted five times.

Footfalls sounded from the hall.

Someone knocked on the door. "Bruce, where have you been—"

Mark? Her heartbeat raced. *Was she hallucinating his voice?*

Turning her head, she jumped from her seat. She wasn't hearing voices. A rush of heat flooded her cheeks. "Mark? Oh my God." She ran to him, hesitating a moment before wrapping her arms around him in an affectionate hug. "It's really you."

"Hailey!" Mark leaned back. "What are you doing here?"

She suppressed a sudden twinge of irritation. "I could ask you the same question. How long have you been staying here?"

He stuttered. "Ah…since I left Virginia."

A scar marked the back of his right hand. Tan-colored fabric covered his left hand and arm.

He wore the same transparent burn mask as the last time she'd seen him, except now a moustache grew underneath. Under his chin, his beard had grown longer. Gray mixed in with the tousled russet-colored hair growing past his blue eyes. Thin patches grew around two scars on the left side of his head. Red, mangled scars streaked up his neck and under his mask.

He didn't have his walking cane anymore.

Had Mark looked like this the last time she'd seen him? Perhaps she'd blocked his scars from her memory. Facing the disfigurement every day, alone, had to affect him. If only she could lock him away from the outside world.

Bruce appeared in the doorway and quietly stepped back.

"Freeze, Bruce!" Hailey rested her hands on her hips. "Why didn't you tell me Mark was here?"

Bruce's face paled as white as his hair, and his hand made the classic move to his chest.

She tapped her foot. "Let me guess. This is the reason you didn't want me involved with your research?"

Bruce massaged his chest more aggressively. "I need to sit down."

"Good idea. I'd like to know what you and Mark have been up to." Hailey sat in a chair and crossed her arms, fighting back a grin. She wouldn't be too hard on them. How could she be angry when joy radiated inside her? She'd found her husband.

After Halley heard their explanations, she stared at Mark. "You've not only been staying here during your therapies, but you're also the chief subject of Bruce's skin regeneration research? Why didn't you tell me?"

Bruce leapt to his feet. "I'll give you time alone." He picked up Hailey's suitcase. "Mark, I'm assuming Hailey will stay with you tonight?"

Mark's posture became rigid. "If she wants to."

Hailey blinked hard. *If I want to?*

Bruce fidgeted with the suitcase handle. "She'll need an electronic key card and fob to access the apartment and main door after hours. I'll start the paperwork in the morning." He shut the door on his way out.

Hailey stepped next to Mark, relaxing her fists as she gazed into his eyes.

"I know what you're thinking." His voice was a thin whisper.

"You do? Then please tell me, because I can't wrap my head around this." A tear slipped down her cheek. "You left…to work on your PTSD. You promised to call me every day."

"I did—"

"For two weeks." She raised her voice. "Then it was every other day. Then twice a week. I could've been here helping you. For weeks! Why do you keep pushing me away?"

"Because I can't bear to lose you."

The back of her throat tightened. Mark was scared, like she had been. Frightened of the unknown, wondering how people would receive his new look and what the future held for him.

She brushed the hair from his forehead. "I love you, inside and out. I'm not going anywhere."

Tears shimmered in his eyes. His dreamy baby blues hadn't changed. "What if my appearance doesn't improve?"

"Then we deal with it together." She held his left hand and kissed the exposed fingers peeking through his glove. "I love you, honey. Nothing is going to change that." She touched his chest. "It's what's inside here that counts."

Mark pulled her closer. "I've made so many mistakes. Don't give up on me. Please."

Goose bumps erupted on her arms. Ignoring the plastic mask outlining his mouth, she leaned in and kissed him, gentle, close-mouthed. Though the touch was quick, it was delicious. "I'll never give up on you."

His arms tightened. "I love you so much."

She kissed him again, more intimately, gliding her lips over his. "I want to stay with you tonight."

"I'd like that. I'll show you the apartment." Mark tilted his head in the same adorable way as when they'd first met. She'd missed his charming mannerisms.

She held his hand and followed him.

****

As twilight settled around José, an uneasy quietness cloaked him. For the past two hours, he'd ridden on the highway, taking in the unfamiliar expanse of land called Texas.

The driver, a contact hired by the commander's migrant smuggler, didn't speak. His jacket was zipped to the neck. Black tar stained his orange, white, and navy-colored baseball cap.

From the back seat, José peered into the rearview mirror. The man's dark sunglasses, short-boxed beard, and moustache hid most of his face. Or was that a disguise?

José obeyed the organization's strict rules to keep the authorities from apprehending his contacts: Paper communications passed in code. Cellular transmissions with burner phones. No conversations during transport. Passenger to duck below the seat when driving through toll lanes. So far, the instructions had gotten him to this point.

The driver parked at the far end of a shopping center lot and passed José a piece of white paper, a key chain with three keys, and a small metal hammer. "Apartment's over there." The man pointed a quivering finger at a gravel pathway that led to an apartment complex on the other side of the hedges. "The key set and hammer will get you into any place."

He drove off before José could say, "*Gracias*."

José fingered the filed-down ridges of the bump keys. Perfect. He jammed them and the hammer into his pocket. Then he unfolded the small note as he strode along the path.

A860P 766 Zabhr Yij

Apartment H#104C. 8:00. White SUV.

He'd memorized the alphabet code during his flights from Venezuela to Mexico. He curved his neck. Left corner of the building. Better arrive ten minutes early for his next ride. One no-show, and the deal was over. Apartment building H was on his right.

José sneered at two teenage boys riding a motorized skateboard in the empty parking lot. In Colombia, boys that age would be insurgents training in his camp.

He adjusted his hat and lowered his chin, turning away from the cameras attached to the entrance posts. At the door marked 104 C, he inserted the correct bump key and struck it with the hammer. He unlocked the door, stepped inside, and flipped the dead bolt.

After three days of traveling, he'd finally arrived in the US. Damn his body for trembling!

He collapsed onto a wobbly recliner and groaned at the TV with a broken screen. Stains streaked across the worn carpet, and dingy faded orange curtains fluttered above the air conditioner unit. A mildew odor hovered over the place, but it had a cozier feel than the other dumps.

All the accommodations thus far were cheap. The hefty fee José paid should've secured rides, rented rooms, and provided food, clothes, and communication via cell phones and walkie-talkies. With the amount of money the migrant smuggler was ripping him off, the man could buy his own country.

Hmm. Maybe he should start his own smuggling enterprise here.

He stepped into the kitchen and opened the refrigerator door. The six-pack would quench his thirst. He grabbed two beers and removed a lukewarm takeout container filled with a grilled hamburger and fries.

No Colombian cuisine? He wrinkled his nose as he sat at the kitchen table with his dinner. At least the food hadn't been in the fridge long.

When José finished eating, he returned to the living room recliner and leaned back with his hands cradled behind his head.

The past few days blurred together. Travel from Venezuela to the US entailed multiple flights, fake IDs, and taxi transports. Getting across the US border was more complex, and for a few shaky minutes, José had grown anxious, wondering if the Border Patrol agents would seize him at the fence. He'd overheard horror stories of migrants' experiences coming across the border.

He should've had more confidence in the chief smuggler. The contacts were careful to stay concealed as they monitored both sides of the border and used cell phones to communicate when to cross. This smuggling operation ran like a first-rate military maneuver; every drop-off and pick-up transpired without any hitches.

In the bedroom, José opened the dresser and pulled out underwear, socks, and a change of clothes in his exact size. Bathroom essentials were spread across the counter. He drew back the moldy shower curtain and rotated the faucet handle.

As the water heated, he walked back into the bedroom and removed his boots. He rolled down his sweat-stained sock, careful to retrieve a tiny paper with Hailey Langley's address. If he could trust the commander's intel, she'd returned to the US the previous week. The blonde *puta* and little girl had to be back in the country, too. The Langley snitch would know where they stayed.

José cracked his knuckles. He'd make her disclose the location before she paid for what happened to Manuel.

He stripped and tossed his clothes into a garbage bag. Passing the dresser mirror, he cringed at his unsightly appearance. More patches of crusted skin had erupted on his face and arms. Damn the Colombian government for spraying chemicals on the coca plants!

He stood under the showerhead and let the water wash away the sweat, mold, grime, and smoke coating his skin. Tomorrow would be another early day. Accounting for the night traveling and car transfers, his trip to Virginia would take two days.

Restlessness flowed through him as he readied for bed and set an alarm. He leaned back onto the pillow. Payback was so close. He'd take the whore's child in exchange for Manuel.

Ojo por ojo.
Or, as they said in the US, eye for an eye.

Chapter Sixteen

Mark breathed in his wife's delicate feminine scent, taking in every beguiling curve of her body. Dang! Hailey was sexier than when they first met. Even her soft snores heated his blood. He should've brought her here weeks ago. After sharing a bed again, he'd do whatever it took to recover and return home.

The shuttle bus would arrive in an hour. He'd wait another five minutes to calm his erection before he prepped for therapy.

He licked his lips. The sweetness of Hailey's honeyed kisses the previous night still lingered. They hadn't made love; the last time he'd slept with Hailey had been almost a year ago. He couldn't push her. Depending on her response to his disfigurement, that element of their marriage might never happen again.

He raised his gloved hand to touch her cheek but then lowered it. Better take things slowly. For now, lying next to her was enough.

Bruce's suspicions had been correct about Hailey encountering hardship in Colombia. Twice during the night, Hailey cried out Mendoza's name.

Mark had comforted her, smoothing her hair, whispering, "I'm here, honey."

He ground his teeth. He should kill that bastard for tormenting her. Thank God she was safe now. Back in the US, away from the Mendoza family.

Hailey's eyelashes fluttered, and a smile spread across her face. "Good morning. What time is it?"

"Quarter after eight." He leaned over and kissed her. God, her sweet lips tasted delicious. He nibbled on her lips again. Like a hummingbird feeding on nectar. "You can use the bathroom first. I'll ask the therapist to change my pressure garments at the clinic. I leave at nine. I won't have much time for breakfast."

She snuggled closer into his arms. "Give me another minute with you. Before the outside world takes over."

His pulse raced. Maybe their relationship hadn't changed that much.

While Hailey showered, Mark stood in front of the bathroom mirror and removed his face mask. He leaned in closer and fingered the scars on his cheek. They were less bumpy. Not as dark. Bruce would be elated at the change. *I hope skipping last night's salve treatment didn't throw me off schedule.*

Mark reattached the face cover, dressed, and applied moisturizer to his skin. Now wasn't the time to include Hailey with his daily care routine. If she were serious about helping him convalesce, she'd find out soon enough how much support he required.

His cell chirped and lit up with a text from his physical therapist.

—Heavy traffic this morning. Shuttle is running 40 min. behind schedule—

Fine with him. More time for breakfast.

He walked with Hailey to Bruce's lab and knocked on the open door. "I told Hailey you'd be working already. Can you spare any time to eat?"

The elderly doctor looked up from the microscope and gave a playful smile. "I wasn't sure you wanted me around anymore since you have a better-looking sidekick."

Laughter spilled from Hailey's mouth. "Don't kid yourself. You're still quite handsome."

Bruce's cheeks blushed a deep red. "Back in the day, maybe."

Mark grinned at their relaxed banter. No wonder Bruce wanted her to be his assistant.

Hailey stepped to the counter. "What are you working on now that your grant project is over?"

Mark held his breath. *Oh boy. She was bound to ask the question sooner or later.*

Bruce flipped off the light at the base of the scope. "Officially, the project's over, but unofficially, I still have one option to pursue." He walked to the sink and washed his hands. "I'll fill you in once we get a bite to eat."

When Bruce finished explaining the specifics of his project, the cafeteria crowd had thinned.

Hailey sat across from the doctor, anger lighting her eyes. "I'm against this. Last night you didn't mention using *Bixa aparra* on Mark." She crossed her arms. "Euphoria has been nothing but trouble. It took my son." Her voice broke.

Mark rubbed her shoulder. "Honey, if the plant has medicinal benefits, we should research it."

She shoved her mug, coffee spilling over. "You're splitting hairs. Do you really believe the plant's flowers can heal skin?"

Bruce nodded. "I've seen it with my own eyes."

Mark nudged Bruce. "Go ahead. Show her."

When Bruce rolled up his sleeves and extended his arms, Hailey gaped. She brushed the hair from his forearm. "This is amazing. Your right arm has no wrinkles or age spots. Mark, have you noticed any difference on your skin?"

Not enough. "The scars seem softer."

Bruce buttoned his shirt cuffs. "It's too early to be optimistic. Unfortunately, we have a limited supply of salve. Maybe three or four days before it's depleted."

Hailey peered at Mark's mask. "Can you get more?"

Bruce shook his head. "The shaman gave me all his oil. There are no more plants."

"Can we make it synthetically?"

"I need to analyze the oil closer, but there's no more specimen."

"Maybe there is." Hailey tapped her fingers on the table. "Mendoza grew *Bixa aparra*."

Bruce's eyes bulged. "Are you sure?"

"He had an entire field."

Mark gasped. "A whole field?"

Hailey frowned. "Until I set it on fire."

Mark slapped his forehead. "Tell me you didn't."

Hailey squirmed like a suspect in the hot seat. "I used the distraction to get away. How was I supposed to know you'd need the plant? Euphoria has caused so much turmoil in our lives. I wanted to destroy any trace of it."

Bruce scratched his neck. "Are you sure the fire destroyed *all* the plants?"

"I dumped over 300 gallons of gasoline on the field and lit the match." She reached in her pocket and pulled out her cell. "But on the off chance, let me call Luis, the man who helped me escape. He might know if the field survived." She brought up his name and put the call on speaker.

Mark held his breath. *Please, by some miracle, let there be some plants left.*

"*Señora* Hailey," a man with a thick accent answered, "do you have more news about Selena?"

"Hopefully soon." She cleared her throat. "I'm calling about something else. When we were at Mendoza's lab, we passed a field of small shrubs—not the coca plants. Do you remember?"

"The one *señor* Manuel used to make Euphoria? The field you set on fire?"

Hailey grimaced. "Yes, that's the one. Did any plants survive?"

"No, *señora*. The fire spread everywhere."

Mark exhaled and closed his eyes. One moment of hope washed down the drain. Damn.

"Why do you ask, *señora*?"

"I need the blossoms for my research."

"Why didn't you say so? The greenhouse has plants. They're in full bloom."

Mark vaulted from his seat. *Now we're talking.* "Ask how many."

Hailey motioned Mark to sit. "How many, Luis?"

"I'd say a few hundred."

Bruce grabbed Hailey's phone. "Are you sure they're blooming?"

Hailey took back the phone. "My colleague is with me, Luis. Sorry for the confusion."

"No worries, *señora*. *Sí.* I saw the flowers two days ago. No one has worked in the facility since *señor* Manuel died."

Bruce whispered, "Ask if he can sneak into the place and send us the flowers." He pulled a pen from his pocket and started scribbling on a napkin.

Hailey read Bruce's note. "Luis, this is asking a lot, but if I obtain the permits to ship the flowers to the US, could you go back to the lab and collect them?"

"*Sí.* I'll go today. It's the least I can do to thank you for searching for Selena."

"My colleague, Dr. Bruce Hanover, will call you in an hour with instructions on how to gather the flowers and where to send the shipment. The blooms are dangerous, so you'll need special gloves to handle them. Be extremely careful. Dr. Hanover will take care of the necessary permit paperwork. I'll reimburse you for the expenses and your time. *Gracias*, Luis."

"*Con gusto.*" Luis ended the call.

"Oh my God! This is fantastic." Mark hugged her and high-fived Bruce, only partly listening as the doctor summarized the shipping timeline and customs inspection procedure. "I'm going to be late for therapy." He planted a light kiss on Hailey's cheek. She was his lucky charm. "I'll see you this afternoon."

Hailey chewed on her lip. "If you'd like, I could come with you."

His feet froze to the ground. *I'm not ready.* "My therapy lasts most of the day. I'd rather you and Bruce focus on shipping the flowers here." He turned to Bruce. "Should you ask Luis to send us some plants, too?"

Bruce shook his head. "I'd rather expedite the blooms first. I submitted a research application this summer on the remote chance I'd bring some flowers back from South America. Importing entire shrubs involve more permits and more customs inspections."

Mark hurried outside and boarded the shuttle bus. If luck was on his side, he'd have enough Euphoria salve for all his scars. Miracles did happen! Everything would be okay now that Hailey was here. She'd only been in town for a day and had already solved a crisis.

As he eased onto the seat, uneasiness cloaked him. In leaving Virginia, he prevented Hailey from seeing his pain and physical impairments. Now she'd see everything. The Herculean task of buttoning a shirt. His difficulty showering. The awkwardness of texting. Even if the salve healed his scars, could he trust their love to survive when he wasn't the same man?

Chapter Seventeen

After Hailey inventoried the glassware needed for the distillation procedure, she walked to Bruce's office and waited until he finished a phone call. "The supplies are here to extract the oil from the *Bixa aparra* blooms. Did you phone Luis?"

Bruce jotted down a note on his tablet. "The shipment's been arranged. Now I need to contact the Department of Agriculture to expedite the paperwork." He passed her two books from his desk. "Before I forget, these will get you up to speed about wound healing and skin regeneration."

She took the books and sat across from him. "So much for 'light' reading. These are heavier than my hand weights."

Bruce winked. "I'm working your muscles as well as your brain." He reached in his shirt pocket and handed her an envelope. "I almost forgot. Here's a lanyard with your keys. The card is for the apartment. Use the key fob to enter the main doors after five o'clock."

She draped the lanyard around her neck. Staying with Mark was now official. "Thank you."

"How did it go last night after I left?"

Hailey sighed. Though seeing Mark had been emotional, sleeping next to him, breathing in his earthy scent, felt perfect. "As well as I could expect. I wish you'd told me Mark was here."

The tight lines around his eyes faded. "I'm sorry, but that decision wasn't mine to make."

No sense in staying irritated with Bruce when he was only trying to help. "Well, I'm here now. While you finish the phone calls, I'll check in with my kids." She laid the books on the desk. "I'll be back in a jiffy."

As Hailey hurried down the hall to the apartment, she pulled up her daughter's contact info on the cell.

Anna picked up on the third ring. "Hi, best mom in the whole entire world."

Hailey chuckled. "Wow. That's a big hello."

"Samantha and Rose called this morning."

"So that explains your cheerful mood. I wondered when you'd hear from them."

"Rose told me that you and her other mom flew to South America and rescued her. Is that true? Why didn't you tell me you were going to South America? I would've come with you."

Fat chance! "She's your friend. I wanted to help."

"Ethan didn't believe me when I told him you were in Colombia. How did you know where to look?"

"I watched a lot of detective shows on TV." She snorted. *If the kids only knew.* "How do Samantha and Rose like living in Boston?"

"They love it. Yesterday, they went on a bus tour, and the bus morphed into a boat. Samantha said they were acting silly and quacking like a duck when the bus drove into the water."

"Maybe we can visit them and do the tour." Hailey picked up an acoustic guitar lying next to the sofa. Strange. Last night when Mark brought her to the apartment, he mentioned the instrument was part of his therapy. "I have a surprise for you."

"What?" Anna squealed.

"Remember when I told you I was flying to Atlanta to visit my friend Bruce?"

"Yes."

"Guess who else is here?"

"Who?"

"Your dad."

"Daddy? You found him? How is he? Is he coming home?"

Joy rushed through Hailey as she visualized Mark reuniting with the kids. "He's working on his rehab, but I hope he can come back soon."

"Can we see him?"

How would he react? The kids needed him. "Let me find a good time when we can all sit down and video chat."

"Okay." The excitement in Anna's voice shot up five levels. "Wait until I tell Ethan. This is the best week of my life!"

When Hailey returned to Bruce's office, the doctor was sitting on a chair with his chin lowered and a book opened in his hands. Did he doze off?

"Ahem." She faked a cough. "I'm back. Is everything arranged with the Department of Agriculture?"

Bruce's head jerked. He took off his glasses and rubbed his eyes. "If all goes as planned, Luis can ship the flowers tomorrow morning."

Hailey clapped her hands. "That's great news. When will the shipment arrive?"

"In a few days. It'll take time to inspect the cargo once it arrives in the US."

"What happens if we run out of salve?"

"Mark's progress will be delayed, or his condition could revert."

She slid into her chair. "Be honest, Bruce. Do you think this treatment can cure him?"

"I think it's his best shot. Herbal products, like the oil from *Bixa aparra*, have different elements to aid in skin repair that you don't find in the synthetic creams on the market." He paused. "Mark didn't want you to attend rehab with him today?"

"Unfortunately, no." Hailey frowned. "I don't want to push him, but family involvement is important to a patient's recovery."

"I agree. You need to see what his therapy requires so you can assist him."

"I saw the splints and pillows he uses in bed. In the bathroom this morning, he applied cream on his skin."

"Did you help him?"

Hailey shook her head. "I offered. Mark said he could do it himself."

Bruce sighed. "He needs you. He's doing well with his walking, but he's frustrated with his other progress."

"I wish he wouldn't push me away."

"Keep offering your assistance. The OT is focusing on activities of daily living, but recovery takes time. Even though Mark's right hand is mostly healed, his movements are slow."

She smacked her forehead. "That must be why he doesn't like to text."

"It's time consuming. The therapist has worked with him to regain that skill, but Mark's in constant pain."

"Will the salve heal his nerves?"

Bruce shrugged. "I don't know. This research is new territory."

"If we don't get enough *Bixa aparra* blooms from Luis, can we use other plants to regenerate his skin?"

"Another good question. There are certainly other possibilities, but *Bixa aparra* is like the gold standard for burns in botanical medicine."

"When will you know if the salve is working?"

"Tomorrow. Once I've tracked the collagen content in the extracellular matrix, I'll have a better idea of what's happening."

****

José glowered at his sneakers as he hiked the block to Hailey Langley's house. Whoever bought him this footwear instead of hiking boots should be shot. He tugged at his jeans and polo shirt. Combat fatigues would've been more practical.

Coughing, he walked up the driveway and removed his ball cap. The broad-leaved trees in the lots provided shade, but the humidity remained high. He brushed back his damp, thick hair and wiped his brow with a bandana. He should've brought his black-and-white striped *sombrero*.

José smirked at the white sedan in front of the garage.

She's home.

He cracked his knuckles. Before killing the nosy snitch, he'd force her to reveal Rose's location. His contact hadn't delivered a gun yet, but there were other ways to murder. He moistened his lips as ideas flashed in his mind. Poisoning? Too slow. Hard blows over the head? Too fast. Strangling—now that would be satisfying. Or drowning. The fear in her eyes would excite him.

His ride would arrive down the block in thirty

minutes. The schedule hinged on how quickly he could make Langley talk. After José killed her, he'd ask the commander to set up a new travel plan to capture Manuel's daughter.

The house looked around fifteen years old, with mildew and dirt accumulating on the siding. Sun-bleached flyers cluttered the shrubs near the bottom porch step.

With a quick glance up and down the street, José prowled past a bed of daisies and climbed onto the porch. His blood pumped with anticipation as he peered through the huge picture window. The place was dark. Maybe she wasn't home.

José removed the keys and bump hammer from his pocket, opened the door, and stepped inside.

He skirted the living room and paused at the family photos hanging on the wall. The daughter had the same hazel eyes and wavy, brunette hair as her mother. The boy looked older than the girl and resembled the father who died in a fire, the one Manuel's ruffians were rumored to have started. The Internet reported multiple stories on the incident.

He walked into a room beside the stairs where partially opened shades gave light to the room. Books and board games filled a bookcase along a wall. A computer and printer sat on the desk next to a stack of mail.

Must be a study. Puny, compared to his. He turned. And more cluttered.

José riffled through the electric bill and credit card statement. Next to the keyboard, he fingered a small green book with the words "Telephone & Address" printed on the cover. He flipped to the letter T.

No listing for Colleen Toole. Her name had to be written in somewhere.

He flicked the pages backward.

¡Ajá! Rose and Colleen's names appeared below Joyce Rogers's information. The former address had been crossed out and changed to a place in Boston, Massachusetts.

The commander can verify the new address.

Lips curling, José tore out the page and slid it into his pocket. Did the blonde hussy think she'd come back to the US with her bastard child—and no consequences? Manuel would be alive to run the family business if Colleen Toole hadn't spawned his kid. She caused his death.

José cracked his knuckles. Once he kidnapped Manuel's little love child, he'd have no time to come back and kill Langley.

Perhaps, she was taking a *siesta*. He climbed the stairs and stalked down the hallway.

The first room had a starfish rug on the floor and a beach-themed shower curtain draped above the bathtub. Basketball posters cluttered the walls of the next room, with sneakers piled beside the dresser.

He paused at the hand-drawn colorings taped onto the door of the second bedroom. One picture depicting three *amigas* was signed with Rose's name. José traced a finger over the smallest figure in the drawing. *She looks exactly like Manuel's daughter.*

He strode into the master bedroom where the comforter was neatly drawn over the bed.

"¡Hijueputa! No siesta."

As a coughing spell overtook him, he scowled at a framed family photo on the nightstand. A loving family was an unrealistic dream. Families were tools to expand wealth and power. Like marrying Camila, and Manuel managing the family business.

José inhaled, fighting to fill his lungs as dryness blanketed his chest. He rifled through the drawers and snapped up $200 in cash. A tiny down payment for the pain Langley had caused. He eyed the clock on the nightstand and headed down the hallway.

The front door creaked.

"Anyone home? Hello? Hailey?"

José stepped back from the top stair and peered through the railing. A *gringo* around sixty-five years old wandered into the living room. "When did you return from your trip? You forgot to lock the door."

Sweat dripped down José's back as he stepped behind the hall bathroom door. His ride would come any minute. *I need a damn gun.*

Chapter Eighteen

Mark stood beside the small pond in the courtyard, gripping a flattened stone. With as much downward force as he could muster, he released his grip forward and counted as the stone dapped along the surface.

Three.

At least it was better than last week. Everything required ten times more effort to reproduce his pre-injury skills.

Two Canadian geese swimming in the water flapped their wings and flew away.

I wish I could join you. He skipped another stone across the pond. Three bounces. He'd never get back to eight.

"There you are." Hailey stepped beside him. "I looked everywhere for you."

Mark's heart pattered. Did she know how hot she looked in her tight-fitting capris and lightweight eyelet blouse? His gaze lingered on her curves. "Just blowing off some steam."

"Are you upset because of what Bruce said?" A gentle breeze blew hair over her eyes, and she tucked the small flyaway strands behind her ears. One day, when his fingers weren't too clumsy, he might be able to brush away her stray hair.

Mark stared at his fingertips peeking from his gloved hand. He'd never ditch these compression garments. "I thought the scars were improving. The salve was supposed to regenerate my skin."

"It is, but the collagen isn't aligning normally. Bruce will run another test in a few days." She slid onto a large boulder next to a patch of black-eyed Susans and patted a vacant space beside her. "Don't get discouraged."

Easy for you to say. He sat beside her. "The salve's almost gone. What happens if the flower shipment is held up in customs? Or never arrives? I *hate* having no control over my life."

Hailey draped her arms around his shoulders. "No one has complete control over their life. I sure don't."

"I really messed up both of our lives, haven't I?"

"Our lives aren't a mess. Messy was when I thought you'd died. You're alive. We need to embrace our second chance." She leaned over and kissed him. "Don't give up hope."

He groaned. "I wanted to come back to you when I was one hundred percent. I wanted us to have a perfect life."

"Nobody's perfect. If you were, you wouldn't want to live with me, because of my imperfections." She traced a finger across his pecs, and the sensation under his T-shirt felt like a feather brushing against his skin.

He squeezed her hand. "I'm glad you're here."

"So am I." Her head leaned lightly against his chest. "Ethan and Anna loved chatting with you last night."

Another bright spot of his day. "They talked as if we hadn't missed any time. They kept asking when I'm coming home."

"They miss you."

"Even Laura was talkative." He shrugged. "I thought everyone would be upset with me."

Her gaze met his. "We love you. We want what's best for you."

As Mark leaned in for another smooch, his cell chirped. He pulled his phone from his pocket. "It's David."

"Put him on speaker. I can't wait to hear his voice when I tell him I found you."

Mark tapped the speaker button. "Hey, buddy."

Hailey leaned toward the phone. "Hello, David."

"Hailey?" David's voice cracked. "You found Mark?"

"Yep." A cocky smile spread across her face. "In Atlanta."

"As in the town where your doctor friend works?"

Hailey nodded. "That's the place."

"Shit. Mark never let on."

Mark rested his chin on her head. "What's up?"

"I have some bad news." David cleared his throat. "Your dad took a tumble down the stairs when he checked on your house today."

"Oh my God. Is he okay?" Mark slid off the rock, his legs shaking.

"He has a concussion and some nasty bumps and bruises, but luckily no broken bones. The doctor's admitting him for observation."

"Where's my mom?"

"At the hospital."

Mark raked a hand through his hair. "How did he topple down the steps? Dad's never had an issue with our stairs."

"Adam insists someone pushed him. His mind isn't the clearest lately. I'm sure Hailey's mentioned that his health has declined."

"She told me."

Hailey reached in her pocket and pulled out her phone. "I'll book the next flight back to Virginia."

"You should stay there, Hailey. Bringing Mark back will do wonders for Peggy and Adam. Only two people are allowed in the room anyway, and Mark's sister Francine is flying in from Arizona to be with them. Laura is staying in New Jersey with the kids."

Mark pressed his lips together. David made a good point. "Are you at the hospital?"

"Left a few minutes ago. I drove Peggy to her house to pack a few clothes and brought her back. She'll stay the night with your dad. Don't worry. I'll check in on them tomorrow."

"Thanks, buddy. I'll phone Mom this evening."

When Mark ended the call, he hurled a stone across the pond. "I should be with them."

Hailey slid off the boulder and rubbed his shoulder. "Your dad's going to be okay."

"What if something happens? I might never see him again."

"Then we'll have to make sure you get better soon."

An image of the ambulance transporting his dad flashed in his mind, sirens blaring like the night of the fire.

His hands started to shake. Dammit!

"Mark? Are you okay?" Hailey's eyes widened. "Oh my God. Do you want me to call a doctor?"

A black hole muted her voice and threatened to lure him in.

"Mark. Breathe in. Look at me. We'll do it together. You're doing great. Inhale and let the oxygen flow throughout your body." She breathed with him. "You're safe here with me. Your dad's going to be okay. Think about Anna and Ethan and the time we rode bikes on the Ghost Town Trail two years ago."

He concentrated on Hailey's comforting voice. Finally, the images faded, and he breathed normally.

"Can I hold your hand?" When he nodded, she slowly brushed her thumb over his hand. "Feeling better?"

He exhaled. "How did I think I could handle this without you?"

"We're a team." She lifted his right arm and pecked a kiss on the back of his hand. "Do you want me to call Dr. Kendrick?"

"No. I'll talk to her tomorrow." Hailey shouldn't have to see him this way.

"How often do you see the psychotherapist?"

"Three times a week." And he hadn't made any breakthroughs.

"Let's walk. A change of scenery might help."

Mark curved his arm around her waist and drew her close. "Thank you. This time wasn't as bad as the others."

He walked beside her into the lobby and pointed to the front entrance. "There's a park with a trail not far from here."

Across the bustle of the city, Mark walked with her to his quiet space, stopping at a bench near a swing set. "Let's sit. My legs are getting sore."

Hailey's pace slowed to meet his. "Should I call a cab?"

"No. I just need to rest a while." He leaned over and rubbed his leg.

"Can I do anything?"

He shook his head and massaged higher on his thigh. "I can handle it. The therapist told me what to do."

"If I knew about your therapies, I might be able to help you. Can you tell me more?"

How much information did he want to share? "The physical therapy helps me rebuild strength and balance for walking."

"I think you walk pretty well."

"Thanks, but it hasn't been easy."

When he described his efforts to move away from the wheelchair and walker, Hailey's face paled. "Gosh! You put in more work than people training for the Olympics."

"I doubt anyone would give me a gold medal if they saw me stand from a chair. I waver like a seasick sailor."

Hailey chuckled. "I've missed your humor. What other therapies do you have?"

He waited as a mother wheeled a stroller past them. "Occupational therapy. The OT helps me work on daily living skills."

"Like eating?"

"Yeah. Holding a fork and spoon." He glanced at his hands. "Texting. Writing. Dressing myself. Shooting a gun again."

Hailey scratched her arm. "Target practicing, already?"

"I'm making some progress, but I'm not strong enough to pull the trigger."

"I'd like to be part of your rehab—if you want me to."

Mark tensed at the empathy in her voice. How could he invite her into his world, a place where hopelessness darkened his soul? It would only bring her down, too. "I can handle rehab on my own. Right now, I wish you'd work with Bruce."

"Okay." Tears welled in her eyes, and she turned away.

Her reaction punched his gut. God help him. Only fools pushed away those who loved them unconditionally. He must be the biggest fool of all.

Chapter Nineteen

"I need a break." Hailey slammed the cover of *Skin Regeneration and Wound Repair*. Processing the information was worse than cramming for a college final. Now she understood why her undergrad students groaned after her lectures. Medical terms swirling in her head, she set the textbook on the desk. "Does the salve destroy the entire matrix and rebuild the skin or does it remodel the existing one?"

"I'm not certain." Bruce scrubbed a hand down his whiskers. "From Mark's test results earlier this week, new collagen fibers are aligning, but the formation is in a single direction."

"Mark's scars look lighter. He must be improving."

"He is, but unless the extracellular matrix reconstructs in random formation, he'll still have scarring." Bruce rubbed his brow. "I think inflammation is interfering with the components of the ECM."

Hailey paced the floor. "The fire was ten months ago. Shouldn't Mark's inflammation have diminished by now?"

"No. Mark's body is trapped in an inflammatory phase. The salve contains all the necessary growth factors, chemokines, and cytokines for regeneration, but we must reduce inflammation as much as possible to support the wound-healing cascade."

"Can you ask for suggestions from the shaman you

met in Peru? He might know of a plant or herb to use."

"I sent a message to his village, but with no cell towers, it might take a few days before he'll respond."

Bruce drew a sketch of the extracellular matrix on a sheet of paper, and he penciled in a big question mark. "We know the salve is restructuring the matrix. The key is to normalize the ECM scaffold while Mark's skin regenerates."

Hailey leafed through another book on Bruce's desk. "Are you sure inflammation is bad? This page says the inflammatory phase is vital for the wound to heal."

Bruce handed her a folder. "The question is still under debate. We'll know more about Mark's progress after we review his latest skin samples."

Hailey gestured at Bruce's forearm. "Did you notice if anything besides your skin had regenerated?"

Bruce brushed his fingers over his blond arm hair. "You mean other than my hair follicles?"

She examined his arm closer. "Yes. I wonder if anything else will regenerate in the skin. Like sweat glands. Nerve cells, perhaps."

"Time will tell."

Hailey's phone buzzed. "It's Luis." She grabbed her cell from the counter and put him on speaker. "Luis? Hello."

"*Buenos días, señora* Hailey."

"You have perfect timing. The shipment you sent is going through customs."

"That's good news. Actually, I called to speak to Dr. Hanover."

Bruce? She lifted her eyebrow. "He's right here."

Bruce's face reddened. "Hi, Luis. Did you take care of the other request I spoke with you about?"

"That's why I'm calling. I only had time to box two plants before the helicopter came for the flower shipment the other day. This morning, I flew back to the lab, but the place was bare. The authorities must've raided the greenhouse. I'm sorry."

Bruce slammed a hand against the desk. "Were you able to ship the two plants you crated?"

"*Sí, señor*, but there's no more."

Hailey sighed. *I caused this trouble.* "We appreciate your help, Luis. *Gracias.*"

"Do you have any more news about my sister?"

The desperation in Luis's voice hit like a hard blow to her face. Should she tell him about Erik's phone call the previous day that linked Selena's pimp to one of India's mafia leaders? No sense upsetting him until she had more information. "Not yet. I'm sorry."

"It's not your fault. I keep hoping..." He sniffled. "The authorities are gathering evidence to charge *señor* José with murder, drug trafficking, human trafficking, and heading a revolution."

"Haven't they arrested him yet?"

"No, *señora*. The authorities are still searching."

Hailey dug her fingernails into her arm and scratched. "Do you think he could have fled the country?"

"I doubt he'd leave his camp. He's probably hiding with the revolutionaries. Don't worry. He'll show up somewhere. He's been stripped of everything. He has nowhere else to go."

Luis was right. If José had left the country, the SCA and CIA would've received an alert.

An hour later, Hailey sat with Bruce at his desk examining the latest slides on a dual-headed microscope.

Bruce moved the pointer over the ECM. "Let me pull up Mark's earlier images and compare." His fingers skated across the keyboard. "Ah! Here they are. This is incredible. Look at the difference from a week ago."

Her stomach flipped somersaults as she zeroed in on the slides. "The change is undeniable. I hope we can make enough salve to treat all Mark's scars."

Bruce moved the slide to another region. "He opted to treat his neck and face first, even though other areas were burned worse."

"Why?"

"Why do you think?"

Hailey didn't need to ponder long. "He's self-conscious about his appearance." She leaned back in her seat. "The other day, Mark grimaced at his reflection in the mirror. He won't let me see his scars. I wish he'd open up. I remember how awful it feels to have a negative body image."

"He's most uneasy about his legs, especially his left side."

She could only imagine what the wounds looked like. Even with his pain meds, Mark cried out at night when his legs rubbed against the sheets. "I'll show him the results after his therapy. He could use some hopeful news."

Bruce increased the magnification and scanned the slide further. "I'd hold off getting his hopes up. The scar tissue is degrading, but the collagen's orientation still isn't what we'd hoped for."

"Do you really believe inflammation is the cause?"

"I do. The sooner we address the problem, the better chance his skin will form properly." Bruce studied a few more images. "When you get some time, can you pull up a list of exotic plants known to reduce inflammation?"

"Of course, but wouldn't it be easier to give Mark ibuprofen or another anti-inflammatory medicine instead?"

Bruce shook his head. "I'd rather stay with natural products."

"There must be dozens of plants that prevent inflammation. How will we know which is the right one?"

"You'll know when you find it."

She sighed. Bruce had more confidence in her than she had in herself. "I'll start the list. By the way, we haven't discussed your phone call with Luis yet. Why did you ask him to ship *Bixa aparra* plants to you?"

"Not to me. To the shaman in Peru, as a thank you for giving me the Euphoria salve. The shaman can plant the seedlings and propagate them in his village." Bruce looked up from the scope's eyepiece. "It's our only hope to prevent the plant from becoming extinct. The Colombian government shouldn't have ransacked the greenhouse. They had no idea how valuable *Bixa aparra* is."

"Tell me something, Bruce. What is it about this plant that compels you to devote so much time? Euphoria killed many people. The drug from the roots almost killed me."

"I know *Bixa aparra* is dangerous, but there are valuable compounds to tap into."

Better not argue. Any benefit from the flowers remained to be seen. "I hope you're right, because Mark needs a miracle." She twisted off the lid of the nearly empty container and breathed in the salve's honeyed scent. "If you skimp, you might tweak out two more

171

applications. When did the flower shipment arrive in Savannah?"

"Ten o'clock last night. The inspection should happen sometime this morning, and the courier will drive it here." He paused. "You look stressed. Everything okay?"

Stressed was an understatement. "There's a lot going on. Mark had an episode last night after he learned his father was admitted to the hospital." Hailey rubbed her temples as she explained the details.

"Did you try slow-breathing exercises?"

"Yes. We walked outside for some fresh air until he calmed down."

"I'm glad you were there for him. Sometimes he's in his room for hours during an episode, and no one knows. Have you asked again to accompany him to his therapy?"

"I have, but he insists I help you instead." She shook her head. "This must be hard on him. He's always felt in control of his life. Now he's worried about his parents and our future. It seems like every time he gets a boost, something knocks him down."

"Maybe his dad's accident triggered flashbacks of Mark's own hospital stay."

She should've thought of that. "It's possible."

"At least his father's going to be okay."

Hailey saved the images of Mark's test results on the computer. "My father-in-law is strong for a sixty-eight-year-old man, but we're still worried."

"Of course. Mark worries about you, too." Bruce wheeled his chair away from the microscope and put on his eyeglasses. "He mentioned you're having nightmares."

Mark had held her the first night when she woke screaming. "I guess Mendoza's death is affecting me more than I wanted to admit." Her voice quavered as rage swelled inside her. "I despised Mendoza for many reasons. He was a monster."

Bruce patted her hand. "It's natural to feel angry, especially after what you suffered because of him."

"My brain is trying to process everything." Hailey wiped her eyes. "Mentally, I'm torn. Despite all the evil, Mendoza gave his life to save Rose. He died having one tiny shred of decency."

"If you need to talk to someone, I can connect you with a counselor."

She could use an entire army of counselors. "Thanks, but I'll be okay."

Bruce switched off the microscope light. "Let's take a walk. We can meet Mark in the atrium at lunchtime. I'll ask the receptionist to page us when the shipment arrives."

****

In the cafeteria line, Hailey put the Mendoza family out of her mind. She paid for the food and laid the tray on the table where Mark and Bruce were discussing the latest Braves game.

As Mark gripped his sandwich, Hailey lowered her gaze. For her husband, the smallest daily tasks were monumental feats. Swallowing seemed difficult, too. *Must be from the orotracheal intubation in the burn unit.*

When they finished eating, Bruce's pager beeped. He gulped the rest of his iced tea. "Perfect timing. The crate's at the loading dock."

Hailey leapt to her feet and collected Mark's napkin. "I'll take your plate, hon."

Mark grabbed the tray. "Let me carry it. You go ahead."

She brushed her lips against his. "Sorry I can't stay longer. Between helping Bruce in the lab and your therapies, we rarely see each other."

Mark stroked her cheek, his gaze connecting with hers, sending an intense thrill through her body. "It's okay. I leave soon for an appointment anyway."

"That's right. With Dr. Kendrick." Would Mark discuss his episode the prior evening? Even if his physical scars healed, he'd need to resolve the private wounds on his soul.

She stole another kiss. Her husband was still a great kisser. He might be a stranger in some ways, but his soft intoxicating lips hadn't changed. "I hope the session goes well."

She followed Bruce into the elevator cart, scratching her arm until white lines remained on her skin. The habit had worsened over the summer. At Bruce's wide-eyed stare, she lowered her hands. Would he say something to her? His habit of massaging his chest, faking panic attacks, was just as bothersome.

Thirty minutes later, Hailey and Bruce pushed a cart from the loading dock into the lab.

"Easy now." She steadied one side of the wooden crate onto the counter.

Bruce grabbed a screwdriver from his drawer and removed the top slats. Wearing thick latex gloves, he sifted through the packaging, careful as he withdrew plastic bags filled with wilted pink-and-yellow flowers the size of hibiscus blooms.

Hailey donned gloves and followed Bruce's example. The work would be dangerous, but this was

Mark's only chance. When she opened the bags, a honeyed scent overtook her senses. "These are beautiful blooms. They smell like a port wine." The kind like Mark and she drank on the rare occasions they dined out without the kids.

Bruce stepped beside her. "Is the steam distillation ready?"

Hailey adjusted a full-face shield over her head. "All set."

"Go ahead and begin. I'll check in on you later." Bruce picked up two unopened bags of blooms.

Hailey shook out the contents from another bag onto the counter. "Where are you going?"

"Downstairs. There's a lab in the basement with equipment for cold pressing. I need to collect raw oil to analyze the chemical composition."

She should've realized steam distillation would inactivate the oil. "Just how toxic is the raw oil?"

"Very. It'll eat right through your skin within seconds. Worse than hydrochloric acid."

Hailey pulled on a second pair of gloves. "I knew the flowers were poisonous, but I didn't realize to what extent."

"The flowers and oil are lethal only if they're mishandled." Bruce lowered his bags onto the cart and waved. "Call if you have any questions."

Hailey began mincing the long, thick silk-like petals. She placed the pieces into a glass beaker and started the distillation, waiting as the pressurized steam forced its way through the petals. Nothing could go wrong today. This collection procedure had to work, for Mark's sake.

Soon, the water inside the glass apparatus changed

to an apricot-orange color as the compounds in the petals opened and evaporated into the steam.

She slid the first flask closer. When the steam cooled, she separated the oil from the water and poured the oil into the glass container. The rich fragrance diffused into the air like a strong perfume. She repeated the procedure for another batch of flowers. Would she collect enough oil to help Mark?

By evening, Hailey beamed at the four full flasks of peach-colored oil sitting on the counter. She cleaned the glassware and shelved the procedure manual. Then she walked across the hall.

Inside Bruce's office, the aroma of greasy pizza permeated the air. A large pizza box had a handwritten note attached to the lid.

Don't forget to eat. ~Love you, Mark

He's so thoughtful. The message was scribbled, but gripping a pencil must be difficult. Another daily living activity her husband worked on regaining.

Hailey opened the pizza box. When she bit into a slice of pepperoni pizza, she moaned. *So good.*

Soon, Bruce shuffled in. "There you are."

She waved him over. "Have some pizza. Mark ordered it." She'd never been more grateful.

Bruce dropped into his chair and grabbed a slice. "I saw the flasks on the counter. Nice work."

Her cheeks heated. Partnering with Bruce again was even better than she'd remembered. "Thanks. But four flasks doesn't seem like much."

"I only need a one percent dilution rate to blend into the carrier oil. With what you collected, we should have enough to treat all of Mark's scars."

Suddenly her appetite grew, and she devoured

another slice. Coming to Atlanta had been the wisest decision she'd ever made. That is, besides saying "I do" on her wedding day.

After Bruce polished off the last slice of pizza, he handed Hailey the near-empty tin on his desk. "Do you mind applying salve on Mark tonight? You can finish it. We'll have plenty now. I'll stay back and make enough salve for tomorrow morning. After breakfast, we can prepare the rest."

Her mouth went dry. Did Bruce know what he was asking? "But—"

He shooed her. "Go. Spend time with your hubby. I'll see you in the morning."

Hailey clutched the container. *This is going to be super awkward.* Especially since Mark didn't involve her with his therapies.

Chapter Twenty

Mark set aside his guitar and stepped in front of his apartment window. Did the trees in Georgia stay green all year? Soon the leaves back home would turn into hues of scarlet, orange, and gold. Nothing beat sitting on the deck with Hailey, admiring the vibrant foliage of the sugar maple trees. Or raking fallen leaves on a cool, blustery day and jumping into the pile with the kids. He could still hear their laughter.

School would start in a few weeks. Hailey would need to get Ethan and Anna back into a normal routine.

I don't want to think about Hailey leaving.

Along the dimmed streets, a few couples strolled, holding hands, pausing at street vendors selling wares. Other passersby hurried along, paying little attention to the musicians and mimes busking on the sidewalk.

He once moved with the same haste, heading home after a long workday in the District.

Damn.

Why didn't he slow down? Buy Hailey flowers from the street vendors near his office. Take her to see more Broadway shows in the city. If he ever made it home, he wouldn't waste another minute.

He tunneled a hand through his hair. The fire was ten months ago. Already, he'd lost too much time with his family. But how could he go home if he still wasn't healed?

His reflection blurred in the window, and he wiped his eyes. Life wasn't the same without his kids. His parents. His family and friends. He needed them. If the salve didn't cure his scars, he'd have to find a way to deal with people's stares. Other people suffered worse traumas.

Peering down at the traffic, he rolled his stiff shoulders. So far tonight, no emergency vehicles had raced down the road blaring their sirens.

Turning, Mark glanced at the wall clock. 10:33 PM. Hailey would return anytime. She'd been engrossed in her work when he stopped by the lab earlier with dinner.

He picked up her soft sweater on the sofa and inhaled the lavender scent. Though she was only down the hall, he missed her laugh, her infectious enthusiasm, her calm stability.

After the fire, he'd blocked all that out, a defensive mechanism in case he'd never see her again.

The door lock rattled.

His pulse raced, and he dropped the sweater.

Breathe. The complex has tight security. It must be Hailey.

A moment later, his wife stepped inside the room, carrying the container of salve in her hand. "Honey, I'm glad you're still awake." Her bright smile didn't ease the dark circles smeared under her tired eyes.

Mark hugged her. "How did everything go?"

"Great." Hailey laid the tin on the counter.

"You look exhausted. Can I get you anything?"

"That would be lovely. A glass of water, thank you." She threw herself onto the sofa. "I've forgotten how exhilarating and exhausting this type of work is."

"Exhausting?" Mark chuckled as he set out two

glasses from the kitchen cupboard. "Says the woman who teaches college classes, handles the household single-handedly, and raises two kids?"

He filled the glasses and carried them into the living room. *Don't spill it. Take your time.*

"Thank you." She took the glass and gulped down half of the water. "Sorry I didn't see you earlier. The pizza was a delicious surprise. Thank you."

Heat radiated through him. "You're welcome."

She curled her shapely legs onto the sofa cushions. "Any news about your dad?"

"He's feeling a little better. Mom said he ate a few bites of chicken for dinner." Mark sat next to her and rolled the glass in his hand. "None of the tests indicated a heart attack. If Dad continues to regain his strength, he should go home in a day or two."

"Thank God. See? I told you. Your dad's a fighter. Just like you. How's your mom?"

"Worried, but she's doing okay." He leaned back on the sofa. Their relaxed conversation felt like old times.

Hailey sipped more water. "How was therapy today?"

"Fine." Mark massaged his upper leg. Good idea taking pain meds after dinner. No sense telling her how much he hurt. "How did the distillation go?"

Her eyes brightened. "Better than I'd hoped. Bruce thinks I collected enough oil to treat all your scars."

"Really? Oh my God. Thank you." He leaned over and kissed her cheek.

A luscious shade of hot pink colored her cheeks. "For what?"

"For making my recovery possible. I was afraid to hope before."

When Hailey explained how she collected the oil, Mark scrubbed his beard. "Are you sure you don't want to go back into research?"

"Gosh, no. Teaching part-time and being a full-time mother and wife are rewarding enough." She yawned. "I'm beat." She set the empty glass on the kitchen counter and held up the tin. "Before we go to sleep, Bruce asked me to put this salve on you. He said to use it all since we're making more tomorrow. Do you want to lie down on the bed?"

He tensed. "Isn't Bruce coming over?"

"He's busy tonight."

"Doing what?"

"Making salve for tomorrow morning."

Shit. If he refused Hailey's help, he'd upset her.

As if she read his mind, Hailey stepped to the sofa and held his hand. "I'm glad Bruce asked me. Let me do this." When he remained silent, she headed into the bedroom. "I'll wash up and get things ready."

Mark frowned. What choice did he have? "Okay."

After he rolled down the covers, he sat on the bed and removed his face mask. *This should be interesting.*

She unscrewed the lid on the salve. "Is the light too bright?"

He leaned back onto the pillow and pointed to the nightstand. "The night lamp is better." *Darker is definitely better.*

Hailey switched on the lamp and flipped off the overhead light. "Are you comfortable?"

Comfortable? What kind of ridiculous question is that?

When he nodded, she leaned over, her lips lowering to his. "I love you."

A lump lodged in Mark's throat. Her lips tasted as sweet as candy.

Hailey's fingers brushed back the long bangs over his eyes. "I'm sorry if this is awkward. I'll go slowly."

Slow would make the situation worse. How much of his body was he willing to let her see?

With careful movements, she spread the salve across his cheeks and forehead, working down to his neck, looking at him often when she applied more salve. "Am I hurting you?"

"No." He waited for her horror-struck reaction, but Hailey remained poised as she worked. *Didn't his garden of scars repulse her?*

She applied salve along his collarbone and leaned in for another kiss. "I'm glad we're together again. I missed you."

He glided his fingers across her arm. "I missed you, too." Leaning on his elbow, he began to reattach the burn mask.

"May I help?"

Heat ran up his neck. "I can do it."

"Please. I want to help you."

The compassion in her soft voice caught his breath. Shit. This experience was entirely different from when Bruce helped. Mark lowered his hand. "Okay."

With the mask reattached, Hailey held up the tin. "There's still more salve. I'll put some on your chest." She wriggled his shirt higher over his abdomen.

He averted his gaze as she exposed pressure garments and sheets of silicone gel. *Why couldn't Bruce be here instead?*

She brushed a lock of hair behind his ear. "Are you okay that I'm doing this?"

"Do you really *want* to do this?"

"I wouldn't be anywhere else." Hailey slid her fingers over his lips and pressed her mouth to his in a steamy kiss that left him delirious. "Let's set the record straight. I've loved you for twenty years, Mark Langley. I'll do whatever it takes to have you for fifty more."

He gulped. He'd be a fool to argue with her logic. "Yes, ma'am."

"Now let's continue." She pointed to his pressure garment. "Is the vest uncomfortable?"

"No. Just tight."

As she removed the gel sheets, she gently thumbed the keloid scars protruding through his sparse chest hair. Was it pity or sadness or anger in her face? Hard to tell in the dim light.

Mark fisted his hand. The scars on his chest looked the worst. If he had an unlimited supply of salve, he'd smother those raised suckers until they drowned in the cream.

She scooped more salve onto the spatula and continued smearing the ointment with deliberate movements.

When she dabbed his nipple, Mark drew in his breath.

Hailey gasped. "I'm sorry. Did I hurt you?"

"It's cold. I need a minute." He held her hand and waited for the icy sensation to pass. Her skin was softer and smoother than his.

"Does it feel cold everywhere?"

"No." He pointed to his left thigh. "I can't feel much on this leg. The doctors said the nerves are damaged."

"Do you have any sensations in your other foot?"

"Just shooting pains. Once in a while, I get them in

my arms, too, along with weakness and tingling."

"I'll ask Bruce if we can heat the salve." She spread the ointment over the rest of his midsection. "Uh, now I need to put this …below your abdomen. Can you take off the sweatpants?"

He shook his head. "That area is off-limits."

She blinked. "Are you serious?"

His cheeks seared, and he inched higher on the pillow. "Hell yes, I'm serious."

"But we're married—"

"No buts. This shit is humiliating enough. Besides, that area didn't get burnt like the rest of my body." He pointed to his lower leg and tugged on his pantleg. "You can put salve on my ankles and feet. I'll take care of…my manhood myself when we have more ointment."

She finished applying ointment on his left ankle and screwed the cap back onto the container. "That's all there is until tomorrow morning. Do you usually rest for a while?"

"Just a few minutes while the salve absorbs into the skin. Can you pull a sheet over me?"

"Sure." She tugged the bedsheet over him. "Do you want the air conditioner turned down?"

"That'd be great, thanks."

Mark followed Hailey's movements as she adjusted the thermostat and sat onto a chair next to the bed. He had been a fool for keeping her away.

He patted her hand. "You make one hell of a nurse."

"You're a great patient."

He winked. "I kind of like having my own private nurse."

Her eyes glistened in the dim light. "Another job to put on my resume."

As fatigue set in, he struggled to keep his eyes open. "Did Bruce tell you I suggested we name the salve Euphoria?"

She flinched as if someone slapped her. "Why?"

"Euphoria's easier to say than the long Peruvian name Bruce called it—*Achachilla si*—you don't look happy."

Tears pooled in her eyes. "I detest that name."

"But this might erase the bad connotation. Give the plant another chance…" *Like our relationship.* "If you're against it, I'll tell Bruce we need a different name."

Hailey's lips tightened into a fine line. "It's Bruce's grant project. Do what you want." She curled a finger through his hair, her expression softening. "Can I come to your therapies tomorrow?"

Mark hesitated. He'd made great strides at therapy, but he was still vulnerable. Sprawled across the bed tonight in front of Hailey was embarrassing enough. What would she think when he struggled to hold a pencil? "I'd rather you stay back with Bruce and make the salve. That's more important." The lie tasted bitter. *Coward.*

Her lips quivered.

God, he was a moron. Why had he refused her?

"Maybe another day. If you'd like, I can trim your hair after your rehab tomorrow."

Mark fingered his disheveled hair. Getting rid of his wild mop would be liberating. A fresh start. "That would be great. But please don't give me a haircut like you used to give Ethan."

She chuckled. "Come on, you'd look cute with a bowl cut." Her fingers stroked his beard below the mask. "Maybe I can shave some whiskers, too?"

He feigned offense. "You don't like my beard?"

She reddened. "I...I didn't—"

He traced a finger across her cheek. "You're adorable when you're flustered." It felt good to tease her again.

"I'm not flustered...I...I'm only trying to—"

"I'm kidding." His finger lingered below her lip. "A trim would be great. No barbershop shave though. The razor might snag my scars."

When fifteen minutes had passed, Hailey zipped the pressure garment and helped him into a sitting position. "How was your meeting with Dr. Kendrick today?"

"It went all right. I told her about last night." *And the two episodes earlier this week.* "The coping mechanisms don't always work."

Hailey sat beside him. "What sets off the episodes?"

"Sirens. Loud noises. Fire. The smell of gasoline." *Feeling helpless.*

"There has to be something we can do to prevent the episodes from occurring." She rubbed his hands.

Her endless love humbled him. Why did he push her away?

Swallow your pride and embrace everything she's offering you.

Tears stinging his eyes, he held her soft body in his arms. "I have an idea."

She lifted her chin, meeting his gaze. "What?"

"Let's call the kids."

Her eyes narrowed. "It's late, and you're exhausted."

He sat. "I got my second wind. Come on, I doubt they're asleep. Hearing their voices is the exact medicine I need."

She grabbed the phone from the nightstand. "Okay. But if we wake them, I'll blame the idea on you."

****

Hailey propped a pillow under Mark's leg, reading his expression for signs of discomfort. He should've been asleep hours ago. "Comfy?"

Mark nodded. "I can't believe we video chatted for over an hour."

"I'm glad the kids were awake." She slipped into her cotton pajamas and walked into the bathroom. "I won't have a problem falling asleep tonight."

"Me, either. Sounds like Ethan and Anna are having a blast." Mark's voice carried from the bedroom. "Movie nights. Beach trips. Amusement parks. Sightseeing. Wow! They're doing everything."

With a toothbrush in her hand, Hailey leaned through the doorway. "Your sister's spoiling them."

He slid his hand under the pillow. "What I wouldn't do to be a kid again and have no responsibilities."

Turning to the sink, Hailey rinsed toothpaste from her mouth. "Reality will set in soon enough when school starts and the kids have an earlier bedtime." She switched off the lights and curled up beside Mark under the covers. At least this part of her routine felt like old times.

Mark's fingers traced circles on her arm. "I'm glad you're here."

"Me, too. Although you can't stretch out and hog the entire bed anymore." She waited for a slick comeback, but his body tensed and silence wedged between them.

Maybe she shouldn't have said that. Did he want her in his bed? She had never asked.

Moments later, Mark exhaled. "I've spent too much of my life in bed." He slid closer, wincing.

"Don't hurt yourself. I'll move to you." She nestled closer against him, laying her hand over his. "This feels much better. I've missed how your touch warms me up."

"I've missed you, too." His voice was a husky whisper. "When I was in the hospital, I doubted I'd ever get out of bed."

For a moment, Hailey froze. *He's opening up. Don't push him.* She carefully chose her words. "How much do you remember?"

"Not much. I have lots of blanks…I remember being scared…and the pain…oh, the pain was indescribable." His body trembled, and he began to cry. "God, Hailey, why did this have to happen? In one moment, our whole world spun upside down."

She closed her eyes, holding him. Mark had always been strong. She stroked the pressure garment covering his arm. Dammit, she couldn't even caress his skin. "We're going to get through this."

A few minutes passed, and Mark cleared his throat. "I remember hearing voices. Most days, I didn't have the energy to open my eyes." His body quivered. "I prayed that God would take me."

A tear ran down her cheek when she opened her eyes again. "Do you remember David visiting you at the hospital?"

"Yeah. David helped me hold my shit together. He kicked my ass when I got discouraged. Cried with me. Told his idiotic jokes."

I should've been there. Not David.

Mark sniffled. "He pestered the doctors about prescribing more opioids. He hated to see me in agony." He sniffled again. "Then I became addicted to the pain meds. It was tough going for a while."

She held him tighter. "I'm sorry."

"I wanted more, but the doctors limited what I took. When the pain got out of control, David threatened to find drugs on his own. It was a nightmare." He shuddered. "When I was finally able to sit up, I saw how badly I was burned. God, Hailey. I'm a freakin' monster."

"You are not." She rubbed her hand over his. If only she could erase his pain. "I won't let you be hard on yourself. I love everything about you. You're a loving husband and a wonderful father to our children. The kids and I need you. You're our world."

"You had a right to know I was alive. I'm sorry I deceived you, but I couldn't hurt you anymore." He wiped his eyes. "This isn't what I want for us."

She didn't want this either. Tears blurred her own eyes, but she dared not wipe them. "We'll get through this."

"I'm supposed to protect you. This isn't fair to you...I may never work again." Mark's voice cracked. "How can I provide for you and the kids?"

"That doesn't matter. The kids are older now. I have a job at the college. I'll take care of us."

"What if I never work again?"

"The DTA won't turn away your expertise. Owen's a pain, but he's not stupid."

Mark exhaled. "I don't know if I'll be able to make love to you again."

She closed her eyes and clung to him. After everything he'd gone through, he was concerned about lovemaking. "We'll find other ways for intimacy. We'll take small steps."

"What if I can't live up to your expectations?"

She let out a small gasp. "Honey, my only expectation is to spend my life with you. Trust me. We'll proceed with whatever you're comfortable with."

He rested his head against her. "How'd I get so lucky to find you?"

"I'm the lucky one." The heat of his body transferred across her skin, soothing her nerves. For eight horrible dark months, Hailey believed she'd lost him. Now her heart pounded obstinately, crying with each thump, "Mark's alive!"

"I want to make love to you," he whispered, "but I need time."

She kissed his head, his hair tickling her lips. "When that time comes, we'll figure it out—together."

Once he drifted to sleep, Hailey slid out of the covers and tiptoed into the bathroom. She switched on the fan and sink faucet to provide background noise as she wept. When she applied the salve over Mark's skin, she'd been a master of hiding her emotions. He was so self-conscious he hadn't noticed her anger as she touched his scars.

She clenched her teeth as bile rose higher in her throat. Mark's injury was barbarous! No one could comprehend his suffering. Thank God David had pulled him from the fire.

Grabbing two fistfuls of hair, she bent over and moaned. Damn Mendoza!

Why hadn't she prevented Mark's attack? Catching bad guys was her career. She should've recognized the danger they'd been in.

At least now Mendoza and his goons were dead. *No one will hurt Mark or my kids ever again.*

Hailey rose to her feet, splashed cold water on her

face, and crawled back into bed. Mark's snores comforted her as she stared at the ceiling.

The sweet scent of salve pervaded her husband's natural earthy scent. How did she feel about Bruce and Mark naming the salve Euphoria? Was it possible *Bixa aparra* could hold some benefit even though it killed her son? Mark had said everything deserved a second chance. An opportunity for redemption. Even Manuel Mendoza died saving his daughter.

She tugged the covers and twisted to her side. The night had been a promising reboot of their relationship. Spreading salve over Mark's body had been emotional, but they powered through the awkwardness. Mark wanted space; he needed time to trust again and work through his insecurities.

A serene peace settled on Hailey's soul. With time, she and Mark could rebuild a stronger relationship. She rested her arm over his chest and waited as sleep overtook her.

Chapter Twenty-One

"Do you think Bruce is awake?" Hailey tested the lock on the apartment door and looped the lanyard and card key around her neck.

"I bet fifty dollars he's already working in the lab." Gray speckles shimmered in Mark's blue eyes, making his irises shine even brighter.

"That's not a fair bet." She laughed.

Mark shrugged, his lips quirking into a grin. "For me it is."

As they walked down the hall, Mark slowed his pace, favoring his left leg. Had Bruce noticed the limp, too? With the severity of Mark's wounds, it might be too much to hope the Euphoria salve could penetrate deep into the dermis and regenerate the nerves.

An optimistic bliss spread over her as Mark opened up about his therapies. Though rehab remained off-limits, he accepted her help in the apartment. He smiled more, too. Hopefully, she was the reason. *Take one step at a time.* Once they reestablished the intimacy, they could find a way to deepen it.

When they reached the lab, Hailey knocked on the door, flipped the light switch, and stepped inside. "Bruce?" She scanned the room. "Looks like you owe me money."

"Very funny. I wonder where he is."

"I'm not sure. He stayed late last night to make salve

for this morning." She pointed to the flasks on the counter. "There's the oil I collected from the distillation." She lowered her hands to her hips. "Now, where did he put the new salve that he made?"

Mark stepped to the treatment area in the corner and began unfastening his mask. "Maybe he hid it somewhere."

"Here it is." Hailey stepped onto a stepstool next to the storage shelves and grabbed an amber volumetric flask from the top shelf. "Bruce already labeled the container and put it away." She twirled the flask, studying how the contents inside rolled. "The viscosity is lower than the salve you've been using. Why would he put it way up here?"

She walked to the corner where Mark sat and removed the glass stopper.

"Hailey, stop!" Bruce dashed into the room, dropping a shopping bag onto the floor.

She jumped. "What's going on?"

"The bottle...don't use it." He clutched his chest. "It's raw oil."

She released her grip like she had spilled acid on her hand. The flask and stopper clunked onto the counter. "Oh my God! I thought this was the new salve you made. It's labeled Euphoria."

"Euphoria, as in raw oil. I couldn't make the salve last night." Bruce stoppered the flask. "The shipment of carrier oil was shattered. I woke up early and drove downtown to the apothecary shop and picked up more. I tried calling, but you didn't answer your phone."

Of all days to leave the apartment without her phone. Hailey covered her mouth, guilt pressing on her like a heavy weight. *I almost killed Mark.* "Oh, honey,

I'm sorry." She slumped into an empty chair next to him. "How could I be so irresponsible?"

Mark whispered, "Shh. It's okay. There's no harm done."

Her cheeks heated. "I should've been more careful."

Bruce set the glass container back onto the shelf and slid it against the wall. "It's my fault. The shaman recommended I store the oil at room temperature and away from sunlight. I figured this was the best out-of-the-way place. I should've marked the flask clearer. I'm sorry I didn't communicate better. I'm used to being the only one in the lab, doing things my way. The regulations aren't as strict here as in other places."

Hailey pointed to the fireproof storage container along a wall. "You could keep the oil in there."

"That's where I'm going to store the new salve. I'd rather isolate the raw oil to prevent confusion." Bruce pulled out three large tubs from the shopping bag and set them on the counter. "We've been pushing ourselves too hard, and now I'm becoming careless. I'll prepare a small container of salve now. After breakfast, we'll make the rest and call it an early day. You and Mark can spend the afternoon together when he returns from therapy. Y'all can come to my house for a cookout. Hamburgers and hotdogs. It's the only food I grill that doesn't end up like a tough piece of leather."

Mark rubbed his hands together. "I could go for a juicy hamburger."

Hailey stared at the flask on the storage shelf. Her mix-up could've been disastrous. Perhaps she did need a break. "Okay. What can we bring?"

****

"Everyone, please start gathering around. We'll

begin the tour in a few minutes." The perky guide with shoulder-length purple hair directed the group of thirty-plus tourists to a spot near the Boston Commons Visitor Center.

José pulled the brim of his blue ball cap lower on his head and donned his sunglasses. He'd become a master of imitating unobtrusive manners of tourists.

His knees locked. *Uh-oh. Another police officer.*

Turning, he bought a water bottle from a vendor. Then he grabbed a Freedom Trail map and skirted to the back of the crowd where he had a better view. The *puta* and her friend spoke to the tour guide while Rose and an older girl romped around the women.

The pistol in his holster band pressed against his waist. He'd read a bumper sticker earlier that morning. "Happiness is a warm gun." *Ha! Wasn't that the truth.*

The *puta* had to die, but abducting the girl was foremost. Revenge hadn't happened as easily as he presumed. The two always hung out with the Rogers woman and her daughter. The foursome even lived in a house together.

So far, he'd followed them to an aquarium, science museum, ballpark, and even a college north of the city. José snickered. Didn't these people ever work?

He loitered in the rear while the tour guide introduced herself and led the group up a hill to the Massachusetts State House. With the large crowd, seizing the child might be another bust. When the guide pointed across the street, spouting off dates and stories of the Revolutionary War, José suffered another coughing spell. People moved away, casting accusing glares. He drifted back, sipping on his water bottle until the hacking quieted.

At a cemetery, Rose and her friend gamboled along the worn-looking headstones.

Tsk. The child had so much energy. Might be hard to restrain this free spirit unless he knocked her out.

When the guide answered more questions about the Boston Tea Party, José scoffed. *What a windbag! Shut up and give me an occasion to grab the girl.*

"Sam, look!" Rose ran through the crowd toward a young woman on the street walking a golden-haired dog. "Can we pet your dog?"

The owner nodded at Rose and the older girl. "He's friendly."

After the woman left, the older friend darted ahead, but Rose stumbled on an uneven brick and fell to the ground.

The tour group had huddled several yards ahead, listening to the guide give the background of an old silversmith's house.

José stepped forward, extending his arms. *Now's my chance.*

The older girl spun around. "Rose, are you okay?"

Rose jumped to her feet, her eyes narrowing at José. She brushed dirt from her palms and darted to the front of the group, gripping her mother's hand. Rose turned her head in José's direction.

¡Hijueputa! He raised the tour brochure over his face. Would the girl recognize him with the sunglasses and cap covering his features?

He shook his head. They hadn't been acquainted in Colombia. He needn't worry.

When the tour ended two hours later, José followed the foursome down the block to a marketplace. While the group dined in a restaurant, he sat across the street under a shaded tree and drank a soda. He had come so close to seizing the girl. Would he get another chance today?

Rose seemed well-mannered and attentive. She had the same dark hair as Manuel's. Not blonde, like her hussy mother. The girl also had a fondness for canines. Manuel used to beg Camila for a dog.

Camila. José's gut twisted as he chewed his sandwich. *She must be grief-stricken.* Though their relationship was strained, he shouldn't have left her the way he did.

On the subway leaving the city, he claimed the last seat on the car and scanned the travelers. *¡Ajá! There she is.* The only passenger who didn't talk or click on a cell phone.

Rose looked his direction, her eyebrows knitting before she spun around.

She doesn't know who you are. No reason to be concerned.

Soon the girl was deep in conversation with her friend, and their giddy, high-pitched squeals filled the air.

He tented his fingers under his mouth. Kidnapping in broad daylight was too risky. He'd have to lure the child away in the early morning or later in the day when Rose and the older girl rode their bikes. Maybe use a mutt as a decoy? Make the *puta* think her daughter ran off and got lost.

As the subway slowed near its first stop, José leaned back in his seat. He'd headed multiple high-profile kidnappings; he could handle this simple one. When the time was right, he'd snatch the girl—and give her to Camila as reparation for Manuel's death.

Chapter Twenty-Two

"I don't know about you, but I'm so hungry I could eat an elephant." Mark sat in the back seat of the taxi and brushed his thumb on Hailey's leg. His poor attempt at a joke didn't even prompt a small scoff from his wife. What was going on in that mind of hers? She'd been distant all day.

At the sound of Hailey's cell chiming, he moved his hand. "Better check that. Francine might be texting about Dad's discharge."

Hailey fished the phone from her purse and scrolled down the screen. "It's only Erik."

"News on Luis's sister?"

She read the text. "The search is going slowly. He needs more manpower to track down the India mafia group who bought Selena." She slipped the phone back in her purse. "I wish Stefan would let me help."

He squeezed her hand. "Try not to think about it. Follow Bruce's advice, and relax this evening."

She avoided his gaze. "I suppose you're right. What's important is Bruce and I made plenty of salve today while you were at therapy."

"Now you're talking." He nudged her side. "If it makes you feel any better, I like my haircut." Mark threaded his fingers through his hair where she'd sheared his overgrown mop and trimmed the sides. "Thank you."

Her cheeks reddened. "You're welcome."

"You never said how you found hair clippers so quickly."

Her lips curved, hinting a small smile. "I have my sources."

"However you managed it, I appreciate your help. You even made my two bald spots look halfway decent. I feel like my old self again."

"I'm glad."

He rubbed his close-trimmed beard below his mask and winked. "I kinda miss my scraggly whiskers though."

She rolled her eyes. "I don't."

The cab driver drove past a sign advertising 55+ Senior Living and turned into a gated townhouse community with exteriors built from stone veneer.

Hailey pointed to the second townhome in a four-house unit. "This is Bruce's address." She paid the fare and walked with Mark up the concrete driveway onto the porch.

"Nice place." Mark whistled as he pressed the doorbell.

A moment later, Bruce opened the door. "Glad you found the place. Come in."

Hailey handed him a bottle of sparkling cider. "Mark suggested wine, but he shouldn't mix alcohol with pain meds."

"Cider's perfect. Thank you." Bruce grabbed the bottle. "Nice haircut, Mark."

"Thanks. Trying to look my best for dinner tonight."

Bruce grinned. "Nothing too fancy here, I'm afraid. I cheated and bought potato salad and baked beans at the grocery store. Make yourselves comfortable while I start the grill."

In the living room, a ceiling fan fluttered air above Mark's head. As he walked past the gas fireplace in the corner, his pulse raced a moment before it settled into a normal rhythm. Thank God the fireplace unit wasn't lit. He stepped away, bumping his shin into a coffee table.

Hailey lowered her purse beside a leather sofa and studied the framed pictures on the fireplace mantel. Eyes glistening, she pointed to a black-and-white picture of three young men. "Mark, look."

He leaned in close. "Is that Bruce?"

"Yes, and my papa and Uncle Henry. I have this picture in our photo album."

She picked up another frame. "Here's one of Bruce with Papa, Uncle Henry, and my grandparents."

Mark lifted a smaller photograph of five young boys standing next to a haggard-looking man. All the boys had Bruce's moon-shaped eyes, thick eyebrows, and broad nose. Bruce looked the youngest, around four years old.

"The grill's heating up." Bruce came through the sliding glass door in the kitchen. "Ah! I see you found my pictures."

Mark set the photo back onto the mantel. "Is this your family?"

Bruce came into the living room. "Sure is. My pa and older brothers. They've all passed away."

"What a handsome family." Hailey gestured to the picture in her hand. "Mark, we have a copy of this one at home, too."

Bruce nodded. "That was taken fifty years ago. Your grandparents had a summer picnic in their backyard to celebrate Henry's birthday."

Mark beamed as Hailey talked to Bruce, bridging pieces of her past.

"I hardly remember my grandparents. What were they like?"

"Mr. and Mrs. Robinson never met a stranger. They always welcomed me into their home during my breaks." Bruce took the snapshot from Hailey and stared at it. "Henry was like a brother."

Hailey turned to Mark. "Uncle Henry and Bruce went to med school together."

Mark feigned surprise. "Is that right?"

The doctor's hands began to shake, and he set the picture on the mantel. "Why don't we go outside on the deck and talk while I put on the hamburgers?" He opened the fridge and pulled out the potato salad bowl, sliced onions and tomatoes, hamburger patties, and hot dogs. "Hailey, do you mind grabbing the cider?"

Mark followed them to the deck, carrying a plate of sliced onions and a pack of hot dogs. His mouth watered at the baked beans and brownies already on the table. He passed Bruce the food and took a seat next to Hailey. "How long have you lived here, Bruce? The place looks relatively new."

"Four years." Bruce raised the grill lid and lowered the ground beef patties onto the grates. "It's a quiet community..."

Woosh! Flames flared up through the grates as the fat hit the coals.

Mark jumped. He began to tremble violently. In an instant, he was transported back to the warehouse the night of the fire.

Run!

His legs hardened to cement.

Flashbacks of the thugs beating him as a punching bag whirled like a movie reel through his mind. Fists smashed against his jaw. Puke spewed out his mouth, the putrid stench assaulting his nostrils.

A high-pitched scream erupted from deep inside him.

"Mark? What's wrong?" Hailey's voice seemed to come from a tunnel. "Oh my God! Mark?"

Air. Someone was stealing his oxygen. Moisture coated his face beneath his mask. He yanked at his shirt. *I can't breathe!*

Dizziness pranked his balance as smoke tormented his throat. Adrenaline pumped through his body on high alert. Someone's hands pulled off his T-shirt. He leapt to his feet, jerking wildly. "I'm going to die!"

"Mark, talk to me."

He slid to the floor, pushing away the flames before they suffocated him. "Stop it!" Wrapping his hands around his ankles, he rocked on the deck planks and wept.

****

"How do we stop this?" Tentatively, Hailey rubbed Mark's shoulder. "Calm down, honey."

Bruce raced and shut off the gas on the grill. "Don't say that to him."

She raised her hands. "What should I say?"

"Tell him you're here for him. Help him calm down."

Hailey stooped down. "Mark! Listen to me! Breathe! Nice and slow. Inhale and exhale. Slow breaths."

Mark lifted his head.

"That's right, breathe with me. Inhale, one, two, three. Exhale one, two, three." She pushed out the air. She could help him through this.

Finally, Mark dragged in deep breaths.

"That's it. Seven, eight, nine, ten. Good." She exhaled as he followed her lead. "Let's do it again."

Slowly, his gaze fixated on her.

"Talk to me, Bruce. What can I do?" Her voice trembled.

Bruce patted her back. "You're doing great."

Mark stretched his neck and held his hands against the sides of his head.

She rubbed his arm. "Would you like to walk around the neighborhood? Get some fresh air? We passed a clubhouse when we drove in."

Slowly his eyes narrowed, as if he were coming out of a trance.

"We'll go as far as you want." She helped him tug the T-shirt over his head.

Bruce leaned over to Hailey and whispered, "There's a scaled-down croquet court down at the clubhouse. I'll finish grilling while you're gone. The flames triggered the episode. I should've known better."

"Take another deep breath, Mark." Hailey held his hand and led him down the deck steps, across the backyard to a walking path.

When they advanced a distance, she slowed. "Do you feel like talking?"

He closed his eyes. "I just need to hear your voice. Can you rattle on about anything?"

"In other words, act normal?"

Mark opened his eyes and nodded.

Hailey exhaled again. The last twenty minutes seemed like five hours had passed. "A croquet court is on the right. Let's see if we can find some mallets and balls."

An hour later, they were back on Bruce's deck. Hailey spooned the last serving of potato salad onto her plate while Mark devoured a second hamburger.

She leaned back in her chair, half listening as Bruce and Mark talked about the upcoming Atlanta Falcons pro-football season. She'd have to be extra vigilant about fire and any sparks around him. No fireworks in July. No birthday candles on the kids' cakes. So many catalysts could trigger another episode.

Mark's PTSD was worse than she'd imagined. During the past few nights, he jumped when an ambulance or fire truck raced down the street. The sirens must've been reminders of the night he almost died. After everything he'd gone through, who could blame him for being spooked? Tomorrow she'd surf the Internet for treatments.

She should've realized life wouldn't just go back to normal. Mark would have to battle many dark days, just like she had done. Recovery would proceed according to his timetable.

A shiver ran through her as the morning's near-disastrous incident replayed in her mind. The raw oil mishap was a wake-up call. Mark trusted her, and she let him down. The only way to keep him safe and rebuild his trust would be to work harder.

Chapter Twenty-Three

Even asleep, his wife looked like a charming enchantress. Ignoring his leg pain, Mark leaned on his side and planted tender kisses along her neck. His thighs grew rigid as he slid his fingers lightly over her curvy ass. Would he have the stamina to pleasure Hailey the way she deserved? For now, sweet caresses and tender touches would have to suffice.

He clenched his jaw. Hailey cried out Mendoza's name again during the night. Even dead, the prick infiltrated her dreams.

Mark brushed a lock of hair from her face. Lately, finding time together hadn't been easy. Hailey spent each evening helping Bruce with his research. Something must've happened to turn her into a workaholic.

The panic attack at Bruce's house the other day must've freaked her out. David had warned him that Hailey might not be able to handle his PTSD.

Get a grip on your life.

Hailey stretched her arms over her head and opened her eyes. "Morning."

He nibbled on her ears. What did he do to deserve such a sweet angel? "Morning, sleepyhead."

His cell chirped on the nightstand.

Mark grabbed the phone and leaned back onto his pillow. "Ethan and Anna are texting."

"Do you want to text them back?"

He glanced at his hands. His clumsy fingers would take an hour to fumble on the keypad. "Nah. I'll do it later."

"The kids are going to the beach later." Hailey extended her palm. "Let me show you something that Anna showed me. It's called voice texting. It might make sending messages easier."

After demonstrating how to use voice text, she handed him the phone. "Go ahead, try it."

Suddenly in a playful mood, he opened Hailey's name and tapped the tiny microphone button. "My wife is smart *and* sexy." He grinned. "Thanks. That was easy."

Another text chirped.

Mark opened the message. "It's Mom. Dad's getting discharged today." He choked on the words as an invisible weight lifted off his shoulders. "Thank God. I was afraid I'd never see him again."

"Have faith. You'll be home before you know it."

"I hope you're right." Mark drank in her sultry eyes. Did she realize her effect on him? She was probably too preoccupied with research to notice. He kissed the dimple on her chin. "I'll catch the morning news while you shower."

****

Why didn't I pack more clothes? Hailey rummaged through the garments in the drawer. Mark liked seeing her in colorful prints. The pair of dark jeans and pink floral blouse would coordinate well. She pulled a brush through her towel-dried hair and swiped mauve-colored lipstick over her lips. No one would ever know she'd been awake half the night. She yielded to the urge and scratched her arm. Terrible time for her nerves to flare up.

Hailey sat on the bed, spreading lotion on her arms as she processed the events of the past few days. Though Mark hinted he wasn't ready to make love yet, he looked at her with the same besotted look as when they had dated. She'd been careful not to push him. Nothing beyond an innocent smooch. When that time came, they'd have to discuss special limitations.

She gave in to another scratch. *Why am I worried? We're married. Sex shouldn't be difficult to discuss.*

They hadn't slept together in almost a year. In some ways, Mark was a stranger. He'd be better off if they remained apart. She was as dangerous to be around as dynamite. Her skills as an agent were waning, and even Stefan refused to have her back at the SCA. *He thinks I'm reckless.*

Was she?

The raw oil incident still made her quake. How could she be so irresponsible? Hailey closed her eyes, reliving the scene. Medication errors were one of the top mistakes in patient care. *I could've killed my own husband.*

Her cell rang from the nightstand.

Hailey swiped her finger across the screen. "Colleen? This is a surprise. How are you?"

"Not so good."

"What's wrong?"

"Oh, Hailey. Motherhood is so difficult. I must be the worst mom in the world."

"Why don't you start from the beginning?"

Colleen exhaled. "Rose had an awful nightmare last night. She dreamt Manuel came to take her."

Hailey winced. "Does she understand he's dead?"

"Yes, but she thinks he came back from the dead. Joyce thought you might have some advice."

Hailey hesitated. Both José and Manuel haunted her dreams. She should be the last one to offer guidance. "After the trauma Rose experienced, nightmares wouldn't be unusual. Has she seen a counselor?"

"I made an appointment with one for later this morning."

"Good. Let me know how it goes." Whether or not Hailey intended it, she was developing a close bond with Colleen. Motherhood required sisterhood. "Hang in there. It takes time to figure out parenting. None of us are pros."

Hailey ended the call and walked into the kitchen.

Mark had set out a banana, cold cereal, and a cinnamon-raisin bagel from the pantry. He shrugged, giving her a wry grin. "This is as gourmet as I get. Sorry."

"This is perfect." Hailey poured two glasses of orange juice and settled into her seat across from him. She'd eat cereal every day if it meant having Mark back in her life.

He chewed a spoonful of oat cereal. "Would you like to walk in the park when I come back from therapy this afternoon?"

"I told Bruce I'd review cell cultures, but I have this morning available. Can I go with you to the clinic instead? Learn some techniques so I can help you at home?" Hailey scratched her arm. Would he allow her be part of his rehab?

"Eh, not today. But I'll be back by two thirty if you finish early."

Lips quivering, she sipped the juice. *Another rejection.* How was she supposed to learn how to assist Mark at home if he didn't involve her in his care? "I'll see if I can get away."

Mark moped. "I never see you anymore."

His words slapped her. "I'm trying to help you."

His spoon dropped with a clank. "I have doctors and therapists for that. I miss hanging out with you."

Hailey bit into the bagel, blinking against the sting of tears. "I need to give three hundred percent toward your recovery." *Make up for almost killing you.* "Bruce and I have to figure out why the salve isn't regenerating your skin the same way it did for the villagers in Peru."

Mark shoved his bowl. "Fuck the research. You're becoming another Bruce Hanover." He closed his eyes, then he opened them and placed his left hand over hers. "I'm sorry. I'm just worried about you working so much."

She glanced down at Mark's hand. The glove's coarse fabric lacked warmth. They were so far apart physically and emotionally. Did she even know him anymore?

Hailey moved her hand and picked at a raisin in her bagel. "I'm fine."

"You look exhausted. The circles under your eyes keep getting darker. You're not sleeping well."

The bagel in her mouth morphed into sawdust. When did the issue shift to her? "What are you talking about?"

"You've been crying out Mendoza's name in your sleep." Mark's eye twitched. "Did that bastard hurt you?"

"No." *But you do when you refuse to include me in*

your life. Hailey clawed her arm hard, white marks trailing her skin. "No one touched me." At least Mendoza's bloody knife didn't stab her like Mark's sharp rejection. She dropped the bagel on her napkin. "I have to go."

"Already?"

"I need to work if I'm going to find a solution to heal you."

"I don't want your help if you run yourself into the ground. You're overworked—" He stared at her arm.

Hailey lowered her head and cringed as blood oozed from her scratches. *God, how embarrassing.* She grabbed another napkin and held it against the arm. "I'll see you later."

"Hailey—"

"Bye."

She raced out of the apartment and ran down the hall, then entered the women's restroom. Slumping to the floor, she bowed her head between her knees and wept. She was a total failure. Why had she come to Atlanta? She hadn't helped Mark at all.

****

After therapy, Mark took the shuttle back to PMI. Grimacing, he shuffled onto the elevator and pressed the button to the second floor. When the doors closed, he leaned over and massaged his left leg.

Therapy was more strenuous than usual, but the iron-fisted nurse refused to give him more medicine when he asked. *Background pain, my ass!* Why did she care if he took more pills? His pain level was past ten on the scale every day. Why the hell bother going to therapy if he returned miserable?

Hailey's heated words that morning only

exacerbated his pain. What was wrong with her? One day she acted lovey-dovey, and the next she was cold and standoffish.

Women!

He'd never understand them.

Back in his apartment, he grabbed a water bottle from the fridge. Cold beer would've tasted better. It had been weeks since Ronnie slipped a six-pack into the building.

Mark eased onto the sofa and drank the water. Then he picked up the guitar propped against the armrest and plucked out the melody to a song he'd written in high school. Not too shabby, but he'd need to rewrite some verses. When his fingers grew sore, he lowered the instrument onto the floor and checked his voicemail.

Hey, Mark. It's Owen. I'm not sure what your therapy schedule is. Call me when you get a minute. We need to talk about your position at the DTA. Beep.

As Mark replayed the message, his blood pressure soared. He'd been afraid of something like this. Owen was going to force him out. *Doesn't he have the decency to allow me to resign on my own?*

He drained the water bottle and chucked it across the room. *It's bad enough Hailey wants nothing to do with me. Now my supervisor wants to fire me. Fifteen demanding years I've given to the agency!*

He powered on the TV, letting the noise of the comedy buffer his loneliness. He closed his eyes. The fire had robbed him of everything. His marriage, his job, his life. *Damn you, Mendoza!*

At five o'clock, Hailey walked into the apartment carrying the salve tin. "How was your day?"

He set the TV remote on the end table. "Fine."

They'd have to talk about their argument eventually, and she'd find out soon enough he'd lost his job.

Her gaze avoided his. "Can I put the salve on now, or would you rather wait?"

"Now's fine." Mark walked into the bedroom and lay on the bed.

Hailey switched on the lamp and applied the salve over Mark's face and trunk in spiritless mechanical movements. She removed the pressure garments on his arm without speaking.

Anger boiled inside Mark like a clogged radiator. Where was the intimacy they had started rebuilding?

Kiss her. Make her want you.

As Hailey reattached the garment on his left arm, Mark pulled her closer, pressing his lips to hers in a burning rush of desire.

Hailey pulled back. "Mark. This isn't the time."

"Then when *is* the time?"

"I don't know." She shook her head. "Not now."

"You've been distant all week. Will you please tell me what's wrong? What did I do?"

She stammered. "Nothing."

"Why are you avoiding me?"

"I'm not." The tin dropped onto the floor.

"Everything was going well between us. Something changed. Was it my panic attack at Bruce's?"

"Of course not." She leaned over and picked up the tin.

"Then what happened?"

"I'm tired, that's all."

"Then please stop working so hard."

Hailey rubbed her temples, her hands shaking. "I can't."

He sat upright, squeezing his fists tighter. "Why won't you talk to me? Argh! You infuriate me!"

She collapsed onto the bed and began to cry.

Now look what you did. Shouting only pushed her further away. Mark smoothed her hair. "Honey, tell me what's wrong. Please. Why are you upset?"

Hailey plucked a tissue from the nightstand. "Everything…I do…is wrong."

He stared at her. "What do you mean 'wrong'?"

"My life is in shambles. Stefan thinks I'm a terrible agent. I feel like a negligent mother. I haven't seen Anna and Ethan in weeks." She sank her head into her palms and cried louder. "And I almost killed you."

"Killed? What are you talking about?"

"The other day—with the raw oil."

So that's the problem. He cradled her in his arms, and the sweet fragrance of her bodywash melted his anger. "That was nothing."

She wiped her nose. "How can you say that? I came within inches of killing you."

"But nothing happened."

"It could've." Hailey scratched her hands. "It was a careless mistake. I'm worried I'm going to lose you again." She closed her eyes, shuddering. "Even in my dreams, José Mendoza tries to kill you."

Her empathy humbled him. She was fighting her own battles, too. Mark traced his thumb across her cheek. "Hailey, look at me." When she opened her eyes, a dark desperation shrouded her face. He kissed her nose. "I promise I'm not going anywhere."

"You don't know that for sure. Everyone I love dies. I'm scared to death something bad is going to happen to you."

"Don't I get a say in this? Nothing is going to happen." He kissed her forehead. "I love you."

"If you loved me, you'd take me with you to rehab."

His muscles tensed. "This again?"

"Yes. It hurts when you don't include me in your life. I'm your wife."

He tucked a strand of hair behind her ear. "I don't want to be dependent on you. It's embarrassing."

"But I can help you with your therapies."

"I don't want another therapist. I want my wife."

"I understand, but family support is important. I've read tons of articles on the Internet about it." Tears trailed down her cheeks. "I'm busting my ass, working long hours, and you keep pushing me away. How do you think that makes me feel?"

"I'm sorry. I thought you worked long hours because I repulsed you."

She sobbed harder. "Repulsed? I've been enamored with you since the day we met."

"Even now?" His throat clogged.

Hailey grabbed another tissue. "Yes, even now. Up until two months ago, I thought I'd lost you forever. I don't care about your scars. I'm helping with this skin regeneration project because you won't come home until you accept who you are. I remember feeling the same way. Your appearance doesn't change who you are on the inside."

Mark crushed her against his chest. Too many emotions raced through his mind. How did he warrant such unconditional love? He smoothed her hair as she cried. "Shh. I'm sorry. I should've realized… Come to therapy with me tomorrow morning. Please. I want you with me."

Chapter Twenty-Four

"You're fidgeting again." Mark's husky voice penetrated the humming of the shuttle bus.

Hailey's cheeks heated as she slid her hands under her legs. "I'm sorry."

Her anxiety level had climbed since Mark agreed she could come to his therapy. She wasn't a therapist. What if she couldn't help him with his rehab?

Mark squeezed her hand. "I love how your eyes sparkle when you're nervous."

Guilt tightened around her like a corset. He was encouraging her when she should've been supporting him.

When the shuttle pulled up to the center's outpatient drop-off, Hailey disembarked and followed Mark to the entrance.

Inside the lobby, the strong scent of antiseptic assaulted her nose. The place resembled a regular hospital. Spotless. Cold. Impersonal. A red-haired nurse sat at the front desk, clicking on a computer keyboard. Staff dressed in green scrubs spoke in low voices as they walked past.

A petite woman wearing scrubs and white sneakers approached them. "Hi, Mark."

She looked about thirty. Her blonde hair was tied into a ponytail, and she wore a name tag on her uniform.

Mark waved. "Brooklyn, this is my wife, Hailey. I

asked her to come and watch how you torture me."

Brooklyn's vivid green eyes sparkled as she extended Hailey her hand. "It's nice to meet you. I'm one of Mark's occupational therapists. He mentioned you're staying in town. I hope he's not telling tall tales about his therapy."

Hailey shook the woman's hand. How exactly had Mark described their living situation? "He hasn't said anything negative. Feel free to show me everything I need to learn."

Brooklyn led them down the hall and opened a door into a large room. "Mark, why don't we start your therapy in here so we can show your wife how to help you at home?"

Hailey surveyed the different adaptive equipment around the room. The place had more sophisticated tools than the colored bands and therapeutic ball in their apartment. "How many different therapies does Mark need?"

"He has OT and physical therapy every day. He'll have aquatic therapy later today, too. That rehab is three times a week." Brooklyn stood beside Mark as he eased onto a chair, and she removed the compression sleeve on his left arm. "We start every session with stretching. This preps Mark for his interventions. It's important he does this throughout the day because stretching keeps the skin from tightening and decreases scarring. Did you take your pain meds this morning, Mark?"

He nodded. "The pain wasn't too bad this morning."

"That's wonderful. Let me know if you feel any pain during today's session." Brooklyn visually examined and palpated the scars on his arm. "The other day, I thought I was imagining it, but your scars are flattening."

She looked closer. "And the coloring is fading… Your injury happened ten months ago?"

"Yes, around then." Mark didn't offer any further explanations.

"Amazing." Brooklyn applied lotion to Mark's skin and elevated his hand, working in the cream. "Since Mark's wounds are healed, we can use lotion to keep his skin soft. I'll show you how to temporarily blanch the skin until it becomes pale. You need to be careful not to overstretch his skin though, because we don't want to tear his tissue and cause joint stiffness."

After the OT modeled different massage techniques, Hailey replicated the steps and rubbed Mark's upper arm. "Does this hurt?"

He shook his head. "Just tingles."

During the exam, Brooklyn massaged Mark's left leg. "How's the itching today?"

Mark lifted his eyebrows. "On overdrive."

She pointed at a tube of cream. "Are you using your lotion at home?"

"You bet."

"Any other changes?"

"I've had some shooting pains—more than normal."

Brooklyn jotted his symptoms on her notes. "I'll make sure the doctor knows."

A mixture of exasperation and disappointment flooded through Hailey. Mark hadn't mentioned his pain to her. He probably hid a lot about his recovery. "Does this mean Mark's nerves are healing?"

Brooklyn gave a hand shrug. "It could signify healing, but it might indicate other processes are occurring. The doctor will examine Mark later today." She pointed to a thicker scar on Mark's forearm and applied lotion. "We use deep pressure massage on these scars to reduce swelling and minimize contractures."

Hailey nodded. "I've seen Mark do this in the morning and evenings when he watches TV."

Brooklyn high-fived Mark's hand. "Way to go." She capped the lotion. "One of Mark's goals is to incorporate these interventions into his daily routine."

Next Brooklyn escorted them into a room that had a large TV screen mounted on the wall. She powered on the console. "I've been practicing my bowling, Mark. I have a strong feeling that I can beat you today."

Mark picked up a controller. "We'll see."

Hailey slid into a chair near the wall. *This should be fun.*

When the video loaded, Mark bent and rolled a virtual ball near the ground.

Hailey couldn't stop smiling as her husband put down ten pins with one roll. What a clever way to improve balance and coordination! "Mark, you never told me you played video games during therapy."

Brooklyn handed Hailey a controller. "Interactive video games are a useful intervention during the rehabilitative phase. Patients enjoy playing a sport that interests them, and they often forget about their pain. Not to mention it's a great way to increase their range of motion."

Mark didn't gloat too much after he beat Hailey by twenty points. Afterward, Brooklyn led them to a room where Mark manipulated fabrics, folding clothes and touching different textures.

At noon, the therapist escorted Hailey to a reception area. "You can wait here while Mark goes to aquatic therapy. He's showing great success with these exercises. Strengthening muscles. Increasing range of motion. Not to mention the water relaxes him."

Hailey waved as Mark walked down the hallway. She collapsed onto a chair and buried her face in her shaky palms. Her husband had gone through so much.

Recollections of Mark dutifully performing his exercises every morning and evening in the apartment spun around her head. What if she wasn't able to help him? What if she did something wrong and hindered his progress?

She stared at the different therapy rooms. So much went into his recovery. Bringing Mark home to their family would go beyond a joyful reunion. Every activity required modifications. The family's entire routine would change.

A tall woman carrying a small electronic tablet strode into the room. "Mrs. Langley?"

"Yes?" Hailey's voice choked.

"It's nice to meet you. I'm the nurse manager. Brooklyn told me you were here." She sat beside Hailey. "I'm glad you could come. Family support is very important. Though Mark continues to make progress here, he'll need your assistance when he returns home."

"I wish it were that simple." Tears pricked Hailey's eyes. "I feel like I'm joining a party right before the last song, trying to catch up on his therapies. Mark tries to handle everything on his own. He doesn't tell me much."

The woman frowned. "That happens with some patients. Men especially tend to keep their fears and other emotions bottled up. Our goal is to get Mark doing many of the activities he used to do."

"Brooklyn used the term 'regain his quality of life.' "

"Your husband needs to regain strength and flexibility in his hands and legs to do everyday tasks. He's fortunate his right side isn't as affected as the left. When Mark first arrived here, I contacted his previous doctor and therapists so we could continue the intervention plan. Counseling for his emotional needs. Physical therapy for his walking and balance." The nurse manager pointed to a table with a marker and portable white board. "Occupational therapy for Mark's daily activities—like writing his name."

Hailey started a mental checklist. When she returned to Virginia, she'd visit a home improvement store and check out handles to replace the doorknobs and faucets. She'd also remove the rugs to avert tripping hazards. "Brooklyn showed me how to help Mark with the stretching exercises. She mentioned his skin graft and other thicker scars can be tight."

"Graft tissues can restrict ROM—range of motion. That's why he needs to work on it throughout the day."

"For how long?"

Compassion filled the nurse manager's dark brown eyes. "Recovery can last years. Even a lifetime. The burn team will keep tabs on his progress. Mark does well at following his exercise program. The long-term goal will be to get him ready to return to work. Meanwhile, we try to do different recreational activities he liked before his accident. Mark told us that he's a government agent?"

"He chased down drug traffickers." It might take years before he'd have the stamina to chase perpetrators in the field. "Do you think he'll ever be able to work again?"

"We'll have to wait and see how he progresses, but the entire staff is on board with his treatment plan.

Brooklyn is working on Mark's trigger movements using plucking exercises."

So that's why he's playing the guitar. "I hope the therapists can help. Mark will be devastated if he can't work again."

The nurse manager stood. "Let's focus on the short-term goals and see how he improves with his range of motion and hand strength. It's important we stay optimistic."

"I will." Pride swelled inside Hailey. Mark was not only strong but also determined. He'd push through with the therapies until he could regain his skills. "My kids and I can't wait for him to come home."

"We'll do everything possible to ease his apprehension about returning to society. We're constantly adjusting his treatment plan." The nurse gave an empathetic smile that put Hailey at ease. "Your input is important, too. We have counselors and therapists to assist him if he can't return to his former career, but in the meantime, we focus on what he's able to do. You won't go through this alone. We'll work together as a team to make Mark's therapy a success."

Hailey's shoulders relaxed. Mark needed her. *I won't let him down.*

****

On the shuttle back to the apartment, Mark fought sleep. Bringing Hailey along had been a bad idea. She hadn't said more than three words since they got on the bus. She had enough on her mind without the therapists weighing her down with tons of information.

He stepped into the elevator, relaxing a little as he caught a whiff of Hailey's lilac-scented body spray. "Thank you for coming today."

A glint of gold glistened in her eyes. "Thank you for inviting me."

Mark yawned. "When we get to the apartment, I need to rest for a while. Want to lie down with me?" The invitation came out as a teaser, but he wasn't teasing. More like hopeful. A sharp spasm of need raced through him.

"Sounds like fun. Give me fifteen minutes to check on Bruce. When I talked to him this morning, he was researching Peruvian plants that fight inflammation."

"Okay, but wake me if I'm asleep when you return." He leaned closer and kissed her, trying to calm his rapidly growing erection. Maybe it was for the best she didn't stay.

When the car opened, Hailey stepped out and checked she had her room card. "Thanks for letting me come today. See you soon." She waved and headed down the hall.

Whistling softly, he walked back to the apartment and unlocked the door. What a stark contrast to Hailey's mood the previous night. His wife hadn't been irritated with him; she'd been angry at herself.

He should've read the signs. Hailey's bad dreams. The obsessively long hours. Her feverish desire to develop a cure for his recovery. She was trying so hard to be a superwoman that Mark hadn't realized she was drowning.

Just like him.

His shoulders slumped. His career was going to deflate soon. Like a big tire blowout.

He paced the living room and listened to his supervisor's voicemail once more. *Don't put off Owen's phone call any longer.*

Mark kicked off his shoes.

Might as well get it over with. It didn't take a rocket scientist to realize he wasn't coming back to the Drug Trafficking Agency. Owen needed an agent who could handle the caseload.

Don't blame Owen for your problems.

Slumping onto the couch, Mark pulled out his cell phone from his sweatpants and used voice command. "Call Owen Kaln."

A gruff voice answered on the third ring.

"Owen, it's Mark Langley."

Owen's voice boomed through the phone. "Mark, how are you?"

How do you think I'm doing? You're about to fire me. "I'm doing better. Thanks."

"Is the new rehab working out?"

"Yes, sir. Going to therapy every day."

"Good to hear."

"How has the agency been getting along without me?" Mark gritted his teeth. *Stop the damn small talk.*

"No one's indispensable. Hell, the agency could function without me."

He was definitely getting the boot. "I suppose you're right."

"I'm always right. Enough chitchat. I want to discuss your future at the DTA."

"I have therapy every day. I'm not sure I can—"

"I don't expect you to go out with your partner and investigate cases tomorrow. Would you be interested in doing research while you're recuperating?"

Mark jumped up from the sofa. "As in a desk job? You want me to keep working?"

"Why not? I said no one's indispensable, but I'm not

going to part with one of my top agents. You have too much expertise to give up and quit. Your CIA friend David Smith called and suggested you might be well enough to collaborate in an interagency human trafficking case with the SCA and Homeland Security. Seems like your wife opened a can of worms when she slipped down to Colombia."

Mark smirked. Hailey's renegade move was gutsy.

Owen cleared his throat. "The director authorized the activity on our end. I'm sure you'll find drug trafficking networks to justify our agency's involvement. If you feel up to working as a liaison, I'll issue you a computer and ship it tonight so you can link into the VPN."

Mark blinked. "Sir, I don't know what to say—"

"Dammit! Say 'yes.' I'll email the SCA contact info. The agent is from the San Francisco field office—Erik Bruno."

Must be related to Hailey's director. "Yes, sir. Thank you."

"Fit in the research between your therapy, but don't dawdle because you're not in the office. I have a shitload of cases I need you to investigate after this one."

Mark ended the call and pumped his fists in the air. *Yes!*

His muscles ached, but his excitement shoved the pain into a forgotten shoebox on a back shelf. He could use the government resources to track down Luis's sister. Pay Luis back for helping Hailey escape and collecting the Euphoria flowers.

His life had a purpose.

Chapter Twenty-Five

Another day of therapy over. Mark slowed his steps down the corridor. No flashbacks in five days. The itching and tingling sensations seemed more prevalent, but the shape, color, and texture of his scars had improved. With the pain lessening, recovery was headed in the right direction. *Stay cautious.*

Once inside the apartment, he powered on the laptop Owen had shipped.

While the computer booted, Mark pulled out a sandwich stowed in the fridge. He'd research Selena's whereabouts and munch on lunch at the same time. Just like a normal day in the office.

Using the adaptive keyboard his occupational therapist had recommended, he logged into the Department of Homeland Security and SCA's databases and searched for Selena Garvez. As the files loaded, he checked his emails and pulled his phone from his pocket. "Call Erik Bruno."

The built-in voice control processed the request, and the line connected.

"Agent Bruno."

"Erik, it's Mark Langley. Did you read the last report I sent on the organized criminal gangs?"

"I did. Can you profile the members of each group? Immigration and Customs at Homeland Security should have more information."

"Already on it. I'm sorting through the database now, collecting files and other intel the drones picked up. There are several migrants in the mafia sectors I'm trying to identify."

"Great." Erik sounded pleased. "This collaboration is working out."

"I'm compiling a list of mafia wives, too. It's possible the mafia leader forced Selena into marriage, or he might've sold her to a fellow gang member."

"Good idea. While you're at it, investigate domestic servitude in that area."

At four thirty PM, Mark powered down the computer and headed to the door. Time for a break. Hailey's bright smile would be the perfect diversion. So would hugging her, pressing against her curvy breasts, and taking in her feminine scent.

In the hallway, Mark waved to Ronnie unloading a trashcan, and he turned to enter Bruce's lab.

Hailey sat at a counter, typing on the computer keyboard, files lying haphazardly across her workspace.

Mark stepped beside her. "Hey, honey. How's it going?"

As she raised her gaze from the computer screen, a cute dimple teased at the corner of her lips.

Yep, she distracted him.

Hailey leaned back. "Slower than I'd hoped. How'd your therapy go?"

"Not bad." No sense complaining how his hands ached.

"Did you speak to Erik?"

Mark dipped his chin. "We're uncovering more material. I ran across human trafficking cases during drug arrests at the DTA, but this ranks at the top. Selena was beaten and traded from one pimp to another. It makes me sick."

Hailey scowled. "Human trafficking is a dirty subject no one wants to talk about."

"It's rampant in every country, including the US." Mark clenched his jaw. "Some victims are the same age as Ethan and Anna."

"It's frightening." Hailey's eyes darkened to a deep amber. "I'm not going to lie to you. When Mendoza's father made plans to ship Colleen and me to the Caribbean, I was terrified."

"Is that why you're having trouble sleeping?"

"Maybe. Who knows how they might've kept us drugged and passed us around? José threatened to sell Rose, too." She scratched her arm. "Nice grandfather."

"He's a jackass." He fisted his hand. *Strange. The skin doesn't feel as tight.*

"José makes his son look like a saint." Hailey logged off the computer. "Manuel's death has stirred up memories of my parents dying."

Mark enveloped her in a hug. No matter how hard he tried, he couldn't stop her pain.

After a moment, he pointed to a white rectangular-shaped instrument on the counter about twelve inches long and eight inches in width and height. "What's this?"

"A microtome. It cuts tissue into thin slices. Bruce brought it out from storage in case the cytology lab took too long to process your latest biopsy. Turns out we didn't need it."

"You got my results?"

Her lips tightened. "Yes. The extracellular matrix is definitely remodeling, but still not in the random cross-weave patterns we'd hoped for."

Hailey might as well kick his gut. "So, nothing's changed. Even though my skin is regenerating, I'm going to have scarring."

"I wish we could do more. Bruce has tried to contact the shaman for suggestions."

"Damn."

"I'm sorry."

"It's not your fault. I should've expected this. Bruce warned me from the beginning this treatment was risky."

"Did I hear someone say my name?" Bruce walked into the lab carrying a tray of glass slides. "Ah! Mark, you're back."

Mark stepped out of the doctor's path. "Hailey was filling me in on the biopsy results."

Bruce lowered the slides onto the counter and gave him an apologetic look. "I believe your skin would heal better if we could minimize the inflammation. Don't give up hope. We're still researching."

"While you're at it, can you find something to hydrate my skin?" Mark scratched his fingers over the pressure garment covering his arm. "Everywhere itches like hell."

The lines deepened on Bruce's brow. "Has the itching gotten worse since we started using the Euphoria salve?"

Mark nodded. "Much worse."

Hailey frowned. "Could it be an allergic reaction? Maybe the salve is building up in his body."

The cell phone inside Bruce's lab coat dinged.

Bruce fished it from his pocket. "Ah! The shaman's returning my call. After I speak with him, I'll examine Mark in my office."

It can't be an adverse reaction. Mind over matter. A

heavy weight pressed on Mark's stomach, and he stopped scratching. He'd tell Bruce the itching stopped. The treatment couldn't end yet, not when the Euphoria salve was beginning to help.

Chapter Twenty-Six

"Grab her!" Manuel Mendoza's hollow voice carried through the trees.

Hailey scrambled down a rocky path, away from Mendoza's jeep. Turning, she gasped. "Papa! Momma!" Why were her parents tied up in the back seat?

She skirted across the road, but the jeep veered over a stream and closed in.

Nothing made sense. How were her parents in Colombia—and alive?

The engine roared behind her. Hailey leapt out of the jeep's path as it plowed over the cliff. Crying, she spun and slammed hard against José Mendoza.

José locked her wrists in handcuffs and dragged her to a burly man loading young women and children onto a boat.

Mark stood, tied to a wood piling, wrenching his arms. "Hailey, run!"

"Say adios*!" José's sinister voice echoed in the air as he pointed a pistol to Mark's head and fired.*

Hailey's legs gave out when she reached for him. "Mark!"

She jerked upright, her breathing ragged. Sweat dripped down her face as her surroundings slowly came into focus. She tugged the bedsheet, wiped her brow, and leaned back onto the pillow. Thank God. It was only another dream.

The red glow on the nightstand clock shone 8:10 AM.

Ugh! Third time this week she forgot to set the alarm.

Hustling out of bed, she slipped into her robe and darted into the kitchen.

Mark sat at the table, already dressed in his T-shirt and gray sweatpants. He turned from the computer screen. "Morning, sleepyhead."

Hailey kissed him and pulled out the other wooden chair from the table. "Why didn't you wake me?"

"You tossed all night. I wanted you to rest." His eyebrow lifted. "More dreams about Manuel Mendoza?"

She massaged the hard knots down the nape of her neck. "I wish I could put Colombia behind me. The worst nightmares involve his father, too."

"I want to rip out both their hearts for what they did to us." He tilted his head in his adorable way and gazed at her like he had when they dated. "Want me to skip therapy today and stay with you?"

No sense wasting his energy on her when he needed to focus on his recovery. "I'll be fine." She gestured to the computer. "What's going on here?"

"I was awake most of the night thinking about Selena's case. At four o'clock, I gave in and turned on the computer."

"Find anything solid yet?"

Mark shook his head. "Erik's fairly certain a mafia group with ties to the Caribbean took Selena to India. There's a chance we can identify her from these photos." He clicked the mouse, and rows of women's faces covered the screen.

"That's a lot of pictures."

"The SCA's been gathering information on India's mafias for years. Now it's collected using drones. If I can't find Selena in these, I'll search pictures of India's organized gangs. A few SCA agents are posted in the country, scoping out the brothels, making contacts. If Selena's alive, she'll show up somewhere."

A spark gleamed in his eyes as he spoke. She'd have to remember to thank David for involving Mark with the case.

Hailey studied the young women's images. "It's been twelve years. Are you using age-progression software?"

"Yes." Mark opened a file depicting a younger and older version of Selena. In both images, she had long black hair, high cheekbones, and curtain bangs framing a golden face. Long eyelashes accentuated her dark-brown eyes in the age-progression photo.

"Gosh, Selena's stunning." Hailey compared the picture to computer slides of different women wearing ghoonghats. "It's hard to tell what people look like under those head coverings."

Mark enlarged the picture. "I concentrate on the tattoo markings."

Hailey pointed to a young Indian woman with an elaborate design extending the whole length of her arm. "Like this mehndi artwork?"

"No. It'd be smaller. The brandings are usually on the chest, back, or arms. Sometimes the pimps engrave images on the women's thighs or genitals. Could be one or two words, initials, or even a barcode."

"A barcode?"

Mark scowled. "Pimps tattoo their victims to mark their property."

She covered her mouth. The women were branded like cattle. *That could've happened to me.* "Oh my God. I'm going to throw up."

A muscle twitched in Mark's neck as he flipped through the pictures. He pointed to a woman with letters above her breast. "Here's a tattoo of a pimp's initials."

Hailey swallowed down the bile rising in her throat. "If you find Selena alive, I can't imagine how she could emotionally recover."

"Luis and his mother deserve closure, one way or another." He closed out of the files. "What's on your schedule today?"

"Same old routine. Just researching ways to minimize your inflammation." She pointed to the Euphoria tin on the counter. "I can put salve on you if you're ready."

"Okay." Mark grabbed a tissue from the box on the end table and wiped the armrest. "I tried putting some salve on earlier, but it smeared on the couch."

She opened the container. "Next time, just ask. I want to help."

Fifteen minutes later, when Hailey finished applying the salve, she kissed him. "I'll take a quick shower and start breakfast. Are you hungry?"

Mark's eyes shimmered. "Extremely."

Her cheeks heated. Was he flirting? He definitely wasn't referring to food.

His gaze focused fully on her as he traced a finger along her pajama top and slowed at her breast. He winked. "Actually, I'm famished."

The touch electrified her even through the cotton fabric. Working this case had given Mark confidence in more than one way. His actions couldn't be more obvious, but so much time had passed since they were intimate. What if she hurt him during lovemaking?

She set the tin on the end table. "I'm glad you have an appetite, but I think eggs are more nutritious."

If Mark was disappointed, he didn't let on. "Don't worry about making me anything. I ate a bowl of oatmeal earlier." He cupped her face between his hands and claimed her lips in a hard, intoxicating kiss. "The shuttle's coming in a few minutes. The weatherman forecasted rain today. Take the umbrella if you go out. I'll see you later."

In the bathroom, she undressed and stepped into the shower. The heat from Mark's lips when he kissed her goodbye caught her off guard. She fingered her mouth under the steamy water. Could Mark be any clearer with his intentions? He wanted her again. Ten months seemed like an eternity. Hot desire flowed through her body. Finally! Their relationship was getting back on track.

When she toweled off, she slipped into a pair of khakis and light-knit sweater. Her cell rang as she brushed her hair.

Anna's name lit up on the screen.

Hailey grabbed the phone from the dresser. "Hi, sweetie. You're not sleeping in today?"

"No. Aunt Laura's taking us to the beach. She said I should call now. We won't be back until late."

"Sounds like a fun day. Remember to use plenty of sunscreen."

"I know." Anna's voice was borderline whiny.

Golly, these teenage years were going to be a trial. "Where's Ethan?"

"He's looking for his shoes. Lost them again."

"Are you two behaving?"

"Yes." Hailey grinned at the inflection in Anna's voice. "David asked the same thing."

"David? Is he there?"

"No, but he's been calling every day. He gives Aunt Laura updates about Grandpa."

Was that all David and Laura were talking about? *Don't let your mind wander.* David was a close family friend. Of course, he'd be in touch with Mark's sister to check in on the kids. "Have you talked to Samantha and Rose?"

"A few times. Rose is still having nightmares."

"Is the counseling helping?"

"Sam didn't say."

"I'll text Colleen later to check on her."

"Okay." Anna quieted as voices chattered in the background. "I gotta go. Ethan found his shoes. He says hello. Love you, Mom."

A few minutes later, the phone rang again.

Hailey tapped her finger on the call button. "Luis. This is a surprise."

"I told *señora* Camila I'd call."

"Camila?"

"*Señor* Manuel's mother. She would like to speak with you."

Hailey hesitated. "Me? Why?"

"I'm not sure, but she said it's important." When Hailey didn't respond, Luis continued. "Camila's a kind lady. She isn't like her husband."

Maybe Camila had news about José. Or maybe she wanted to check on Rose. "Okay. Text me her number, and I'll call before I head out this morning."

"*Gracias, señora.* I'll send you her number now." He paused. "Any leads on my sister?"

"I can't divulge details, but Erik is actively working on the investigation."

"I understand."

"Hey, keep the faith. If Selena's alive, he'll find her." Luis's text containing Camila's contact info appeared on Hailey's screen. "Have the authorities arrested José yet?"

"No, but don't worry. A lot of people are searching. He'll surface eventually."

Hailey ended the call and walked into the living room. The place was quieter with Mark at therapy, but with him back in her life, everything felt right again.

Chapter Twenty-Seven

"Sorry I'm late." Hailey rushed into Bruce's office and grabbed her lab coat on the door hook. "I've been on the phone all morning."

Bruce lifted his gaze from a book he'd been reading. "You're a busy woman."

She buttoned her coat. "First, Luis called. Camila Mendoza—Manuel's mother—asked to speak with me, so I called her."

"What does she want?"

"She asked if I'd give Colleen her contact info. Camila wants to video chat with Rose."

Bruce frowned and laid the book on his desk. "I wouldn't trust her. One Mendoza is as bad as the other."

"I thought the same thing at first. But Rose is Camila's last link to her son."

"That's even more reason not to trust her."

"I understand what you're saying, but the decision isn't up to me. I'll call Colleen later. If she's interested, Mark's CIA friend David could secure a line for a chat. In the meantime—" Hailey spread her arms wide. "—I'm here to help."

"I thought you'd be at rehab with Mark."

"He asked me to go tomorrow."

Bruce gestured to the empty seat across from his desk. "How are you two getting along?"

Heat flowed to Hailey's cheeks as she slumped onto

the chair. "Better, but I feel like I'm walking on broken test tubes when I'm around him. Enjoying the good moments, waiting for him to explode the next minute. Sometimes, I think we're reviving our relationship. Other times…I don't recognize my husband." She shook her head and rubbed her temples. "I don't know if we can get back what we had."

"Did you talk to him about your concerns?"

"He has enough on his mind."

"Mark thinks the same about you. He's concerned you're still having nightmares."

Hailey shrugged. "I don't want to upset him."

"How so?"

"Every night in my dreams, someone close to me dies. Most of the time, it's Mark. I stand there, helpless." She sank her head between her palms. "Sometimes I feel like I'm a burden to Mark by staying here."

"I think you're helping Mark. His outlook has improved since you've arrived."

She raised her head. "What if my dreams are an omen Mark will leave me again? Or that he'll give up on our marriage? I'm scared I'll lose him again."

"You won't. Look at the love you share."

"But what if our feelings have changed? Mark's no longer the same man that I married. I'm no longer the same woman who married him."

Bruce patted her arm. "Do you still love him?"

"Of course I do." She picked at a fingernail. "Our relationship is different, though."

"I'm no expert, but I think change is normal. Don't be afraid to let go of old dreams and forge new ones."

"I miss what we had *before* the fire. I don't know how to start again."

"I imagine Mark feels insecure about the future, too."

Such valuable advice. "Thanks for the pep talk." She stood. "I'll be back in a few minutes. I need to do something."

In the hall, Hailey pulled out her phone. No sense in putting off Camila's request any longer. Just as Hailey had lost time with Mark, Rose was losing time with her grandmother.

Colleen answered on the fourth ring. "Hailey? This is a surprise."

"I thought I'd check in. How's Rose?"

"She's still not sleeping well."

"The poor girl. Has counseling helped?"

"No. Now Rose wants a dog to protect her. I don't want to add that responsibility to our life right now."

"I spoke with Camila Mendoza this morning. She misses her granddaughter and would like to video chat with her." How lucky Rose was to have a grandmother who was alive.

Colleen cleared her throat. "Rose mentioned her *abuela* bought her toys and read books to her at bedtime."

"Maybe seeing her grandmother on video would ease Rose's nightmares. Camila said you can be on the phone when they talk. She's not trying to take Rose away. She only wants to build a relationship."

"I'll think about it. Will you text me her number?"

Hailey smiled, envisioning the video chat. "I will."

"Thanks. When you hear from Mark, tell him I said hello."

A heaviness overcame her as she ended the call. Years ago, Colleen and Mark had been close. With

Hailey and Mark's future so unsettled, she wouldn't risk relaying Colleen's message.

****

This itching is driving me crazy! Mark stepped off the shuttle, reached in his backpack, and squeezed more anti-itch ointment over his arms. His skin prickled like a million tiny ants were crawling underneath. What if the itching sensation was a reaction to Euphoria salve?

Mark gave a quick wave to the receptionist at the front desk and rode the elevator upstairs. He stopped in the doorway of Bruce's lab and stared as Hailey pipetted a solution into a glass test tube. Her face glowed as she worked at the counter. If she stopped teaching at the university, which career would she pick given a choice between medical research or working cases as an SCA agent? Tough decision. He'd support her as long as she was happy.

He tapped on the door. "Anyone up for a late lunch?"

Hailey shook her head. "I can't—"

Bruce looked up from his microscope. "Go ahead, Hailey. I'm fine here."

"But—"

Bruce's bushy eyebrows lifted over the rims of his wire glasses. "You haven't taken a break since this morning. Go."

Hailey nodded at Mark. "Okay, but can you give me a few minutes to finish?" She broke open a small ampoule and started pipetting its contents into the test tube.

Mark repressed his desire to take her in his arms and mold her sexy body next to his. "I'll be outside."

In the hallway, he waited as Hailey collected the

reagents on the counter. Might as well use the time and call his parents. When no one answered, he used the voice feature and texted Francine.

—Hey, sis. Checking on Dad. Is he doing OK?—

The phone chirped a reply within seconds.

—Perfect timing! I was settling him into bed.—

—How is he?—

—Edgy. He's been agitated since he came home. Still insists someone pushed him down your stairs. He wants to check your house.—

The cell vibrated for an incoming call, and David Smith's name lit up on the screen.

—Hey, Mom needs me. Got to go.—

—Tell Dad to stay home and rest. I'll text again later.—

Mark hurried and tapped the screen before it went to voicemail. "David? What's up?"

"Hopefully the stock market. How have you been?"

"Good. Thanks for suggesting to Owen that I work on the Selena Garvez case."

"Glad he's giving you work. Any leads?"

"A few. One pimp trafficked Selena in the Caribbean for three years until she went into hiding after a hurricane pushed across the islands. Her pimp eventually found her and beat the crap out of her. Ended up selling her to another shitbird, a mob boss from Goa." Mark sighed. "There's a slim chance she's still alive. I'm searching through photos from organized crime families."

"A reason for hope, even if a small one."

Definitely a long shot. "What's up with you?"

"Work is busy as usual. I spoke with Laura yesterday. Updated her about your dad. She's having fun keeping your kids busy." David chuckled. "She's as sweet-natured as I remember."

Mark grinned. David never outgrew his soft spot for Laura. "She's been a lifesaver." He leaned against the wall and peered into the lab. Hailey had moved and was wiping down the counter. "When you were at my house after my dad fell, did you notice if anything looked suspicious? Dad's convinced someone pushed him down the stairs."

"I arrived after the ambulance came. There was no sign of an intruder."

"Just thought I'd ask. It's not like him to be so stubborn. He's very careful about holding on to the banister when he climbs stairs."

When Mark ended the call, he tucked the phone into his sweatshirt pocket. Now Hailey was dawdling by the storage cabinet. What was taking so long? She moved slower than a garden snail. He turned to the floor-length windows overlooking the town.

Down the street a high-pitched siren blared, and two firetrucks sped past. Windows rattled as a parade of police cars ran sirens through the traffic lights.

Mark jerked. The saliva in his mouth went dry, and his windpipe closed. He grabbed his hair and slumped onto the floor. *Please God, not again! Why won't it stop?* He covered his ears, shivering as flashbacks darted through his mind. The thugs were relentless, beating on him. Clobbering his head. Punching.

A hand clasped his shoulder. "Mark? Are you okay?"

He swung his fist. "Don't touch me!"

Hailey stepped back and rubbed her arm. "I…I'm sorry."

The hallway spun as he fought to regain control. He lurched at her. "What took you so long!"

Her eyes and mouth opened in shocked disbelief.

Bruce rushed into the hall next to her.

Pressure built inside Mark like a volcano on the brink of eruption. He punched his hand against the wall. "Fuck this place!" His voice resonated through the hall as he stormed toward the stairwell.

Pain shot through his legs with each footfall on the stairs. At the bottom step, he fought to keep from falling apart. His knuckles throbbed, and his hand ached like his bones were broken. Somehow, he managed to open the door and stagger into the courtyard.

Dammit! Practice your breathing techniques.

He paced across the lawn, inhaling, exhaling, trying to match his breathing with his steps until his shaking subsided.

What a fucked-up life!

As he brushed past a rose bush, a thorny branch snagged his arm.

Mark yanked the flower to rip it off the stalk, but his finger rubbed the velvety petal, and his anger muted. The floral scent smelled like Hailey's shampoo. He snapped off a small branch with three roses and clumsily scraped off the spiny thorns with his fingernails.

"Mark. Wait!" Hailey opened the glass door and dashed toward him, slowing as she advanced.

He lowered the flowers to his side and swiped pricked fingers against his sweatpants. Heat crept across his cheeks. "I...I...I'm sorry. I don't know what happened in there."

Concern softened her hazel eyes. "Your PTSD is getting worse. You're losing control at the slightest trigger. Any trigger…a sound…a smell…a…I don't know." She threaded her fingers through her hair. "Can I call your counselor?"

He massaged his temples. "Give me a few minutes. I'll be fine."

"You're not fine. You need help." She touched his sleeve. "What about the EMDR therapy your therapist mentioned?"

Mark had read the brochures a million times. Nothing could help him. *You'll lose Hailey if you don't do something.*

She brushed his bangs away from his eyes. "I read up on EMDR. It can have positive results. Why don't you try it?"

He scrubbed the wiry bristles below the burn mask. What did he have to lose? "I'll think about it."

She moved closer and brushed her lips against his. "Don't give up hope. There's got to be some kind of therapy available that can help you."

The tenderness in her voice calmed him. Hailey was the most put-together person he'd ever known. He passed her the scanty bouquet he'd picked minutes earlier. "Here. These are for you. Roses always make things right between us." He tilted his head, begging for absolution.

Hailey fingered a petal and inhaled the flowers. Her eyes grew wide, and she leapt in the air. "Oh my God, you're a genius!" She rolled on her tiptoes and kissed him. "An absolute genius."

"What are you talking about?" The roses weren't that special.

"Come on." She headed toward the building. "I'll explain inside."

He jogged up the stairs, grimacing through the leg pain as he chased after her. What had he said that elated his wife?

When he reached the second level, she was already holding the door wide open. He leaned over the railing and dragged in a deep breath.

Hailey rubbed his back. "Almost there, honey. Can you make it?"

"I think so. Can you give me a clue about what's going on inside your pretty head?" He hobbled alongside her down the hallway.

Hailey charged into Bruce's lab. "Roses." She lifted the flowers in the air. "We need to use roses."

Bruce lowered the microscope slide in his hand. "For what?"

"We've been trying to find exotic plants native to Peru to reduce Mark's inflammation. Roses can reduce inflammation and hydrate the skin. Let's distill rose petals and dilute the oil with a carrier oil—similar to how we made Euphoria salve."

Mark's gaze darted to Bruce. Could the solution be so utterly simple? Was it kismet that brought him to send his wife roses all these years?

Bruce's eyebrows lifted. "It's worth a try. Roses and Euphoria might even work in synergy. Let me do some research to find where we can buy organic roses or rose petal extract."

Hailey's arms encircled Mark in a tight hug. "Oh, honey. You're amazing."

Grinning, he curved his arms around her waist and kissed her. "I don't know what the hell just happened, but I'll take the credit."

Chapter Twenty-Eight

Gritting his teeth, Mark limped onto the elevator cart. As the door closed, he bent and massaged his leg. Must've worked too hard at rehab. Or maybe all the rose water Hailey had been pushing on him caused the ache.

His cell phone rang as the doors opened.

He pulled the phone from his pocket and tapped the screen. "Don't you ever work?"

"If you only knew how many cases I juggle." David chuckled. "I had a few minutes. Thought I'd check in."

"I haven't freaked out since the other day, if that's what you're hinting at. I wish Hailey hadn't mentioned it."

"She was concerned about the PTSD. We care about you, buddy."

"I know you do."

"I imagine it's nice having your better half with you again."

More like perfect. "We're settling into a routine."

"I hope you're doing more than that."

"Funny. You know Hailey. She can be a little obsessive. Last week, she talked to the nutritionist and started only cooking healthy food. I kind of miss the greasy burgers you used to bring me."

"Glad she's taking better care of you."

"You have no idea. Yesterday, she put specialized sheets on the bed to ease the friction against my skin."

David laughed. "Okay. That's extreme."

"Tell me about it."

"Have you noticed a difference?"

"Well, yeah. They are more comfortable. My itching isn't as bad, either. But come on, bedsheets?"

David laughed harder. "Count yourself a lucky man that your wife cares about you. I envy you. By the way, anything new on Selena's whereabouts?"

"I've been searching photos, but nothing definitive yet."

"Hey, a call's coming in. I need to take it. Talk to you later."

Mark slipped the phone into his pocket and sighed. Life would be a whole lot better if Hailey showed more interest in him romantically. Kissing was nice, but they were married, for crying out loud. Between his therapy sessions and her research, he barely saw her. *Hailey and I should be more affectionate—like we used to be before the fire.*

He smiled at a memory of them sneaking back into bed after the kids had gone to school. Did Hailey remember their trysts? Someday they might be intimate again.

He plodded down the hall to his apartment, unlocked the door, and flipped the light switch. "Hailey?"

She must be with Bruce.

Mark powered on the computer and opened the fridge door. The leftover chicken fettuccini would hit the spot. As the pasta heated in the microwave, he grabbed the pitcher of rose water from the fridge and took his pain medication.

He set the food on the table and opened the classified file containing India's crime families.

Zero in on beautiful women with dark black hair. He leaned closer toward the screen. *With possible tattoos on the forearms.*

Mark zoomed in on every image. A woman with a contoured jawline and thick eyelashes looked to be in her early thirties. She'd be the right age. Her brown eyes seemed somber under her dark eyebrows.

He searched more photos. Hmm. That same woman he noticed earlier was standing next to a man and two children. Wind had swept up part of her blouse. He increased magnification on her chest. A crown tattoo. "No way!"

Mark cropped the woman's pictures and logged into his email. Picking up his cell, he pressed his voice command. "Call Erik Bruno."

Erik picked up on the second ring. "Agent Bruno."

"It's Mark Langley. I'm emailing you pictures of a woman from Uttar Pradesh. Could be Selena. I think you were right. She might be in a forced marriage or working as an indentured servant. Can your staff confirm if the tattoo matches the description from her pimp you tracked down in Haiti?"

"I'll put an agent right on it, and I'll also push the pictures through facial recognition. Send me details of the crime family. I'll alert the agents stationed in northern India."

"If this woman is Selena, you might want to use her brother, Luis, to convince her that your men are safe. She may be hesitant to trade into a worse situation."

"Good thinking. I'll be in touch."

A few minutes later, Hailey walked into the apartment. "Sorry I'm late—" Deep lines carved into her brow. "What's wrong?"

Mark greeted her with a hard kiss. "You're never going to believe this."

"What?"

"I think I found Selena." He smiled so widely his cheeks pinched. "Hot damn. I know I did!"

****

Hailey leaned back on the sofa and relaxed her head against Mark's chest, a feeling of weightlessness flowing through her. The mystery woman in the pictures definitely looked like Luis's sister; even the age progression image was similar. "What will happen if Selena is the woman you found?"

"Erik's agents will work with the authorities in India to free her."

She burrowed deeper into his embrace. "I can't get the image of those two young children out of my mind. If Selena's their mother, will she leave them? Gosh, what a terrible dilemma." Hailey scratched her arm. "Is Erik going to tell Luis?"

Mark's hand covered hers, stilling her scratching. "He needs to investigate more. Verify it's really her."

What a cruel blow if they were mistaken. "Assuming it is Selena, she'll need counseling once she's free—and medical care."

"There are international organizations that will give her support. The Colombian government has resources, too."

Hailey shuddered. Therapy helped after her kidnapping, but memories remained. "I wonder if Selena asked for help. She might've learned a few words in Hindi."

"Who could she turn to? Trafficking victims feel trapped. Often, they're beaten and robbed of their identifications and passports." His voice choked. "The dipshit owner probably brainwashed her into thinking she'd go to prison if she was caught, or maybe he threatened violence to her family."

Hailey's heart warmed. This was the man she had married. Kind. Compassionate. Supportive. She turned her head and kissed him. "Thank you."

"For what?"

"For caring. And for finding Selena. I assumed after all this time she had died."

"We still need to wait for confirmation."

"Either way this turns out, I'm proud of you."

His lips curled upward. "I must admit, this case gives me hope that I can work again—in some capacity anyway. Obviously, I wouldn't be working the streets, but a desk job won't be too bad."

"Don't sell yourself short. Your OT said she's focusing on your career skills so you can go back to work."

"What else did Brooklyn tell you?"

She shrugged. "Just tips to help put on your pressure garments and treat your dry skin." No need to tell Mark everything they discussed.

"Speaking of skin"—he scratched his neck—"this itching is worse than chicken pox."

"I thought you said it was getting better."

His hand shifted to his chest. "Somedays are worse than others. Today's one of those days."

She gripped his hand. "Stop scratching. You'll damage your new skin."

"That's easy for you to say." Mark snuck in another scratch before she pulled his arm away. "Do you have any idea how miserable I feel?"

"I have a pretty good idea." She glanced down at her arms. "Trust me, scratching doesn't relieve the misery."

His dreamy blue eyes dimmed. "I'm sorry. That was inconsiderate of me."

"Don't apologize." At least her itching was confined to her upper limbs. Mark was miserable all over.

Hailey stood and grabbed a tube of lotion sitting on the countertop. "Let's try this moisturizer Dr. Wright recommended." She unscrewed the cap. "Show me the worst places."

He pointed to his shoulder, gazing at her with a longing in his eyes. "Thank you for taking care of me." His husky voice sounded like a desperate whisper.

Unable to stop the heat flooding her face, she lowered her chin.

Mark picked up her hand coated with lotion and kissed her fingers. "I know this is difficult for you, but I enjoy when you touch me."

Her heart fluttered at his tender touch. Mark was still the same man—on the inside.

What was wrong with her? He was the same on the outside, too. How many times had she touched his scars and rubbed the salve over his thickened skin? The marks didn't define him.

She set down the anti-itch cream and unscrewed the lid from the salve container. "Now that Bruce added in rose petal oil for inflammation, he wants you to start afternoon applications of Euphoria into your routine. Which reminds me, did you drink your water today?"

Mark made a fist with his thumb raised. "Already drank three glasses. Believe me, nobody wants this treatment to work as much as I do." He removed his T-shirt and lay on the couch. "Do you mind putting the salve here instead of the bedroom? I'm too beat to move. With all the commotion about Selena, I skipped my afternoon nap."

"Sure." Hailey scooted beside him and began applying the salve on his left shoulder. "Has anyone noticed changes in your scars other than Brooklyn?"

"A couple of nurses commented. The aquatic therapist said the scars looked better. The PT jotted down some notes on the chart about them fading."

"Does Dr. Wright know you're using Euphoria salve?"

"Bruce consulted him before we started." Mark yawned. "No one else knows. Bruce doesn't want the news getting out to the public."

"What has Dr. Wright said about the change in your scars?"

"He's cautious, but he admits the skin is undergoing extraordinary healing." Mark lifted his arm as she spread the salve along his side. "In your opinion, if my skin continues to heal at this rate, how long will I need to wear the mask and pressure garments?"

Tough question. Weeks. Months. Any wrong estimate, and he'd be disappointed. "I'm not sure. Depends on how quickly your new skin grows." She traced a finger over a scar on his left thigh. "I see improvements every day. Even the scars on your legs are starting to change."

When Hailey finished applying the salve, she wiped her hands on a paper towel. "How's the pain today?"

"About a four."

He was lying. His pinched expression was all the proof she needed. "I ran into one of your nurses when I left today—the one with the short, wavy black hair. She seems very sweet. She said you're a prize patient."

Mark chuckled. "What else did she say?"

"Not much. We talked about your pain meds, and she warned me about thermoregulation."

"Brooklyn reminds me about my body temperature, too, especially when I exercise and shower." Mark adjusted a pillow under his head. "I think you've met everyone at the clinic now."

"I haven't talked to your counselor yet."

"That's right. She usually comes in the early afternoon. I saw her today after PT."

"Did you talk about EMDR?"

"Yeah, she scheduled it for tomorrow."

Hailey clapped her hands. "That's great. Why didn't you say something?"

He shrugged and trailed his fingers up her arm. "I was busy thinking about you."

Goose bumps surfaced on her arms. Was Mark giving her one of his pickup lines?

Hailey unsnapped his workout pants and raised the bamboo fabric higher on his legs. Whoa. The changes weren't only in her imagination. Even the deepest wounds were lighter in color.

"Do you—" She smiled, trying to ignore the erection tenting his briefs. "Do you want me…to uh…to go with you to the EMDR session?"

He grinned and slid his hands behind his head.

Did he enjoy seeing her flustered? From the heat hammering her cheeks, her face must be cherry red.

"I'd rather go alone. At least the first time."

"That's fine." She wouldn't push him. Making the appointment was a big step. "I'm glad you decided to try it."

Mark dipped his finger in the salve and playfully rubbed some on Hailey's cheek.

"Why did you do that?" She brushed her skin where he dabbed.

"Don't take it off. I'd like you to have the salve for your scars, too."

Heat ran up her neck. Her scars were miniscule compared to his. "This salve's for you. Wait until we can make more before you start giving it away."

"It's not right that I use it all. Ronnie could use Euphoria for his psoriasis."

"More people, including Ronnie, may get the chance when this study is over and Bruce identifies the compound that regenerates skin. We'll mass produce the salve for anyone who needs it."

His eyes misted over. "Other patients at rehab need the salve more than me."

"I understand. But ethically, Bruce can't use this salve on anyone else until he's completed more studies. Technically, he shouldn't even use it on you." How could she convince him? "Look at it this way. You're the guinea pig taking all the experimental risks that will eventually benefit others. Be patient."

Mark breathed out a long sigh and removed his burn mask. "I'll try."

She feathered her fingers across his jaw. "This is amazing. The scars on your face and neck are blending in with your normal skin."

He nodded. "I noticed it, too. I can't wait until I don't need this damn mask anymore."

Hailey spread salve on the scars between his patchy whiskers. "Are you going to shave the beard after your skin heals?"

A roguish smile curled his lips, and Mark scrubbed a hand over his whiskers. "I don't know. I kind of like my beard and moustache. Makes me look like Robert Downey Jr." He leaned upright on the sofa and reattached the mask.

She'd never admit it after all her teasing, but the facial hair was growing on her, too. "Go ahead and nap while I buy groceries for dinner."

Hailey set the half-empty tin of Euphoria on the counter and blew a goodbye kiss. At the rate they were using the salve, Mark might need every ounce to regenerate his skin.

Chapter Twenty-Nine

A cool wind gust snapped across José's cheeks as he strode down the sidewalk from his secret hideout. Shivering, he bent over in a fit of coughing and peered up at the sky where dark gray clouds blocked the sun. He should've worn a jacket. The temperature in Boston was at least ten degrees cooler than Colombia.

He thrust his hands into his pants pocket and walked into the sandwich shop across from the gated property where the *puta* and her friends resided. A ham sandwich and hot coffee would sate his hunger. He paid the server with a twenty-dollar bill he'd pinched from the Langley house in Virginia and moved to the side.

Cold air blowing from a vent stung his lungs. He coughed again and ignored the accusing glares. The pandemic still frightened people. Not many in the US would associate hacking coughs with illnesses like herbicide spray poisoning.

He picked up his order, settling into a booth at the far end of the room. He barely registered the food as he bit into the roll.

Three times this week, the *puta* had driven off at eleven AM. Hard to tell if Rose was with her, but each trip lasted an hour. Yesterday, while José waited, he bought a burner phone at a nearby drugstore.

He swallowed the last bite of the sandwich and stared out the window.

Why did they stop taking a subway into the city? Were they sick?

He snickered. Did he care?

Maybe he did care—just a little. He couldn't avenge Manuel's death if he lost the girl.

José sipped the coffee and let the hot, bitter brew slide down his throat. He'd coughed so much lately that his lungs had to be bruised.

Sliding a hand into his jeans pocket, he pulled out the newly purchased burner phone, now fully charged. The blank screen stared back at him. Buying his own phone went against the commander's rules.

Like I give a shit.

Camila would probably be at the orphanage. If he called, she might refuse to speak to him.

Luis might know how she's managing. José pressed in the underling's number and cancelled the call. Luis's phone might be tapped.

¡Hijueputa! Only one way to find out. He dialed Camila's number and waited.

On the fifth ring, his finger hovered over the screen to disconnect.

"*¿Hola?*"

"C—Camila. It's me." He conversed in Spanish. Would she hang up? He'd have only a short time to talk in case the police were tracing the call.

"José? Where are you?" Her voice squeaked as she rushed her words.

"Never mind that." How would she react if she knew he was in the US? "I'm sorry about Manuel."

"Oh, José." She sobbed. "My baby's dead…I've lost everyone—Manny…Rose—they're gone."

A hard lump swelled in José's throat. *¡Maldita sea!*

Hearing her cry was harder than he anticipated.

"Why aren't you home?" Her voice broke for a moment, then she regained control. "The police raided the mansion and ranch house. They confiscated all the computers."

"I'm not worried." The security administrator he'd hired protected José's computer passwords, expunged his name off the bank records, and added firewalls. Any paperwork the authorities would uncover was solely in Manuel's name.

She wept again. "My heart hurts so much."

"Don't cry. I'll make it up to you."

"How?"

"I plan to bring your granddaughter home to you."

Camila gasped. "You'll do no such thing."

Had he misjudged her feelings toward the child? "Don't you want to see her?"

"Of course I do."

He squared his shoulders. "Then I'll bring her back to Colombia."

"Wait…you're in the United States? Are you crazy? My God, José! Don't you dare lay a hand on that child. Manny forbade you any contact with her."

"But—"

"Do not hurt Bella or Rose, do you hear me? Promise me, José. If you ever loved me, ever felt one speck of love…respect this request. Rose belongs with her mother. God knows we don't need another orphan in this world."

He gnashed his teeth. "Don't tell me what to do, woman."

"I…I…I'll turn you in. I have photos of you and your men. Tapes of your schemes to murder the FARC leaders and kidnap the government politicians." Her words strung together. "Your name is mentioned as the leader. There's enough evidence that you'll never set foot outside of prison."

José fisted his hands. "No one blackmails me!"

"I'm warning you. Leave Rose and her mother alone."

"Don't give me orders."

"I'll let you run the estate again if you do."

José tightened his lips. He'd be back in power. He could unseal his hidden bank accounts. Run the camps and gain control of the drug routes. "Okay. You win."

"Say it, José. I have to hear it. Promise me that you won't hurt Bella or Rose. If you hurt them, the deal's off. I'll bequeath everything to the orphanage."

¡Hijueputa! She backed him into a corner like a trapped puma!

But he'd have control. "I promise."

"Thank you. Now please come home."

The call disconnected.

José coughed until his ribs hurt. No sign of movement at the house across the street. If he killed Manuel's *puta*, would Camila find out?

He drained his coffee cup and stood. He wouldn't go back on his word—yet. Not until he regained control of the cocaine production and trafficking. His wife held too much over his head. He could kill Camila later. Set up an accident, after he coerced her into signing over the property.

The *puta* and little reject might be off-limits for now, but he never vowed anything about the nosy bitch in Virginia.

Heavy raindrops speckled his jacket as he hurried

back to his place. Once inside, José locked the dead bolt and texted his contact on the designated burner phone.

—Need a ride to northern VA—

Chapter Thirty

When Mark woke, the sun cast long shadows across the carpet.

"Hailey?" He rose from the sofa. Stabbing pain radiated up his leg as he searched the apartment. Her lanyard with the fob and room card were gone. *Must still be grocery shopping.*

Mark massaged his thigh. *Damn pain.* It was getting worse. He'd have to tell Bruce. He scrawled a short message, left it on the kitchen table, and locked the door.

More twinges ran through Mark's legs as he walked down the hall. He checked Bruce's office and, finding it vacant, limped to the lab.

There he is.

Guilt pricked his heart as the elderly doctor shuffled to the counter and fidgeted with the knobs on a broken analyzer. Bruce had been working these long hours for him.

Mark knocked on the door. "Bruce. Have a minute?"

Bruce turned. "Is everything all right?"

"You told me to let you know if my leg pain got worse." Mark hobbled into the room and winced. "Well, it's worse."

"How long has it been going on?"

"A few days."

Bruce scratched his head. "Hailey didn't mention it."

"She doesn't know. I thought it would go away, but it hasn't. Dr. Wright called them 'breakthrough pains.' Whatever the fancy term, the pangs are occurring more often."

"Why didn't you tell me sooner?"

Mark scratched his arm. "I was afraid you'd make me stop using the Euphoria salve."

Frowning, Bruce pulled two gloves from a box. "Have a seat on the exam table."

Twenty minutes later, Mark reattached his pressure garments. Bruce's expression was harder to read than a skilled poker player. "Give it to me straight, Doc. Am I having a reaction to the salve?"

Bruce peered over the top of his eyeglasses. "I don't think it's an allergic reaction. There's no sign of irritation. Your scars are diminishing, and the texture's smoother. The change is even more noticeable than last week."

"Then what's causing the sharp twinges?"

"I'm hesitant to speculate until I do more testing. I'll call Dr. Wright, and we'll schedule a punch biopsy to get a better idea of what's going on."

"What does that entail?"

"Dr. Wright will remove tiny pieces of skin. Don't worry. It can be done as outpatient surgery. It's a low-risk procedure. You'll be given local anesthesia."

Mark fastened the flaps of his jogging pants. "When?"

"It'll take a few days to get on the schedule. With the way your skin's responding, this salve should make a substantial impact for many burn patients."

Mark pointed to the amber vessel on the top shelf. "Any update on the supply chain delay?"

"No, but once the analyzer part arrives, I'll start testing the raw oil."

Mark's neck hair bristled as he glanced up at the shelf and eased off the bed. "Just keep that oil away from me."

Grinning, Bruce gestured to the door. "Let's talk more in my office."

Across the hall, Mark settled into a padded chair and tapped his fingers on the armrest. "I scheduled an EMDR session for tomorrow."

Bruce's eyes brightened. "That's wonderful! The therapy has had favorable outcomes."

"That's what everyone tells me."

"Did Dr. Kendrick explain what to expect during the session?"

"We worked on prep skills today. Dr. Kendrick will guide me using different movements to process painful memories the night of the fire."

"Bilateral stimulation." Bruce removed his eyeglasses and set them on the desk.

Mark nodded. "She'll move her fingers back and forth like she's hypnotizing me. I might have to tap my shoulders or cross my arms over my chest." He demonstrated the movements.

"She also might have you use little devices that pulse or vibrate."

"Oh, yeah. The tappers. She showed me. They're only about two inches long."

Bruce leaned back in his chair. "The alternating buzzing or vibrations will help process your memories."

Mark nodded again. "Exactly what Dr. Kendrick said. We identified targets that upset me the most, and we talked about different ways I can reduce stress."

"Sounds like you're all set."

"I hope it works." It had to work. He was running out of options. Mark glanced at the wall clock and stood. "I should get back to the apartment. Want to come over tonight? Hailey's cooking a special dinner."

Bruce shook his head. "I don't want to intrude."

Mark sighed. "Believe me, you're not interrupting anything."

"Is something going on with you two?"

"More like what's not going on. We act more like friends than a husband and wife."

Bruce buffed his lenses with a tissue from his desk. "Have you talked to her?"

Did Mark want to start that conversation? "I don't want to push her."

"I'm not an expert on marriage, but I think you and Hailey need to sit down and have a long talk. Tell her what you need. She might be holding back on you, as well."

"I get the vibe she's not interested in me in that way anymore. I can't blame her. She's been thrown into the role of my caregiver."

"And you think she doesn't want to cross that line?"

"I don't know what to think, but I can't handle that rejection right now."

Bruce arched his eyebrow. "Seems to me, you're the one holding back."

****

Hailey walked out of the grocery store with a bag in each hand. The fresh-baked bread would go well with the chicken cordon bleu. This dinner had to be perfect. *I need all the help I can get to put Mark in a good mood before tonight's discussion.*

As she passed a toy store, her lips twitched, and she reversed direction. Mark would love his gift.

Back at the apartment, she read Mark's note on the kitchen table:

Went to see Bruce. Be back in a few minutes.

She'd better hurry.

Hailey preheated the oven and prepped the chicken in the casserole dish. Next, she julienned the carrots and boiled them on the stove. Diced cucumbers and tomatoes topped fresh spinach salads.

The door lock clicked as she laid the last silverware onto the napkin. Perfect timing.

Mark walked into the kitchen. "Hi, honey. Dinner smells delicious."

"Thanks. We're having chicken tonight." She stepped closer and hugged him.

The aroma of baked chicken wafted through the room as she poured rose water into two glasses. "We have a few minutes before dinner's ready. Let's sit." She led him into the living room and lifted a wrapped box from the floor. "I bought you a present."

His eyebrow arched. "What is it?"

"Open it and find out." Hailey handed him the gift. She'd missed this part of their relationship—the fun stuff.

Mark sat on the sofa and tore into wrapping paper, like their kids opening gifts on Christmas morning. He looked at the picture on the box, and his jaw dropped.

She slid beside him. "It's like the motion-controlled video gaming system you use in OT. I thought we could play in the evenings." Was he pleased, in shock—or both? "I enjoyed bowling with you at the burn center. The kids will love to play, too, when you come home."

A wide smile spread across Mark's face. "I don't know what to say." He pulled a white handheld controller from the packaging. "Thank you."

She should've come up with the idea sooner. "You're welcome. The system has twenty games. Want to try one after dinner? After…" An itch prickled around her arm, and she scratched it.

Mark set down the controller and stilled her hand. "Honey, what's wrong?"

He'd become more perceptive than he used to be. "I got an email this morning. Ethan and Anna start school in two weeks. Orientations are coming up."

Mark blinked hard. "You're leaving?"

She fisted her hands. "I don't want to, but school's starting."

"My treatments are going so well. I need you here."

"I don't like this situation either. Life's starting to come together for us."

"I need at least another month or two before I come home." He rubbed his forehead. "Is it the money? I'll call Owen. I have workers' comp."

"Money's not the issue." When Hailey explained she was the sole beneficiary to Parker's life insurance, she squeezed Mark's hand. "He would be pleased the money was being put to good use."

"Parker didn't give you money so you could support me. *I* should be providing for you."

"He told me you were alive. He wanted us together." Hailey raked a hand through her hair. How could they resolve their predicament? "The dean might consider letting me take off a semester or teach online classes, but the kids need to start school. Couldn't you do therapy in Virginia?"

Mark shook his head. "I'm not leaving while Bruce is researching a cure. My scars look better, but I want to wait until I'm completely healed."

"I know the timing's bad." Hailey groaned. "Ugh! I don't want us to separate again."

"Then don't leave." He pulled her close against him. "My parents can watch the kids for a month."

"They have enough on their plate. Your dad just got out of the hospital."

"Ethan and Anna could help them around the house. Shop for groceries. Do yardwork."

"Maybe." They were getting older. It was one option.

"Or we could enroll our kids in virtual school and ask my sister to keep them at her place."

"That's another possibility, but we'd uproot the kids from their friends." Nothing was ideal. "Or we go with my original plan, which makes the most sense."

Mark heaved a long sigh. "When do you go back?"

"End of next week. Saturday at the latest. The kids need school supplies."

He scratched the whiskers under his chin. "So, this is the reason for the fancy dinner."

Busted. "I want to make some special memories before I leave."

He winked. "Here I thought you wanted to seduce me."

Her cheeks heated. "Don't joke about that."

"I'm being serious. I'm not much to look at—"

"Stop. Don't say that." Her own insecurities when she was seventeen came flooding back. She couldn't look in a mirror for months after her attack. "I don't care about the scars. I love *you*."

"I love you, too. It's just—" Mark shook his head and exhaled. "Shit. This is hard to talk about."

With her finger, she lifted his chin. "Spit it out."

His eyes closed. "I'm afraid I won't be man enough for you."

She gaped. *Man enough?* How could she wipe away his insecurities? "Trust me. That is not a problem. You were man enough for me the day I met you, and you still are. You're everything I want."

"Look at me." Mark looked at his legs. "How can I satisfy you?" His deep voice rasped. "I want to caress you—all over. Make you yearn for my touch. Feel your touch in return. I miss how close we used to be. I want *you*—all of you." He wiped a tear from his eye. "Please. Stay in town a little longer. I can't do this without you. You're an important part of my treatment."

Isn't that what she wanted? To help Mark recover and bring him home? Why was life so complicated?

She held his hand. "I haven't been completely honest with you."

"What do you mean?"

She brushed back his stray locks of hair and gazed into his eyes, searching his soul. Yep. He was the same man she fell in love with. The same man who patiently waited for her when she needed time. "I've avoided…getting closer…because I'm afraid I'll hurt you."

Mark pointed at his legs where an erection tented his sweats. "You're not hurting me now."

She chuckled. "Come on. I'm being serious."

"So am I." Mark's thumb caressed her hand. "Don't worry. I'll tell you what hurts and what doesn't. I won't break." He kissed her forehead. "I'm not saying we have to make love tonight, but can we cuddle and explore? Be open to romance when the time feels right? I want to be close to you."

Hailey bit her lip. Maybe they could find their way back together after all. "I want that so badly."

Mark raised his hands to his head and removed the burn mask.

"What are you doing?"

"I'd like ten minutes where I can make out with my wife without feeling like the Phantom of the Opera." He leaned closer and pressed his lips to hers, sweeping his tongue between her lips.

As Mark's mouth took bold possession, his breath ignited a buried hunger, curling her toes.

Hailey moaned into his mouth. His sweet caress rocketed through her restless body. God, she wanted him—ached for him. His touch felt marvelous. She returned his invigorating kiss with her own sweeping invitation. Her mind reeled with desire at his earthy scent. As Mark slipped his arms tighter around her waist, she trailed her fingers down the nape of his neck and parted her lips for more.

****

José cracked his knuckles from the back seat of a sedan, breaking the silence between him and the scrawny guy behind the steering wheel. José's foray into the States was getting closer to winding down. Soon the commander would finalize the details with the migrant smuggler for a return passage.

Since José returned to Virginia the previous night, uneasiness needled his soul. Nothing was going as easily as he'd anticipated—especially exacting revenge for Manuel's death.

As the car neared Langley's wooded development, José patted the firearm in his slacks. The troublemaker had outsmarted him too many times. He wouldn't be made a fool of again.

The driver followed a garbage truck down the block. He tugged a flat cap lower onto his head and glanced into the rearview mirror. His gray eyebrows raised above his sunglasses as he handed José a folded paper.

José took the note and exited the car. He barely registered the driver speeding away as he opened the paper. OUNPD YRQNW 8856. He checked his watch, readied for a black sedan at 11:20, and walked to the house. Thirty minutes would be plenty of time.

A coughing spell overtook him as he walked to the property. He hacked a glob of sputum at the white sedan parked in the driveway. A few days had passed since he'd been there. She had to be home now.

He peeled some weathered paint from the garage trim and peered through a window panel. *The trashcan is still in the garage!* He kicked the door. Today was pickup day. He'd passed the garbage truck down the road.

Where the hell did she go?

Had someone cursed him so that nothing worked out? For two weeks he'd chased down the *putas*. Now he had to return to Colombia empty-handed? Never! Langley was the only person left he could seek revenge on.

Near the porch, José balled a sun-faded flyer lying in the overgrown bushes and hurled it into the trees. He fished the bump key from his pocket. *¡Maldita sea!* The tiny hammer must've fallen out. What else would go wrong? He picked up a cobblestone from the flowerbed and struck it against the bump key in the front-door lock.

Once inside the house, he marched straight into the study and flipped through the address book on the desk. Langley had scads of acquaintances. Would she be visiting with a contact from out of state? She might be on vacation. From the condition of the house, she didn't have money for a hotel or to be away for too long. Better chance she was staying with someone.

He tore out the pages of the out-of-state addresses. With his shirt, he wiped off fingerprints and replaced the book on the desk. He'd be back in Colombia before anyone realized the pages were missing.

José locked the front door and headed to the meeting place, coughing until his lungs spasmed. Circumstances had changed. He wouldn't leave the States until he killed Hailey Langley. No one made an ass out of José de Mendoza.

After the driver dropped him off at the safe house, José collapsed onto the couch. His chest hurt like wild horses had trampled over him. He closed his eyes. Rest a few minutes, then decide how to proceed.

When he woke, three hours had passed. His cough had subsided, but his entire body ached. He dug into his pocket for the pages he'd ripped out from the address book. He flicked the loose, scaly skin from his forearm and unfolded the pages. Someone had to know where the snitch was staying. He'd make some calls. One way or another, he'd find Hailey Langley and make her pay.

Chapter Thirty-One

Mark tapped his fingers on the sofa in Dr. Kendrick's office. Was he wasting his time in trying EMDR therapy? The psychotherapist had tried different therapies with him already, but today felt different. The pressure to have this treatment succeed was palpable.

The room's professional décor exuded a cold, clinical vibe. A stepladder bookcase containing neatly staged books, puzzles, and faux succulents leaned against a wall. Three indoor palm trees flourished near the full-length window.

Dressed in a navy dress and beige pumps, Dr. Kendrick plucked a folder from her desk and settled into the leather chair across from him. Her long, blonde hair was pulled back in a French twist that emphasized her high cheekbones. She adjusted a gold chain around her neck. "Nervous?"

"A little." Mark shifted his shoes on the oversize rug underneath the sofa. Butterflies, no, more like angry dragonflies buzzed inside his stomach.

"That's normal. You're going to do fine." The psychotherapist set the folder on her lap. She looked to be a few years younger than Mark, maybe mid-thirties. "I have your history from our previous sessions. Yesterday, we worked on setting reasonable expectations, and we established your self-control techniques. Do you remember your stop signal?"

Mark pounded one fist over his other fist. If he ever needed to stop, this movement was his way out.

"Very good."

The calmness in Dr. Kendrick's silvery voice soothed him. Somehow, he'd handle the disappointment if the therapy didn't work.

"It's important to remember that you have control in your treatment. I'm going to give you clues at certain points during this session, asking you to think about a particular painful memory from that event—the target memory. You'll use different techniques to help process the memory. Then I'll ask you to take a breath and open up to tell me what you're thinking…"

Mark registered fragments as Dr. Kendrick spoke. His insides rattled like he'd drunk fifty cups of coffee. The pep talk sounded fine, but would this therapy work? He slowly relaxed as he practiced his breath strategy.

Dr. Kendrick pulled notes from the folder. "Today we're going to process the memory of the assault, the night of the fire. Do you remember that night?"

"Yes."

"Can you tell me the image of the worst part of that specific memory?"

He started trembling. The picture was so vivid. "Three brutes tied me to the chair. They punched me in the gut…bashed in my face…broke my nose. They wouldn't stop. Some of my teeth fell out, I tried not to swallow them. I was helpless…trapped."

"What emotions do you notice when you think about that night?"

Pressure built in his lungs as a bunch of different feelings swirled in his mind. "Fear…anger…panic. Mostly panic. I…I didn't think I'd survive."

"On a scale of zero to ten with zero being no distress and ten being the worst, what number are you holding for these negative emotions?"

Ten. Don't be a wuss. "Nine."

"When you're thinking of that image of your assault, are there any negative beliefs that go along with that image?"

A hundred-pound weight swung onto his chest.

His brain screamed, "Flee!"

His hands shook. *Don't go back to that memory again. This therapy is bullshit.*

Try. Do it for Ethan, for Anna. For Hailey.

"I'm helpless. I should've found a way to overcome the thugs."

Dr. Kendrick leaned forward. "Is there a belief you *prefer* to feel about yourself that would go along with that image?"

Mark exhaled. What did he want to feel? "I want to be strong. In control."

"As you continue that image in your mind, of you being beaten, think about 'I'm strong. In control.' How true does that feel on a gut level, on a scale of one being completely false to seven, completely true?"

"Maybe a one." Was zero an option? God, even now he was hopeless.

Dr. Kendrick's brow furrowed. Was she judging him? "As you hold that image in your mind and say 'I'm weak,' what feeling comes up?"

"Fear." Mark bowed his head. "I'm a coward. I'm worried I won't be able to protect my family."

"Where do you feel that in your body?"

"My chest." Mark pointed.

"How strong is that feeling from zero to ten, with

zero meaning no distress, and ten being the worst?"

Mark's throat tightened. "Ten."

"Can you pair the image, the negative belief of being weak and embarrassed, and let your mind go with that as I begin the stimulation?"

He nodded, concentrating on his breathing. *Here I go.*

Raising two fingers, Dr. Kendrick moved her hand to the right and left and continued the motion.

Mark followed her fingers, letting his mind wander to the goons pummeling him. Blood dripped out his nose, his mouth. He couldn't catch his breath. He wrenched his fists against the ropes binding him to the chair. There was no escape.

Oh God, help me.

A weight as heavy as the Titanic slammed against him. This therapy was a bad idea.

Show the damn stop signal. Dammit! Show it!

"Take a breath." Dr. Kendrick's voice dissolved the harsh image. "Open up."

"I'm anxious. I don't know what's going to happen to me."

"Go with that." She moved her two fingers back and forth again.

The men's images were clearer. Dark angry eyes. Tanned faces. One foul-smelling, bald man with a scarred face. A heavy guy with bulging biceps and a black beard. The tall one at the door with a black moustache and maple-leaf tattoo. They came at him, taking turns beating him.

"Take a breath."

He struggled for air, his lungs heavy.

"Open up."

275

"I'm panicking. I can't stop them. My head jerks whenever their fists come toward my face." He choked.

"Go with that." She moved her hand, guiding the process.

Mark followed the movement. He pleaded with the thugs, crying as they taunted him. More images flashed across his mind. The men held his chin upright and punched his head. Something snapped. The pain in his jaw was unbearable.

"Take a breath."

He inhaled.

"Open up."

"I feel helpless… I can't stop them… They threatened to go after my wife and kids."

"I'd like you to cross your hands over your shoulders, like the butterfly hugging position we talked about yesterday." Dr. Kendrick modeled, crossing her arms over her chest.

Mark copied the position, resting his fingers over the opposite arms.

"I want you to tap back and forth when I say 'Go with that.' "

He demonstrated tapping his shoulders, alternating the patting left and right.

"Now think about the helplessness, the panic you felt when you thought your family was in danger and go with that."

A metallic taste of blood stung Mark's tongue. Voices jeered, overpowering his other senses. More and more punches…

"Breath. Open up."

He gasped. "The men keep coming. I'm defenseless."

"Go with that."

He tapped his arms, the pungent odor of gasoline filling his nasal passages. Flames clawed his lower legs, burning his feet. Fire latched onto his pants. The heat seared his skin.

Please, God, help me!

"Breath."

He blinked twice. The image seemed distant now, broken into little pieces.

"Open up."

"I want to be strong for my family."

"What about the original image?"

He searched his memory. Where was the image? "It's gone."

"Go with that."

Mark closed his eyes and tapped. Sensations overwhelmed him. High-pitched voices screamed. Heat latched onto his limbs. He gasped for air. So hard to breathe. Fire snapped. Gunshots blasted. David's voice shouted above the chaos. Mark's chair slammed to the floor. David shielded Mark, cut him loose, and carried him out of the building. Mark's body shivered as cold air shocked his skin.

"Breath. Open up."

Mark paused. His mind was an ocean of rolling waves.

Dr. Kendrick seemed to study him. "Do you remember the positive image in your mind showing how you want to feel?"

"I'm strong. I'm in control." Amazing. He felt better just saying the words.

"How true does this feel on a scale of zero to ten?"

Mark paused, reassessing his answer. "Five."

"Let's try the tappers." Dr. Kendrick reached on the table and gripped her controller.

Mark picked up the black oval-shaped pulsers on the coffee table and clutched one in each hand.

Dr. Kendrick nodded. "Go with that."

The vibrations alternated in his hands at different speeds as memories ran wild.

At some point, the doctor stopped. "Breath. Open up."

"I want to be in control like I used to be."

"Go with that." She adjusted a knob on her controller. The speed of the vibrations decreased. In a few moments, she lowered her hand. "Okay. Breath."

The pressure on his chest lightened. The anxiety faded. He was at his job, arresting drug dealers. Owen appeared, encouraging him. "I was a skilled agent. I was never frightened of anything."

"Go with that."

With each twenty-second mini segment, time seemed to pass quicker.

"I want Hailey and my kids to see me as a protector…"

Dr. Kendrick's monitor clicked. "Breath."

Mark opened his eyes. The exercise was getting easier.

"Open up."

"I'm crying…and angry."

"Go with angry."

More images brought more emotions. Visiting Colleen in prison, putting her happiness before Hailey's. Arguing with Hailey the morning of the fire. Lying to Hailey about his casework. Keeping Colleen's secret. Hurrying out the front door as Hailey shouted at him.

Waking up in the burn unit, begging David to kill him. His body wrapped in sterile white bandages. The sharp, stinging pain that never ended.

"Breath."

Mark inhaled.

"Open up."

"I'm terrified I won't be able to hug my family—to tell them I love them. I need to be a better father and husband."

"Bring up the original image again." Dr. Kendrick maintained eye contact. Was her voice softer, or was he calmer? "Do you notice any disturbance?"

Mark shook his head. "Not a lot."

"On a scale of zero to ten with zero being no distress and ten being the worst, what number are you holding for these negative emotions?"

"Two."

Dr. Kendrick nodded. "Let's concentrate on your rehab memories."

The images swirled around him. Taking slow steps beside the physical therapist. Walking with a cane. David's visits. Hailey standing inside the apartment when she first arrived in Atlanta. Holding her hand as they walked in the park.

"Breath. Open up."

"I'm a survivor."

"How do you feel?"

Mark concentrated. What was his body saying? Where was the 52K ton weight pushing on him? He exhaled. He could finally breathe. "Better. Freer."

Dr. Kendrick smiled. "That's terrific."

Chapter Thirty-Two

In the reference department at the city library, José stood behind a black-haired woman herding her two young children dribbling apple juice over their picture books.

He hadn't paid too much attention to the local library in Colombia before he dropped out of high school. Times had changed since he and his comrades lingered behind bookshelves with the sole purpose of selling drugs.

When the family in front of him left, he stepped forward to the middle-aged librarian with a small ladybug tattoo on her wrist. "Excuse me. How do I reserve a *computadora*—a computer to do research?"

The woman picked up a clipboard and pointed to the computer area. "Cubicle number five is available for another forty minutes. Do you have your library card?"

José frowned. He needed a library card to use a computer? "No, ma'am."

She scribbled some letters and numbers on a small piece of paper. "Here's a temporary log-in slip with the information you'll need. Trash it when you're finished." She pointed to the empty computer stall. "I'll be right here if you have any questions."

He dipped his head in appreciation. "*Gracias*—" *Uh-uh. You aren't in Colombia.* "Thank you."

With his shoulders back, he strode to the computer.

His English wasn't as polished as Manuel's, but the librarian hadn't seemed to notice when he fumbled over a few words.

José muffled a cough and glanced at the wall clock. Forty-five minutes before the next driver arrived. Better hurry.

Sliding onto a chair at the desk, he clicked on the mouse, and the screen brightened. He tapped his fingers as the computer fan churned.

He entered the log-in information the librarian had handed him.

José reached into his pocket and removed the pages he'd torn from Hailey Langley's address book. His fingers clicked across the keyboard. Tom Parker, Chicago, Illinois.

Minutes ticked by as he read the man's obituary followed by several newspaper articles reporting on a shootout and kidnapping of a five-year-old girl. *Must have been Manuel's kid.*

Next, he searched two women who once had the same address in Fairfax, Virginia. Mark Langley, the snitch's dead husband, was associated with their names. Were they sisters? Two phone calls could confirm whether his target was at either location.

Eyeing the computer clock, José typed the last name. Bruce Hanover.

Several medical journal articles authored by a Dr. Bruce Hanover showed up on the search-engine results. The doctor once worked in Austin, Texas before he moved to Georgia. *A researcher. Interesting.* When Manuel lived in the US, he funneled monies to a doctor in Texas for Euphoria research.

José licked his lips.

SCA headquarters was in Austin, Texas. Hanover might've worked with Hailey.

José cleared his search engine history, logged off the computer, and patted the handgun in his pocket. Elderly people were easier to intimidate. Perhaps he could persuade Dr. Hanover to make some calls and find out where the bitch was staying.

****

"How's my brother?"

Hailey put Laura on speaker and picked up a guitar pick from the living room carpet. "Doing better. He's getting a biopsy in two days to check his scars."

"Do you think the salve is really a miracle cream?"

"Yes. I see improvement in his scars every day."

"If the salve works the way you hope, pharmaceutical companies will be beating down your door."

Hailey skimmed the room for tripping hazards and tucked the video cables behind the game console. "I'm afraid to get my hopes up. I'm just happy to see him every day."

"Has Mark had any more episodes? You know…with his PTSD?"

"Not since the other day. He had another EMDR session this morning."

"Is the therapy working?"

"I think so." Hailey smiled, recalling how Mark picked her up and twirled her after his first session. "Although nothing's one hundred percent."

"We're due for some good news. How come I haven't heard of this therapy before?"

"EMDR is rather new. It has only been around since the late 80s."

"And he's okay doing this?" Laura sounded as skeptical as Mark's parents.

"At first, he resisted, but now he's noticing improvements." Hailey stacked bowls in the dishwasher and added detergent. "He might need a few more sessions until we know more. Some people need a dozen."

"I hope he continues to see progress."

"Me, too." Hailey carried the phone into the laundry room behind the kitchen.

"Did you talk to Mark's therapists about what he'll need once he comes home?"

"Yes. We've gone over the modifications. David offered to install grab bars in the bathroom so Mark can get in and out of the shower. I need to remove the tripping hazards, like the throw rugs in the kitchen and bathrooms. The case manager will talk to us again before Mark comes home. He has a whole team assigned—doctors, nurses, PTs, OTs, counselors, and social workers."

"I never realized how many people were involved in his care."

"I didn't either. The nutritionist even gave me a food list for Mark's diet."

"Home-cooked meals taste way better than fast food any day."

"I don't know if Mark would agree." Hailey laughed. "Enough about Mark and me. Are Ethan and Anna behaving?"

"Oh, yes. They even help with chores. That reminds me. Someone called asking for you."

Hailey folded towels from the compact dryer. "Who would call your house looking for me?"

"I don't know. He called on the landline while Kayla was vacuuming. She told him you weren't here."

"Did he give his name?"

"No. I was upstairs talking to David on my cell. The kids usually don't pick up if they don't recognize a number, but Kayla said the phone kept ringing."

Hailey arched an eyebrow. "That's strange. Maybe the secretary from school found your info in the emergency contact forms. I haven't been home to get any back-to-school information. Classes are starting soon."

"Yeah, my kids go back in three weeks. I'm not ready for the summer to end." A click interrupted the connection. "Hey, Mom's calling. I'll talk to you later."

"Thanks for everything, Laura. Tell the kids Mark and I will call tonight."

When Hailey ended the call, she put the towels in the bathroom and looped the key lanyard around her neck. Time for a quick run in the park before Mark returned.

Grabbing her cell phone, she skimmed a new email from the university detailing instructions for the fall semester. The middle- and high-school schedules would come out any day, too. She groaned. The summer flew by too fast.

She scrolled down to the next email and read Brooklyn's message:

Sure, I can meet with you and Mark about your intimacy concerns.

Hailey and Mark's heart-to-heart conversation the previous night had been replaying in her mind. She'd assumed he hadn't the desire or energy to be intimate, but now he gave a different vibe. When the time came to make love, she'd need to be mindful of his mobility and pain and be careful of his body image, needs, and feelings. Communication was essential.

Her cell chimed an incoming call with Colleen's name on the screen.

Hailey hit speaker while she slipped her feet into the sneakers. "Colleen, this is a surprise. How are you?" She leaned over and tied the laces.

"Terrible. I'm sorry to bother you, but Joyce is busy taking care of her father, and I have no one else to talk to."

Hailey slid a chair from the kitchen table and sat. "What's wrong?"

"Rose has been a wreck. She refuses to eat or play outside. She's convinced Manuel's coming to take her."

"She's still having issues?"

"Yes. She insists he's following her."

"Oh, the poor child."

Colleen sighed. "Her imagination's on overdrive. She balks when we go anywhere."

"Is she still seeing a psychologist?"

"Yes. Three times a week. The doctor thinks Rose is traumatized from seeing Manuel die."

Would a psychologist try EMDR on a child? If the therapy made a difference in Mark, it might help Rose. "I hope you're sitting down, because I'm going to tell you something that will knock you off your feet."

After she told Colleen about finding Mark, Hailey explained the EMDR sessions. "The therapy might help Rose, also."

"It might. Thank you." Colleen's voice quivered. "It couldn't have been easy to tell me about Mark. I'm sorry for all the strain I've caused you and your family."

Six months ago, Hailey wouldn't have believed her.

"You're not to blame. Focus on helping Rose get better."

"Your suggestion makes sense. I'll ask her doctor."

"Here's another idea. Rose likes to draw. Have her draw a picture of the man from her dreams. It might help her process what's happening in her memory."

A loud sniffle came across the connection. "At this point I'll try anything."

Chapter Thirty-Three

Mark twisted the single red rose in his hand that he'd bought from a street vendor, and he opened the apartment door.

The adage was true. You didn't appreciate something until you lost it.

The place didn't feel like his home in Virginia. No backpacks strewn about the room. No sneakers kicked under the end table. No foul-smelling basketball clothes tossed into a corner or dance bag open by the sofa. No bickering. He missed it all, especially Anna and Ethan's laughter.

Thank God, Hailey was here. At least for two more weeks. *Better make the most of the time we have together.*

"You're home early." Hailey called from the kitchen as she diced mushrooms on a cutting board. "Hope you're hungry."

"Ravenous. What's for lunch?"

"A leafy green salad topped with roasted rosemary chicken."

Another salad. "Sounds delicious."

Grinning, he nudged the rose stem between his lips and leaned against the table.

Hailey divvied shredded cheese onto two plates and looked his direction. "What are you doing?"

Mark stepped toward her, resting his right hand on

her lower back. With his other hand, he removed the rose from his lips and tossed it onto the table. Extending his left arm in the air, he offered his best sexy Spanish accent. "I want to tango."

With a lighthearted laugh, she assumed the dance position.

His leg throbbed with a dull ache as he led her across the floor, but the pain was worth it.

For several minutes, Mark and Hailey fumbled through the dance movements. Unable to resist any longer, he leaned over, his tongue teasing hers in a private tango.

Hailey surrendered with her own long, drugging kiss and slowly pulled back. "You're a good dancer."

She was a good liar. He'd play along. "I know."

"And an exceptional kisser." She pecked a kiss on his lips. "How did everything go today?"

Mark's body stirred at Hailey's flowery perfume. His pulse raced just looking at her smile. "Fine. Dr. Kendrick said the session went well, too."

"Feel any different?"

Where should he begin? "I don't feel as frustrated or uptight."

"You seem happy."

Was that the feeling? "I guess for the first time in a long time, I am."

"I'm proud of you."

He'd missed her tender embraces, the encouragement. "You being here has made all the difference. I was a fool to think I could do this without you."

She gazed at him with a longing that rocked him inside. "Are you hungry?"

"Starved."

Hailey picked up the dinner plates overflowing with garden greens and carried them to the table. "Let's eat while we talk."

He extended his arms. "Can I help? Food prep is one of my short-term therapy goals."

"You can be my sous chef." She pointed to a plate of whole-wheat bread. "Mind getting the bread?"

Mark set the plate onto the table and pulled out her chair.

Once they were seated, Hailey lifted her glass filled with rose-petal water and clinked it against his. "Cheers to us. The tango duo. Now tell me about your day."

When he finished recapping his latest EMDR session, he wiped a napkin across his mouth. "I can't explain how it happened, but the belt squeezing my chest is gone."

Flecks of soft amber danced in her eyes as she studied him. Like she was looking into his soul. "This is wonderful news."

"I wish I'd done the sessions sooner." He stabbed a piece of chicken with his fork. "Afterward, Brooklyn took me to the gym, and we played basketball. Real basketball, not the video game."

"Really?" Hailey's mouth opened. "How did it feel to play again?"

"My dribbling wasn't the best, but I made two baskets." He massaged his bicep. "It was a rough start. Boy, my arms are sore."

"You're doing terrific." She buttered a piece of bread. "Have you talked to your parents?"

"I called them while I waited for the shuttle. Dad's doing better. He sounds more lucid."

"That's great news." She patted his hand.

Hailey's cell phone buzzed.

"That might be the kids." She opened her purse on the end table and fished out the phone. "I'm wrong. It's Luis. He might have news on José." She tapped on the screen and put the call on speaker. "Luis. I'm surprised to hear from you."

"Actually, I called to speak to your husband."

"Mark?" Hailey's eyes narrowed. "He's right here."

Mark lowered his glass. "Hi, Luis."

"*Buenos días.* Agent Erik Bruno called. I identified Selena in the photos you sent him. Erik invited me to join the rescue mission. He said you suggested I go along. *Gracias, señor.* The State Department is fast-tracking approval so I can participate."

Mark glanced at Hailey. Her expression was priceless. Erik had made a smart decision including Luis. Without his presence, Selena wouldn't trust the good guys. "I'm glad plans are coming together. I can't wait for you to bring her home."

"Me, too." Luis choked.

Tears filled Hailey's eyes. "Please keep us posted."

"I will, s*eñora.* I owe you both."

Hailey wiped her cheek. "Any news on José?"

"Not yet. He didn't show up for Manuel's funeral. I'm sure he's hiding at his camp, waiting for events to die down. I'll text if I hear anything before I leave." Luis disconnected the call.

Worry lines etched on Hailey's brow as she slowly scratched her arm.

Mark stood and carried his dishes to the sink. José's whereabouts still bothered her. She needed a distraction. "Feel like losing in a game of bowling?"

Hailey laughed. "Aren't we confident? Go ahead and set up the game. I'll wipe down the counters and help with your stretches before we play. Oh, and we should also call Anna and Ethan before we bowl."

In two hours, Mark collapsed onto the sofa. "That's three games for me. One for you." His legs behaved like wobbly noodles, but his balance and reaction times had improved.

Hailey slumped next to him. "I'm totally worn out."

Mark reached over the armrest and picked up his guitar, resting it on his leg. "Relax a minute. I have a surprise for you." He tuned the low E string and tweaked the next string.

"What are you doing?"

He adjusted another string. "Be patient."

When he finished tuning, he strummed a chord. *Here goes nothing.*

Mark shut his eyes. Soon his fingers skated along their own path, skipping over frets, playing the intro he'd composed years ago in high school. Gaining confidence, he began singing, pledging his love to his soulmate who refused to give up on him.

His tremulous voice steadied into a solid mellow tone during the refrain. The words flowed effortlessly from his soul. After Mark strummed the last chord, he waited a long moment before he opened his eyes.

Tears rolled down Hailey's cheeks.

She leaned forward and kissed him so tenderly dizziness swept over him.

"That…was the most amazing song I've ever heard. Why didn't you tell me you could play—and sing?"

He lowered the guitar onto the floor. "It's nothing. I played a little in high school, but I wasn't that good.

When Brooklyn suggested plucking strings to simulate pulling a gun trigger, I decided to try the guitar again."

Hailey wiped her nose with the back of her hand. "That was the best gift you've ever given me. Thank you."

She liked it. His hard work paid off in dividends. "You're welcome."

"Can you sing it again? Please?"

Mark flexed his fingers. "My hands are sore. How about tomorrow?"

She glanced at her watch. "Oh my. I didn't realize the time. I'll get the salve so we can get ready for bed."

"Sounds good. Skipping my afternoon nap two days in a row is taking its toll." He positioned a pillow on the sofa's side arm. "Mind putting on the salve out here again?"

Hailey twirled a finger in his hair. "Not at all. I'll put on pajamas and get the salve." She stood and walked toward the bedroom.

Yawning with a sound of a roaring grizzly bear, Mark removed his pressure garments and facemask. He'd rest his eyes for a few minutes...

"Mark?"

He blinked, staring at the shadows settling in the room.

Hailey stood over him, holding the tin in her hand.

He rubbed his eyes. "What time is it?"

"Nine o'clock. You were sleeping so soundly; I didn't want to wake you." She switched on the lamp and unscrewed the tin.

With slow strokes, she spread the salve across his cheek, her warm fingers a stark contrast to the cold ointment. "The scars flatten more each day."

Blood rushed to his manhood. "Your touch feels nice."

"You can feel my fingers on your scars?"

"Yeah. I guess I can."

She leaned back. "Is it a dull sensation or more intense?"

What did he feel? "More than dull." He fingered his cheeks and neck. "I feel a little sensation all over."

Hailey fingered a tuft of his tousled hair. "That's a promising sign."

He scratched his calf muscle and slid his leg over the seat cushion. "My leg's still a mangled mess."

"Your legs might take longer to heal since the burn penetrated deep into your dermis. How's the pain?"

"The throbbing isn't as sharp, but the itch on my feet and legs is driving me crazy."

Hailey bent over and glided her hand over his abdomen, her loose-fitting nightshirt drooping over his bare skin. "Bruce is curious if the salve will regenerate hair follicles and sweat glands."

Mark breathed deeply as her creamy-colored breasts jiggled on top of him. Damn. What a view. If his sweat glands were working, he'd be drenched in perspiration.

He lifted his hand and teased a finger down her cleavage. He could easily spend the night caressing her.

Her cheeks reddened. "You're distracting me. Let me finish so we can go to sleep." She rubbed salve over his abdomen and continued lower. When she reached his engorged manhood, she blushed a deep crimson, but didn't say anything.

Her silence stirred his arousal even more. Was his wife going to ignore the elephant in the room? Dammit. He'd been a fool to declare his groin area was off-limits.

Should he be blunt and tell her that all areas needed attention?

She skipped to his lower extremities. "New skin is forming everywhere. Did Bruce advise you to continue wearing your mask?"

"Yes. He wants to see the biopsy results before I pitch any pressure garments."

Hailey stroked a keloid scar on his chest and met his gaze. "Does this hurt?"

"No. Wherever you touch feels nice." Mark covered his hand over her fingers as she traced the new skin closing around the bumpy scars. If he moved, the pleasure might end. "Remember the last time we made love?"

She whispered, "The night before the fire."

"After you showered, you crawled in bed, smelling like honeysuckle. You looked so sexy... You still do."

She wiped her eyes. "I remember everything about that night."

"Honey, don't cry." Mark brushed a tear from Hailey's cheek. "The memories of you and the kids pulled me through when I wanted to give up. I thought of you every day." God, how could he erase the pain he caused? He touched her soft lips. "I want to make love to you."

She leaned back. "You said you weren't ready."

A fresh confidence spread through him. Mark smiled, unable to ignore the aching bulge between his legs. "That was before. Now I'm ready."

****

Hailey gulped at the directness in his husky voice.

Am I ready? Intimacy was an important step in rebuilding their marriage. Would she hurt him as she moved on top of him? Would he cry out if she caressed him where his skin was healing?

Don't rationalize the situation. He wants you. Figure out everything as you go along.

Mark's finger traced under her chin. "If you don't want to—"

"Oh, I want to. There's never been a time when I didn't want to make love to you. I'm just…nervous." *More nervous than when we first made love.* She inched her mouth closer, letting her next caress linger. "We'll take things slowly, according to what you can do. Tell me if you're in any pain."

"I will." He grinned. "I already talked to my doctor and OT."

"About what?"

He rubbed the rough pad of his thumb over her cheek. "Sex."

"You talked to Brooklyn about sex?"

Mark winked. "It *is* an activity of daily living."

She should've known he'd ask. "Aren't you full of surprises?"

"I try to be."

He cupped her face in his hand and kissed her so fiercely she longed for more. Tonight would be about Mark. His needs. His desires. "Are you sure? I don't want you to get—"

"You're stalling."

"Don't set any expectations—"

He placed a finger on her lips. "If you don't come to the bedroom with me now, I'll undress you right here and make love to you on the floor."

She helped him sit against the cushion. "Okay. But what happens tonight stays between us. I'm not sure how

I feel about Brooklyn, or anyone else, knowing about our sex life."

Mark pulled her chin down and pressed his lips against hers in a hungry kiss. "No one needs to know."

Butterflies fluttered in her stomach. Lovemaking over the past years had felt rushed with their hectic schedules and the kids. Tonight, they had a new opportunity to slow down and savor the experience.

Mark rose to his feet and wrapped his arm around her. As he guided her into the bedroom, his hand slid to her derriere. "Lead the way."

Hailey giggled. She'd missed his feisty playfulness. "Why do I feel like we're sneaking off for a secret rendezvous?"

His warm breath brushed against her ear. "The longer you delay, the more aroused I get."

Heat rushed through her. She'd make the evening one to remember.

Chapter Thirty-Four

Dawn crept over the horizon as Mark gazed at his wife sleeping next to him, and he brushed a wisp of stray hair from her cheek. Last night had been perfect.

He stared at the ceiling, unable to stop the tears.

Dear God, thank you.

Hailey had made him feel loved. Worthy. Normal. What had he done to deserve this incredible woman?

Drawing in a deep breath, Hailey turned her head, and her eyelashes fluttered open.

Mark wiped his tears on the bedsheet and planted a tender kiss on her forehead. "Good morning."

A saucy grin spread from ear to ear, and Hailey nestled her sensuous body against him. "Did last night really happen?"

He rested his hands on the curve of her hips and nuzzled his nose against her neck. "I don't think we were dreaming."

She traced a finger across the scant hair on his chest. "In that case let's do it again."

He drank in his wife's smoldering eyes and kissed her sweet swollen lips. His manhood was at full attention. What new way would they share intimacy this morning? His voice rumbled as he pulled her closer. He was the luckiest man alive.

****

Hailey stepped out of the shower and toweled

herself dry. Heated memories from the past twelve hours replayed through her mind. Mark's affectionate caresses had swept away all her reasoning. She'd never imagined sharing intimacy again would reconnect them so quickly.

The covers were pulled over the pillows. Mark usually watched the morning news while he did stretching exercises. After last night's lovemaking, he probably fell asleep in the living room.

She wrapped a towel around herself and cracked open the bedroom door. Her hand covered her mouth as she gazed at Mark on the couch, plucking his guitar.

Brooklyn deserved a lot of praise for suggesting a fun activity to help Mark regain his finger strength. At the rate he was going, he'd be able to shoot his firearm in no time. Would Owen give him another assignment now that Selena's case was almost over?

Hailey's pulse raced. If Mark did return to fieldwork, she'd be a nervous wreck.

She closed the door. She had another hour before the shuttle bus arrived. Plenty of time to cook a hearty breakfast and refuel Mark's energy.

In the closet, she chose a pair of flared slacks and pulled a formfitting top from a hanger. After she dressed, she brushed her hair back into a ponytail. Once the kids started back to school, she'd make a hair appointment to deal with the gray hairs.

Her cell rang.

When Colleen's name appeared on the screen, Hailey tapped the phone. "Hello?"

"It's not Manuel." Colleen's words ran together as one.

"Pardon?"

"It's José."

Hailey shook her head. "What are you talking about?"

"Rose drew a picture of the man who's been spooking her. It's José."

Hailey collapsed onto the bed. "Has Rose ever met José?"

"No. Manuel didn't allow his father near her, but they look alike. He must've followed us. I already notified the police, but I wanted you to know."

"What are you going to do?"

"I'm leaving town. I need to protect my little girl from that deranged psychopath!" Colleen's taut voice echoed in Hailey's ear as the call disconnected.

Hailey squeezed her trembling hands. *José's here in the US?* Would he be desperate enough to go after her and Colleen?

Her stomach hardened. José had the resources to move around.

She stretched her fingers. The joint pain and brain fog had finally diminished from when José had poisoned Hailey last spring. He might blame her and Colleen for Manuel's death. And for burning the crops. They—and Rose—would be his targets.

The Colombian authorities had been searching for José for three weeks. Rose's nightmares began two weeks ago. The timeline fit. He could've been following Rose in Boston this whole time.

Hair prickled on Hailey's head as the room began spinning. *Oh my God, José could be anywhere. He could be here. He could find Mark.*

I have to leave.

She ran to the window and closed the blinds.

Fleeing was the only way to keep José away from

her husband, from finding out he was alive. Mark had suffered too much already. Plus, she couldn't risk harming Bruce.

She wheeled her suitcase from the closet and heaved it onto the bed. Back and forth, she dashed around the room, gathering her clothes.

"What's going on?" Mark stood in the doorway, panic filling his gravelly voice.

She jumped. "Shit! You scared me!"

He marched across the room and pointed at the suitcase. "Where are you going?"

She rushed past him into the bathroom, collecting her hairbrush and toiletries from the counter. "I have to go."

"What? Why? I thought you were staying another week."

"There's no time to explain."

"Did I do something?"

Hailey massaged her temple. "No. Of course not."

"Then why are you leaving? Are the kids okay?"

She shook her head and let out a deep breath. "Sit down. I'll tell you."

When Hailey told Mark the details of Colleen's conversation, he paced the floor. "We can't jump to conclusions."

"Of course we can!" She stood and zippered the suitcase. "If José's here, he could go after you. Me. The kids." She threaded a hand through her hair. "Oh my God! I have to protect the kids."

Mark lowered his hands onto her shoulders, the pressure reducing her anxiety like a weighted blanket. "Hold on. Even if José's in the US, he doesn't know where the kids are."

"How did he figure out where Colleen and Rose were? No one knew they were staying with Joyce. I just updated their info in my—"

Hailey sank onto the bed and smacked her palm on her forehead. "The address book. I left it out on my desk. All my contacts were in it."

Mark's face tensed. "Call David and ask him to check the study. See if anything looks out of place."

Hailey pulled up her contacts on her cell. "José better not go after our babies."

Rage stormed in Mark's eyes. "Call David."

****

Hailey's voice trembled as she finished relaying her suspicions to David. "José and Manuel look alike. It's logical Rose would think her father was alive. What if José broke into the house and saw my address book?"

David grunted. "That would explain how he found Colleen and Rose's whereabouts so quickly. Maybe Mark's dad wasn't imagining things when he said someone pushed him down the stairs. Give me an hour. I'll drive over to your house and check it out. Can you call Camila? Find out José's weaknesses—what makes him tick."

"I will. Be careful." Hailey ended the call and dropped the phone onto her lap.

Mark set it on the nightstand and wrapped his arms around her. "Don't worry. Everything's going to be okay."

She pulled away. "How can you say that? There's no guarantee. Not with that madman on the loose."

"Honey, we can figure this out—together."

He made a good point. They were both trained agents. "Should we warn Laura?"

Mark shook his head. "Not yet. Wait until David calls. If José broke into our house, you're better off staying here."

"I won't put you and Bruce in danger."

"José doesn't know I'm alive, and he doesn't know Bruce."

"What if you're wrong? Bruce once worked for Manuel."

"That was six years ago. Besides, José didn't hire Bruce. Manuel did. José has no reason to come. Even if he does, we have the upper hand. We'll catch him off guard." Mark's lips pressed into a thin line. "We need to work as a team. Trust each other. No more taking off."

"Okay, I'll stay—at least until I hear back from David." She opened the phone's contacts. "I better call Camila."

An hour later, David called. "You could be right. The address book is on your desk."

Hailey increased the phone's volume and sat beside Mark on the bed. "And?"

"Some pages are torn out."

A painful lump rose in her throat. "Which ones?"

"Looks like the letter R—"

Hailey gripped the phone. "Rogers. I added Colleen and Rose's name under Joyce's address. That's how José found them. Are there any other pages missing?"

"I'll start from the beginning." The ruffle of pages echoed through the connection. "Ah…the letter B is ripped out."

"Mark's sister. I'll call Francine and warn her."

"Dammit!" David tacked on a string of colorful curse words.

"What?"

"He tore out Laura's page, too."

Hailey's hand covered her mouth. "Oh my God! A man called Laura's house looking for me."

Mark blinked hard. "When?"

"I'm not sure. Yesterday or the day before. Kayla told him I wasn't there." Hailey leapt to her feet and grabbed her purse. "I have to get Anna and Ethan."

Mark stood. "I'm coming with you."

"No. Both of you, stay where you are." David's directive stifled Hailey's natural inclination to rebel against orders. "If José's only looking for Hailey, Laura's daughter might've bought us some time. I'll protect Ethan and Anna. Call Laura. Have her and the kids pack some clothes. Laura's kids should come, too. I have a friend who owns a cabin in the Poconos. We'll hide there while the authorities look for José."

Hailey shook her head. "I want to see my kids—"

"Hailey, listen to me. Mark's not strong enough to face José alone." More pages ruffled through the connection as David spoke. "Oh, shit. He has Bruce's address, too."

His words hit her like a gut punch. "Are you sure?"

"The page for H is missing. José may try to contact your doctor friend, too. Bruce and Mark can't fight him alone. You need to stay."

David was right. Mark and Bruce would never be able to overtake José. "But the kids—"

"Will be fine." David's voice softened. "I'll guard them with my life. I swear. We'll let them think it's another vacation."

Hailey closed her eyes a moment. No one was more competent than David. He loved her kids like they were his own. She turned to Mark.

A sad resignation filled his eyes. "Let him do it."

David cleared his throat. "I suggest you both start thinking like agents again. I know you're working through your own battles, but get prepared just in case."

Hailey nodded. "We can handle things here."

"I know you can. Laura and I will hold down the fort. I'll call when we arrive, but don't text specifics in case José gets access to our phones. Talk in code. I'll ask my supervisor to contact the other agencies and pool our resources in the search. I'm sure Owen will assign some agents. Hailey, I have to notify Stefan."

She frowned. "He won't be pleased that I'm involved."

"He'll get over it. If José's in the country, we must work together to apprehend him. Does your building have security?"

Mark rubbed his neck. "Yes. There are always two guards."

"Good. I'll circulate José's picture with them and ask the Atlanta police to be on the lookout. I'll put twenty-four-hour surveillance on Mark's parents and his sister's family in Arizona. Text me Colleen's number. I'll assign her security, too."

Hailey exhaled. At least they had a plan. "I'll call Laura. How can we ever thank you?"

"Not necessary. Don't worry. José's in our jurisdiction now. We're going to nail this son-of-a-bitch's ass into the ground."

****

A gray-haired man wearing a frayed beanie wheeled a battered shopping cart in front of the bench where José sat. "Hey, buddy. Can you spare some change?" The beggar held out his grubby hand. His filthy coat reeked of smoke and booze, and dried spittle streaked his straggly beard.

José wrinkled his nose and slid farther away on the bench. If a scrounger dared accost him in Colombia, José would've beaten him up and thrown him to the dogs. "No, you lazy ass. Get off the fucking bench."

The man swept his long hair from his face, wiped his nose across his coat sleeve, and hobbled down the street.

A coughing fit overtook José, and he hacked up more bloody phlegm. He leaned back, massaging his chest. He'd see the doctor when he flew home. Who could he designate to manage his rebels? Manuel was no longer an option.

I still can't believe Manuel's dead... He disappointed me in so many ways.

What had the Colombian government done with the cocaine lab in the mountains? The insurgents could set up another lab—one without the Euphoria plant. Manuel had been foolish to spend his resources searching for a drug with lower overhead.

José walked toward the two-story brick building across the street where Dr. Bruce Hanover worked. Shuttles had been picking up and dropping off people and packages throughout the day.

The firearm weighed heavily in his pocket. *My options are running out.* Once he identified Dr. Hanover, José would follow him to his residence and force the doctor to track down Hailey Langley's location.

He hacked again, ignoring the disconcerted stares as people scurried past.

Chapter Thirty-Five

Hailey scanned the lobby, holding the Glock she'd bought from a friend of one of the PMI researchers. "Okay, it's clear." She walked beside her husband into the elevator cart.

Mark waved to the receptionist and leaned over to Hailey. "Make sure no one's hiding in the bushes."

She peered through the opening as the doors closed. So many people to keep track of. "What's that woman's name again?"

"Desiree. You should remember it by now."

Hmpf. "I'm too stressed to remember everyone's name. How long has she worked here?"

"Six years." Mark frowned. "Come on, Hailey. You're being paranoid. She's not working with José."

"We don't know that. José could be working with anyone. He could be here right now."

"It's been three days. José's probably not in the country anymore. Even if he were, David has it covered. He has three agencies searching for the man. An undercover agent is posted in the building, and one is outside across the street." Mark yawned. "You were restless last night."

Guilt gnawed at her like a rat. She shouldn't have told Mark the grisly details of her latest nightmare where José killed him. He had enough going on.

The doors chimed and opened.

Hailey raised her firearm and peered into the hallway. "I'm glad Bruce agreed to stay in the apartment across the hall instead of at his house. Makes protecting both of you much easier. Except now Bruce is literally here all day." She stepped out of the cart and raised her thumb. "All clear."

As they walked down the hall, Mark waved to the tall custodian wheeling a cart.

She lowered her voice. "Do you recognize him?"

"Ronnie's been here since I came. Don't go overboard securing the place. This research complex has its own tight security." Mark bent and rubbed his calf muscle.

"Is your leg still sore from the biopsy?"

"A little."

"Should you tell Bruce?"

"It's only been two days. I'll give it more time." He scrubbed the long whiskers poking out under his burn mask. "It's supposed to rain this afternoon. Why don't we stay inside and nap together after lunch?" Humor coated Mark's sly voice.

Changing the subject. Very smooth move. "Depends. Do you want to sleep or snuggle?"

He brushed a finger across her cheek. "I want to cuddle next to my sexy shadow and then nap."

Hailey smiled at his playful tease. "I'm not your shadow. I'm your bodyguard."

At the apartment, Mark inserted his card key and opened the door. "You're too attractive to be a bodyguard, but you can safeguard my body any day."

His earthy scent calmed her anxieties. "Just be glad this bodyguard is enamored with you. My only goal right now is to keep you and Bruce safe." She massaged her neck. They couldn't keep living like this—fearful that José was waiting at every corner. She blocked the entrance with her hand. "Wait while I check the place."

Mark rolled his eyes. "You're taking this safety escort to extreme measures. I was an agent, too, you know."

"It's better to be careful." If José were inside the small apartment, he wouldn't have many places to hide. She searched the rooms, tilted her head, and listened. The ear implant registered the soft hum of the refrigerator and the street traffic below. "Okay, we're clear."

Mark unzipped his sweatshirt and directed her to the kitchen table. "Please, sit down and rest. I'll make lunch today."

"Thanks." She slid onto a chair and set her phone on the table. "I wish you'd carry a gun."

He frowned. "How can I fire a gun when I can't squeeze the trigger? I'd be a hazard."

Mark put up a confident front, but stress weighed on him, too. He checked in with David three times a day and more often with Ethan and Anna.

"During your aquatic therapy, Camila finally returned my call. She said the herbicide sprays used for the coca plants have affected José's health and mental processes. She seemed genuinely upset over everything that's happened."

"I wouldn't trust her. José and Camila have been married for fifty years. There has to be some kind of loyalty in their relationship."

"I disagree. Camila lived a sad life with him. She spent her days managing an orphanage while José trained revolutionaries. Manuel was her one joy. She's clinging to him through Rose."

"At least the security guards David posted in Boston will protect Rose and Colleen." Mark poured two glasses of rose water and handed her one. "What did you decide about taking a nap this afternoon?"

"I'd love to, but first let me check if Bruce needs my help."

"Bruce will be fine."

"I'm worried about him." Hailey drank her water. "He works long days. Have you noticed the dark bags under his eyes? He's got to cut back on his hours."

"Age is catching up with him."

"He takes twice as long to do his tasks. I don't like seeing him slow down."

"I understand—especially now that my dad's health is declining."

"More reason to protect you both." She finished drinking her water. "After lunch, I'll review the camera footage in the security office with the agent Owen assigned. We should rethink David's suggestion to use me as bait. Draw José out in the open—"

"Absolutely not! You are not putting yourself at risk. The authorities are going to find him." He kissed her forehead, his shaggy beard tickling her cheek. "What would you like for lunch?"

"A garden salad's fine."

Mark scowled. "How about a sandwich? I feel like I'm on a diet with all the salads we've been eating."

Hailey chuckled. "A sandwich is perfect. I'll check in with David while you prepare lunch." She turned on her cell and began texting.

—*Having fun with Laura and the kids?*—

David's reply chimed.

—*No time for fun*—

Frowning, Hailey messaged back.

—*What's going on?*—

—*Watching 6 people isn't easy. Very stressful. Don't say anything to Mark.*—

Her fingers skated across the keypad.

—*Do u need my help?*—

An itch spread under her forearm. Perhaps this commitment was too much on David. If Ethan and Anna weren't cooperating, she'd have a stern talk with them.

Mark set a bowl of red grapes on the table. "What's going on with David?"

She stopped scratching. "Nothing."

His gaze lingered on her arm. "Why are you scowling?"

Hailey nibbled on a grape. "No reason. Maybe I am a little tired."

"Aha! You *do* need a nap." Mark winked and passed her a plate with a turkey sandwich on rye bread and sliced cucumbers.

"Honey, this looks scrumptious."

"Sorry it's not any fancier." He sat and opened his napkin. "Our roles may switch once I come home."

Home. Her stomach fluttered. "Don't worry about working when you come home."

"I have to work somewhere. I don't know if Owen can keep me on a desk job forever." He bit into his sandwich. "Actually, I kind of like cooking."

She laughed. Where had he been the past sixteen years? "I'd be happy to take turns with meals. Anna will want to be part of the rotation, too, though I doubt Ethan will be interested."

"You never know. Maybe I can teach him a thing or two." He ate a grape. "One of the first things I plan to do when I get home is play basketball with Ethan and Anna. I lost a whole year with them."

Hailey's cell chimed again.

She glanced at the screen. "Bruce doesn't need my help this afternoon, but he would like to see us later today. He has the biopsy report on your leg."

Mark groaned. "It must be bad news if he didn't text the results."

Her thoughts exactly. "Keep positive. Whatever happens, we'll deal with it together."

****

José prowled in an alley behind a bistro and pulled out a crumpled paper bag from the dumpster. Swatting flies, he smeared food remnants over his pants. Stains on his clothing would blend in with homeless people on the street. His lip curled as he adjusted the tattered ball cap on his head. The drunk down the block probably hadn't realized it was missing from his cart.

At the rumble of thunder, José glanced at the dark sky. Another police car drove down the street. Fourth patrol check since the morning. The couple inside the sedan parked near the alley hadn't gotten out all day. Undercover cops?

Stop being paranoid. No one knows you're here.

He pulled his burner phone from his pocket, typed in a phone number, and waited.

"Posterity Medical Innovations. How may I help you?" A woman with a singsong voice answered the call.

José contrived a cheery voice. "Yes, is Dr. Bruce Hanover available?"

"May I ask who's calling?"

"This is Dr. Asting from Indianapolis." Three days José had waited for the elusive doctor to exit the building. Desperation called for chicanery to smoke him out.

"Hold on while I transfer you."

The connection clicked and began to ring.

José hung up. Tugging the cap lower on his head, he joined a group of pedestrians at the crosswalk and walked to the side of the building where tall bushes provided cover.

Bruce Hanover's inside.

Now he'd wait.

****

"We're late." Mark patted Hailey's shapely butt as they strolled down the corridor to Bruce's lab. "Our afternoon snuggle session wore me out."

She grinned. "Even with a nap afterward?"

No amount of sleep could revitalize him that fast. "I could've slept longer, but Bruce is going to wonder what we've been up to."

Hailey's cheeks reddened under the hallway's bright fluorescent lights. "I think he can figure it out."

The door was ajar, but Mark tapped lightly on the doorjamb. "Hi, Bruce. You wanted to see us?" He gave a quick wave to the doctor typing on the computer and followed Hailey into the room. The trace of antiseptic in the air had the same sterile smell as the burn center.

Standing, Bruce walked to the counter. "I have your biopsy results, Mark. Histology sent me slides this afternoon. I'll put them on the screen."

After Bruce powered on the microscope and connected the monitor, he looked in the eyepiece and moved a built-in black pointer over the image. "This is taken from your left leg where you've been noticing issues. Check out this area right here."

Mark squinted at the pink fingerlike loops tunneling across the image. He might as well have been back in high school biology again. "All I see is a pink smudge with loops and big purple dots."

Hailey chortled. "Oh, honey. There's more going on in this picture than a smudge." She nodded at Bruce. "Go ahead. Tell him."

Bruce pointed at the screen, tracing the stained dark-purple smudges at the rounded ends of each loop. "This lighter-colored area here is what I'm focused on. The dermal papillae."

Even the word—papillae—sounded grim. Whatever the diagnosis, he'd get through it. Mark swallowed his fear. "What are dermal papillae?"

Bruce lowered his wire-rimmed glasses. "Without getting too technical, they're specialized cells at the base of hair follicles."

Mark tilted his head. "But I don't have hair on my legs anymore."

Bruce beamed. "You will soon."

When the words sank in, Mark dropped his jaw. "I'm going to have hair again?"

"Yes!" Hailey's eyes shimmered like sunshine on the ocean. "On your head. Arms. Legs. Chest… Everywhere."

"There's more." Bruce pointed to another section on the screen. "These clear sections are new sweat glands. They're on all the slides. Your dermis is regenerating, Mark. Your sebaceous glands, the blood vessels—"

His skin was growing back. "Oh my God! Yes!" Mark wrapped his arms around Hailey and twirled her.

She laughed. "Honey, put me down before you hurt yourself!"

Mark lowered her to the floor. "Bruce, I can't thank you enough." He pointed to the bottle of raw oil on the top shelf. "When you find the chemical composition someday, you can help burn patients everywhere. This is huge!"

"It's bigger than the state of Texas." Bruce collapsed onto his chair. "After fifty years, I finally discovered a beneficial use for *Bixa aparra.*"

Hailey's eyes narrowed. "You mean *ten* years."

Bruce jerked his head. "Pardon?"

"You've only been researching *Bixa aparra* for ten years." She stepped toward Bruce. "You said fifty years."

"Y…y….yes, of course." Bruce's face paled, and he massaged his chest. "I've been working too much. I got mixed up. I meant ten years."

She crossed her arms. "Something's going on. Your mind is as sharp as a scalpel even when you are tired. Fifty years ago, you were in med school—"

Mark stiffened. *Uh-oh.*

"—with my Uncle Henry." Hailey gasped. "You and Uncle Henry researched *Bixa aparra* in med school? Is that how he died?" She rubbed her brow. "I asked you six years ago about rumors of Henry dying from a drug overdose. You wouldn't explain." Scarlet streaks spread up her neck. "How did he die? Tell me!" She swayed, steadying herself against the counter.

"Hailey, are you okay?" Mark led her to a cushioned chair. "Bruce, bring her some water."

"I don't need water, and I don't need to sit. I need the truth." She kicked the chair. "Henry died from Euphoria, didn't he?"

"What? No—" The creases in Bruce's brow muted,

and his coloring faded to a pasty ash gray. Rather than deny the accusation, he sank his head into his palms.

Mark legs hardened like steel. Hailey didn't need to deal with this news on top of everything else going on. "Honey, let's talk about this another time."

"No! Tell me what happened, Bruce. The truth." Her sharp tone demanded an answer.

The doctor raised his head but avoided her gaze. "During med school, my lab group worked on a research project we hoped would catapult our careers. One of my classmates convinced the group to use a plant he'd smuggled in from the Amazon. *Bixa aparra.* He told us stories about how the aborigines used the plant as a recreational drug. After he found a way to extract the drug from the leaves, we pulled straws to see who would test it. Henry got the shortest straw."

She gripped Mark's hand. "He died from the same drug that killed my son?"

Bruce stuttered. "We didn't realize the drug was so potent. I'm sorry."

She recoiled into her chair, tears banking against her eyelids. "How many times is Euphoria going to hurt my family? How could you not tell me? I thought you were my friend."

Bruce's face crumpled. "I am your friend—"

"Stop!" She grabbed the hair on the sides of her head. "You were nice to me because you felt guilty about my uncle's death."

Bruce flinched. "That's not how it was."

Mark stepped beside her. "Honey, hear him out."

Her nose wrinkled. "To think I used to feel sorry for you…always working late into the night. You're nothing but a worn-out scientist chasing fame."

The light in Bruce's eyes dimmed. "Please, let me explain."

"You had fifty years to explain—or ten. Either way, your time's up. How dare you use me to ease your guilt." Rising to her feet, she brushed a tear from her cheek and ran out of the room.

"Hailey, wait!" Mark limped down the hall, needle-like pains shooting up his leg. When he lost sight of his wife, he returned to the lab.

The elderly doctor waited by the door. Deep lines etched the man's face, and his lips quivered. "We need to find her. I have to explain."

Mark needed to explain his part in the deception, too. "Let's split up. I'll check the apartment. Notify security and search downstairs."

Chapter Thirty-Six

Show yourself, Hanover! José paced behind the tall evergreen hedges near PMI's main entrance as lightning flickered overhead. He took off his cap and wrung out the rainwater. When a clap of thunder rattled the ground, he dodged under the roof overhang.

What's taking him so long? He peered through the condensation clouding his watch crystal. 6:20 PM. Bruce Hanover had to exit eventually.

The temperature had dropped since early afternoon, but sweat dripped from his forehead. A shiver ran through his body, and he rubbed his elbows. The damp, earthy scent of the shrubs dominated the air. José coughed until his lungs cramped in a spasm. Weakness and muscle aches drained his energy.

As another torrent of rain hit, he lifted his head to a band of gray clouds. Was exacting revenge on Hailey Langley worth this aggravation?

The front door opened, and a woman stormed out of the building.

José raced from behind the hedgerow to the entrance, grabbing the door handle before it closed.

Turning, he stared at the lady who gave him access. She had brown shoulder-length hair and looked to be middle-aged. Hmm. Something was familiar about her. He rubbed his eyes as she sprinted across the crosswalk and headed downtown.

¡Maldita sea! Hailey Langley had been inside the building the entire time. *Must be working with Dr. Hanover.*

He pulled out his gun. Too much distance. With no purse, she'd be back. Wait and catch her off guard.

José stepped inside the lobby and traced his finger along a wall. Silver pendant lights hung from the atrium's high ceiling. Water cascaded from the top of a ten-foot-high travertine panel fountain. *Impressive and expensive.* Eyeing the security camera above the reception desk, he dodged behind the tropical shrubs growing in an inset on the marble floor.

When an elevator chimed, he scuttled farther back into the shadows. The loud car horns from the street traffic muffled his cough.

Two uniformed men raced off the elevator and disappeared out the main door.

José gripped the cold handgun in his pocket. He'd need it before the night was over. With most of the staff gone, he'd have an easy time to explore and plan his attack. Surprise the bitch before he killed her. Licking his lips, he crept down the stairwell.

****

Through the city streets, Hailey dodged passersby steadying wobbly umbrellas. Wind whipped her face as heavy sheets of rain pummeled the sidewalks. Hot tears mixed with the cold rain, blurring her path as she fled from the horrid truth.

Bruce had deceived her, keeping his dark secret for years, never saying a word. How dare he! His lie was a knife in her heart, and it hurt more than Mendoza stabbing her.

The betrayal felt like a sadness strangling her soul.

Bruce hadn't wanted her friendship. He wanted prestige. His lofty ambition had played a large part in Henry's death.

She choked back a sob. Her uncle's death was a senseless tragedy. Like her son's. Both died too young. Dammit! Euphoria had robbed her again.

Her sneakers skidded on the roadway as she turned a corner and picked up speed. She ran until her legs wobbled like rubber bands. Her lungs burned as she struggled for fresh air. For good measure, she pushed forward a few more blocks until numbness seized every muscle in her body. Slowing, she caught her breath.

With wet clothes clinging to her skin, she hiked back to PMI and waved her key fob in front of the door sensor. The lobby was dark as she passed through. Elevator or stairs? She headed into the stairwell. After the distance she had run, a few more steps wouldn't hurt.

On the second floor, a custodian cart was parked at the far end of the hallway.

Ronnie must be working overtime.

Turning left, Hailey plodded toward the corporate apartments. She unlocked her door and flipped on the light switch. "Mark?"

The bowl of grapes from lunch sat on the table.

"Mark?" Was he hanging out with Bruce? Giving her time to calm down?

Maybe he texted. She patted her wet jeans and fished out the phone from her pocket. The screen was rain-streaked. "Please turn on." Holding her breath, she pressed the power button. When the screen brightened, she exhaled and typed in her password.

David's text was the last message. He'd seemed overwhelmed earlier. Protecting six people was a big responsibility. Strange that Anna and Ethan hadn't mentioned David was stressed.

As she walked past the living room, the rain hammered the window. She leaned against the wall a moment, steadying herself. Any minute, she might collapse from sheer exhaustion.

In the bedroom, she shivered under the wet clothes. Loneliness nipped at her as she kicked off her rain-soaked sneakers and tried to process the day's events swirling through her mind.

Mark, I need you.

She toppled onto the bed as a wave of fresh tears released.

****

Adrenaline pumping in his veins, José shut the doors to the surveillance office and shoved his gun into his pocket. The two security officers hadn't noticed him waiting in the corner when they found their colleague killed in the room. Spilled blood had a satisfying smell.

He lurked through the corridor, testing the locks and peering through small window openings in the doors. After searching the basement and first floor, José stole up the stairs.

Dusk was settling in, but the city street lights illuminated the dark hallway. The overhead signs pointed to more research rooms.

Hmm. He should've searched here first.

José crept beside a custodial cart in front of an office with the door ajar. He gripped his gun and inched closer.

Two men stood near a desk. An older man with white hair on the sides of his head matched the Internet pictures of Dr. Hanover. He looked to be in his mid-seventies. José's age. The other man was younger and thinner with black, coiled hair—maybe in his fifties.

"Doc, I can stay longer if you want me to keep looking for Mark's wife."

"No, Ronnie. It's late. Go home." Dr. Hanover drank from a coffee cup on the desk. "Security called an hour ago. They haven't seen her either."

"I hope she shows up soon. It's pouring buckets out there." Ronnie tucked his shirttail into his jeans. "By the way, are you using some kind of magic potion on Mark?"

"Why do you ask?"

"His skin looks better. I overheard him tell his wife that Euphoria was going to cure him."

José stifled a cough. *Mark Langley's alive? And he's using Euphoria? A fire allegedly killed him a year ago. Interesting. Was Euphoria responsible for the man surviving?* Manuel had always insisted it had medicinal properties.

Dr. Hanover yawned. "I can't say too much until the study's over."

"I understand. Can't have other companies stealing your discovery." Ronnie plucked a keychain from his pocket. "Whatever experiment you're doing, Euphoria must be a miracle drug to help Mark."

"The treatment does look promising."

With a half grin, Ronnie rubbed his hands. "Think I can try some for my psoriasis?"

Bruce picked up a rack of test tubes and walked to the back of the room. "I don't have much left—only what's in the other room for Mark. If I make more, you'll be next."

Ronnie replaced a bag in the trash can. "Don't worry, Doc. He needs it more than me. I won't tell anyone about your miracle oil."

José stared at the scaly lesions on his forearm. He raised his gun and kicked open the door. "You'll tell me."

Chapter Thirty-Seven

Mark halted in the bedroom doorway and peered into the darkness where streetlights cast shadows across the room. Hailey lay on the bed, crying.

Thank God!

He rushed to her. "Honey, are you all right?" He switched on the bedside lamp and sat beside her, smoothing his hand over her damp, tangled hair.

"Hold me. Please." Her brittle voice was barely a whisper.

He cradled her against his chest, keeping her safe from the world. "You're soaking wet."

Her teeth chattered. "It's raining outside."

"I'll get your pajamas." He gathered the sleepwear from the top dresser drawer and helped her peel out of her clothes. "Thank God you're okay. Where were you?"

Hailey plucked a tissue from the box on the nightstand and wiped her nose. "Running."

"Outside? At night?"

"I needed to clear my head."

"When you didn't come back, I thought maybe José—" Mark held her against him. "Please don't scare me like that again."

"I'm sorry." She wrinkled her nose. "I smell like a wet dog."

He kissed the top of her head. "I love the way you smell."

She was quiet for a moment. "Did you know about Bruce's secret?"

How could he explain without driving her away again? "It wasn't my place to say anything. We didn't want to upset you. I found out six years ago—when you were in a coma. There was never a good time to tell you."

She rubbed her eyes. "It's not your battle. I'm just…"

"Hurt?"

"I've known Bruce since I was seventeen. He was more than a close friend. He was like my father. I trusted him." She pressed deeper into his arms. "I can't help but wonder how much of our relationship was a sham."

Mark tilted his head. "Maybe none."

"How can you say that?"

"You weren't even alive when your uncle died. Yes, Bruce and Henry were close friends, but Bruce could've moved on with his life and never looked back. Instead, he helped you recover when you had no one. He didn't have to do that." Mark traced his thumb over her cold hand. "Look, I'm not telling you how to feel. We can't change the past, but we have control over the present. You're the family that Bruce never had. You call each other during the holidays. Consult with his research. Check in on each other when you're sick. Your uncle would be overjoyed that you and Bruce are there for each other."

Hailey sniffled. "Do you think so?"

"Yes." He kissed away the salt-laden tears weighing down her eyelashes. "I also think your uncle wouldn't want you to be at odds with Bruce right now."

She scratched her hand. "Perhaps you're right."

"Bruce is miserable because he hurt you. All

evening, he's searched the building, trying to find you."

"He did?"

Mark raised his right hand. "I swear. Now he's pacing in his office. We were all worried. Bruce even asked security to search outside. Ronnie stayed to help, too."

"I wondered why his cart was still here."

"He stayed to cheer up Bruce. Which reminds me…I need to text Bruce that you're back." Mark pulled out his cell phone and used the voice command to send a message. Then he brushed away the wisps of damp hair covering her eyes. "Things happen for a reason. If Bruce wasn't in our lives, we wouldn't be here right now. We wouldn't have the Euphoria salve."

She clutched her head. "This is a lot to process."

"I know. What's important is you're all right." Mark gently booped her nose. "I love you—more than anything."

Her lips pursed. "How can you be so calm?"

Mark kissed her. "Why shouldn't I be? I have you. You have me. What else matters?"

"José's out there somewhere. We shouldn't let our guard down."

He slid his hand under her pajama top and brushed a finger over her nipple. "José is the furthest thing from my mind right now. He's probably already back in Colombia."

"Whoa!" Her eyes widened. "Who are you? What have you done with my husband?"

"You make me a better person. I'm relaxed around you." Mark shifted on the bed as his rapidly growing erection pulled against his pants. *Oh, the irony.* He held her tighter, plucking kisses from her lips. When she didn't respond, he dragged his mouth from hers. "Okay, what's bothering you?"

Hailey frowned. "I'm worried about Anna and Ethan. David's having a hard time keeping everyone safe."

"David?" The man could juggle ten cases at one time.

"He's overwhelmed. He asked me not to tell you."

"You're kidding, right?"

"He didn't want to worry you." She grabbed her phone from the nightstand. "Read his texts if you don't believe me."

After Mark put down the phone, he shook his head. *What a sly move.* "Trust me. Don't worry about David. Ethan texted me this evening and said everyone spent the day playing video games." No sense in divulging Owen posted extra agents around the cabin.

Hailey planted her hands to her sides. "Well, judging by David's texts, I think he's sinking fast."

"David's the oldest of eight. He babysat siblings all the time. He's playing you for sympathy—probably so you don't suspect he's enjoying his time with Laura."

Her eyes narrowed. "Are you serious?"

"Yes. He's living the dream right now being with my sister. He's fine."

"I don't know…"

"Remember the other day when we discussed getting protection for everyone? David assigned agents for Colleen and Rose, my parents, and Francine. He could've assigned security detail on Laura and the kids, but he didn't. The only protection he wanted on them was himself—in a secluded cabin in the middle of the Poconos."

Her lips tightened into a fine line. She wasn't buying it. There had to be a way to convince her.

He held out his hand. "Please give me your cell."

She passed it to him. "What are you doing?"

"I'll prove it to you." Mark used the voice activation. "Call David." He put the call on speaker.

David picked up on the third ring. "Hailey? Is everything okay?"

Hailey gave Mark a puzzled look. Had she noticed the soft music playing in the background?

"Yes. I…I…wanted to check on you. You sounded frazzled before."

"Oh yeah." David's voice became deeper, quieter. "It's been crazy here."

"Can I talk to the kids?"

"Uh… They went to bed."

"Is Laura around?"

"We're—uh—I mean she's reading the kids a bedtime story."

Mark held back a laugh. *Yeah, right.* A bedtime story to a twelve-year-old? He didn't need Hailey's ear implant to recognize the smooching going on in the background.

Hailey grinned. "You sound tired. Are you getting any sleep?"

David cleared his throat. "Not too much. I'm on constant alert."

Mark shook his head. With Laura and David making out, the only thing on alert was David's lower half.

A devious glint glimmered in Hailey's eye. "This is more than you bargained for. I'll call Stefan in the morning and ask him to send a replacement so you can get back to your job."

"No, no, no, no." A loud thud sounded through the connection, like a phone dropping. "Everything's under control. Don't bother contacting Stefan."

"Are you sure?"

"Yes. I'll be fine."

Hailey winked at Mark. "Okay. If you change your mind, let me know—"

"Bye." David disconnected the call.

Hailey settled into Mark's arms. "Looks like your friend has a wild side. Did anyone ever tell you that you're a genius, Mr. Langley?"

"Actually, someone did last week." Grinning, he hugged her tighter. "We've had a long day. Will you put on the salve so we can go to sleep? I want to crawl under the sheets and collapse in your arms."

Hailey helped him take off his compression gloves, and then she grabbed the tin on the nightstand. "Oh, crap."

He removed his face mask. "What's wrong?"

"We need more. I emptied the container this morning. I meant to grab another one from the cabinet before we left for therapy. I'll change clothes and run down to the lab."

Mark set the mask on the nightstand. "I'll go with you. My shadow's not leaving me behind again."

****

With her gun secured in her waistband holster, Hailey walked beside Mark to the lab. At the door, she pointed down the hall where light shone underneath Bruce's office door. "Bruce is still here."

"He was pretty upset. Probably wore a rut into the floor by now with all the pacing he's done."

Her stomach twisted. How could she go to sleep

when Bruce was so miserable? Life was too short for grudges. "Honey, do you mind if—"

Mark smiled. "I'll go with you."

"I need to do this alone."

"Okay." He switched on the lab's overhead light. "I'll get the salve from the storage cabinet and wait for you here."

"Thanks." She passed him the gun. "Take this."

Mark stepped backward. "Hailey, I can't shoot—"

"Please. Just in case. I'll be back soon."

"Sure, you will." Mark flashed a knowing grin like he didn't believe her, but he took the firearm and walked into the room.

Pivoting, Hailey hurried down the hall. She tapped on the office door. "Bruce?"

When he didn't answer, she knocked louder. "Bruce? It's Hailey. Can we talk?"

Hmpf. That's strange.

She nudged the door open and stepped inside. The overhead fluorescent lights brightened the room like a sunny day.

"Bruce?"

Where'd he go?

Over the soft hum of the ventilation system, a voice moaned from behind the counter.

"Bruce?" Hailey rushed to the other side of the room, stepping over tossed scientific manuals, broken microscope slides, test tubes, and glassware.

She stared at the mess and shrieked.

Sprawled on the floor was Ronnie, blood oozing from his shirt. Bruce lay face down across Ronnie's legs.

"Oh my God!" She knelt beside the men, wincing as glass shards pierced her knees. Dread tightened around her chest like a shark clamping down on its prey. The custodian's dark-green eyes stared into emptiness as she placed two fingers against his carotid artery. No pulse.

Hailey turned to Bruce and pushed away the broken glass. Rolling him onto his back, she rested a finger on his neck. She choked back a sob. He had a pulse, but it was weak.

"Bruce?" She tapped his cheek. "Come on! Say something."

"Aawh." The grunt was barely audible.

"Bruce! Thank God." Tears welled in her eyes as she wiped blood from his cheek.

He winced. "My hip…I think it's broken."

"Don't move. I'll call for help." She pulled her cell from her pocket and dialed 911 on the keypad. "What happened?"

His eyelids fluttered. "José."

The air deflated from her lungs, and she fell backward.

The operator answered on the first ring. "911. What's your emergency?"

"I…I need an ambulance at Posterity Medical Innovations on 1481 Clint Ave. My co-worker's hurt. He's on the second floor. Room 2104. Turn left off the elevator. And send the police. José Mendoza is inside. There's an APB on him. One man's dead."

Warm fingers grabbed her arm.

She jerked. "Aaaahh!"

Dammit! It was only Bruce. Her nerves were on overdrive.

"Ma'am, are you okay?"

Bruce touched her arm again. He murmured, "José's…looking…for you."

Oh my God. Mark.

"Ma'am, are you in danger?"

Hailey barely registered the operator's voice.

Bruce coughed. "Go. I'll be fine."

"Ma'am?"

"Yes, I'm in danger." Hailey hushed her voice. "There's a psychotic killer on the loose. Send help now. Posterity Medical Innovations on 1481 Clint Ave. Hurry."

Hailey put the phone on speaker and set it on the floor next to Bruce. "Stay on the line. Tell them to notify Stefan. I need to warn Mark."

She crouched behind the countertop, her heartbeat pounding against her chest. Was José hiding in here? No, he would've attacked her by now. She scanned the room. There had to be something she could use for protection. Something sharp. Or heavy enough for her to manage. She opened a drawer below the counter. Vinyl gloves, boxes of them. She slammed it shut and opened another drawer. Dammit! More gloves.

Brushing away tiny glass shards stuck to her slacks, she crawled to Bruce's desk and rummaged through the top drawer, scooping a pen and handful of paper clips into her pocket. If nothing else, she'd have something to poke out José's eyes. She ransacked the side drawers and clutched a utility knife. "Bingo!"

At the door, she scanned the hallway and listened for any sound her hi-tech implant registered. José could be anywhere. Satisfied at the silence, she raced to the lab and slowly opened the door.

Mark faced the window, staring out at the cityscape, oblivious to the bedlam in Bruce's office fifteen yards away.

Thank God, he was safe. "Psst. Mark. We have to get out of here—"

Behind her, a hand clamped her throat like a vise. The cold metal of a gun pressed against her temple. "Don't leave on my account." José's hot, foul-smelling breath pricked the hair on her neck.

Quick on the draw, Mark turned with his gun raised, determination etched on his tense face. "Drop your weapon."

"I don't think so." José pushed his firearm's muzzle harder against Hailey's head. "After I shoot her, you're next."

Hailey slipped into training mode. With her thumb, she moved the slider across the utility knife and extracted the blade. She met Mark's stare and lowered her gaze to her hand. Their eyes locked in a shared understanding.

With a hard elbow in the gut, she plunged the knife into José's arm and rammed the blade deep into his flesh.

José released his grip on her and dropped his gun.

Hailey dove to the floor. "Now!"

Mark's face strained, like he was preparing for the gun's recoil. He squeezed the trigger and flinched.

Bang!

The noise sounded like a bomb detonating. The shot went askew, hitting the metal sprinkler head in the ceiling. Perfect shot—if that was Mark's actual aim.

Water sprayed the room.

José picked up a vortex mixer from the counter and hurled it at Mark.

Mark jerked to the side. He fired again, hitting the storage shelf. Beakers and flasks toppled over, crashing to the floor. Hailey held her breath as the amber flask of raw Euphoria oil teetered.

Grunting, José charged full throttle at Mark.

Hailey screamed. "Mark! Watch out."

He steadied the gun with his other hand and pulled the trigger a third time.

José stumbled, clutching his chest. His eyes widened, and he gaped at his bloodied hand. Then, like a scene shot in slow motion, he collapsed onto the floor.

A shiver ran through Hailey as she stared at José Mendoza's pallid face. The man terrorizing her and her dreams was finally dead. He'd been the vilest man she'd ever met.

She rushed over to Mark, careful not to slip as the sprinkler sprayed water in every direction. "Are you okay?"

"I'm fine." He slid the gun into his pocket. "Are you?"

Sirens blaring in the near distance muffled her reply. Police and paramedics would arrive any minute.

Hailey gasped. "Oh my God. I forgot about Bruce. He's hurt!" Turning, she ran out of the room, Mark matching her stride. She stopped at the elevator and pressed the down arrow. "Go to the lobby and let the paramedics inside. Notify security and the agent on patrol. I'll wait with Bruce in his office."

Water dripped from Mark's hair. "Be careful."

His clothes were drenched. She glanced down at her wet clothes. They both looked bedraggled. The sprinklers would soak everything in the lab. She smacked her forehead. "How could I be so stupid!"

"What?"

"I forgot to grab Euphoria."

Mark stepped into the cart. "The salve doesn't matter anymore. Skip it."

Hailey shook her head. "I can't."

"Dammit! Go help Bruce. Everything's ruined by now anyway."

"The salve in the cabinet will stay dry, but the raw oil is the only sample Bruce has left for his research." Hailey leaned into the cart and hit the down button. "This project's too important to him." She stepped back as the doors began to close, and she bolted down the hall.

When she reached the lab, water was already streaming into the hall. She gasped. How could this much destruction happen in three minutes? The tile floor inside the lab looked like shiny glass. Water dripped down the walls, puddled on the countertops, and dribbled over the equipment and computers.

Fine mist from the sprinkler blurred Hailey's vision as she splashed across the floor to the storage shelf. She blinked away water droplets weighing down her eyelashes. Lifting on her tiptoes, she stretched her arm, blindly grabbing for the oil.

Where did it go?

She slid her fingers along the shelf's ledge. Nausea gripped her as she lowered her gaze to the floor. *Did the flask fall over?*

Someone behind her coughed. "Looking for this?"

Chapter Thirty-Eight

José?

Hailey sucked in her breath and slowly turned.

José wheezed like he would collapse any moment. Blood streaked down his face. Dark bloodstains marbled his shirt. He held the flask of raw Euphoria oil in one hand, a utility knife in the other. Adjusting the items in his hands, he slammed the door and set the lock. His venomous glare bore into her.

Goose bumps cropped up on her skin. *How on God's green earth was this man still standing?* She thrust a hand into her pocket and fingered the pen she'd taken from Bruce's desk drawer.

José staggered toward her, raising the flask. "This must be important if you came back for it." He spat on the floor and limped closer. "Manuel tried to convince me Euphoria had potential. Your doctor friend confirmed it."

Hailey grabbed for the oil.

He raised it out of her reach and pointed the knife at her chest. His eyes blazed like a wildfire. "You took everything from me."

Hailey stepped back. *Stall him.* Security would come any moment and unlock the door.

She eyed the fire extinguisher hanging near the door. Spraying him with foam might be another option.

He coughed. "Manuel should've killed you when he

335

had the chance. He was nothing but a gutless coward."

"He was not a coward. He died saving his daughter."

José brandished the knife closer to her face. "Shut up, *puta*!"

If she was going to flee, she needed to run *now*. Hailey dashed toward the door.

He lurched forward and stabbed the knife into her arm.

Heat burned down to her fingers, but she grabbed the pen from her pocket and rammed it hard into his cheek.

Moaning like a hurt animal, he shoved her with a force that lifted her into the air.

When she landed, her feet slipped. She skidded backward, crying out as her head hit the floor. White stars circled her vision.

"*¡Hijueputa!*" José smacked Hailey's head. He moved on top of her, pinning her legs as he straddled her hips.

Pain radiated inside her skull. José's rancid stench suffocated her. She scratched his arms, struggling to breathe.

Holding the amber flask in his hand, José bit the rubber stopper and spat it onto the floor. He raised the container over her head, the raw oil sloshing inside. A cruel smirk spread across his face. "I will enjoy watching you die."

She flinched as his spittle landed on her face. Was he going to pour the oil over her? Where the hell was security?

José sneered. "Your precious husband will have to find his own cure. Euphoria is mine." He drew the flask to his mouth and chugged the oil, draining the contents in two gulps. He pitched the bottle onto the floor, shattering it into tiny pieces.

Hailey gulped. *Oh my God! He drank the oil.*

José lowered the knife to her neck.

"No!" She twisted beneath him.

A loud pounding banged against the door. "Hailey? Are you in there? Open the door!"

"Help—"

José's calloused hand clamped over her mouth.

Her lungs strained for air. She bit his bony finger, tasting salt and iron. "Mark!"

José struck her jaw. His bloodshot eyes flashed revenge as he pushed the blade against her throat.

Hair prickled on her scalp. The blade would pierce her windpipe in one slash. She braced for the impact.

Instead, a wet gurgle sound escaped José's throat.

His knife dropped with a hollow plonk onto the flooded floor.

Writhing in pain, he clutched both hands around his neck. The skin on his face darkened to a forbidding purple. A river of bright red blood gushed from his mouth.

Hailey gagged as an acrid metallic smell stung her nose.

Dark clots spurted from José's mouth. His pupils enlarged, masking his irises, and his eyes rolled back into his head. He collapsed onto the floor, his body jerking in a violent seizure.

Hailey shrieked as she wriggled away.

The door kicked open and four police officers charged into the room with their weapons drawn.

Behind them, Mark darted straight to Hailey and scooped her into his arms.

She couldn't decide whose heartbeat raced faster. "Mark, put me down. The floor's slippery."

"Not on your life. I'm never letting you out of my sight again." He held her tightly, capturing her mouth in a fierce kiss.

While the police worked to shut off the sprinkler system, Mark carried Hailey into the hallway and eased her onto the ground. He pulled off his sweatshirt and draped it around her shoulders. "I'll get a paramedic to look at your arm."

"Let them help Bruce first. I can wait." Every nerve ending in her arm spasmed, but the nightmare was over. She let Mark's earthy scent comfort her. "I thought I was dead."

His arms tightened around her. "Shh. You're safe now. I got you."

Hailey nuzzled deeper into his arms, faintly aware of the chaos surrounding her.

When two paramedics wheeled out a gurney from Bruce's office, Hailey rose and reached for her friend's hand. Bruce's eyes were closed. Dried blood speckled his face and arms. A belt had been strapped around his hips. He looked like a feeble, old man.

Hailey fingered the tape securing the IV on his arm. He couldn't die yet. She needed him too much. "How is he?"

One paramedic stayed back as her partner loaded Bruce into the elevator. "Looks like a fractured pelvis. His EKG showed a fast heart rate, but his vitals are stable now. We gave him some pain meds to help him rest. He'll be at the hospital downtown."

"Did he have a heart attack?"

"More likely a panic attack. The hospital will run

tests. Dr. Hanover said he collapsed after his co-worker was shot." The paramedic shrugged. "The gunman might've thought Dr. Hanover died when he hit the floor. In any case, your friend's a very lucky man."

Should she laugh or cry? Bruce had been having panic attacks since she met him. Maybe this one saved his life.

The paramedic examined and bandaged Hailey's arm. "You'll need to get this looked at in the ER. I'll call for another ambulance."

Hailey shook her head. "I'm fine—"

Mark rubbed her back. "You should get checked out. Besides, this way we can be with Bruce. Make sure he's taken care of."

Her heart warmed. Mark knew what she wanted before she did.

After the paramedic left, goose bumps prickled her arms. She could've been killed. She would've lost Mark, Anna, and Ethan.

Mark sniffed. "Ronnie didn't make it."

"I'm sorry. I know he was your friend."

"He was a good man." Mark framed the sides of her face with his hands. His touch warmed her skin like a heating blanket. "Are you sure you're okay? Another ambulance should be here in a few minutes."

"I'm fine." With Mark beside her, she was more than okay. "By the way, you took some good shots tonight."

Mark winked. "I had to protect my shadow."

The wailing of sirens intensified as they stared out the window at the beams of red and blue lights battering the darkness.

Mark bowed his head and laughed.

Hailey turned. The stress must have gotten to him. "What can you possibly find amusing right now?"

As he raised his gaze, gray flickers shone in his eyes. "Listen. What do you hear?"

She shrugged. "The police talking in the lab?"

He pointed outside. "And what else?"

What sound was he referring to? Hailey gazed out the window where onlookers, police cars, and firetrucks lined the streets. The sirens blared...like a loud rockfest... She gasped. *His PTSD.*

"I'm doing okay. All this"—Mark waved his hand—"all this noise didn't trigger me. I'm getting better."

Her pulse raced. "That's the best news I've heard all day. I have a feeling everything's going to get better from now on." She traced a finger over his cheek. With or without scars, Mark was hers to love. They'd face each new day together.

He pulled Hailey in closer, kissing her with a hunger that took her breath away.

Epilogue

With his wife at his side, Mark walked out of the Dulles Airport terminal and followed the signs to the rental car lot. The routine felt like past work trips. Almost like he was going back in time, but stepping into his old world with new feet. An encouraging sign, even if he walked with a slight limp.

Hailey wheeled her suitcase over the pavement. "Nervous?"

"More like excited." He lowered the ball cap, shielding his eyes from the cool October sun.

"This is our spot." She pointed to a red coupe parked next to an SUV. "I'm glad I didn't drive to the airport when I flew to Atlanta. My car battery would be dead."

Mark walked to the rental. "The booster cables are stowed in the back. I could've jumped it."

Hailey popped the trunk latch with the key remote. "Both cars will need battery charges when we get home. Maybe Ethan can help you, seeing as he's anxious to get his learner's permit."

He loaded his suitcase and guitar. "As soon as I get the okay, I'll teach Ethan how to drive." A milestone he'd looked forward to for a long time.

"The doctor's clearance won't be too far away. Your reflexes are coming back, especially with all the rehab you've been doing." Hailey stacked her luggage beside his.

After Mark pulled down the trunk, he curved his arm around Hailey's shoulders and breathed in her flowery perfume. "Did I ever tell you how remarkable you are?"

She blushed. "Only about a million times."

And he'd tell her a million more.

He lowered his gaze to her lips and kissed her, drinking in her sweetness. How could his heart carry so much love? Surely, it would burst any moment. Hailey belonged with him. They were a team. He'd welcome whatever the future brought.

As they inspected the rental car for dents and scratches, Hailey's phone chimed.

Mark leaned against the driver's side door. "Who's texting? Anna and Ethan already texted five times today. Everyone else should be waiting at the house."

"Imagine how often the kids would text us if David hadn't brought them to visit last month." She dug the phone from her purse. "It's Luis. Oh, look. He sent us another picture of his mother and Selena." She held up the phone.

Another encouraging family picture. "What else did he say?"

"He thanked us again." Hailey's eyes misted. "I hope Selena can overcome this ordeal."

"She's been home for six weeks. The worst is behind her. Luis is getting her every resource available. Selena's a fighter."

Hailey brushed a tear from her cheek and slipped her cell into her purse. She sat in the driver's seat and fastened the seat belt. "Luis wouldn't have found Selena if you and Erik hadn't gotten involved. You two saved her life."

He pushed his shoulders back and found his way to

the passenger seat. Playing a part in locating Selena redeemed his self-esteem. Since the rescue, Owen had assigned Mark more cases and reserved him time at a firing range.

Mark secured his seat belt. "It's ironic the consigliere in India who paid off the mafia boss saved Selena's life."

Hailey tried out the turn signal levers. "I wouldn't call it 'saving' her. Forcing Selena to marry was as bad as prostituting her. The creep preyed on her emotions and made her feel obligated to pay off the debt he incurred for taking her from another trafficker. Thank goodness she was not the mother of those kids she watched. Selena was trapped in that household. She had no passport and didn't speak the language. How could she ask for assistance?"

"Honey"—he waved his hand in front of his chest—"we're on the same team."

"I know we are. This subject just boils my blood. When will the exploitation stop?" Hailey adjusted the side mirrors. "I suggested to Stefan the SCA investigate more human trafficking cases."

"Will he take your advice?"

"About that." A sly grin spread across her face. "Stefan asked me to come back."

"Oh Lord Almighty." Would he be ready if she returned to her former career? "I thought you planned to teach in the spring. Your department head only approved taking off this fall."

"I'm not sure I'll have time to work at the university or the SCA. My primary focus will be to create two scholarship foundations."

"Two? You finally made up your mind?"

She nodded. "I put a lot of thought into it. Medical research and law enforcement, in memory of my son Justin and Parker. I think they'd be pleased. Parker's life insurance is enough to fund both."

Whatever she wanted. Mark would make the situation work. "I'm proud of you, honey."

"Thanks. That means a lot."

He stared out the window as they exited the terminal parking lot. The past year felt like thirty.

Hailey patted his arm. "How are you doing?"

"I'm fine." Who was he kidding? He was nervous, excited, anxious, apprehensive—there wasn't an emotion he didn't feel. When he reunited with his family, another deluge of emotions would hit him. He peered at an airplane flying in. "Did you remember to text Bruce when we landed?"

"Yes." Hailey merged onto a toll road and weaved into traffic. "I wonder if he'll miss us."

"I don't know, but I'll miss him. At least Bruce is home now and out of rehab. His injuries could've been much worse."

Hailey chuckled. "I always thought he faked his panic attacks."

Mark scrubbed his beard. "Too bad he broke his hip when he fell."

"He plans to cut back on his hours when he goes back to PMI."

Mark laughed. "That means a twelve-hour workday instead of sixteen."

Hailey looked into the rearview mirror. "The agency that awarded him the skin regeneration project offered him another grant to continue studying *Bixa aparra*."

"But the plant is extinct."

She signaled and changed lanes. "Actually, it isn't. Before the Colombian government demolished Mendoza's lab, Luis shipped two plants to Peru. The shaman propagated a few dozen saplings so far. Bruce intends to fly to Colombia to search the fields around Mendoza's lab for any Euphoria plants that might've survived."

"When does he plan to do this?"

"After he visits us next spring."

Mark leaned his head against the headrest. "Oh, good grief!"

"Don't worry. I'm not going along."

Thank God for small miracles. "Maybe Colleen and Rose will fly with him. They can visit Rose's grandmother."

Hailey shook her head. "Colleen won't feel comfortable going back for a while, if at all. Besides, Camila has offered to visit them in Boston. Now that Rose's nightmares have subsided, they can tour the city again."

"Do you still want to visit Colleen and Rose over Christmas? I don't blame you if you decide not to." *Especially considering the thorny history with Colleen.*

"Anna has her heart set on going, and it'll be nice to see the puppies. Ester and Ase."

Mark scratched his head. "Odd names for dogs."

"Not for a family of science gurus. Colleen's father, A.C. Toole, would've loved the names." Hailey eased off the gas in a construction zone and maneuvered through heavy traffic. "I get the impression Colleen will stay in Boston."

"I hope she puts down some roots." He glanced at the car clock. They'd be home soon.

Goose bumps pricked his arm—a nice sensation to experience again. "Are you sure everyone's at the house?"

Hailey nodded. "Francine and her family flew in from Arizona yesterday. Laura drove to our house last night after Ethan and Anna finished their assignments. The virtual school keeps a tight schedule."

"I'm grateful Laura offered to take care of our kids. At least Ethan and Anna could meet with their friends a few times during Laura's house-hunting trips."

"I hope Francine will decide to move back to Virginia, too."

"Maybe eventually she'll move back." Sunday dinners with his sisters at the table flashed through his mind. "It'd feel like old times."

"I, for one, am thrilled Laura wants to move closer to your parents."

He snickered. "That's not the only reason she's moving." If Ethan's daily updates about Laura and David becoming cozier were true, Mark would see her a lot more often.

"Are you okay if your sister and David get together?"

"Heck, yeah. They flirted all the time in Dad's garage. They should've hooked up years ago."

Hailey signaled and exited the highway. "This summer was definitely one for the books."

It certainly was. He leaned his head back and closed his eyes. Of all the emotions he needed to process, gratitude was top on the list.

****

Hailey braked at the stop sign at the entrance of her neighborhood. Mark could sleep another minute before she'd wake him. With all the brouhaha of returning home, neither she nor Mark had slept well lately. She was as nervous as he pretended not to be.

The summer had seemed like a bizarre dream. In the two months that passed since José drank the raw Euphoria oil, Mark's skin had completely regenerated, except for a section on his left leg where skin was still healing. Occasional twinges of pain still shook Mark, but he had no scarring. The treatments took every smidgen of salve. Earlier in the week, a barber cut Mark's full head of hair and styled a neatly trimmed beard. Who would've thought Euphoria would turn out to be a blessing?

Hailey sighed. With deforestation around the globe, what other pivotal medicines and cures might never be realized?

She turned into the driveway lined with cars, and she nudged her husband. "Honey, wake up."

He rubbed his eyes. "Let's get this party started."

Her heart swelled. Mark had battled the fight of his life and suffered more than physical scars. He couldn't recover the time lost with his family, but today was a new beginning. *Every* day would be a new beginning.

"Mark, look." She pointed to the house.

A welcome home banner stretched across the yard. Red, yellow, green, and blue balloons dangled over the porch railing. Mark's parents walked onto the porch; their faces wreathed in smiles. Behind them, David draped his arm around Laura.

Heat radiated through Hailey's chest. Finding new love was as exciting as revitalizing lost love. Strange how Euphoria had robbed her of so much happiness, but brought it back in other ways.

As she unbuckled her seat belt, Ethan and Anna claimed the front rail area of the porch, Mark's niece and nephews crowding behind them.

Hailey turned her head. "Looks like mayhem is about to erupt any minute. Are you ready for this?"

He grinned. "Oh, I'm more than ready."

Mark was finally home where he belonged. Her chin trembled as she squeezed his hand. "I love you."

"I love you, too." He gazed at her with a longing that made her insides flutter. His dreamy blue eyes could still seduce her. "I knew you were the one for me the first day you walked into my life."

Hailey waited to get out of the car until Mark opened his passenger door. Today was about him, standing on his own.

When she walked to his side, Mark tilted his head in the adorable way that made her soul dance. He cupped her chin with his hand. "Thank you for not giving up on me."

Hailey drew in the fresh autumn air. Their relationship was stronger than before the fire. Hope filled her future.

Holding hands with their fingers interlocked, they crossed the driveway into the yard.

Ethan jumped off the porch rail and ran toward them.

Anna squealed and bounded down the steps, dashing ahead of her cousins.

The two leapt into Mark's open arms. "We missed you, Dad!"

Similar greetings echoed through the air as the rest of the family rushed toward them.

Tears rolled down Hailey's cheeks. Her family was

together again. Her life might not be perfect, but it was perfectly wonderful.

She pressed a kiss on Mark's cheek and whispered into his ear, "Welcome home."

A word about the author...

A native from western Pennsylvania, C. Becker earned a B.S. degree in Medical Technology and MT (ASCP) certification. C. Becker has worked in clinical settings testing drugs of abuse, among various lab responsibilities. The author has published multiple stories in different genres.

Thank you for purchasing
this publication of The Wild Rose Press, Inc.

For questions or more information
contact us at
info@thewildrosepress.com.

The Wild Rose Press, Inc.
www.thewildrosepress.com